Just What the Doctor Hired

by

Amanda Nelson & Lisa-Marie Potter

Plus One

Copyright Notice
This is a work of fiction. Names, characters, places, and incidents are either the product of the author's imagination or are used fictitiously, and any resemblance to actual persons living or dead, business establishments, events, or locales, is entirely coincidental.

Just What the Doctor Hired

COPYRIGHT © 2025 by Amanda Nelson & Lisa-Marie Potter

All rights reserved. No part of this book may be used or reproduced in any manner whatsoever including the purpose of training artificial intelligence technologies in accordance with Article 4(3) of the Digital Single Market Directive 2019/790, The Wild Rose Press expressly reserves this work from the text and data mining exception. Only brief quotations embodied in critical articles or reviews may be allowed.
Contact Information: info@thewildrosepress.com

Cover Art by *Teddi Black*

The Wild Rose Press, Inc.
PO Box 708
Adams Basin, NY 14410-0708
Visit us at www.thewildrosepress.com

Publishing History
First Edition, 2025
Trade Paperback ISBN 978-1-5092-6160-4
Digital ISBN 978-1-5092-6161-1

Plus One
Published in the United States of America

Dedication

To Leanne Morgena, without whose knowledge, patience, and support, we wouldn't have grown as authors; and to Jeremy Nelson, whose tech support and encouragement have saved us and our manuscripts on many occasions.

Medical Prescription Form

℞

Patient Information
Patient name : *My favorite reader*
Patient address : *Your imagination*

Directions:
Read to the end and leave a review

Signature *Dr. Edwowza*

www.NelsonPotter.com

Chapter 1

Autumn

Seattle's Rock Bar was like no other establishment I'd ever seen. While one half was ultra-modern with minimalistic barstools and tables, the other half was organic—a backlit wall with varying hues of peach and gold rock salt. Even the pendant lights were rough-hewn cubes of the natural mineral, giving the whole place a soft orange glow, like a photo filter. I wouldn't have been surprised to find incense burning in the corner; it would have fit the vibe. Instead, I was greeted by the standard pungent aroma of spirits and beer.

I took a seat in front of the glowing wall facing the entrance, laying my gray pea coat over the back. A man, with a deeply creased smile and thatchy brown hair I'd bet my next paycheck was a wig, approached.

"Can I bring you a drink? Beer, wine, cocktail?" He laid a square brown napkin on the table.

I shook my head. "Um, just a water for now. I'm waiting for a friend." I shifted my gaze to the light wood plank door. Still no client.

The server nodded and strode away.

I glanced around. The environment was precisely the type of place I'd expect to meet a personal life consultant—the listed profession of my newest client. However, Josh Anderson's photo didn't match how I'd pictured a twenty-seven-year-old inspirational guru. If I hired someone to oversee my mental well-being, I'd expect them to be a linen-wearing, happy person with a sense of empathetic energy. In the profile Josh submitted to my boss, Ruth, at the Plus One Companion Agency, he wore a navy suit and tie with neatly coiffed, coffee-colored hair. The leery smile was what threw me, though. Not to mention, his naturally smoldering dark eyes appeared way too aggressive—a common expression from most of my cocky, workaholic clients whose personal life only consisted of occasional one-night stands. However, Josh's choice of venue had me doubting my first impression. Maybe he was a tranquil person who knew the secrets to happiness.

Last night, I checked out Josh's website, The Life Lexicon, and found the homepage busy and gimmicky, filled with cheesy, uplifting quotes, hollow promises, and a link to register for his online classes. His site listed no qualifications and a disclaimer releasing him of any responsibility. Yet, Josh had over two million followers. As my lawyer father would say, something wasn't adding up. I picked up the miniature wooden tool and raked swirls in the white sand of the Zen garden embedded in the table.

The server returned with a glass and small carafe of water. "I'll check back in a few minutes."

"Thank you." Throwing him an apologetic smile, I curled my shoulders. I knew servers hated tables that wouldn't generate a profit.

The man gave two sharp raps on the table with his knuckles and left.

I glanced at my watch. Fifteen minutes tested the limits of the no-show boundary—if Josh didn't arrive soon, I'd bail.

Just then, the entrance door swung open, and in swayed my client. The pronounced hunch in his shoulders deemphasized his tall, lean build. Nodding acknowledgement, he flopped into the black chair across from me, almost slipping out the other side, and shifting his unbrushed hair over his sunglasses.

"Damn. You're even hotter in person." He wore a wrinkled black suit over a wine-stained, white cotton T-shirt. Josh wobbled and grabbed onto the edge of the table. "Whoa."

Tonight is not *going well.* His breath was rank—the fermented stench of someone who'd already had several drinks. I leaned back in my booth, putting as much distance between him and myself as possible.

Josh dragged the back of his hand across his mouth. "So, how does this work?"

His slurred question was a standard from all my clients. *I wish Ruth would put instructions on the website.* "Well, we exchange pertinent information about ourselves and the expectations for tonight." *He might as well take off those damn sunglasses because they're not disguising his wandering gaze. I feel dirty even talking to him.*

A salacious smile crept over Josh's lips.

"I got tested three weeks ago. I'm clean."

Jerking my head back, I scowled. "What? No. I don't need to know your medical history."

Josh scratched his head, further mussing his hair. "You don't?"

Ugh. Here we go again—he thinks I'm an escort. Moments like this made me frustrated with myself. If I could swallow my giant pride and accept financial help from my dads, I wouldn't have to put up with clients like Josh to earn the additional income from Plus One. Swallowing the rising bile, I fought to keep the repulsion from my expression. "No. Your sex life is not relevant to a country club fundraising dinner."

He barked a laugh. "I lied. We're not going there. Country clubs are for people like my father."

Sweat trickled down my back, and I readjusted the neckline of my burgundy wrap jumpsuit, covering as much of my cleavage as possible. "Then why *did* you hire me, Josh?"

He aggressively leaned forward, finally removing his sunglasses, his bloodshot eyes dark and cheek lifting. "A dare."

I clenched my teeth. "What kind of dare?" *Don't say it. Don't say it.*

The rough pressure of his dress shoe tugged on my pant leg under the table, rubbing my calf. "The only kind I'd accept." He winked.

Gross! I jerked my leg away and straightened, bracing my hands on the table. "What do you think you're doing?" Heat rose up my chest, and I couldn't stop my heart from pounding.

Josh reached forward and squeezed my wrist.

Twisting my left arm from his grip, I rested a hand on top of my purse, taking comfort in the bulk of the taser under my palm.

Josh leaned back, exhaling in a huff, and rolling his eyes. "Oh, come on, sweetheart. What do you think I'm doing? I'm cutting to the chase."

Shaking my head, I collected my coat and bag. "Clearly, you didn't read the constraints of the Plus One policies." I stood, ensuring a safe distance. "Your contract is canceled. Good night." Adrenaline raced through my veins, and I had to restrain myself from running toward the exit. When I got onto the sidewalk, I inhaled deeply, clearing Josh's foul stench from my lungs—replacing his unpleasant odor with the familiar scent of downtown's asphalt and brine. I strode to the corner away from the bar, with one hand on my taser, the other clutching my phone.

—*Lil, leaving Rock Bar, keep an eye on me. Client was a creeper*—

Since I'd started at Plus One, Lilly Huang—a fellow nursing student, Plus One companion, and my best friend—and I had worked out an anti-creeper system. She and I shared companion appointment calendars and location statuses via our phones to keep each other safe. I glanced over my shoulder like a skittish cat. The vibration of Lilly's response made me jump.

—barf emoji *I got you. Do you want to talk about it when you get home?*—

—*No, it's okay. I've got my taser. I'll fill you in tomorrow during class*—

—Thumbs up emoji, wide-eyeball emoji—

Switching out of messages, I tapped on the app for my Plus One portal. I opened Josh's contract and clicked *cancel*. A text box popped on the screen.

Are you sure you want to cancel this contract?

Hell, yes!

****

Scrubbing my face in the shared bathroom of my downtown apartment, and lamenting for the millionth time at not having my own, I fumed. *What a giant waste of my time!* If I'd had a dime for every douche bag who confused my profession with an escort, I could quit my second job at the Seattle Ferries tollbooth. I yanked on my pajamas and tiptoed past Alyssa's room, avoiding the creaky spots in the wood laminate so I wouldn't wake my roommate. Alyssa was quiet and kept to herself. Aside from the info on our rental agreement—her name and previous address—I didn't know much more about her, and she never seemed inclined to share any additional information despite having lived together for over a year. She'd shut down every conversation I instigated as if I was collecting data to steal her identity.

Taking a seat at the kitchen table, I pulled out my Anatomy of Circulation textbook and uncapped my highlighter. Reading through the paragraph on phlebotomy, I streaked the bright-yellow marker across the page. At least something good would come from tonight. Usually, I used the anonymity, privacy, and intermittent stretches without commuters during my tollbooth shifts to do most of my homework, which lightened the studying I had to complete in my free time, and therefore opening additional options for companioning. Tonight was an exception—I'd swapped shifts with a coworker to take Josh's contract. My income from Plus One was three times that from Seattle Ferries. Now, however, thanks to Josh's misinformed assumptions, I would only receive half of my expected income—still more than a night at the docks, but disappointing nonetheless.

An email from Plus One glowed on my screen. Retrieving my phone, I expected to see the canceled contract informational survey when I tapped the alert but found a new contract instead. I glanced over the details. "Well, that's a new one." A woman wanted to hire me for her friend, Jensen Edwards—a doctor who needed a date for a formal event this coming Friday. When I reached the end of the email, I spotted the name of the hiring party, Molly Covington, and it rang a bell. I doubted the renowned writer—the one who'd just gone viral on social media for falling in love with her own Plus One companion—was the same woman initiating the contract, but the coincidence would've been fun to tell the folks.

I responded, first to Ruth to let her know I'd received the email and would contact the client, and then to Miss Covington to accept the contract. After hitting the *send* button, I returned to reading an explanation on how to locate an acceptable vein through touch. My phone glowed again. I had another email and tapped on the alert—Molly Covington had already responded.

Dear Autumn,

It's lovely to hear you're available this weekend. When I had to cancel on Jensen at the last minute, I was gutted. Dr. Edwards is such a nice guy, and I think you'll be the perfect date because, according to your profile, you're also in the medical field. Hopefully, your knowledge will come in handy at the "Best Doctors In Seattle" recognition dinner, where he's receiving an award.

I will give Jensen your contact information to arrange a place and time to meet before the event. I've already taken care of all the Plus One fees.

Attached is a link to Jensen's professional profile. He doesn't keep on top of his social media.

Have a great time, and for the record, he's not as stuffy as he seems in his bio, I promise. Winky face

emoji
Sincerely,
Molly Covington

A doctor who can't get a date? And how much medical knowledge will I need for this event? Luckily, I only had three semesters of school to finish until I received my Bachelor of Science in Nursing—I should be good. Steeling my shoulders, I clicked on Jensen's bio and felt my heart kick up a beat. I took a few deep breaths. After reading Molly's email, I pictured a mature gentleman with gray hair, a beard, and glasses; but the photo on my screen displayed a gorgeous man who appeared around my age—early to mid-thirties, with a stubble beard, light brown hair, green eyes, and a sharp jawline that could cut glass. "Well, hello, Dr. Edwowza!"

Chapter 2

Jensen

As I approached the incubator in my patient's room, I rubbed my hands together to warm them after washing in the sink. The tiny baby girl inside appeared perfect, despite being less than three pounds. Unclipping one of the doors covering the holes cut into the side of the plastic shell, I reached in and held one of her delicate hands with a gloved index finger.

Swallowing the lump in my throat, I marveled at Amy's little form. The intricate details on these tiny humans in the neonatal intensive care unit never ceased to amaze. Every time I had a patient in this department, I gained a new appreciation for their fight and determination, though each time my heart would break because I knew these babies had to struggle from the start. These precious kids would have enough hard things to deal with in this world, and fighting for their lives as infants shouldn't be one. "Hey, Amy. How's the little princess today?" Using my free hand, I grabbed her chart. "Look at you gaining an ounce." I bounced the finger that held her hand. "It looks good on you." Her skin had lost its translucence, and her limbs were taking shape, plumping and becoming less skeletal—more like a healthy newborn.

Amy was a fighter. Born at twenty-seven weeks with significantly underdeveloped lungs and a slew of other medical issues, she'd already been in Seattle Children's NICU for over eight weeks, but she was improving daily. Not by much, but any little bit of progress was all I could wish for.

Retracting my hand, I donned my stethoscope. I grabbed a heated baby wipe from the cupboard under her incubator and cleaned the round surface. Opening the second door, I extended both hands. "Sorry if this is cold." I rested the pad against her bare chest.

Amy flinched.

"Oh!" I cringed. "The stethoscope wasn't warm enough. Sorry, little lady." Her heartbeat was strong, despite the murmur. "We'll keep an eye on your valve. But for now, let's work on getting those breathing tubes removed." I glanced at Amy's chart again. "If you keep progressing this way, then your parents can take you home before we know it." I retracted my hand with the stethoscope, stroking the soft fine hair on Amy's shoulders with the other. Physical touch was crucial in these early stages, and I made sure to visit patients like Amy as often as my schedule allowed.

Glancing over my shoulder, I saw no one in earshot, then turned back to Amy. "I don't suppose you're free Friday night?" The beeping of the monitors and the soft whooshes of Amy's breathing machine were my only answers. "I didn't think so. You see, I'm attending an awards banquet in my honor, and the invitation came with a plus one." Sighing, I recalled the circumstances which had gotten me into my current predicament. "At first, I planned on going stag. But then my mother caught wind of the extra ticket and insisted I take a date—the daughter of one of her friends. My meddling mother arranged this whole family barbecue thing and cornered me into asking the woman. I hadn't minded, though, she's a beautiful, renowned author, but the situation was still stressful.

"At first, the author said *yes*. However, that changed when Molly got back together with her boyfriend, now fiancé, Jared, and former employee of a company who contracts companions for events such as my doctors' dinner." I made a notation on Amy's chart of the frequency of her murmurs. "For reasons I'm sure were half-guilt-half-pity, Molly generously offered me a complimentary extension of the Plus One's services for my congratulatory function. This whole situation has been one big blow to my ego." Molly swore Jared's former agency was above board and professional. No prostitution involved. Potential headlines reading *Hard Up Doctor Hires Date* blazed across my vision, and I protested her offer. But Molly assured me, as long as I kept my mouth shut, no one would know she paid for my date—including our mothers. After some additional "come ons" and "pretty pleases," I'd reluctantly given in, and Molly did the rest.

Amy's tiny body shivered, and she threw out her hands.

I ran a soothing finger down her arm to calm her. "Right? I don't know how to handle this, either. I'm more than capable of getting a date, believe me. It's just after the nasty breakup with my ex, my heart hasn't been in it." I twisted my lips to the side. "Now I've lied to everyone, including my mother. They all think my date with Autumn is a legit setup by a friend." I leaned toward the side of the clear hard plastic unit. "Just so you know, what I said about Autumn being a companion is just between you and me. Okay, cutie pie?"

A swirl of antiseptic-scented air ruffled the pages on Amy's chart. I spun to see Nicola with her blond spiky hair, one of the neonatal nurses, pause in the doorway before strolling to the sink.

"Hello, Dr. Edwards. How is our Amy doing this morning?"

"She's doing great. A little too attached to the breathing tube still." I brought my gaze back to the infant girl. "But we're working on getting rid of it, aren't we, Amy?"

Nicola smiled. "She's a trouper, for sure." The nurse veered toward another incubator.

I checked Amy's other vitals and made a notation on her patient chart.

Nicola left with a wave.

"Phew." I wiped a hand dramatically across my forehead. "It doesn't seem like she heard me. The last thing I want is for the nurses in this hospital to be any more into my business. After breaking up with the hospital pharmacist, Kayla, I felt like I was on a reality show and about to be voted off the island, despite *her* cheating on *me*."

Amy shuddered again.

"Thank you. It's not just me." I stroked her budding hairline. "I'm glad you're on my side. You're a good listener, you know?" Withdrawing my hand, I tilted my head and regarded Amy again. "Next time I see you, I want the breathing tube out. I know you can do it." Patting the top of her incubator, I removed my gloves and pumped some hand sanitizer into my palm and strode into the hallway, almost colliding with my chief of staff. "Dr. Anderson!" I grabbed onto his arm to steady us both. "I'm so sorry."

Gary straightened his crisp lab coat. "No worries, Edwards. It happens." He clapped me on the shoulder. "You all set for Friday evening?"

I repressed a grimace, dread gnawing at the pit of my stomach. "Yes, sir. I'm picking up my tux from the dry cleaners tomorrow morning."

"Excellent!" Gary beamed. "Is your guest someone from the hospital?"

Sweat formed in my armpits. "Uh, no. It's someone new I've been dating." *Lies. Lies, Lies.*

"Well, I know Meg will be excited to meet her."

"Yeah, me, too." Autumn and I agreed to meet before the event Friday night—something that both turned my stomach and filled me with adrenaline.

Gary's brow furrowed. "I'm sorry?"

I gawked like a deer caught in headlights, scrambling for a way to extract my foot from my mouth. "I meant, I'm excited for Meg to meet my date, too."

"All right then." Dr. Anderson gave a curt nod. "I've got a meeting with the head of orthopedics." He clapped my shoulder again. "I'll see you around."

As I watched Gary march down the hall, I gave a vague wave, deflating like a balloon. How on earth would I pull off Friday night? I had a hard enough time dealing with the backlash from my breakup with Kayla—the nurses' cold shoulders, the not-so-hushed conversations stopping when I approached, and the pitying expressions on the other doctors' faces when her cheating came to light. The situation had gotten so bad I dreaded even coming to work. I was living a nightmare—I wasn't sleeping well or eating; I lost weight. If my co-worker and best friend, Dan, and his wife, Kristine, hadn't intervened, I would still be in that dark place. They faithfully stood by my side, buoyed my confidence, and got me from a hot mess to just a mess.

Thinking about Autumn meeting Dan and Kristine felt like I was leading a lamb to the slaughter. They'd see right through the charade. I'd never pull off a fake date. But I couldn't back out now; I just told Dr. Anderson I would introduce Autumn to his wife.

Chewing the inside of my cheek, I turned to the nurses' station to grab the chart for my next patient. When I approached the counter, I heard the three women and one man, all wearing varying cartoon character scrubs, stop their low murmurs. I raised an exasperated brow, nabbed the paperwork, and hurried down the hall, feeling the daggers from their stares in my back. If I couldn't pull off this date, I'd request a transfer.

Chapter 3

Autumn

Watching Lilly's delicate fingers insert the needle into the vein at the crook of my arm, I winced, staring as my deep-red blood filled the vial.

"Nice." Professor Ross pushed up her thick, black-rimmed glasses before making a note on her electronic tablet.

I nodded, appreciating Lilly had hit a vein on the first attempt—quite an improvement since the last time when I'd felt like a pin cushion.

"Thanks." Lilly beamed, her black winged eyeliner elongated with her smile. "Hopefully, this means I've mastered my technique."

"Hopefully." Professor Ross nodded with a tight smile, her wispy blonde hair brushing her cheeks. "I'll be back for Miss Haze's turn in a few minutes."

Lilly withdrew the needle, pressing a cotton ball over the injection site, and leaned close to my ear. "Now that we have a second, wanna tell me about last night?"

I kept the pressure on my arm until Lilly got a bandage and discarded the syringe in the red plastic needle box. "Yeah, he was a real jerk." I stood and let my best friend take my place in the plastic chair, then unwrapped a new needle and laid it on the silver tray with a *clink*. "The client either had no clue or didn't care about the no-sex policy."

Lilly's breath came out in a whoosh, and she threw her head back, her long black ponytail swishing the top of the next table. "But it's in bold print on the website."

"I know. I don't get it, either; you're preaching to the choir." Scanning the room, I noted Professor Ross still had three more groups to observe before returning. "When I asked the douche bag for pertinent information about himself, he told me he was free of any sexual infections."

Lilly shuddered.

"Tell me about it. The jerk hired me as a dare." Hopefully, the misunderstanding saved some poor escort from an awful experience.

"Gross." She shoved up the sleeve of the white shirt she wore under her turquoise scrubs. "I'm going to mention something to Ruth about making the policy more prominent on the website."

"What's she gonna do, Lil? It's already in sixteen-point font."

"Still, we've each had a misinformed client in the last six months, and even one"—Lilly held up an index finger—"is too many."

"Miss Haze. Are you ready?" Professor Ross stood to the right, marking on her tablet, then raised her light-colored brows.

"Yes, ma'am." After donning my rubber gloves, I retrieved the tourniquet and wrapped it around Lilly's arm, securing it with tug.

As Professor Ross made a quick notation with her electronic stylus, scratches clicked against the plastic screen.

I took a deep breath. "Okay, Lilly, please clench

your fist."

Lilly gave a few squeezes, balling her fingers.

Feeling the crook of my friend's elbow with my index and middle fingers, I located a good vein. Next, I ripped open an alcohol wipe packet and swabbed her skin. Picking up the syringe with a steady hand, I carefully positioned the needle at a thirty-degree angle and pushed it into the vein. Deep crimson fluid filled the attached vial.

"Now withdraw." With an index finger, Professor Ross adjusted her glasses.

I released the rubber band tourniquet and grabbed a cotton ball. Pressing the round white fluff against the injection site, I withdrew the needle.

Professor Ross smirked. "Full marks again, Miss Haze." She stepped to the next set of students.

Lilly replaced my fingers on the cotton ball and rolled her eyes. "Show off."

I dropped the syringe into the plastic needle box. While she might have been jealous of my phlebotomy skills, I was half the person Lilly was. She selflessly worked as a Plus One companion to earn money for her educational fees and to support her multigenerational Vietnamese family. I met Lilly in my pathophysiology class ten months ago, when she made fun of me for using my highlighter in a textbook.

"You know we're in the twenty-first century, right? Professor Lowry gave us access to the e-book?" She glared through her narrow almond eyes during our first lecture together.

"Oh, yeah, I know. But I just love the feeling of marking and taking notes in a physical book." I grabbed the edges of my textbook and shook it for emphasis.

Lilly swiped her tablet screen with a scoff. "The app has a notes function, too."

I laughed.

Lilly introduced herself.

To this day, even though we'd been through many classes together, Lilly still hadn't persuaded me to the electronic side. "Whatever, you know I'm just gifted." I shoved Lilly's shoulder and handed her a bandage. "I got another contract for tonight."

A crease formed on Lilly's brow, and she scooted to the edge of the plastic chair. "What? It's not in the calendar."

The concern in my friend's tone was palpable. That was why I loved her—she cared. "I know. Ruth sent the request late last night, and I only just confirmed." Retrieving my phone from my scrubs pocket, I pulled up Jensen's bio picture and showed the photo to my friend.

Lil squinted at my screen before her eyes widened and her jaw dropped. "Hello! Yummy!" She pulled my phone closer with a hand. "Cancel his contract; I'll take this one for free."

"You wish." While Josh had been good looking, he didn't exude the sincerity and kindness Jensen did with his smile. *With any luck, my gut will be right about this contract, too.*

"Of course, I do. Now I see why you didn't put it in the calendar yet—to rub it in my face!"

I scoffed, and my cheeks heated. "No. I was too busy studying last night, but I'm still keeping to our agreement to stay safe." While I didn't think Jensen would be a problem like last night's date, the real danger would be my instant attraction to his rugged good looks. During my early days as a companion, I promised myself not to date any clients, but I extended that rule into my social life, as well—no men until my BSN. Which meant no real dating while I was in school—period.

Lilly barked a laugh. "Whatever; you could have texted me last night, but you always show me the hot ones in person."

"No, I don't!" Running a finger over my mouth, I examined Jensen's picture again. "He is cute, though, but I'd bet he's boring to talk to."

"I can only hope he is." Lilly pursed her lips.

Huffing, I planted my hands on my hips. "What are you implying?"

"You know."

I did know. Clients as hot as Jensen were few and far between. "You're just jealous."

"You're right. I am. Maybe I'll even use his picture for a screensaver." Lilly laughed. "Seriously, though, I'll be diligently following your GPS location and living vicariously through you on this one. I'll set a reminder to check on you throughout Friday, and don't forget I have my lonely boomer client for his Sunday brunch ritual."

Rolling my eyes, I smiled at the reminder of Lilly's wealthy seventy-three-year-old widower who just liked her company for a weekly meal. He'd been her client for the past year, making him hard to forget. "Is there any point in me still tracking you on those dates?"

"You remember the harmless bunny on that British medieval comedy—you never know. He could be a killer."

I snorted. "Okay, if you say so. Anyway, I'll text

you from my rideshare before my date."

"If you kiss the hottie on Friday, boring or not, I want details—his lips look delicious."

Yeah, they do!

Chapter 4

Jensen

Standing in front of the full-length mirror in my bedroom, I huffed while fumbling with my bow tie. Why I'd let my parents talk me into getting a "real" one when I'd landed my top-pick residency, I'll never know. Sure, black silk was considered better than a clip-on and screamed class and sophistication, but getting the bow to sit right was always a pain. My dad had the looping, circling, and tugging down to a science long before he passed five years ago, but I had yet to master the technique in my decade of owning the damn thing.

Of course, my father—having been recognized as one of the best orthopedic surgeons in Seattle, servicing some of Washington's collegiate and professional sports teams—had attended many fundraising and sports recognition events, which undoubtedly helped his neckwear-tying skills. However, I'd had far fewer invitation opportunities as a pediatric hospitalist. Which was why being honored at the "Best Doctors in Seattle" event had my shoulder muscles in knots. No, that was a lie. Receiving recognition wasn't what had my armpits testing the limits of my deodorant. That honor belonged to my date—Autumn Skye.

I shifted my weight from foot to foot, swallowing to clear my dry throat, and tugged on the corner of the smooth fabric again. This wasn't a completely blind date. When Molly secured the contract the same day she'd canceled, she sent a link to the Plus One website. Seeing the company's homepage was professional eased the knot in my stomach. Their play-on-words name was clever, which earned them some bonus points, too. I'd even scanned their reviews. Hundreds of five-star ratings agreed with Molly—the company was upstanding and credible.

Reassured I wouldn't be humiliated, I visited Autumn's profile. The companion Molly chose was an eleven out of ten in the looks department, and not at all what I'd predicted from her hippie name. I'd expected a woman who went by Autumn Skye would have flowers in her hair and a billowy tent dress. Boy, was I wrong. Autumn's style was tailored and neat. Her long, wavy brown hair was sleek and well-managed—even her makeup was trendy yet conservative. She was a far cry from the bohemian image her name had conjured. I'd spent an ungentlemanly amount of time staring at her sultry dark-brown eyes and well-defined lips. Her photos—Autumn in a black cocktail dress showing off her legs, another with her hitting a punching bag in tight workout clothes, and a third of her reading a book in a cream blouse and charcoal-gray pencil skirt looking like a sexy librarian—all made my mind wander to forbidden places, considering the circumstances. I'd visited her profile so frequently, I practically had the page memorized. But when the bio listed Autumn had a belly button ring, my body hummed. Thank goodness the agency website was explicit in the rules I had to follow, stating:

Plus One does not provide any form of sexual

service. Our employees offer companionship only. Please do not make lewd requests. Any contact of this nature will not receive a response. Furthermore, all personal information from the client and the companion will be held strictly confidential within the guidelines of the Plus One contract.*

In other words, no funny business, emphasis on the "fun," on tonight's date. I scratched my cheek. The policy was explicit about sex, but how would that translate into faking chemistry with a total stranger posing as my girlfriend? Depending on Autumn's brains and personality to get me through the event was a gamble. What if she'd lied to beef up her online persona? Autumn was listed as working toward a nursing degree. However, the mention didn't guarantee she was a serious student. I knew plenty of unemployed parents of my patients who described themselves as "between jobs."

I pulled on the edges of my bowtie, adjusting its symmetry with a final tweak, then checked the time. Needing to leave, I strode past my small living room. The original restored wood flooring of my 1932 brick cottage-style home creaked under my feet. Entering my newly remodeled kitchen, I grabbed my tuxedo jacket off one of the cream breakfast table chairs that contrasted with sage cabinets and made a mental note to thank my interior designer again for doing such a good job. I patted my pockets to ensure I had my keys and phone before descending the stairs to the basement garage.

Seated and secured in my luxury sedan, I backed out of the short driveway, the engine's purr calming my pounding heart. As I boarded the ferry to head into

Seattle, I received a call from my mother, sending my chest back to thrumming like a dance club. "Hi, Mom, I'm in the middle of the Puget Sound. What's up?"

"Hi, honey. I just wanted to wish you good luck tonight. Who are you taking again?"

Sighing, I shook my head. The minimal amount of information I'd supplied about my date was obviously killing her. "Remember, Mom? I told you. Her name is Autumn."

"Right." She dragged out the word.

Her judgment was evident in her tone.

"And you haven't met this woman in person?"

I just told you her name. "Correct." I parked behind a white minivan. "She's a friend of Molly's. I'm on my way to meet her for drinks before the recognition dinner."

"Uh-huh."

The short, non-committal, no-inflection reply was condescending. I could almost hear the wheels in my mother's head turning, searching for an angle to obtain more details.

"And how does Molly know her exactly? Does she work with Molly? Is she a writer, too?"

My mom was getting dangerously close to the truth. While Autumn didn't work with Molly, she kind of worked with Molly's fiancé, Jared, in a roundabout way—he'd previously been a Plus One employee. And while my mother *said* Molly hiring Jared to be her fake boyfriend and muse for her novel but ended up falling in love in real life was romantic, the twitch in her eye whenever she'd conveyed the sentiment indicated otherwise. "The ferry's docking, Mom; I've gotta hang up." More lies. "I don't want any frowns from the harbor workers." I talked fast, making sure not to give her room to get a word in. "I'll call you tomorrow and let you know how the night went. Love you, bye." I jabbed the *end* icon on the console display with a heavy sigh, letting the briny air fill my lungs. My mother thought anytime after six a.m. was an appropriate time to call in the morning. I'd have to remember to silence my notifications when I got home later tonight—just to be safe. No thirty-seven-year-old man wants to be woken up by his mother.

While following my GPS to the upscale bar, The Stalker's Tango, in downtown Seattle, I marveled at how Molly could overlook Jared's previous profession. Logically, I knew being a companion wasn't something to be ashamed of. We were in the twenty-first century. Still, with Molly's career as a famous author, the situation sounded like a tabloid scandal waiting to happen. Surprisingly, when the headlines came out concerning their relationship earlier in the week, the publicity had the opposite effect and cemented Molly's switch from thriller to the romance genre.

As a children's doctor, however, I wasn't anywhere near being in Molly's position. If anyone leaked I'd hired Autumn, I'd be done for, and my reputation would plummet. I'd probably be labeled a pervert and be terminated from the hospital. A ripple zinged through my body, and I shuddered. I wanted to speed back to the ferry. But showing up without a date to my own recognition event would be pathetic—like going to a movie theater alone. Not to mention, I'd told my chief of staff I was bringing someone, and my ex, Kayla, would be there with her newest victim, Dr. Andrew Lee.

Finding out the whole hospital had known Kayla cheated with Andrew before I did was bad enough. But when I overheard one of the nurses ask why Kayla left for the esteemed oncologist, the answer was like a punch in the gut. The whole thing was a numbers game to my ex—she'd been with me for my money, but Dr. Lee earned more. When I learned Andrew was dating Kayla, I went numb. He must have heard she was a gold digger. To each his own.

After my phone call with Molly, I knew if I showed up at this recognition dinner alone, I couldn't handle Kayla's smug expression. Not to mention, the gossip which had spread through the hospital following the end of our relationship made me never want to date another coworker again. At least with Autumn, I could trust her motives. Sure, she agreed to be my date for my money, or rather, Molly's money, but business was business. That alone gave me the courage I needed to hand my keys to the bar's valet.

Opening the door to the establishment, I enjoyed the faint scents of fruit and oak washing over me with the cool air-conditioning. A few moments passed before my eyes adjusted to the dimmed lighting of the cozy atmosphere, but once my vision adapted, I scanned the large wooden counter stretching along the right side of the room. Autumn wasn't among the bar stools. I surveyed the leather booth spanning the length of the dusty-red-papered wall and accompanying tables on the left. As I spotted her in the second-to-last seat, my breath caught. She was seated closer than I'd expected. Holy bats, she was gorgeous. A wave of heat flooded my torso. I couldn't get enough of Autumn, and I approached her table.

She stood and smiled.

Her silky, little red dress with spaghetti straps draped nicely over her breasts and hugged her slender curves. The hem stopped just below her knees with a slight flare at the bottom, showing off tanned, toned, and smooth-looking calves. I forced my gaze back up, landing on her perfect lips covered in a velvet-looking lipstick that matched her dress. My head told me I needed to look her in the eyes, but the simple gold chain dipping down Autumn's chest drew my gaze back toward her cleavage. My stomach clenched. I was grateful she extended her right hand, breaking my line of sight and allowing my brain to override my lustful thoughts. What had I gotten myself into?

Chapter 5

Autumn

Jensen gripped my right hand, giving a firm shake—strong and masculine at the same time. His skin was soft, and his nails were well-manicured. "Hi, Jensen. It's nice to meet you." His mossy-green eyes and rugged jawline would have fit perfectly in one of those expensive cologne ads in an overpriced fashion magazine. I was impressed I could form a coherent sentence.

"Yeah, hi. Um, it's nice to meet you, too, finally." He stammered slightly, shifting his gaze to the chair in front of him. "Should we sit?" He gestured to the wooden table.

"Absolutely." I slid into the black leather booth. Considering Jensen seemed as nervous as I did, I dove right in as soon as his butt hit the wooden chair. "My understanding is, you'd like me to pose as your girlfriend tonight?" A job which, so far, I wouldn't mind.

With a half raised hand to hail the server, Jensen glanced out of the corner of his eye. "Um, would you like a drink first?"

I could tell he needed one, as did I, but because I was abstaining, I channeled my inner superhero woman to bolster my confidence. "I don't allow myself to drink on the clock. But a ginger ale would be nice."

As he waved at the server with his right hand, Jensen's jacket strained against his bicep.

I shuddered, feeling shivers running down my spine. Thank goodness, I had the no-alcohol-with-contracts rule. This guy wasn't someone I could trust myself to be around while drunk. He was too attractive.

Jensen got the petite server's attention.

The dark-haired woman wove her way through the crowd to our table. After taking our orders, she made herself scarce.

Smoothing my dress, I returned my gaze to Jensen. "So, as I was saying, I'm to be your girlfriend?"

Jensen scratched at an imperfection in the grain of the table. "Yes, if you don't mind?"

His shyness made my nerve endings tingle, alleviating my anxiety. I gave him my warmest smile, hoping to put him at ease. "Of course not. That's what you hired me for." I leaned forward, resting my chin on the back of a hand. "In order to establish how familiar we should be, how long have we been *dating*?"

Jensen swallowed hard, his gaze firmly fixed on the table. "Most of the doctors at the hospital know me well enough they wouldn't buy I could keep someone like you"—he gestured across the table, his cheeks turning pink—"a secret. So, not long? Maybe a few weeks?"

My chest fluttered. *Cha-ching!* He found me attractive. Pursing my lips, I chastised myself for liking the win. "Okay, so I don't need to worry about having met your family, but how did *we* start dating?" I gestured between him and myself.

Jensen met my gaze and blinked. "You mean, like a backstory?"

I nodded. "Yes, unless you want to go with the truth." No one ever went with the truth.

Jensen's eyes went as wide as saucers. "Hell no!"

I laughed. "I didn't think so." A light flickered in his eyes.

"Hey, I have a suggestion."

"Okay, let's hear it." I sat back, schooling my features and hoping his response didn't sound as ridiculous as some other meet-cutes offered by previous dates.

Jensen straightened. "Picture this"—he fanned out his hands—"your car gets a flat tire. You're stranded on the side of the freeway. After watching several cars pass by, I see you and pull over—a knight in a shiny sports car. What do you think?"

His dramatic presentation of his scenario was endearing, but unrealistic. I traced a finger around the edge of the circular coaster on the table, pinching my lips together, and tried not to laugh at his expense. "There are so many holes in your story it's not even funny. That meet-cute sounds like a Christmas rom-com in the making."

Jensen's breath came out in a whoosh. "What? It's a great story."

"Sure. But it's impractical."

Jensen opened his mouth.

I shook my head. "First of all"—I held up an index finger—"I can change my own tire." I raised a second finger. "Two, if for some reason I couldn't, I have a cell phone." My ring finger joined the other two. "And three, I'm not some damsel who needs saving."

His shoulders slumped. "It could happen."

Not in today's day and age. I gave him a blank

stare.

Jensen crossed his arms over his chest, averting his gaze. "It's how my parents met."

I sputtered a laugh, throwing a hand over my mouth. "I'm so sorry. I had no idea."

He sighed deeply, dropping his defensive posture. "It's fine. The accidental meeting *is* old-fashioned. I hadn't taken cell phones into account." Jensen gestured toward me. "What do you suggest?"

I leaned against the booth, running through my catalog of meet-cutes, and hoped to match a situation to one where I might bump into this gorgeous, upper-class doctor. "Okay, scenario number one—you sat beside me on the ferry. We got to talking, talking evolved into flirting, and you asked me on a date." I touched his forearm, meeting his gaze to ensure consent.

He didn't flinch.

"You were very charming, by the way."

Jensen's cheeks flushed. "Uhh, I don't think my colleagues would buy that, either. They know I rarely get out of my car on the ferry. Most days, I spend the sailing time catching up on phone calls and emails."

"Me, too." Although I remained in my car to do homework. "But I'll tell you the advice my Papi gives me, 'Get out and enjoy the skyline or daydream about which house you want on the islands.'"

Jensen ducked his head. "Actually, while I don't take advantage of the Seattle skyline on the ferry, my kitchen window sports a great view of the Sound."

A pang reverberated in my chest as green clouded my vision. "Oh my gosh, you live on one of the islands?" This man was checking all my boxes. I almost regretted having sworn off dating. His cheek quirked up in a sexy half smile I felt in my toes.

"Bremerton."

My ribs squeezed tight with longing. "Very nice."

The server arrived with our drinks, set them down, and left like the ninja she resembled in her all-black attire.

I took a sip, letting the tangy ginger bubbles douse my libido. "Back to business. Scenario number two—we met in the produce section of your local grocery store. We both reached for the same apple—*awkward!* Then, we ran into each other several more times throughout the store. Finally, you asked me out when we ended up in the same checkout line."

Jensen's lips screwed to the side. "Again, my friends know better. Eating takeout is my go-to, or I order my groceries online."

Swing and a miss. My heart sank. "Okay, not option number two, either." Why was I bothered I'd never meet this man at a grocery store? We'd likely never see each other after the contract ended.

Jensen rubbed the back of his neck, his face flushing again. "Sorry, I don't mean to be difficult. It's just…most of my dates are setups."

I worked to keep my brows from touching my hairline and stretched across the table, touching his forearm again. "Don't be. It's no biggie."

Jensen placed a hand over mine.

I was shocked to find the spark from his touch lit up my body like a firework.

"Wait." He closed his eyes briefly. "I know how my answer sounded, so I feel like I should clarify. As a general rule, I don't have a problem asking a woman on a date." Jensen drew a deep breath, his gaze drifting to the next table. "I just have a mother and a few well-intentioned nurses at the hospital, who, recently, feel the need to fill up my social schedule. And despite this situation being another set up"—his gaze returned to mine, and as he removed his hand to indicate to the two of us, his complexion deepened—"it's unconventional and a little intimidating."

I dipped my chin and laughed. He had to be joking. "You're a handsome, successful doctor, and you're the one who's intimidated?"

Jensen scratched his scruff with a timid smile. "Well…"

I mentally chided myself for letting my thoughts leave my mouth. With my free hand, I fidgeted with my necklace and cleared my throat. "I'm just giving you a hard time. I understand; it's not your typical blind date. And stop worrying, you don't come across as someone who would have a problem getting a date on your own—regardless of the circumstances." He was far from it. I squeezed his arm, reveling in its hardness before I removed my hand. Jensen relaxed like he was melting into his chair.

"Thank you."

"Plus, you've just pointed out our meet-cute—we were set up on a blind date by our mutual friend, Molly Covington."

Jensen's eyes lit up, and his back straightened. "Perfect! Despite her being a famous Seattlite, none of my friends know her, but they know I do."

Letting my jaw go slack, I leaned forward and felt my heart kick into overdrive. "She's *the* Molly Covington?"

He nodded, beaming. "Yep, the one and only."

I forced the smile from my face, trying to remain neutral. "Hmm, her notoriety might change things." I bit my lip, counting my breaths to slow my heartbeat. "Famous people have fans, and sadly, they do their research. Is there someone more obscure we can have as a mutual?"

Jensen frowned, examining his hands. "We could always use Molly's fiancé, Jared. He was the one who used to work for Plus One, after all."

I furrowed my brow and shifted in my seat. "Are you sure you want to use someone associated with my agency?"

His eyebrows shot up. "Oh, for sure, no. But he no longer works there. He owns the Sky's the Limit in Manhattan."

"True, but his name went viral along with Molly's this past week." The connection would be made in an instant.

Jensen rubbed the back of his neck. "What about Molly's cousin, Fin? He works at that swanky Brazilian steakhouse just up the street." He thumbed over his shoulder.

My nerves settled. "Bahia?"

Jensen nodded.

"Perfect. My Dad and Papi love that place." The plan came together, and I nodded. "Fin set us up, and we've been dating for what? Two weeks?"

Jensen took a swig of his beer. "Sounds plausible. What would we know about each other from those two weeks?" The crease in his forehead disappeared.

"First and foremost, which hospital do you work at?"

"Mmm." Jensen swallowed his mouthful. "Good

question. I work at Seattle Children's Hospital."

One of my top choices for after graduation. "And how long have you been there?"

"Five years." Jensen put the bottle on the table and leaned forward. "Where do I say you work?"

I cleared my throat, glad my tollbooth attire was a prescribed fluorescent yellow vest and harbor worker baseball cap. No one ever recognized me. Even Jensen, living on one of the islands, hadn't ever spotted me during his commute. "For obvious reasons, I'll avoid my employment status at Plus One and stick with the truth of being a nursing student, but pretend my dads are paying my way through school so I don't have to work." Like they did with my first degree after I'd ended things with my high-school boyfriend, Matteo. Shaking my head, I pushed my ex to the back of my mind.

Jensen nodded again. "How much longer until you graduate?"

My chest swelled. "After this semester, I'll have one year left."

"Two- or four-year degree?" Jensen's chair scuffed the cement floor as he pulled closer.

I sat straight on the edge of the booth. "I'm fast-tracking for my Bachelor of Science in Nursing."

Jensen folded his arms on the table. "Oh, what's your first degree?" The corners of his eyes crinkled with his smile.

I rested an elbow on the table and fiddled with my earring. "Psychology."

His smile broke into a low chuckle. "Please tell me you're not analyzing me."

Too late. I skimmed my tongue across my teeth,

having already decided Jensen was every inch my type. "If you want my official diagnosis, I'd have to send you a separate bill."

"In that case, I'd be happy to pay." He winked.

I shivered, hoping he'd wink again.

"When you get your BSN, do you think you'll work at a hospital or doctor's office?" He raised his brows.

He appeared genuinely interested in my answer—a refreshing change from most of my clients. "Hospital." *Preferably yours.* "The oncology department, if I have my choice."

Jensen's head reared back.

I realized we'd been unconsciously gravitating toward each other, and my body hummed.

"Wow, you picked the one department I wanted to avoid when I chose my specialty."

Not surprising. "I understand; oncology isn't for everyone." My classes were much smaller now that my classmates and I had all chosen our preferred areas of interest.

Jensen gave a short huff. "Yeah, I knew I couldn't handle the emotional turmoil that comes with oncology. And I'm even more grateful now I hadn't chosen that specialty."

"Oh?" I raised an eyebrow, and I placed a hand over my heart. "Do you have a loved one with cancer?"

Jensen held out a hand. "No, nothing like that." He rubbed his fingers over his brow. "That makes my excuse sound pathetic."

While I was relieved no one close to him had died, his response made me even more curious. "Don't leave me hanging." Jensen deflated like a punctured tire.

"It's because of my ex, Kayla"—he peeked from under his lashes and locked gazes before studying his beer—"cheated and left me for the senior oncologist at my hospital, Doctor Lee. The breakup was messy."

I cringed. That was not the answer I expected to hear him say, but I empathized. When Matteo stole money from my wallet to "go out with the boys," he'd hammered the final nail in our relationship's coffin. That breakup had been messy, too. Especially since I'd followed Matteo to Arizona, and my dads had to pay for my return to Washington. "I'm sorry. Will she be there tonight?"

He nodded. "Yep. Doctor Andrew Lee is getting an award, too."

Jensen's voice was heavy with sarcasm. "Am I allowed to *boo*?"

He cracked a smile, a hint of color touching his cheeks. "If I had some rotten tomatoes to give you, I would." He wrapped a hand around his drink. "But seriously, I'll point Kayla out, and when she's close…."

"You want me to ramp up my game?" I smirked. Showing the cheaters what they were missing was the best part of my job. And getting to do it with Jensen had butterflies swarming in my stomach.

His smile broadened. "Yes, please. And just to be clear"—he held up a hand—"I'm not trying to win her back. When we broke up, everyone started gossiping, making work unbearable."

"That must have been horrible." What was wrong with her? How could she cheat on Jensen? He seemed perfect. What was the crazy in Jensen's basement I was unaware of? Something had to exist.

"Work is getting better. I'm glad Kayla showed her

true colors." His eyes searched my face. "Having you by my side tonight will stop me from looking like a pathetic loser. Thank you."

"No need to thank me. I don't think that could ever happen." Taking a sip of my drink, I brushed my fingers over the front of my satin dress. "Wow, she went for another doctor—in your same hospital. What? Is there some medical dating app I'm unaware of?"

Jensen chuckled. "If something like that existed, she'd be on it. But no." He shook his head. "She's got easier access than an app."

I tilted my head to the side. "How so?"

"She's a pharmacist at my hospital, so she sees doctors every day."

No wonder the breakup had been a scandal—they couldn't escape each other. "Her constant proximity must be uncomfortable for you." At least, Matteo was still in Arizona.

"Sometimes." Jensen shrugged. "When we were together, I interacted with her one-on-one when I had questions about a patient, but after the breakup, I pass my messages through the nurses and residents."

"I don't blame you." I toasted him.

He clinked my glass with his beer bottle. "Thank you. I was very proud of myself for coming up with that."

I smiled and checked the time. "Oh, wow. It's already after six, and we need to be there by seven, correct?"

Jensen glanced at his watch and nodded.

"Since we'll need to get moving soon, how about we do some rapid-fire facts? I'll go first."

Jensen crossed his arms and relaxed in his chair,

one brow cocked.

My stomach dropped through my thighs, but I ignored my desire. "My favorite color is red, my favorite food is Indian cuisine—*naan* is to die for—and my favorite movie is *Dirty Dancing*. I like to listen to any genre of music"—I held up a finger—"except jazz. If you put it on in the car, then I will change the station—consider yourself warned." I narrowed my eyes with a playful pout. "I'm an only child—adopted; I have two dads. One's a lawyer, and one's a musician."

Jensen's eyes widened. "Wow, they say opposites attract…"

"Shh, no, no. I'm not done." I winked to soften my chastisement.

He pinched his lips together, repressing a smile. "Sorry, continue."

"My favorite drink is a dirty martini, but when I'm not drinking, like tonight, I stick with ginger ale"—I pointed toward my glass—"or a Shirley Temple."

Jensen's forehead creased, and he cocked his head to the side.

I answered his unasked question. "You'll need to know if I ask you to get me a drink tonight."

"Ah." Jensen tapped his temple. "Noted."

I glided my fingers along my braided necklace and reviewed my facts. "Oh, and I love to dance. If we get the opportunity tonight, know I'm in, if you are—but no pressure." I finished my ginger ale and gestured. "Okay, your turn."

Jensen cleared his throat, then took a deep breath. "My favorite color is navy blue, and I love Mexican food—the spicier, the better." He peeked from the corner of his eye, and a smile tugged at Jensen's lips.

"Jazz is my favorite kind of music—"

I shot him a dead stare. "You're joking, right?"

Jensen laughed. "One hundred percent. I couldn't agree more about jazz. It's awful." He made a gagging motion. "Alternative is my go-to. Um"—he tugged at his collar—"what else do you need to know about me?"

"What about your family?"

"Ah, yes. My mom is a widow, and I have a younger brother, Billy, who's studying dentistry at UCLA. My favorite drink is a beer"—he jiggled his bottle—"but at events like tonight, I feel like I need something more professional—like bourbon, but I nurse the liquor because it burns."

He rasped the last word. I sputtered a laugh. "You think a bourbon sounds more professional?"

Jensen scoffed. "Yes. I've never seen any of the other doctors order a beer at these events. Besides, I hide the grimace, and the crying stays inside." He thumped his chest. "Nobody will know but you."

He was a winning lottery ticket—handsome and funny. I shivered against the tingle on my skin. "I'll keep tissues handy in case a tear slips out."

"Ha. Ha." Jensen slowly shook his head with each syllable.

"Okay, what about dancing? Is it on the table for tonight?"

"Oh." His eyebrows bounced. "I didn't realize this evening would be a table-dancing kind of night."

Biting my lip, I closed my eyes at the swagger in his tone. As long as I didn't drink alcohol, table dancing wouldn't happen.

"I'm kidding; I'm kidding." Jensen chuckled, but his ears went bright red. "However, I have something embarrassing to admit about dancing."

I leaned forward, resting my elbows on the table. Spilt tea was always entertaining. "Ooh, do tell."

"My mother was adamant I know how to dance properly, so I had three years at the Bellevue Dance Academy."

He winced, looking as if he'd bitten into something sour. "Three years? Really?"

Jensen gave a slow nod with a grimace. "Yep, top of my class." He laid a couple of twenties on the table and stood.

Electricity whirled up my spine. He might have been embarrassed, but I was quite the opposite. "Hopefully, tonight's venue has a dance floor." As I rose from the booth, I texted Lilly.

—*Be jealous. Be very, very jealous*—

Chapter 6

Jensen

I drove Autumn to the Bleu Harbor International Conference Center, peering at her in the passenger seat. The streetlamps illuminated her petite features. She had a beautiful profile, but after our conversation at the bar, I knew Autumn had more than just her distinctive looks. She had a quick wit and a plan for her future. I was ashamed to say I hadn't expected those qualities from a companion. She also gave the impression she worked for Plus One, not as a last resort or an easy job, but more a means to an end. I turned into the venue's parking lot and waited in line for the valet.

Autumn rotated in her seat. "One last thing before we go inside, how affectionate and adoring do you want me to be tonight? Are you okay with public displays of affection?"

I froze. "Yes." My voice cracked, and I cringed. Coughing, I cleared my throat. "Yes."

She smiled and brushed a hand down my arm.

Tingles propelled through the rest of my body.

"Are you sure, Jensen? We can pretend to be a conservative couple. Whatever makes you the most comfortable."

"No!" The word came out sharper than I'd intended. I swallowed, reining in the mixture of nerves and desire. "What I mean is, look at you." I swept my gaze over her sexy curves, and I had to force myself not to linger. "I don't think my colleagues would believe our story if I *wasn't* touching you." I rubbed at the heat radiating up the back of my neck. "I think the more important question is—how are *you* with PDA?"

Autumn blushed. "In case you haven't noticed, I'm a touchy person." Her gaze darted to her hand still holding my wrist. "So, as long as your actions are appropriate for the situation, we're good. Okay?"

I nodded, and my mouth went dry. As I agonized over how to touch Autumn, I felt like I was about to take a test I hadn't studied for. The balance of what my body wanted versus what people expected and what was considered appropriate was tricky. One wrong move could cancel the contract and ruin the night. I decided to veer on the conservative side of PDA. With any luck, I'd match her comfort level. The last thing I wanted to do was touch her too much and earn myself a slap. After putting the car in Park, I exited the vehicle.

The dark-green vest-wearing valet opened the door for Autumn.

She stepped out of the car and waited on the curb.

I passed off my key fob to the gangly attendant.

Autumn wrapped an arm through mine and squeezed my bicep. "You ready?" She beamed.

How did she appear so calm? I could hear my heartbeat pounding in my ears, and my movements felt stiff. "I hope so." My words came out as a question.

Yanking my lapels, Autumn forced my gaze to her eye level. She placed her hands on my cheeks and rested her forehead against mine. "Stop overthinking it, Jensen. Do what comes naturally, and they won't doubt a thing."

Autumn's aggressiveness made my body react ungentlemanly, and I had to force myself to concentrate on comprehending her advice. I escorted Autumn to the event room, reveling in her soft vanilla scent and silently repeating the phrase *do what comes naturally*. My plan to have the mantra sink into my subconscious wasn't working. My gut told me to crush my lips against Autumn's and see where the night led. However, I was sure I was just one of a long list of hopeful clients who wished they hadn't agreed to the constraints of the contract.

Inside the conference center, I let my thoughts drift back to my time with Kayla. Everything that came naturally was wrong—Kayla didn't like my arm around her at the table; she never wanted to hold hands, and kissing was completely off-limits unless *she* allowed it. Conversely, Autumn appeared at ease with her arm through mine, and we were basically strangers.

A woman wearing a conference center name badge that read *Juli* opened the door to the presentation hall for Autumn and me.

Entering, I took a step before stopping in my tracks and brought Autumn to a halt. The opulence of the venue blew me away. The space felt like we'd hopped through a magic portal into an interior decorating magazine. Thin, reeded wood panels covered three of the ballroom walls, matching the color of the vinyl wood flooring. The ceiling had a grid formation, with wavy metal lattices between the gaps, reflecting its lights behind, and gave the room a shimmering glow. Dotted around the floor stood round, white-cloth-covered tables with assigned numbers in the center. The location was way nicer than I'd expected.

At least half of the attendees were already mingling with drinks in their hands.

I spotted Dan, my best friend and coworker, at the bar across the room by the final wall made of windows overlooking the Sound. I released a cleansing breath. "Okay, let's do this."

Autumn gave an opened-mouthed wink. "Bring it on, baby."

My stomach flipped. Her term of affection caught me off guard, like finding a twenty in the pocket of your jeans. Kayla never liked pet names. I put a hand on the small of Autumn's back—something else my ex also never allowed—and escorted my date toward Dan. "See the guy with the cropped, light-brown hair?" I spoke low and quietly in her ear. Autumn's musky perfume riled my senses. "His wife is the blonde with her hair up in the sparkly silver dress at the bar?"

Autumn bent closer and followed my line of sight. "Yep. Who's he?"

I leaned back to keep her proximity from jumbling my thoughts. "That's my best friend, Dan, and his wife, Kristine. He's a fellow pediatric hospitalist. I've known him since our residency together." I gave Autumn a pointed stare, locking our gazes to convey the gravity of the situation. "His wife will be our toughest sell."

She gave a curt nod followed by another wink. "Got it."

I swore I could feel my heart skip a beat. Reining in my innate longing for Autumn, I purposely led her the remaining few feet between us and the couple. "They'll let anyone in here, won't they?" I smacked Dan on the back.

He turned, laughing.

I watched him catch sight of Autumn and do a double take.

Dan kept his gaze on my date. "Jensen, whom do we have here?"

Autumn stuck out a hand. "You must be Dan; I've heard all about you. I'm Autumn." She gave a warm smile to his wife. "And you must be Kristine?"

Dan and Kristine took turns shaking Autumn's hand, their jaws slack.

My friend grabbed the back of my neck. "You dirty dog, where have you been hiding this beauty?"

"Yeah, Jensen." Kristine gave me a shove. "I can't believe you've kept her from us."

I glanced down, shuffling my feet.

"That's my fault. I've been monopolizing his time and unwilling to share." Autumn put her free hand on my chest and gazed into my eyes. "But tonight I will, so everyone will get to celebrate what I've come to know and love about this amazing man."

Dan threw his hands in the air, palms forward. "Well, I don't know if I would go as far as calling him 'amazing.' " He air-quoted the last word.

"Stop, Dan. You're just jealous he's getting an award, and you're not." Kristine swatted her husband's arm playfully. "It's that kind of mentality that kept you off the best doctor list in the first place."

Dan opened his mouth.

Kristine splayed a hand in front of his face.

Taking his wife's hand, Dan laced his fingers through Kristine's and shrugged off the gesture.

"Anyway, I want to hear about you two. How did you meet?" Kristine's gaze bounced between Autumn and me.

It's go time. I inhaled a deep breath, channeling Autumn's confidence. "We were set up, of course."

Dan and Kristine nodded.

I smiled at Autumn. "A mutual friend matched us on a blind date."

Autumn dropped her gaze and nudged me with her shoulder.

My smile was unrestrained at her girlfriend-like reaction.

"I have to say, I was a little leery when Fin told me about Jensen. I mean"—she met my gaze and held it—"if he's a handsome young doctor, why doesn't he have women falling all over him?"

Dan barked a laugh. "Hardly."

I glared at my friend, not appreciating his jibe.

"But, when I met Jensen"—she readjusted and brushed my jaw with her fingers—"I couldn't believe my luck that this guy was still on the market." She tapped my nose, her gaze dancing between my eyes before dropping to my lips.

Unexpected waves of heat ran through my torso. Autumn was good, and I found myself willing her words to be true. I tightened my grip on her waist, pulling her against my chest.

She gasped, her pupils wide.

I was aware of every place our bodies touched.

"Wow! Do I need to throw cold water over you two?" Dan shielded his wife's eyes. "Jensen, you're making me look bad."

Kristine batted her husband's hand away. "You don't need his help."

"Edwards! Falkner!"

Turning, I spotted the Chief of Staff and his wife

sauntering in our direction. I released Autumn.

She smoothed the front of her dress with a hand, a bit of color in her cheeks.

Gary's laugh lines deepened as he shook hands with Dan first, then Kristine.

The Chief's wife, Meg, air-kissed both my cheeks, then clasped her fingers together, rattling the numerous gold bracelets adorning her wrists. "Jensen, aren't you going to introduce me to your beautiful lady friend?"

I presented my date to my boss and his wife. Autumn didn't even flinch at Meg's overly plastic, almost alien-looking face, complete with lips which barely moved. In fact, Autumn's engagement with our whole group came off as genuine and natural. I was shocked she hadn't gone into acting. Her performance was flawless; if I hadn't been a part of this whole charade, even *I* would have bought our story. Molly chose my date wisely.

"What line of work are you in?" Gary directed his question at Autumn.

As she gave the details of her education and the status of her nursing degree, she didn't hesitate.

I listened to their conversation, unable to keep from smiling.

Dan leaned close. "Dude, well done."

He spoke low into my ear.

"Even the boss likes her." He nodded toward Autumn. "Plus, she seems like a nice person—what you see is what you get, unlike a certain money-grabbing pharmacist we both know."

I coughed to cover my laughter at the irony of his statement. Besides Autumn working toward her BSN, nothing else was true about this evening. "Yeah, I won the jackpot."

Dan slapped my shoulder and took a sip of his drink. "Not gonna lie, we were worried you would show up alone since you rejected the date with Kristine's coworker, and with Kayla coming…."

He didn't need to finish his sentence; I knew what Dan meant. Not wanting to go stag at the last minute was why I'd agreed to this arrangement with Autumn in the first place. "You're telling me." I forced a grin. When Autumn discussed her intentions to enter radiation oncology as opposed to medical or surgical, the passion in her eyes matched her smile.

"Beating cancer is a team effort—everyone needs to work together. The majority of people have no idea the discomfort chemotherapy entails."

Autumn's enthusiasm was captivating, and as she shared her grandmother's battle with pancreatic cancer, our whole group hung on her every word.

"Knowledge and awareness are key. When I'm an oncology BSN, I hope my experience will benefit my patients."

Meg toasted Autumn. "I couldn't agree more. When my sister was diagnosed with breast cancer, none of us knew what to expect or what to do." She took a sip. "A nurse like you would have been very helpful."

The lights flickered. The dinner and presentation would begin soon.

Gary gave my hand a final shake. "Hold onto this one." He smiled at Autumn. "Otherwise, when I hire her for our oncology department, it will be awkward."

I chuckled, fiddling with my bowtie. If Gary hired Autumn, work would become complicated again. This lie would never end.

Chapter 7

Autumn

Throughout the meal, tension radiated off Jensen in waves. The ridged slant of his shoulders appeared as if he was chiseled from stone. I couldn't decide if his nervousness was over receiving his Best Doctor's award or the awkward remark his boss had made before we sat. Either way, I didn't break character. We were seated at a table with three other doctors and their partners, none of whom appeared to know each other, making the majority of the dinner conversations inconsequential small talk.

Once the servers cleared everyone's plates, the bespectacled presenter stood at the podium onstage. The introductions began, starting with surgical, but before long, we'd gotten to oncology. When I heard Dr. Andrew Lee's name called, I leaned toward Jensen. "Is that him?"

Jensen's lips drew into a hard line, and he nodded.

"So, where's Kayla?" I scanned the audience, wondering which of the women was his ex.

Jensen shook his head. "I don't see her, but I know she's here."

The master of ceremonies cleared his throat and moved onto the next specialty.

I sagged in my chair. Getting a peek at my supposed opponent would have been nice.

"Our next doctor is Jensen Edwards. He's from Seattle Children's Hospital." The host continued, describing Jensen's work with Doctors Without Borders, his fundraising efforts for the hospital, and his other charitable volunteer work. With each mention, I could feel my respect for Jensen grow. Seeing him rise to accept his award, I stood, too, clapping and bouncing on my toes.

Jensen received his plaque, then met my gaze before acknowledging the crowd with a wave.

The gratitude in his expression made my knees go weak, and I had to lean on the table for support.

Jensen returned to his seat.

I nabbed the award from his hands. The black wood brandished a silver plate etched with Jensen's name under the words, *Best Doctors in Seattle*. I trailed my fingers over the letters. "Congratulations, Jensen. This is an incredible honor."

He ducked his head, pink blotching his cheeks. "Thank you."

Straightening in my chair, I blinked several times. Witnessing Jensen's humility, I felt a twinge behind my ribs.

"I liked seeing you in the audience." Jensen leaned in close.

His breath fanned my neck. Repressing a shiver, I bit my lip.

"I know you're getting paid to clap and whatnot, but the gesture made me feel good all the same."

Putting a hand over my pounding heart, I hoped to convey my sincerity. "The applause was genuine." I glanced around but didn't see any prying eyes. "Contract aside, I couldn't help but be impressed with your volunteer work, in addition to your job. With all the hours you put in at the hospital, the extra efforts are no small feat."

Jensen averted his gaze and scratched his cheek. "We are required to do a certain number of community service hours."

He was being modest. "But your list was longer than many of the other doctors."

Jensen bobbled his head. "Well, sure, but…."

I shoved him playfully, a ripple of want pulsing through me at the firmness of his shoulder. "See? So, take the compliment."

Jensen's mouth slanted up, the corners of his eyes crinkling. "Fine."

The presenter removed and pocketed his glasses. "Let's give one final round of applause for all our doctors this evening."

I clapped along with the crowd, my gaze snagging on Jensen's hitched-up cheek, sending liquid heat through my veins. He caught me looking.

Jensen tilted his head and raised a brow.

I turned back to the elderly presenter, my ears burning.

"Thank you all for attending. Please feel free to head onto the roof for dancing and drinks."

Jensen stood and offered a hand. "Care to celebrate with some dancing?"

I popped out of my seat like he'd hit the eject button. Grabbing my clutch, I looped my arm through Jensen's. "Can't let your three years of dance lessons go to waste." I had no intention of passing up the opportunity to press myself against his stellar physique. Plus, I loved dancing.

The convention center rooftop was stunning, with the glistening lights of the Seattle harbor as the backdrop. The center of the gray-and-white checkered patio was a designated dance floor with the DJ toward the back, edging the view of the Sound. Along the side railings sat high bar tables scattered among a few shorter seating areas, with a wood-slatted bar off to my right.

"Should we claim a spot so I can set down my plaque?" Jensen hefted the rectangular piece of wood and motioned to a table on his left. "Or Dan and Kristine are over there." He jutted his chin in their direction. "Want to sit with them, instead?"

I gave a slight shrug. "You're the boss tonight. I'm happy with whichever you decide." Despite my motto to swear off men, I knew which I would prefer, and I had to fight the suggestive smile threatening to give away my feelings. Jensen's cheek quirked in a wolfish grin, causing my stomach to free-fall like the first drop of a roller coaster. Adrenaline filled my veins as I followed him to the table on our left. I was giddy at the thought that perhaps his choice meant he wanted me all to himself. *Calm down, Autumn!*

After depositing my clutch and Jensen's jacket along with his award, he took my hand and led me into the middle of the dance floor.

The bass reverberated through my chest, and I swayed my hips to the rhythm.

Jensen placed a hand on my waist, his body undulating with the beat.

I bit my lip. He wasn't lying. Jensen had moves, and I had to stop my mind from wandering to other scenarios where his smooth actions might apply. For several songs, our bodies collided to the music, the salty sea air cooling the heat building in my belly.

Jensen undid his bowtie, letting the silk dangle from his neck. The top two buttons of his shirt hung open.

I caught a glimpse of his glistening chest, the dampness of the white cotton melded to his muscles, leaving little to my imagination.

Jensen's heavy-lidded eyes roamed over my curves.

Heat coiled up my thighs, and I needed to quell the sparks of desire sprinting towards becoming an inferno before they got out of hand. I was feeling too comfortable, and the situation was becoming a little too real. I angled toward his ear. "I'm going to grab a drink." I shouted over the music. "Do you want one?"

Jensen's throat bobbed once. "Let me. What would you like?" He took my left hand again.

I followed him to our table. Sliding my clutch from its hiding place under Jensen's jacket, I fanned myself. "Just water would be fine. Bottled, if they have it."

Grabbing one of the cloth napkins on the table, Jensen mopped the sweat from his brow and the back of his neck. "Water, it is." He gave a wink and sauntered backward toward the bar. "Be back in a minute."

A sensual smile played on his lips. Jensen was *so* sexy. Flirting was part of the job. Just because I was enjoying myself, and he made me quiver, didn't make what I was doing wrong. In fact, the ease I felt with Jensen made the situation easier to sell. As long as he and I knew where the line was, I'd be fine. At least I was making Jensen comfortable, which is more than I could say for the chick in the unflattering gold dress chatting with him at the bar. I watched Jensen order our drinks. His back was so straight I thought he had a pole up his backside.

He turned his head and gave me a side-eye.

Oh no! She's his ex. I finger-combed my hair, giving the strands a few poofs, and smoothed my dress, strutting over to a wide-eyed Jensen.

The bartender handed him the drinks.

Rubbing a hand down Jensen's back, I took the glass of ice water. "Thanks, babe." I pecked him on the cheek, then turned to the wannabe Margot Robbie, complete with shiny plastic breasts. "I don't believe we've met." I stuck out my right hand, keeping eye contact. "I'm Autumn, Jensen's girlfriend."

Her head reeled back, and she glared at Jensen. "Girlfriend? Wow, you didn't take long to move on."

Jensen downed his bourbon, slamming the glass onto the bar. "At least, I waited until we weren't together."

Kayla put her left hand on her hip. "Maybe if you'd specialized, we wouldn't be having this conversation."

"Maybe if you weren't so shallow, you'd have realized what you had. Lucky for me"—Jensen jerked his head in my direction—"Autumn does." He slipped a hand around my waist.

His grip, rough and possessive, did a number on my insides.

"Come on, Autumn, let's dance." He ushered me back toward our table.

I took a few swigs of my water before abandoning the glass with my clutch and followed Jensen into the fray with an eager skip in my step.

Tension radiated along his jaw, and his gaze

appeared to be a mix of determination, anger, and lust.

Whatever he was feeling, his reaction had me salivating—a bad-boy attitude but still a nice guy—I wouldn't have thought he had it in him.

Jensen leaned forward, his lips rasping against my ear. "Make me look good—she's watching."

I shook, an involuntary shiver running down my neck and into my spine. *This will be fun.* "You got it." I licked my lips, slow and seductive, before wrapping my arms around his neck, my hips pressed against him, and swayed to the beat.

Jensen's hands slid down my waist.

I felt his fingers dig into my skin, and I couldn't stop my heart from racing. Jensen's performance had me coiled like a spring, ready to jump at any moment. If Kayla was watching, she couldn't deny my chemistry with Jensen. I chanced a glance. The woman's deep scowl and curled lip was all the answer I needed. *A+* for Jensen's performance. "She looks furious."

"Good."

His response was a growl, and I tightened my grip. I couldn't help myself. "Want to send Kayla over the edge?"

"What?" He blinked, his gaze darting everywhere but my face. "How?" Jensen swallowed hard.

He appeared nervous, but honestly, so was I—eager, too. Throwing caution to the wind, I voiced my thoughts. "Grab my backside."

Jensen coughed a couple of times. "I'm sorry?"

"You heard me." I jutted my chin, my confidence building. "Grab. My. Backside."

Jensen's eyes darkened, and his hands slid from my hips to my butt, cupping my rear.

Desire took over, and my instincts kicked in. I leaned forward and crushed my lips to his.

Jensen froze.

I'd taken him by surprise—him and me both.

With a sexy low moan, Jensen's mouth moved ravenously over mine.

He tasted like bourbon and mint. One of his hands slid to my lower back, and he crushed me against his chest.

His breathing became ragged.

My insides were on fire.

Jensen's teeth grazed my bottom lip.

I couldn't stop the yearning that ran through my body.

He paused, pulling away. Jensen studied my face.

Hunger swirled in his gaze. The primal part of me begged for more, but I needed to rein my desire in before either of us got out of hand. I averted my gaze, breaking Jensen's stare and took a deep breath. Glancing over my shoulder, I checked for Kayla. She was gone. Clearing my throat, I loosened my hold around Jensen's neck and took a step back. "It worked." I thumbed over my shoulder where his ex had been. "Good job, Jensen. She couldn't take it."

He shook his head, and his gaze fell back on my lips. "What?"

"Kayla"—I nodded my head at the space where she once stood—"she's gone. She's no longer watching. Our performance must have gotten under her skin." *I know it got under mine.*

Jensen blinked rapidly.

The pressure of his touch lightened.

"Oh. Yeah, yeah. Good. I'm glad." He rubbed a

hand over his mouth. "Thank you." Jensen breathed heavily.

"No thanks needed. Kissing you was hardly a chore." The words just came out, and heat invaded my face. "Besides, my job *is* to make you look good." My chest squeezed. When I'd kissed him, I hadn't given a thought to his contract.

He dipped his head and let out a low chuckle. "I'm glad I wasn't torturing you."

"Not even." The kiss made me putty in his hands, and my body was all too eager to get back on the potter's wheel. "Should we take a break from dancing and be more social?" *Put out the fire you ignited in my core?* He schooled his features into a polite smile.

Jensen pulled at his collar. "If that's what you want."

It wasn't, but space was what I needed. I spotted Jensen's friends at a nearby table. "Look, Dan and Kristine are still sitting over there. Why don't we join them?" *Let them be a buffer.* "After you."

The mischievous smile on Jensen's face told me being around his friends wouldn't change a thing.

Chapter 8

Jensen

The drive back to The Stalker's Tango flew by. *How am I hitting every green light?* I didn't want the evening to end. With every passing intersection, I couldn't keep dread from churning in my stomach. I kept reliving my kiss with Autumn on the dance floor. Had the interaction been a performance? The chemistry felt so real. She'd even admitted the kiss wasn't a chore. Which meant Autumn enjoyed herself, too, right? The passion couldn't have been all one-sided. Aside from the kiss—she'd also handled the whole night well. If tonight was all an act, she deserved an award. Autumn was flawless in her conversations with the other doctors, she'd clicked with Dan and Kristine, and even Gary and Meg thought she was intriguing. I glanced at Autumn in the passenger seat doing something on her phone. Watching the intermittent streetlights illuminate her beautiful features, I realized something. "Let me pay for your parking."

"Hmm?" Autumn glanced up. "Oh, I didn't drive. For anonymity's sake, Plus One requires us to use driving services, so I took a rideshare to the bar."

"In that case, why don't you let me take you home?" The ache in my chest lightened. "Dropping you at the bar just so you can call for a ride seems silly."

She inclined her head, lowering her gaze. "Thank

you. I appreciate your chivalry, but accepting wouldn't be appropriate."

I gripped the steering wheel, desperate to change her mind. Having to part with Autumn was bad enough, but abandoning her to depend on someone else to get her home was out of the question. "My only motive is to get you home safely."

She sucked in a deep breath and held it for a beat. "I know. But it's against company policy for you to know where I live."

I winced. The subtle reminder Autumn was paid to be my date left a hollow feeling in my chest. "Of course, I'm so sorry. I didn't mean to make you uncomfortable." I drove alongside the curb in front of The Stalker's Tango. Putting the car in Park, I got out and jogged to open her door. Offering Autumn a hand, I helped her onto the sidewalk. "Would you mind if I waited until your ride shows?" It was the least I could do.

The night had gone better than any of the actual dates I'd had in the past six months. Then again, maybe my time with Autumn was fun because her job was to be a good date. An uneasy feeling settled in my stomach. That explanation didn't sit right. Throughout the night, Autumn talked to my colleagues about her education, aspirations, and her family life. The stories never changed, and since lies were hard to keep track of, I could assume those facts had to be genuine. So what parts were fake?

"Thank you. I'd appreciate it." Autumn rechecked her phone, rubbing her hands up and down her arms.

Is she cold? "Do you want my jacket?"

She demurred with a shake of her head. "No, I'm

fine."

"I can see the goose bumps on your arms." I slouched out of my tux coat. "Here." I draped the jacket over her shoulders, ignoring her protests.

Autumn scrunched her shoulders and inhaled deeply.

My breath caught. Women in the movies did the same thing when they enjoyed a man's scent, right? Did Autumn enjoy mine? She couldn't still be acting—the date was all but over.

"Thank you. You didn't have to. I'm not on the clock anymore."

Score! The reaction was a genuine appreciation of my cologne. "Clock or no clock, I'd be a jerk if I watched you shiver to death." Plus, I liked seeing her in my jacket.

Autumn's head tilted, her gaze roaming my face. "I don't get it, Jensen. Why don't you have a girlfriend? You'd said it's been a while since Kayla."

I didn't want to read too much into her question and fought the hope threatening to fill my chest but found coming up with an answer difficult. "I don't know." Shrugging, I sighed. Honesty was the best policy. "I've been too busy." My response sounded like a question. "With work, checking in on my mother, volunteering, upkeep on my house, and medical conferences, I just haven't had the time to date." Not to mention, I hadn't found anyone as fascinating as Autumn.

She pursed her lips, tugging the lapels of my jacket tighter. "You should make time. You're cheating some nice girl out of your company." Autumn's face softened. "And you deserve someone nice in return."

She placed a hand over my sternum. "Someone who deserves *you*."

I swallowed slow and hard, the heat from her touch spreading through my insides. *She likes me.* My heartbeat picked up, and I was sure she could feel it, too.

Her gaze landed on my lips.

My body instinctively responded, leaning forward of its own accord.

"Autumn?"

A deep male voice with a heavy Southern accent arose from the far side of my car. I turned to see a black coupe double parked, a bearded man with a beanie and heavily-rimmed yellow glasses behind the wheel. The illuminated sign on the dashboard indicated he was her ride.

Autumn took a step back, glancing at the rideshare driver and held up a finger in his direction before turning back. "That's me." She stared wide-eyed at my tux jacket covering her raised arm, then slid the garment from her shoulders, and handed it back. "Here. Thanks again." She held the jacket at arm's length.

This was good-bye, and I was torn. Instinct begged me to kiss her good night, however, considering the circumstances and my willing desire, I was sure the action wouldn't be appropriate. I rocked back on my heels. "Um, I'm not sure what to do here."

"Look, this isn't a real date. You don't owe me anything. You're off the hook." She extended a hand. "Thank you for a wonderful evening."

I stared at her smooth, slender fingers for a moment before wrapping my hand around Autumn's and guiding it to my lips. I placed a soft, lingering kiss on the inside of her wrist and met her gaze. "The pleasure was all mine."

As she withdrew her hand, Autumn averted her gaze, biting her lip, then scuttled to the rideshare. Opening the door to the car, she glanced back. "Good night, Jensen."

Her wistful expression strangled my heart. "Good night, Autumn."

****

Thirty minutes later, I sat in one of the cushioned seats at the back of the ferry, watching the Space Needle, downtown skyscrapers, and the Seattle Great Wheel shrink away out the back window of the boat. Autumn was right; I shouldn't deprive myself of these views. I recalled the evening, fixating on the kiss. Autumn's lips were like velvet, tasting of mint and salt. As we danced, the subtle curves of her body against mine had me undone. I blew out a breath and focused again on the vanishing city lights. Fixating on a woman I couldn't have wasn't appropriate. After regaining control of my desires, I obsessed over my good-bye. *Why did I make the moment so awkward?* She'd extended a hand to shake, and I kissed her wrist? My attraction couldn't have been more obvious.

Autumn contracted dates for a living, and kissing was fair game according to the Plus One website. Did that mean she made out with all her clients? Red filled my vision, and I shook my head to clear the irrational emotion. No, the kind of kiss I shared with Autumn couldn't be the norm. Otherwise, rules would get broken, or the companions would be in danger from overzealous clients.

Plus One hadn't given me a background check

before my date with Autumn. I could have been a sex offender for all they knew. Hopefully, Autumn's actions tonight meant I made her feel safe enough to have allowed *that* kiss. She'd even asked me to grab her backside, which likely wasn't typical protocol. I ran my hands through my hair, gripping my scalp, more confused by this fake date than any other setup in the past. "Damn it, Molly! This is your fault." My words came out too loud.

A gray-haired man in a newsboy cap side-eyed me over his book.

I ducked my head, my ears heating. My outburst gave me an idea. If anyone could make sense of tonight, it would be Molly. I got out my phone, scrolling through my contacts until I found her name. Tapping on Molly's number, I glanced at the clock on the wall of the ferry. Great, I was calling after midnight. I jabbed the *End* button, terminating the connection. Opening my calendar, I checked my schedule for tomorrow morning, searching for an opportunity to squeeze in a call. Pressing the plus sign in the corner, I selected 9:45 a.m., poising my thumbs to type when Molly's profile appeared on my screen. She called back. *Guess I didn't hang up fast enough.* "Hello?" I cringed.

"Hi, Jensen. I had a feeling you'd be calling."

Her tone was smug, and I widened my eyes. "You did?"

"Of course, Jared and I had bets going on what time you'd call." She laughed. "He owes me a foot massage."

I leaned forward, resting my elbows on my knees, and scrubbed a hand through my hair. "Well, since you expected this, I'm sure you know what I want to ask."

"I figured you were either calling to thank me or chew me out. Which is it?"

"Neither." She had no idea how perfect her choice was in Autumn.

Molly gave a high-pitched grunt. "Okay…"

Hoping she had a magical answer, I tapped my fingers on my thigh. "It's about you and Jared. How did you know what was real?"

Chapter 9

Autumn

The line of cars at my tollbooth snaked around the ferry lot, through the traffic light, and onto Alaskan Way. I didn't mind, though. During these rush hour moments, most of the commuters had Puget Card ferry passes, which made my job easier. But every now and then, a vehicle would still pay with cash or credit.

A silver luxury car similar to Jensen's caught my eye. As the vehicle approached my booth, I thought of my date from last weekend, just like I had every other day this week. The heat from Jensen's kiss still lingered in my veins, and I couldn't stop thinking about his rough grip on my backside. Making his ex jealous was fun. In fact, I'd enjoyed the night a little too much. Jensen starred in more than one of my dreams this past week, which had never happened before with a client. I was angry with myself that the fantasies even happened at all.

Midterms were just weeks away. Jensen was a distraction—one I couldn't afford right now, reminding me I needed to block off my Plus One calendar as soon as possible. Studying was my top priority—no men until my BSN, because, while getting my psychology degree, I'd learned the hard way that putting my personal life before my studies stalled my future.

My ex, Matteo, could have been a Mediterranean

hottie poster child with his olive skin, silky black hair, and smooth personality. We'd dated my senior year of high school, and I convinced myself we were meant to be. Hence, when he got a baseball scholarship to Arizona State, I followed him like a lost puppy.

Instantly, I fell in love with Arizona. Tempe was heaven—the sky was always blue, the weather was always warm, and the only rain came from the intermittent, fifteen-minute monsoons. Sure, I lived in a sketchy apartment close to the university and enrolled at the local community college while Matteo lived it up on campus, but I was happy—or so I thought. The fact my boyfriend was okay with my living situation should have been my first red flag.

As I spent every possible moment with Matteo outside of his practices, I was blinded by my love. However, as the baseball season ramped up, Matteo's availability became infrequent—not just physically, but emotionally, too. He texted less, he rarely talked on dates—if he ever took me on one—and eventually, he stopped coming over altogether.

Reflecting, I realized I should have seen the end coming. If I had a nickel for every time he'd said, "It's a team-building experience—no girlfriends allowed" or "It's a guys-only night," I would've had enough money to fund the rest of my first bachelor's degree. But when I caught him stealing from me to "go out with the boys," I decided Matteo hammered the final nail in our relationship's coffin.

By the end of the first semester, my dads had heard enough of my tear-filled drama, and they offered to pay for my return to Seattle. Reluctantly, I took them up on the deal, returned home with my tail between my legs, and finished my psychology degree at the University of Washington.

That was six years ago, and my faith in men still hadn't been restored. In truth, working at Plus One hadn't helped, either—some clients were genuinely selfish, but it didn't matter; I had a plan. Thanks to Matteo, I vowed to achieve my nursing degree independently, put my love life on hold, and not rely on any man, including my dads. Dad and Papi were gracious enough to bail me out the first time; I couldn't—or, more like, wouldn't—let them help me again.

Unfortunately, my altruism left me strapped for cash. The minimum wage I earned working at the tollbooth wasn't enough to live on. Not if I wanted to be an independent full-time student in Seattle and not live at home, making my second job at Plus One a necessity. And while Lilly chose companioning as her full-time income, watching the emotional drain and her lack of time was all I needed to convince myself that Plus One was a weekend-only deal.

As I opened my register to get the Middle Eastern businesswoman at my window her change, I heard my phone ping. I chanced a glimpse at the screen—another alert from Plus One. *Damn it!* I was too late in blocking off my calendar. Making a mental note, I promised myself I'd contact Ruth later and ask her to reassign the job, even though I could've used the money. Extending my hand holding the bills, I inhaled the crisp scent of the rain, allowing the cool air to fill my lungs.

The next several cars all had Puget Cards. Each scanned and drove into the waiting lanes. Another vehicle just like Jensen's pulled forward. From what I could see past the swishing wipers, even the driver's messy brown hair resembled Jensen's. *If only it were him.* I opened my drawer and retrieved the stack of twenties, flipping and rotating them to all face the same direction, scowling at the musty smell of mildew and concrete mixed with hot plastic permeating my cashier stall despite my open windows.

"Autumn?"

I knew the rich tenor voice speaking my name—I shouldn't, but I did. Holding my breath, I spun to see Jensen beaming through his open car window, with a twenty and a ten in his hand, fluttering in the breeze.

"You work here, too?"

"Don't you have a Puget Card?" I pursed my lips, my stomach knotting over my accusatory tone. Being seen in my horrid florescent vest and cap by the star of my recent fantasies sparked my defensiveness.

His smile faltered for a second. "Yes, but the card seems to have fallen under my seat, and I can't find it." Jensen shrugged. "So, I'll pay with cash today."

Jensen let out an uncomfortable laugh, further screwing up my insides. *Get it together, Autumn!*

"How many jobs do you have?"

"Just the two." The tightness in my chest since he'd recognized me eased. *This run-in isn't a big deal. Bainbridge is your regular booth. You probably won't see him again.* "One ticket to Bremerton?"

Jensen's eyes lit up. "You remembered."

He'd set up camp in my brain this past week—of course, I did. I took his cash and slid it into my register, convincing myself the butterflies in my stomach were from surprise, not excitement, at seeing him again.

"Were you contacted by Plus One? Are you okay

for Saturday night?"

What is he talking about? I froze mid-count—the Plus One alert was Jensen. "I noticed I had one, but I've been busy and haven't had a chance to check the details. It's from you?" I handed him his change, wracking my brain for a way to turn him down politely.

"Yeah, I'd requested you as my Plus One again for this weekend. It's a catered hospital benefit, and they invited *all* the doctors." His head bobbed.

His mocking tone and emphasis on the word *all* had me wrinkling my nose. I knew what Jensen meant—Dr. Lee would be there with Kayla. As much as I couldn't afford to take time out of my study schedule, I also didn't feel like I could say *no* and leave Jensen to the wolves. Kayla wouldn't have the last laugh at Jensen's expense if I could help it. Besides, wasn't I just lamenting I'd miss the money this date would provide? The decision was settled. "I'll be there." I shut my register, frowning at my traitorous rapid heartbeat. "What's the dress—"

The white truck behind Jensen honked in two short bursts.

Jensen glared at his rearview mirror before opening the satchel on his passenger seat. He withdrew a business card from one of the pockets and passed it through his window. "Call me; I'll give you all the details." He drove forward, joining the queue for Bremerton.

I stared at his card, zeroing in on the dark-blue digits consisting of his cell number. With Jensen being a doctor, I knew he didn't pass out this information to just anybody—a cell was a private number. Now, Jensen had given it to me and expected I would contact him outside of the Plus One messaging portal. My mouth went dry; this faux relationship just got personal.

****

The next day, I met with Dad for lunch between classes at his favorite café, Grind Grandeur. I sat across the woodblock table with my hands in fists. "I'm so mad at myself for accepting this client for Saturday night. I have midterms coming up." At least, that was the lie I'd been reciting was responsible for my clammy hands and loss of appetite I'd had since Jensen gave me his personal info.

Dad's heavy brows lowered behind his thick, black-rimmed glasses, his bald head shining in the pendant Edison lights. "I told you to request the break sooner."

"I know, and I meant to. I just didn't have the time." *And I felt like I couldn't say* no *to Jensen.*

He pursed his lips. "Didn't have the time, or didn't make the time?"

I cringed. Dad was right. Accepting the date with Jensen was my choice. The fact I'd allowed the contract to take up too much space in my head was my fault, but I wasn't about to admit my faux pas. "Whatever."

"Hmm, mature answer." He took a sip of his hazelnut latte. "How about you admit you're wrong for once?"

"Never." I gave him a playful sneer. "It just means I have to manage my time better from here on out until midterms are over." I'd complete my contract with Jensen tomorrow, stash the cash, and then I could put him out of my mind and use Sunday and Monday to concentrate on my studies.

Dad adjusted his light-gray waistcoat, shaking his

head. "Then I can assume you've already contacted Ruth, and there won't be any other contracts until June?"

"Not exactly, but I will." As a wave of nausea washed over me, I pushed my grilled-cheese-and-black-cherry sandwich away, the scent of burnt mozzarella assaulting my nostrils.

A frown settled on Dad's brow, and he jutted his chin at my plate. "Why aren't you eating? Isn't their grilled cheese your favorite? Is something wrong with it?" Dad shifted, glancing toward the server.

I shot out a hand. "No, Dad. Really. It's fine. My stomach's just upset." I shrugged and rubbed my belly. "It's just the stress of midterms." The intermittent ache in my midsection since last night had nothing to do with the fact Jensen contracted me to be his girlfriend again with the potential I'd have to kiss him to make Kayla jealous—no way.

Dad's phone vibrated on the tabletop, bouncing against his plate and rattling his silverware. As he retrieved the device, he glanced at the screen. "You know"—he set his cell on the table—"if this is stressing you out too much, you can still cancel Saturday's contract and let Papi and I pay for your schooling."

I felt the back of my neck prickle. "No, Dad. I can't cancel, and I won't let you pay." My pride was too big.

Dad's dark but peppered eyebrows shot up.

"You've already financed my first degree and bailed me out of the 'desert fiasco.'" I used the code name we substituted for Matteo since Dad banned his name upon my return. "I can't take any more of your money. I'm a grown adult. I can make it on my own."

"The money is always available." Dad patted my hand. "But why can't you cancel tomorrow?"

My heart squeezed, knowing my answer would be futile—it didn't even make sense in my head, but I tried anyway. "It's the same guy from last week. You know the one whose author friend hired me? The hospital is putting on a benefit dinner, and everyone I met last week will be there, so he can't show up alone. They're expecting me."

Dad nudged his glasses up his nose. "This man had a friend hire you because he couldn't get a date of his own, and now he can't go to a dinner by himself?" He closed his eyes and shook his head. "And you think Papi's dramatic?"

"Oh, stop!" I swatted his arm. "He's not being dramatic. If Papi cheated and left you for another lawyer at your firm, and then you had to attend a function where Papi would be there with his new beau, you'd be okay going alone?" *Let him wriggle out of this one.*

"First of all"—Dad held up a finger—"Papi would never cheat. Besides, if he did, our prenup would destroy him, and he wouldn't have the money for the new outfit he'd need to attend. And second, there's no one better than me at my firm. Not to mention, the rest of the law partners are women." Dad gave me a wink.

"Ugh, Dad." I closed my eyes and sighed. Of course, he wouldn't take my scenario seriously. "You know what I mean." I crossed my arms and leaned back in my chair, just like the petulant child I was being.

His phone buzzed again. After he checked the message, he collected his trash and piled everything on his plate. "I don't know, Autumn. This still sounds like a 'him' problem."

My mouth went dry, and I took a sip of my water, redirecting the conversation. "Is the jury back in?" I folded my napkin and balanced it over the half of the sandwich I couldn't finish.

"Are you canceling the date?"

"Dad, I told you. I can't." My insides felt like they were in a vice grip, and I pinched a spot over my hip to dull the pain. "Not with such late notice."

"Hmm." He grabbed his plate, eyeing my sandwich with a crease between his brows. "Are you sure you're feeling okay?"

I forced a smile and lied through my teeth. "I'm fine."

"As long as you're sure."

I nodded.

Dad gave me a peck on the head before turning toward the door. "Take better care of yourself. Love you."

"Love you, too." I waved, the stitch in my side tightening. Staring at my father's retreating back, I puzzled over his comment. Why did I want to defend Jensen? Why didn't I feel like I could cancel? He was just another client, wasn't he?

Chapter 10

Jensen

I made a note on Beckham's chart before turning to his parents—both preppy blonds in pastel button-down, fitted dress shirts. "Okay, I've changed your son's medication. The downstairs hospital pharmacy will have his new inhaler ready in thirty minutes. And you"—I ruffled the boy's cornsilk hair—"congrats on making the soccer team, but make sure you keep the inhaler handy on the field. I'm glad you're not letting your asthma slow you down."

Beckham flashed a gap-tooth smile.

As I gave him a fist bump, I felt my phone buzz in my pocket. "Excuse me." I focused on the screen and read Autumn's name in the text. My lips twitched. Raising my cell, I shook it. "I'm sorry, folks, but I have to take this. If you have any other questions, or if Beckham has another attack, here's the direct number to my answering service." I fished a card from my pocket and passed it to the boy's mom. "Call that number, and one of my nurses or I will get back to you."

The parents shook my hand, and with a wave at Beckham, I escaped into the break room to respond to Autumn in private. I shut the door before I sat on the worn leather couch and read her text.

—*Hi, it's Autumn. I'm just checking the dress code*

for Saturday—

—Hi, it's Jensen. Winky face emoji. *The attire is business casual. Thank you for agreeing to do this. I hope you don't find my hiring you for the same role creepy—*

I tapped on her number and created a new contact, planning to attach one of her Plus One profile pictures alongside her name.

—No worries, Jensen. It happens more often than you'd think—

My grip on my phone tightened. For some reason, the thought of her being with other men gave me heartburn, but I forced myself to laugh off the implications.

—You're saying, I'm not the only pitiful dumpee out there trying to save face?—

—Don't be silly. You're not pitiful. Besides, if I didn't show up, then everyone at the hospital benefit would wonder what you did to drive me away—

My throat felt thick. She was right; my colleagues adored her. Therefore, if I didn't bring Autumn as my date, the blame laid with me.

—I'm not gonna lie. I'd look like a walking red flag if you didn't show up—

Not to mention, I wanted her there by my side.

—As if you could ever be a red flag. You're pretty much every girl's dream—

Sweat trickled down my back, and I shrugged off my lab coat, laying it over the arm of the couch.

—Tell that to my ego—

Stop. Being. Needy. Change the topic.

—Seeing you at the toll booth was a pleasant surprise. How long have you been working there?—

—When I started nursing school. I'd hoped with my scholarship, grants and the wages from Seattle Ferries, I would have enough to live on, but no such luck, so I supplement with Plus One—

—How come I haven't seen you there before? I travel through the Seattle Port every day—

—I was just subbing there this week. Usually, I'm at a different location—

—Which one?—

The next few seconds contained crickets. Had I overstepped? I *was* still her client. Before I could rip my hair out, I noticed three dots appeared on my screen. I watched them, holding my breath.

—My typical post is at Bainbridge—

Just one island over.

—I might have to change my commute. Winky face emoji—

Great, another overstep, except now I also sound like a creeper.

—Just kidding. I'm not a stalker. Smiley face with sweat—

Her reply was immediate.

—I know—

Relieved, I sighed and leaned back, the leather creaking under my weight. Why was I flirting with a woman I'd hired to be my pretend girlfriend? She did this for a living—she wasn't interested in me personally. While the logic was sound, I couldn't fight the nagging hope I was wrong. To convince myself, I pictured her rolling her eyes at our conversation. I needed to back off.

—Sorry, I'll let you go. I'm sure you're busy. I'll stop bothering you—

I've transitioned to pathetic.
—You're not bothering me—
Dopamine flooded my veins.
—You're helping me avoid studying for my midterms—
My short-lived high was quickly replaced by cortisol.
—Oh right, midterms! In that case, I NEED to let you go. One last question. Where would you like me to pick you up tomorrow evening?—
Your place?
—You can pick me up at the same bar—
Damn!
—Perfect! I'll see you at The Stalker's Tango. But if you need someone to quiz you on your studies, you have my number. Smiley face emoji—

As I stared at my screen, I hoped she'd take me up on my offer, knowing in the back of my head it was a long shot.

The break room door opened.

Dan staggered in on a crash course for the coffee machine with purple bags under his eyes. "Hey, Jensen. I thought your shift was over at seven." He glanced at the clock above the door. "That was more than an hour ago. What are you still doing here?"

Fantasizing over a woman I can't have. I stood from the couch, grabbed my coat, and stretched. "One of my patients was admitted with an acute brittle asthma attack."

"And you didn't want to let Michaelson handle it?" After filling a mug, Dan set the coffeepot back on the hot plate.

The scent of his dark brew made my mouth water.

"This poor kid deals with enough. He doesn't need to deal with Michaelson's big head on top of it."

Dan laughed. "Fair point." He sipped from his mug. "Will you and Autumn be there tomorrow night? Kristine's dying to see her again." He gave me a flat stare over his coffee. "She wants me to set up a double date with you two."

My pulse thudded in my ears, relieved I had an excuse at the ready. "Kristine will have to wait. I had a hard enough time getting Autumn to agree to the benefit. She's got midterms coming up."

"Okay. I'm just glad you're dating again. You were pretty mopey these past six months." He studied the inside of his cup. "I know you had reason to, but still."

I slid on my lab coat to hide my damp armpits, despite being minutes away from heading home. "I wasn't that bad."

Dan scoffed. "Kristine was prepared to have an intervention, especially during your hermit stage."

Right after I'd discovered Kayla cheated, I stayed at home except for work, refusing to watch Orcas pro football games at Kristine and Dan's like normal. However, if Kristine thought my previous behavior was bad, she'd flip if she found out Autumn worked as a companion, and an intervention would be the least of my worries. "I'm glad it didn't come to that."

Dan flopped onto the couch and rested his head against the back cushions. "Well, tell Autumn to keep her schedule clear after midterms. You know Kristine won't forget."

I laughed uncomfortably, opening the break room door. "Yeah, I'm well aware." Scurrying into the hallway, I swallowed the bile creeping up my throat. If the truth of my situation with Autumn came to light, the repercussions would be worse than what happened with Kayla. How would I tell my best friend I lied? Kristine would never forgive me. But I couldn't keep Autumn on retainer indefinitely. As if the situation wasn't bad enough, now Kristine wanted to double. How would I get out of this one?

Chapter 11

Autumn

Entering the library's private study room Saturday morning, I took a seat at the workstation. I spread my textbooks and highlighters next to my laptop before powering on the interactive display board in case Lilly and I needed it during our cram session. She agreed to meet me here for a quick brushup on Microbiology before our midterm next week. I logged into my laptop.

Lilly dropped her backpack on the laminate surface with a *thunk*. "Sorry I'm late." As she sat across the table and pulled out her computer, she kept her voice low.

"No worries. I just got here myself." I wheeled my commercial grey office chair across the concrete floor, tucking myself into the desk.

"You're so lucky to have the next two weeks off work." Lilly redid her messy bun, securing coarse black strands on the pile atop her head. "I've got contracts four out of the seven days next week and another one tonight. Did you get the text and picture?"

"Yeah, I got it." I tugged on my ear, keeping my gaze on my laptop screen. "I have a date with a client tonight, too." As I recalled my conversation with Dad from yesterday, I felt queasy.

"What?" Lilly's slender fingers sprinted across her keyboard, her fake nails clicking loudly. "You haven't texted me anything. How are we supposed to keep each other safe if I don't know whom to send the cops after?"

I shook my head, smiling. "Ruth would know, but you already have his details anyway."

Lilly's eyes widened, and the clicking came to a halt. "Ooh, a repeat offender. Which one?"

Heat rose up my neck. "The doctor from last week." My voice pitched higher, like I was asking a question. *She'll see right through me.*

Her jaw dropped. "You mean the hot one whose kisses melted your—"

"Yes, that's the one." I pinched my lips together, focusing intently on my stack of notes.

One of Lilly's perfectly manicured eyebrows rose. "Do you think accepting the second contract is a good idea after the last time?"

Her salacious tone brought the memories of Jensen's lips on mine to the forefront of my thoughts. My internal temperature spiked. "No, I don't think it's a good idea. So, talk me off the ledge, please?"

"Talk you off? If I wasn't a good friend, I'd push you over." Sliding her laptop to the side, it shuddered across the white laminate surface, and she narrowed her gaze. "He's an EGOT."

"He's a what?" Lilly was all about the acronyms, but I never understood what half of them meant.

Lilly rolled her eyes. "You know, Emmy, Grammy, Oscar, Tony—he wins in all the categories."

I tipped my head back and scoffed a laugh. "Don't you think I know, Lilly?" I met her gaze, my ears on fire. "He pushes all my buttons, checks all the boxes, and gives me all the feels. I shouldn't even be going on a second date because the chemistry feels too real. But I also couldn't say *no* because, deep down"—I cringed a shrug—"I want to see him again." I peeked from the corner of my eye. "You gotta help me, Lilly. We made a pact—no men until our BSN. I've still got another year left. I can't fall for a guy now."

She squinted and gave me a hard smile. "So, it's not just a physical attraction?"

I drew in a deep breath. "No. Yes." Exhaling, I closed my eyes and shook my head. "I don't know. And that's the point—I shouldn't want to find out, but I will because I agreed to his contract." My stomach rolled. I was in over my head. "Is now too late to cancel for tonight?"

"You know Ruth won't let you cancel within twelve hours unless you're sick." Lilly chewed on her bottom lip. "My advice, fasten your chastity belt, eat something garlicky, and don't go on a third date."

I laughed. "Fair enough." I kneaded my forehead.

"Look"—Lilly extended her arms across the table and took my right hand in both of hers—"you need to recenter yourself. You're letting some stupid hot guy get under your skin. Need I remind you of what happened the last time?"

An echo of the hollow ache from Matteo's betrayal squeezed my heart—a pain I never wanted to relive again. "No." I was no longer the silly young girl who let her feelings for a man dictate her life or her decisions.

"You're a year away from achieving *your* goal." Lilly jabbed a finger. "*You* want this. Let me play devil's advocate. Maybe this guy isn't an EGOT. Perhaps he's just a good actor, like you and me. It's not hard to be a gentleman for an evening. Like you've said, even Matteo could fake interest when he wanted something."

My heart sank. She had a point. "But the Hot Doc's response to my kiss was real." Men couldn't fake physical reactions like that.

Lilly pursed her lips. "You're a beautiful woman, Autumn. Of course, he responded well." She tightened her grip. "Just remember it's business, and we're all playing a part. Will you promise me something?"

I nodded numbly, unsure I could live up to her expectations.

"No initiating kisses tonight. If he kisses you, fair enough, but you keep your mouth to yourself. Deal?" Lilly lifted and extended a hand.

If I was being honest, when it came to Jensen, I had no idea if I had enough self-control, but I shook her smooth grip anyway. "Deal."

****

As I waited for Jensen, I paced the sidewalk in front of The Stalker's Tango, the crunch of grit under my heels distracting me from my nerves. Lilly's pep talk was just what I needed. I'd been reciting the protocol—no men until my BSN—silently on a loop since we'd parted ways at the library. *Everything will be okay. For Pete's sake, I've only been on one date with Jensen.* While he acted like a gentleman, Lilly was spot-on when she pointed out anyone could fake good behavior for one night. This dinner would be no exception.

The gravelly sound of tires against asphalt drew my attention to the curb.

Two men in dark jeans and blazers hopped out of a

cab.

I continued my revolving path on the sidewalk. When I got close to the entrance to the bar, I nodded at the taller man holding open the door.

"You going in?" He connected gazes.

I paused my pace. "Oh, no. Sorry. I'm just waiting for a friend."

A smile crept across his face, dimples sinking into his stubbled cheeks. "Do you want company while you wait?"

He was an attractive man, taller than me in my heels, with chocolate-brown eyes and short-cropped hair of the same color.

"No, I'm okay. Thank you, though." I gestured toward the street. "They'll be here any minute."

He sucked in a breath through his teeth. "I don't know if I feel right letting a beautiful woman wait on the sidewalk alone at night."

Behind me, the soft purr of another car pulled to the curb, followed by the slamming of a door. I opened my mouth to object to the man's offer, but a hand wrapped around my waist, and a pair of lips landed on my cheek.

"Hi, honey. I'm sorry I kept you waiting."

Jensen's familiar scent, musky with a hint of citrus, filled my lungs, awakening all my senses.

The other man excused himself and entered the bar.

I spun to thank Jensen. His adoring green eyes met mine and turned my insides to goo. Despite all my earlier pep talks, I was in trouble.

Chapter 12

Jensen

When I spotted a tall guy with dark hair talking to Autumn at the entrance to The Stalker's Tango, I couldn't exit my car fast enough. The mischievous smile on the man's face had my neck hairs standing on end. Autumn's body language—straight backed with her arms crossed over her chest—told me she wasn't interested, but it didn't stop the burning jealousy within. I sprinted onto the sidewalk, making a split decision on how I would handle the situation and hoping my impromptu plan didn't backfire in my face. Sliding an arm around Autumn's waist, I kissed her on the cheek. "Hi, honey. I'm sorry I kept you waiting."

The muscles in Autumn's back softened under my touch. In my peripheral, I glimpsed the other man hold up a hand, and he backed away.

She swiveled to meet my gaze.

I couldn't read the emotion swimming in her brown eyes, and my mouth went dry. "Hey, I hope my actions were okay. From what I observed, I assumed you wanted him to leave you alone."

Autumn slid from under my arm and cleared her throat, swallowing hard. "Yes, um, thank you. He was just offering to wait with me until you arrived and didn't take my *no* for an answer."

I glared at the bar's entrance, wondering if I

needed to have a word with the man ensuring he understood *no* means *no*.

Autumn held up a hand. "It's fine, Jensen. He wasn't forceful or threatening. He was polite."

I relaxed my jaw and let my gaze sweep Autumn from head to toe. She looked incredible in a skintight, one-shoulder gray dress which hitched my breathing. I reminded myself this wasn't real. Repeating the reality of the situation several times in my head, I recalled my conversation with Molly. This date was all an act, and I couldn't let the unintentional attraction get to my head. I cleared my throat, hoping to find my voice. "You look amazing."

"Thank you." She skimmed her hands along her sides, her cheeks flushing. "I've been dying for a reason to wear this. I found the dress on sale last year and just had to buy it."

"You did good." Selfishly, I allowed my gaze to linger, hoping she'd think I was appreciating her outfit when, in reality, I was stuck on her curves. "I'll be the envy of every guy at the benefit."

A shy smile spread on Autumn's lips. "You're too sweet."

Before I said something stupid, I gestured toward my car. "Shall we?"

"We shall."

Taking her hand, I felt my core tighten. *I'm done for.*

****

After relinquishing my keys to the valet, I opened the door of the Bleu Harbor Convention Center, escorting Autumn inside. This time, I led her to the Atlas Ballroom. A white table with a black runner sat next to the entrance, with event staff in formal attire waiting to check guests in with an array of lanyards.

Holding back my tie, I leaned over the table. "Dr. Jensen Edwards and Autumn Skye."

The blonde, pony-tailed attendant made a mark on her clipboard before finding our corresponding lanyards and pushed them forward along with a place card. "You're at table number four."

I donned my name badge, careful not to mess my hair, and helped Autumn do the same.

Tugging my elbow, she brought her lips to my ear. "I forgot to ask—same deal as last week?"

A bolt of electricity shot through me, and my fingers twitched. I ached to take Autumn into my arms, but I knew better. "Yes, all my coworkers you met last week will be here, along with some new faces."

"Got it." She winked.

Again, as I ushered her into the room, I couldn't deny that her confident demeanor and warm, vanilla scent had my heart thundering like a storm. Three walls, the majority of which were made of windows, supported a ceiling sporting a giant 3D world map. I leaned into Autumn, prepared to comment on the décor, but I noticed her eyes were narrowed and focused on something across the room.

Autumn nodded at a lone man with black hair sitting at table four. "That's Dr. Lee, correct?" She kept her voice low and spoke out of the corner of her mouth.

Following her gaze, I clenched my right hand into a fist. "What are the chances?" While I had no problem with my fellow doctor, whenever I interacted with Kayla, she wasn't very civilized. Now, I'd be forced to endure an entire evening with my ex up close and personal. Bile rose in my throat.

Autumn grabbed my arm, turning me to meet her gaze. She brushed at the shoulders of my heathered-blue suit jacket, then slid her hands along the lapels, stopping when they hit the button. "He's watching. Yes, having to sit next to Kayla and her boyfriend sucks." Autumn rubbed a thumb over my bottom lip.

The heat in my veins went south.

"But we've got this." She slid a hand to the back of my neck and tugged until our foreheads touched. "We're the same power couple from last week." Autumn took my hand and led me to table four where Dr. Lee sat. "Andrew, how are you?" As she passed him, Autumn touched Dr. Lee's shoulder, then took a seat across the table.

I smiled at her bravado, positive she left out the title of doctor to get under his skin.

"Hi. I'm Autumn, Dr. Edwards' girlfriend. I was at the awards ceremony last week. Congratulations, by the way."

Andrew gave a strained smile and tugged on his collar. "Oh...Thank you." He nodded in my direction. "Jensen."

Shaking his hand, I flashed a tight smile. "Hello, Andrew. Are you here alone?" I took my seat next to Autumn, knowing there was no way in hell he wouldn't be, but I could hope—for my sake and his.

"No, no. Kayla's here." He waved a hand over his shoulder.

My ex appeared out of nowhere like he'd conjured the witch. Her frosty demeanor made me feel like the room had dropped a few degrees.

Kayla stood at the edge of our table in a drapey,

rose-gold dress that tied around her neck, showing off her bare shoulders and enhanced cleavage. "Andrew, I thought you were saving the table for the rest of the oncology staff."

Dr. Lee sighed heavily. "It's assigned seating, honey, remember?"

Kayla's deep-red lips tightened into a thin line. "I asked you not to call me 'honey.'" She squeezed his shoulder, her knuckles turning white, and flashed a toothy smile. "But I'm sure Dr. Edwards wouldn't mind switching seats so you can be with your team?"

She met my gaze with a cold stare. I liked seeing Kayla squirm. She didn't want to sit with me either, but I puffed out my chest, noting she was the one who appeared more bothered by the situation. I shook my head. "But if Autumn and I switched tables, then I'd be required to notify the waitstaff and rearrange the meal assignments." I waved a hand in the air, dismissing her suggestion. "It would just be a big mess." I tried but failed to keep from smirking.

Dan, in a charcoal-grey suit, and his wife, in a cream floor-length dress, appeared at the door.

I waved them over to my table.

Stopping beside my ex, Dan greeted her with a half-cocked smile. "Kaylaaaa."

She shifted to face my best friend and his wife, and although she kept a stoic expression, Kayla's shoulders were stiff.

My ex eyed the two of them from head to toe. "Dan, Kristine."

"This'll be fun."

Dan's comment wasn't quiet, and his intentional jab at my ex solidified him as one of my favorite people.

He pulled out the chair next to Autumn for Kristine.

Kayla held up a hand, her gold bracelets clinking. "It's assigned seating."

Dan's eyes twinkled. "I know." He waved his *Table 4* card at Kayla and sat on Kristine's other side.

Autumn swiped her hair behind her ear. "Hey, you two, good to see you again."

Kristine scooted into the table. "Your dress is to die for!" Her gaze flitted over Autumn's outfit.

Dan leaned back in his seat, waving a hand behind the ladies' chairs. "Tonight seems to be going well. Can't wait for the show." He waggled his eyebrows.

The final couple assigned to our designated table approached—a tall, dark-haired woman and a balding man with a buzz cut.

I tried not to laugh at Dan's enthusiasm over Kayla's discomfort and chastised him with a glare.

"Dr. Lee, it's so good to see you." The newcomer put a slender hand on her date's arm. "This is my husband, Todd."

Andrew shook their hands and turned. "Kayla, you already know Dr. Meleka Stanton, right?"

Meleka gave a pinched smile. "Of course, who hasn't heard of Kayla?"

Autumn coughed to hide a laugh.

I leaned in, my lips at her ear. "Guess she's heard the gossip."

Autumn squeezed my left knee.

The hairs on my leg stood on end.

Dr. Stanton focused her attention on the rest of the table. "Hello, as you've already heard, I'm Dr. Meleka

Stanton, and this is Todd."

Her husband pulled out her chair.

Meleka sat, adjusting her tight purple dress. "And I know from the *Best Doctors Magazine*"—she nodded in my direction—"you're Dr. Jensen Edwards?"

"Guilty." I placed an arm around Autumn, and I couldn't slow my speeding heart. "This is my girlfriend, Autumn Skye."

"Nice to—"

"Ha!"

Meleka was interrupted by a mocking scoff from Kayla.

"Skye? Your name is Autumn Skye? Sounds like a stripper name."

Kayla's laugh sounded more like a witch's cackle. I clenched my jaw.

The whole table gawked at my ex.

Red flooded my vision, and angry comebacks filled my head.

Autumn squeezed my knee again, leaning in. "It's okay, *honey*. I've got this."

The use of Andrew's pet name for Kayla was deliberate, giving me a high like a sugar rush.

Autumn smirked at Kayla. "If you must know, I only strip for one person." She twisted to meet my gaze, tugged my tie, and pulled me close. "And you love it, don't you?"

With our lips almost touching, my mind felt muddled, and I mustered all my energy to form a reply. "You know I do." Images of Autumn's suggestion raced through my mind, bringing my body to attention.

Autumn's silky pink lips quirked up in the corners, and her gaze fell to my mouth.

The urge to kiss her overwhelmed me. I closed the small gap and claimed her lips. My mind felt fuzzy, and I couldn't think straight. Cupping Autumn's cheek, I breathed in, desire burning through my veins. I didn't want to let go.

Dan coughed.

The sound brought me back to my senses. With Herculean effort, I willed myself away from Autumn. As I did, I couldn't help myself and nipped her bottom lip with my teeth. Seeing Autumn's dilated pupils stoked the fire within me.

"Take that, Kayla."

Amen, Dan!

Chapter 13

Autumn

My lower lip tingled from the graze of Jensen's teeth. I was grateful I was already sitting; otherwise, my knees would have given out. *Holy bats, his kiss was hot.* But Lilly couldn't be mad—I hadn't initiated it. With a shuddering breath, I let go of Jensen's tie but didn't avert my gaze. A thin ring of green surrounded his black pupils, and his ragged breathing made every nerve in my body hum. As I watched him readjust his tie, I almost imploded at Jensen's roguish smile. Because even though my contract scripted our circumstances, the electricity I felt for Jensen was all too real. Tonight would be harder than I'd expected.

Jensen scooted his chair closer. "Sorry, folks." The edges of his mouth twitched, and he draped an arm across the back of my seat. "I can't help myself around her."

Kayla's eyes narrowed. "Try."

Please don't. The thought popped into my head unbidden, and my skin tingled. I willed my body to behave. *Remember your promise to Lilly.* I sat back in my chair, letting Jensen's arm brush my shoulders. At least, I had gotten under Kayla's skin. Watching her tight expression across the table, I realized, maybe getting Jensen to want me was exactly what tonight called for. Jensen hired me to continue the charade from last week—be his girlfriend so he wouldn't be alone in front of his ex. Not to mention, Jensen asked me to up my game in front of Kayla, and if PDA was the way, I had no objections. My contract practically required me to do so. The damn rational voice in the back of my head screamed at my justification, but I ignored her. Reaching over, I stroked the stubble on Jensen's jaw with the back of a finger.

Jensen grasped my wrist and held my fingertips to his mouth, kissing each one lightly.

I shuddered at the electricity running down my spine and let my lips part.

"Aww, young love." Dr. Stanton clasped her hands against her chest and tilted her head.

The sound of glasses hitting silverware rang out.

I jolted. For just a moment, I forgot we had an audience.

"Drat!" Kayla threw her napkin onto the table and mopped a spilled water puddle.

Did we rattle her with our flirty behavior? I decided to test my theory. Scooting back my chair, I rose. "Excuse me. I need to visit the ladies' room." I leaned in, cupped Jensen's chin, and brushed my lips against his. "Miss me." His delicious musky-citrus scent awakened all my senses. The goofy expression on Jensen's face was priceless.

"Oh, please." Kayla sneered.

As I sashayed away from the table, I squared my shoulders with a smug smile. Entering the bathroom, I approached the mirror and reapplied my lipstick. My mouth tingled from the pressure, and I paused, replaying Jensen's teeth on my lip. I swallowed hard. *Why am I so stuck on him?*

The door flung open.

Kristine flashed a wide smile. "You and Jensen are too cute." She swatted a hand in my direction and stepped to the adjoining sink.

I dipped my head, hoping to hide my blush. "Thank you."

Kristine rotated her head, patting her chignon. "I remember those early days when Dan and I couldn't keep our hands off each other." She reinserted a bobby pin into the back of her blonde locks. "Don't ever lose that."

I wasn't sure how to respond. Jensen and I weren't an actual thing.

"However, I don't think Kayla likes it." Kristine's crystal-blue eyes twinkled.

A rush of adrenaline flowed through my veins, making me almost lightheaded. "I know, right?" I smiled conspiratorially. "It's fun to see her get so flustered." The catty comradery was better than an energy drink. I threw my lipstick back into my clutch. "Andrew seems nice and all, but he ain't no Jensen."

She laughed, running a finger under her eye and clearing a smudge. "You got that right, but it's not like Kayla cares about his looks."

My stomach hardened. "She doesn't?"

Kristine's gaze locked on mine in the mirror, and she smoothed her dress. "Wait. You don't know?"

I shook my head. "Know what?"

"Kayla left Jensen because Andrew makes more money."

I slapped a hand over my mouth. "No! I thought she'd fallen in love with Dr. Lee, which is why she cheated." *She left Jensen for money? How shallow can she be?*

Kristine scoffed, waving a hand in the air. "Please! I doubt she loves Andrew at all. Hopefully, when Kayla's done with him, she'll be kinder than she is to Jensen."

The air freshener in the corner hissed, and the smell of lavender filled the rose-wallpapered space. The overwhelming scent turned my stomach. "Yeah, she's not even being civil. You'd think at a function like this, she would be."

Kristine nodded and gave the back of her hair one last pat. "You'd think, but I'm glad they broke up." She met my gaze again, the corners of her eyes crinkling. "Because now, he has you. I've never seen Jensen happier." She squeezed my arm and then left the bathroom.

I stared at the dark oak door, the breath whooshing from my lungs. Was Kristine right? Did my presence make Jensen happy, or was his smile a result from ruffling Kayla's feathers? I threw back my shoulders. *Stop overthinking the situation!* Jensen was a fun client. Why I was allowing myself to get into my own head was ridiculous. Whatever the reason for Jensen's happiness, it didn't matter. He was enjoying himself, and I was getting paid. With a final check in the mirror, I marched back to the table.

Jensen stood and pulled out my chair, one cheek pulled in a half smile. He leaned over my shoulder, his nose grazing my ear. "Welcome back."

As I sat, the feel of his breath conjured goose bumps along my arms, and I smiled demurely, rubbing them away. "Thank you." *Just a client. Just a client. Just a client.*

The dinner salads were already on the table. As I picked up my fork, I noticed Jensen's plate sat untouched. "You could have eaten. You didn't have to wait."

"Nonsense. I didn't want to be rude." He gave me a wink.

My stomach fluttered. I dug in, and we finished our salads in amiable silence.

Servers in white jackets and black bowties cleared our plates.

Jensen wiped his mouth with a napkin. "I hope you don't mind, but I needed to preorder our meal choices beforehand." He shrugged, his voice low. "I wasn't sure what you'd like, so I ordered a different option for each of us. We can always trade, if you don't like what you're served."

He was so thoughtful. The only other person I knew who was as considerate was Papi. "Thank you." I smoothed the rough cloth napkin over my lap, unable to meet his gaze. "As a general rule, I'm not picky, but if they serve me pork, I'll take you up on that." I was fortunate and received the chicken breast with asparagus, although I wouldn't have complained if I'd gotten Jensen's filet with broccoli. But when I watched the server set a chocolate cake in front of me while Jensen received the crème brûlée, I had to object. I bumped his elbow. "Can we trade? Crème brûlée's my favorite."

Jensen smirked. "This?" He pointed a finger at the caramelized custard. "You want this?"

His tone was heavy with sarcasm. I narrowed my eyes and fought the upturn of my lips. "Yes."

"So you'd be bothered if I"—he took his spoon and

carved out a generous portion—"ate some?" He popped the bite into his mouth.

"How dare you eat *my* dessert." I loaded my fork with the rich brown sponge with creamy icing. "Don't you want *your* chocolate cake?"

"Of course, I do." With one swift movement, Jensen took my wrist and shoved my fork into his mouth. "Mmm." He closed his eyes momentarily. "It's delicious."

I dropped my jaw in mock offense, bubbles filling my chest, and warmth pooling low in my belly. "You can't have both."

Jensen gave a heavy-lidded gaze. "Just did."

He leaned in aggressively, inches from my face. My breath caught in my lungs.

"Will you ever forgive me?" His gaze dropped to my lips.

His actions told me he wanted a kiss, but I didn't trust myself. Instead, I offered him an alternative. "If I can have the rest of *my* crème brûlée, I will."

The corner of his mouth hitched up, but his eyes dimmed. "Deal." He switched our plates.

Glancing up, I caught Kayla giving me the stink eye.

"Honey"—Dr. Lee raised his fork over Kayla's plate—"can I have a bite of your cannoli?"

Kayla scowled. "Eat your own damn dessert."

I suppressed my delight. *Flirting with Jensen is paying off on so many levels.*

Chapter 14

Jensen

As I drove Autumn to The Stalker's Tango from the conference center, I couldn't sit still. The night went even better than the last time. But after the desserts were cleared away and I slow danced with Autumn was where she seemed most at ease. Her smile was serene, and her eyes were bright. When Autumn laid her head on my shoulder, and I held her in my arms while we swayed to the music, I couldn't deny how my heart swelled. Our bodies fit together, we clicked on an intellectual level, and we even shared the same sense of humor. She was perfect for me—exactly my type, or at least she appeared so.

Not knowing if whatever was going on between us wasn't simply an act had me pulling my hair out. Autumn could have lied about some of the things she told me she loved. Like, what if she wasn't an Orcas fan or she didn't like hiking in the Olympic National Park? What if those were lies to feed my ego and make her seem compatible as a couple for our audience? *What the hell is real, and what isn't?* I arrived at the bar and rubbed the back of my neck, feeling conflicted. Exiting, then walking to the other side of the car, I opened the door and held out a hand for Autumn.

As she stepped onto the sidewalk, she winced, teetering on her silver heels.

I looped a hand around her waist, steadying her, while simultaneously eager for an excuse to touch her again. "You okay?" My doctor's brain kicked in, and I mentally catalogued possible causes for dizziness and pain.

Autumn gritted her teeth. "I'm fine. I think I ate too much." She rubbed her belly. "I just need to get home and lay down." Retrieving her phone from her purse, she opened the rideshare app.

I furrowed my brow. "Why don't you just let me take you?" If she was truly sick, she'd be better off with me by her side.

Autumn cocked her head. "Jensen, you know it's against company policy."

Her complexion appeared ghostly under the warm glow of the streetlights. "Don't take this the wrong way, but you're not looking so well." I placed the back of a hand against her forehead—a little warm, but nothing too bad. I reached for her wrist and checked her pulse.

Autumn ripped herself from my grip and bent over, bracing her hands on her knees. "I'm not feeling so well." She waved her phone. "Can you arrange my ride? The app's open."

Like hell I'm letting someone else take you home. I pocketed her phone, holding her elbow and bracing her back. *If this is serious, I want to be close. I wouldn't leave anybody standing in the street in this condition.* "Done." I ushered her back toward my car.

Holding her hunched position while shuffling along, she glanced out of the corner of her eye. "What are you doing?"

I kept her moving forward, pausing to open the

passenger door. "Stop protesting. Our contract ended the moment you left the car. Now, I'm acting as a doctor and your rideshare driver."

Autumn's forehead creased before cupping her mouth and holding back a gag.

"I'll take that as a *thank you for taking me home.*" Shielding her head with a hand, I helped her lower herself back into the passenger seat.

Autumn leaned against the headrest, her eyes closed. "Since I don't have the energy to protest"—she took a labored breath—"thank you." She rattled off her address.

After following the navigation system's directions to her apartment, I parked in a temporary loading space in the front and helped Autumn from the car. With an arm tight around her waist, I ushered her toward the door of the building.

"I've got it from here." Breaking away, Autumn took a step, wobbled, and vomited into the flower bed next to the entrance.

"That's it. I'm helping you to your apartment, and I won't take *no* for an answer." Retrieving Autumn's keys from her hand, I waved the fob at the sensor, opened the door, and escorted an ashen-faced Autumn into the lobby. *Could be food poisoning? Maybe she has irritable bowel syndrome. Or perhaps it's simply a stomach virus?*

She exhaled through her nose, wiping her lips with a pinched brow. On the elevator, Autumn leaned into my shoulder. "I'm sorry you're seeing me like this."

I exhaled a laugh. "I'm a doctor; I've seen worse." *Please don't let this escalate.* The elevator arrived on her floor, and I helped Autumn to her apartment.

She hunched over and flinched. "It's the square gold key."

Examining the metal ring, I spotted a Blast the Orca mascot keychain flash in the light. I smiled. At least now I knew she wasn't lying about being an Orca's fan. Opening the door, I led Autumn inside.

She flipped on the lights and illuminated the bright white entryway. Autumn kicked out a foot to remove her heel, but the strap held tight, making her wobble.

I swooped to steady her with my hands on her hips. Autumn's fingers dug into my biceps. My face was mere inches from hers, and my heart hammered from both concern and proximity. "What can I do for you? Do you want me to help you take off your shoes?" *Give you a full medical evaluation?*

"Yes, please." Autumn braced herself, resting her back against the door.

I crouched, lifting her right shoe onto my thigh. As I slid the heel off her foot, I grazed my fingers over the smooth skin of her ankle bone, and I repeated the gesture with the other shoe. Grabbing both heels, I stood and handed them over. "There you go."

Autumn's cheeks were flushed, and a sheen of sweat shone across her forehead. "Thank you." She swatted her hair out of her face. "I'm going to change. This dress is suffocating."

"Of course." *Hopefully, a looser outfit will ease her symptoms.*

She shuffled down the hallway.

"I'll wait right here to make sure you don't need anything else before I go." I couldn't stand the idea of leaving until I knew her symptoms had abated.

Autumn responded with a non-committal grunt

before changing direction and heading for the bathroom straight ahead.

While I marched into the kitchen to look for a sick bowl, I scanned the tidy apartment. As I passed the fridge, I noticed some photos taped to the white surface. The first was of Autumn and her dads. She was somewhere around five years old with pigtails in a black-and-silver dress, sitting on Santa's lap. The two men beamed at the camera. The second one must have been her Papi, because he held a guitar on a stage, playing his heart out; he'd even autographed it.

But the last one stole my attention—Autumn and Papi in front of Marymere Falls. I'd know that waterfall anywhere; I'd hiked the trail at least a thousand times. I scrubbed a hand down my face. The picture and the keychain were proof Autumn was genuine in her conversations earlier. Did the culmination of those two things mean I could trust everything she'd said? The possibility seemed unlikely. For Autumn to show her true self on Plus One dates would be risky. I'd be a fool to think I was different from all the others.

Opening the cabinet under the sink, I pulled out the trash can. *This will do.* I grabbed a spare bag from the box next to the oven cleaner and replaced the stinky half-full one. No need to aggravate Autumn's condition with the foul stench of rotten food.

The door to Autumn's bathroom swung open.

I rushed to her side with the makeshift bucket.

She waved a hand. "I'm okay now." She patted her belly. "I think whatever upset my stomach has gotten out of my system."

Thank goodness, it was just the food. I was worried it might be appendicitis. "Is there anything else you need?" I hated leaving her, even though she was feeling better, but staying wasn't my place, either. Because I didn't know if we'd ever see each other again, I selfishly couldn't leave it there. "A study buddy for midterms? They're coming up, right?"

She sighed heavily. "They're next week, but I have a study group. Thank you, anyway." She swiveled toward the door.

Damn. "And that's my cue." Letting my shoulders drop, I trudged to join her. I felt awkward. Leaving without some sort of goodbye didn't seem right. I didn't want her to think she'd ruined the night by eating something that disagreed with her. Filling my lungs, I leaned in and brushed my lips on Autumn's cheek.

She smiled weakly. "Thank you for everything. I enjoyed doing business with you."

My heart sank to my core, but I kept the corners of my mouth from dipping.

Autumn opened the door. "Good night, Jensen."

I traced her features with my gaze. Unfortunately, reality wasn't like the movies. I couldn't change her mind with a grand gesture or a passionate kiss. Instead, I committed her to memory. "Good night, Autumn." My words were just a whisper.

Chapter 15

Autumn

As soon as Jensen left, I crumpled to the floor, a pain stabbing my right side like a hot poker. I was in agony but didn't want Jensen to see me this way. Doctor or no doctor, he didn't need to witness me any longer in my current state. Sweat covered my brow, and I gritted my teeth, grasping a spot next to my right hip. Nausea riled my stomach, and I quickly tabulated the possible causes. I hobbled toward the bathroom again, barely reaching the tile this time before retching. Panting, I heaved myself to the basin and wet a washcloth to wipe my face.

This was not good. All my symptoms pointed to appendicitis. Crawling back to the entrance, I grabbed my phone from my clutch I'd dropped next to my shoes at the front door. Of course, this was the week my roommate visited her parents; otherwise, I'd have her drive me to the hospital. I examined my remaining options. I could call 911, but the ambulance bill and an emergency room visit would empty my bank account and then some.

Another white-hot spike of pain jabbed my side, and I doubled over. I debated calling my dads, but what could they do? They lived over thirty minutes away, and they weren't doctors. In hindsight, I shouldn't have shoved Jensen out the door. I glanced at the time on my phone screen: 11:15 p.m. The last ferry didn't leave Seattle until 12:50 a.m., meaning Jensen was still in the city—he was my best bet. I opened his contact.

—Can you come back?—

A few agonizing seconds ticked by as I sat on the cold entryway tile with tears streaming down my face.

—Of course. On my way—

—I think I have appendicitis—

My phone screen lit with his call. "Hey, Jensen, sorry about this." I panted into the speaker.

"Don't be sorry. Did you call an ambulance?"

"No"—*breath*—"I hoped"—*breath*—"you could confirm my diagnosis"—*breath*—"before I have to spend my emergency money." The last thing I wanted was to be one of those patients the staff laughed at because I went to the ER only to find out I was suffering from painful gas or kidney stones.

"Autumn, don't be ridiculous. You know how serious this can be."

A dart of pain so intense my vision blurred pierced my abdomen. I had no doubt in my mind I would need to go to the hospital. And, if Jensen confirmed I had appendicitis, I was sure he'd drive me himself. At least then, I wouldn't have the ambulance bill.

"Autumn?" Jensen's voice called out from my phone. "You there? Stay with me."

Wiping the sweat from my brow, I blinked several times, then widened my eyes, focusing on the screen.

"I'm here. Can you buzz me in?"

In so much pain, I struggled to register Jensen's voice. Through gritted teeth, I rose to my feet, crouching. As I pushed the button and unlocked the deadbolt, leaving the door ajar, I clutched at my hip before I dropped my phone onto the rug and curled into the fetal position, the carpet fibers scratching my cheek.

"Autumn!" Jensen rushed inside and gathered me into his arms, kicking the door closed before half carrying me over to the couch. He gripped my shoulder, pushing to straighten me on the cushions.

Pain rippled through my torso, and I moaned, staying on my side.

"I need you to relax so I can examine you."

His voice was soothing. I pinched my mouth shut against another roll of nausea and shook my head. "Can't." Jensen's cool fingers glided along my arm, ending with a gentle pull on my wrist. An echo of pain erupted from where he prodded at my right side. I screamed.

"I'm calling an ambulance." Jensen's phone screen illuminated his face in a greenish glow.

"No!" I shot out a hand. Not having to spend my emergency money was the whole point of why I'd asked him to come back.

"Autumn, you need to go to the hospital. I believe your appendix has ruptured."

I squeezed my eyes shut against the intense pain. "Big deductible."

Jensen smoothed a lock of hair out of my face. "We'll worry about money later."

"No!" He didn't understand. I could barely manage my monthly expenses, and a huge medical bill would put me on the street.

He huffed, and the green glow extinguished. "Fine. I'll take you to the ER myself."

Gratitude filled my chest before the world went dark.

Chapter 16

Jensen

When Autumn came back around, she squeezed my hand so hard it was numb by the time I got her to the hospital. I arrived at the emergency room entrance and raced to grab one of the wheelchairs by the automatic sliding glass doors. As I helped Autumn out of my car and into the chair, I registered her warm skin that blazed against my palms. *A high fever—not good.* I looped her purse strap around my hand and wheeled Autumn forward.

Retching, she leaned over the side of the chair and vomited onto the sidewalk. "Sorry." Autumn wheezed between pants.

"It's okay. Don't worry about it"—*hurry, hurry, hurry*—"happens all the time at hospitals." My chest was tight, making getting the words out hard. "Let's get you inside." *Get you into surgery.* Rushing over to the check-in desk, I rapped my knuckles on the counter and read the brunette receptionist's name badge. "Hello, Shawna, my name is Dr. Jensen Edwards from Seattle Children's. I need an emesis bag."

The eyes of the early twenty-something-looking woman in pink scrubs widened, and she dove into the cabinet under her desk, resurfacing with the collapsed blue plastic sack. She shoved the receptacle across the counter.

I passed it to Autumn before returning my attention to Shawna.

She held out a clipboard. "Fill these out, and I'll need a driver's license and insurance card."

I huffed but took the paperwork. "She has appendicitis with a high fever and has been vomiting for the last half hour. I'm worried it's ruptured." *Just take her back.*

Shawna gave me a tight-lipped smile. "Okay, sir. Just complete the paperwork, and I'll take her to triage. What's her name?"

Hearing the receptionist's clipped tone, I gritted my teeth. "It's Autumn, but she doesn't need triage; she needs surgery." I was acting like one of those neurotic patients who thought they were too important to wait in line. Which was ridiculous because I knew how this process worked, but I'd never been on this side. I didn't like it.

Shawna held up a hand, repressing a sigh. "Sir, I'm going to need you to calm down."

"I am calm." My tone was more severe than I'd intended, but I didn't care. Autumn needed to be seen, STAT. *So help me…if she got peritonitis.*

Shawna's brow furrowed. "Sir, I understand you're worried for your friend, but I ask that you wait here and fill out the paperwork while I take Autumn back to triage to assess her condition."

My pulse thundered in my ears. "I told you her condition." *No wonder patients and their families get so mad in the emergency room. This wasn't some sprained ankle, this was a true emergency.*

The woman's nostrils flared.

Autumn grabbed my hand. "Jensen." She'd rasped

my name in a whisper through clenched teeth.

Hearing her struggle, the fight drained right out of me. I took a deep breath, clearing my lungs, and directed my attention at Shawna. "I'm sorry."

The receptionist's features softened. "I understand you're worried, sir, but we'll take good care of your friend." Shawna patted Autumn's shoulder.

Watching Autumn get wheeled away, I felt helpless. *I'm a doctor, for crying out loud.* Shuffling to the nearest black chair, I flopped on the cold plastic surface, placing the clipboard over Autumn's purse, which rested on my lap. I watched my hands tremble and flexed my shaky fingers before releasing the pen and reading the first line of the admission form.

Last name of patient.

The back of my throat constricted. Skye wouldn't be Autumn's given surname but rather a pseudonym. Was her first name even Autumn? Hanging my head back, I stared at the ceiling. *How can I fill any of this out?* I didn't know anything about her. I shifted in the chair. The corner of Autumn's purse dug into my thigh. I lifted the clipboard and stared at the sparking jeweled bag. Her driver's license would be inside with all her pertinent details.

However, as her client, would rifling through her belongings to find her personal information be crossing the line? Surely, this was a special circumstance. As a doctor, I wouldn't have any reservations, but I hesitated now. Staring at the automatic double doors they'd taken Autumn through, I jumped to the worst-case scenario. What if something went wrong? What if they needed to contact her dads? Was I really too chicken to dig inside her purse because I dreaded breaking the terms of the

Plus One privacy clause? What was more important—Autumn's health and safety or a stupid agreement to save my dignity?

****

I stood vigilantly at the foot of Autumn's post-surgery hospital bed, scanning the latest rounds of vitals marked on the room's dry-erase board for the fifth time, unable to concentrate. While she was in the operating room, a lot transpired, and I had some explaining to do. But when she woke up, I didn't know where I would start.

Autumn groaned.

My chest loosened, but the tension hadn't left my shoulders. *She's okay.* "Good morning, sleepyhead." I pushed away the roller table beside Autumn's bed and approached her side. "How ya feelin'?" I kept my tone breezy, even though my nerves were a tangled ball of yarn.

"Better." Her voice was raspy, and her eyebrows rose, although she kept her lids closed.

"Are you in any pain?" I let my hand hover over the nurse's call button, just in case she needed more painkillers.

"Surprisingly, no."

What a relief. "I bet the anesthesia is still in your system." *Which means now is not the right time to bring up that I took care of her hospital stay.*

"Good. I'll take it." Autumn rubbed her eyes. "What time is it?"

I checked my watch, the beeping of the monitors and sensors filling the room's silence. "Eight thirty-eight a.m. It's only been nine hours."

Autumn sighed. "Thank you."

I grasped the railing on the side of her bed. *Was her gratitude because she knows I paid her bill? No, I'm being stupid. She was in surgery, and she only just woke up.* "For what? The time?"

"No, for"—she opened her eyes, squinting and turning away from the fluorescent lights and gestured at herself, the hospital room, the monitors, and the equipment—"this."

She knows? My face prickled with heat. *She couldn't. Be cool. Don't jump to conclusions.* "If I left you at home to die, I wouldn't be much of a doctor." I laughed, tugging at my shirt collar. Recalling the image of her in so much pain made me feel sick. However she reacted to my generosity, I made the right decision.

Autumn's mouth curved into a smile.

Despite the hospital gown, pallid complexion, and dried sweat in her hair, she was still beautiful. My chest tightened. I hoped when she learned I knew her true identity and she was free from the hospital debt, she would still be grateful.

Autumn peeked out of the corner of her eye. "Can I still wear a bikini?"

Okay, I'm safe for now. I choked out a laugh, and my worry was replaced with the image she'd conjured in my head. My heart stuttered. "Definitely. The surgery was laparoscopic. You have two small incision sites about half an inch long. Most times, they fade, and you can't see them."

She pressed a button, and as she readjusted her bed into the sitting position, a hum sounded throughout the room. Autumn winced. "I need to see." She gathered her gown in her hands.

I averted my gaze and turned, giving her some

privacy, the back of my neck growing hot.

"They're covered in gauze."

She sounded surprised. "Of course, you just had surgery." I smirked, talking over my shoulder. "But you can remove the tape and look under the bandage."

Her breathing hitched before becoming labored. The heart monitor beeps increased. "A little help?"

I spun. Autumn's face had a green tint. "What's wrong?" I mentally raced through the possibilities of her discomfort and held out my hands, ready to help with whatever was ailing her.

She put a hand on her forehead. "I'm not feeling so well."

I nudged her fingers aside and rested my palm on her brow. She didn't feel hot. "In what way?" Her surgeon assured me everything went well, so she shouldn't be septic.

Autumn's head shifted from side to side under my touch. "No, it's not what you think."

I removed my hand and heard my heartbeat pounding in my ears. "What do you mean?" I checked her IV and monitors. Everything appeared normal.

"This is going to sound stupid."

Her tone held an embarrassed edge. "What is?" I let my gaze scan every inch of her form, searching for the problem.

Autumn sighed. "Well...I can handle any kind of injury"—her shoulders rose to her ears—"as long as it's on someone else." The end of her sentence raised an octave.

Relief filled my veins, but I couldn't stop my eruption of laughter. "You're feeling faint from looking at your *own* incisions?" I found her choice of vocation hilarious, considering this tidbit of information.

She covered her face with her hands, peeking through her fingers. "I haven't even removed the gauze yet."

I pretended to wipe tears from my eyes. "Ahh, you're hilarious. You just made my day." I found her adorable.

Autumn dropped her hands and squinted, a slight smile on her lips. "I'm glad I could be of service." She beckoned with a hand. "Now help me."

I quirked up my cheek. "Should I have the smelling salts ready?" I winked and leaned over her bed.

She slapped my shoulder, her color returning. "Just hurry before I lose my nerve." Autumn held her gown, the covers on her bed edging the top of her lower abdomen.

I swallowed hard. The smooth landscape of her stomach was interrupted by two large white cotton squares, one over her belly button and the other farther down—a tantalizing sight. As I gently held taut her silky-soft skin, I tried not to let my hands shake while I peeled back the surgical tape to reveal her incision. My fingers tingled from the contact.

Autumn sucked in a breath, leaning her head against the pillow with a hand raised to block her view. "Give me a moment."

I bit back my smile, listening to her shaky exhales.

Clenching her jaw, Autumn raised her head, her eyes pinched shut. "Okay." Squinting through one lid, she peeked at her incision site. Her jaw went slack with a scoff. "They removed my belly button ring."

I fixed my gaze on her torso, a hunger building in my midsection. "Of course, they did." I pointed at the glued, puckered red line bordering the top of her navel. "That is where Dr. Montgomery made her incision." I reapplied the tape, covering the tiny wound, then lowered her gown and readjusted her covers. As I vaguely waved a hand at the location of the second bandage, I breathed deep, heat flooding my cheeks. "The other will be the same."

Autumn dropped her head back again and pouted. "Can I wear the ring again?"

I nodded once. "Absolutely." Her worry was cute. I had to admit, when she had the jewelry back in place, I wanted to see. "If you can't handle looking at your tiny incision, how did you cope when you had your navel pierced?"

She brushed a wild hair back from her face. "The same way people who don't like needles get tattoos."

"Touché." Autumn had a point. My cousin fainted at the sight of blood but had several tattoos.

Her gaze drifted to the door. "When do you think I can go home?" Autumn kneaded her forehead. "I'm anxious to see how much this will cost."

There it was—the moment I dreaded. "The nurse is on their way with the discharge paperwork." *And the paid invoice that will out me as her benefactor.*

She bobbed her head. "Okay, one night. Hopefully, the cost won't be too bad. I'll have, like, what? Six weeks before I receive the bill? They have payment plans, right?"

I fiddled with the cuffs of my sleeves, still wearing the clothes from last night's event. *Bite the bullet, Jensen. Time to confess.* "You won't be getting a bill."

Her head jerked, eyes narrowing. "Huh? What do you mean?"

I put my hands into my pockets, kicking my toe at a black mark on the cream tile. "Well, when they whisked you away for surgery, they handed me the paperwork. Only then did I realize Autumn Skye wouldn't be your real name." Averting my gaze, I shrugged. "I'm sorry, I dug in your purse for your insurance card and license but could only find the latter." Glancing up, I gave her a tentative smile. "And because you called me instead of an ambulance, I paid the bill." While I didn't regret my actions, I could see how they appeared excessive from the outside.

But last night, when I filled out the forms, without any insurance information to provide, I spiraled down a jealous rabbit hole, and now the deed was done. Autumn was clear that her financial situation was tight and she had a big deductible. Therefore, I knew an appendectomy bill would take a long time to pay off, meaning she'd be forced to work more hours. Plus One paid substantially better than the toll booth—which meant more dates. Picturing her out with other men almost gave me an ulcer. My two options were to either book her for all those extra dates myself or put the hospital bill on my credit card. So, I bit the bullet.

"You did what?" Her mouth hung open.

The tops of my ears burned. I had no idea if she was more upset because I knew her identity or that I took care of the bill. "Violated our contract. I know. I'm sorry."

"No." Autumn waved a hand in the air. "I don't care about that. But you paid my bill?"

I couldn't read her reaction. Was she grateful or mad? "It's fine. You're not one of my patients." I studied my cuticles. "There is no moral ambiguity."

"Yes, but I'm also not *your* responsibility."

Her words and sharp tone pulled at my heart. "When I returned to your apartment last night, I took you on as my responsibility." Jealousy aside, I cared about her, and she still had finals to get through.

Autumn wrinkled her brow and crossed her arms. "Maybe for me, but not for the bill."

I held my hands out, palms up. "Can't you just be grateful and accept my generosity?" *Please?*

Autumn gaped, but when the door to her room swung open, she froze.

A tall, dark-skinned male nurse in navy-blue scrubs entered the room, followed by two shorter men. The first had an olive complexion, was bald, and well-dressed. The other I recognized from the picture on Autumn's fridge—Papi. He was a few shades lighter than the nurse, with leather pants, a drapey shirt, and dreadlocks. The latter two were arguing with the hospital employee.

Autumn gritted her teeth and pointed a finger at my face. "This isn't over."

I swallowed hard, and my chest tightened.

The nurse turned toward the bickering men and made a stopping motion with a hand. "Look, I told you it's not my department. If you want more details, go downstairs to billing."

My stomach bottomed out. *Damn it! I hadn't considered how my generosity would be interpreted by her dads.* From what I'd just heard, the situation was about to go south.

"Dad! Papi!" Autumn's hands flew to her cheeks, and her eyes became glassy. "What are you two doing here?"

Both men rushed to the bed, each grabbing for her left hand, Dad deferring and settling for a spot on her arm.

"The hospital called us. We're still your emergency contact"—Dad spoke to his daughter but shot me a glance—"in case you've forgotten. But because we leave our phones on *do not disturb* at night, we only just got the message."

"We've been so worried." Papi caressed Autumn's cheek. "You don't even want to know how fast Dad drove to get here. I was terrified." He placed a hand over his heart.

Dad gave Papi a thin-lipped glare before turning back to Autumn. "When did this start? Was this why you didn't eat anything at lunch?"

She shrugged. "Maybe? Remember I'd thought my lack of appetite was stress? But last night, after I'd completed my Plus One contract"—her gaze darted to the side—"the pain came on suddenly and was *intense*." Autumn's eyes widened on the last word.

As I recalled her collapsed form on her entryway floor, I rubbed where my chest ached but the feeling was overshadowed by the sickness churning in my gut. *Not only will her dads question my motives for paying the bill, but now they know I'm a client.* This hole was getting deeper by the second.

Papi's brow creased. "Thank goodness, you had your wits about you enough to call 911."

She pinched her lips together.

"Autumn Summer Haze, I know *that* look." Papi crossed his arms. "What's the guilty expression for?"

Again, her gaze darted to mine before she cringed away from her father. "I...didn't call 911."

Both men scowled.

"You called a cab?"

"You drove yourself?"

At the simultaneous replies from her dads, Autumn shook her head. "Neither."

As if in slow motion, her parents gaped, mouths slack.

"My friend drove me. Dad, Papi, this is Jensen." She gestured the introduction with a hand. "Jensen, meet my dads, Karl and Rob."

Sweat dripped down my back, and I extended a hand. "Nice to meet you both."

Papi nodded.

Dad's grip was firm. "Thank you for getting our daughter to the hospital."

Ouch! I dipped my head, flexing my fingers before shoving it back into my pocket. "Of course."

"Excuse me. I need Autumn to sign the discharge paperwork." The nurse cut into the conversation.

Rob's eyes went wide. "You're kicking her out so soon?"

The nurse shook his head. "No, the doctor still needs to do a final examination. She'll be here for a few more hours."

I was grateful for the nurse's impatience. The hospital bill was bound to be the next hot topic, and when the subject came up again, I didn't want to be around. Knowing everyone's attention was on the paperwork, I took advantage of the diversion, ducked my head, and slipped out the door, guilt pooling in the pit of my stomach. *I am such a coward.*

Chapter 17

Autumn

Fifteen minutes had passed since Jensen escaped, and the nurse left my room with the hospital discharge paperwork, but my dads were still on my case.

"I can't believe we almost lost you, all because you didn't want a bill." Papi's voice broke, and he swept his dreadlocks behind his left shoulder.

"Yes, how could you be so irresponsible?" Dad wrapped Papi in his arms. "I know you want to be independent, Autumn, but this is too far."

I shook my head. "No, I *was* being responsible. That's why I called Jensen. He's a doctor, and he was still close by." Besides, I doubted my dads would have been so understanding about a huge ambulance bill if my condition hadn't been an emergency. And because my insurance deductible was through the roof, it wouldn't have covered anything anyway. Not that my dads or I needed to worry about an invoice. I couldn't believe Jensen paid for everything. Sure, he was a pediatric hospitalist and made good money, but an emergency room fee and surgery weren't cheap. Why would Jensen spend his money on me, anyway? I was just some companion he'd hired to masquerade as his fake girlfriend for two events.

Dad and Papi pulled apart.

I noticed a look pass between them—a silent

conversation I was glad I couldn't hear.

"And who is this *Jensen* to you, by the way?"

Dad's inflection made the quotation marks in his question obvious. Not to mention he was using his courtroom voice. As I struggled for a good explanation, I felt my mouth go dry, and I fiddled with my blanket. Admitting Jensen was a client was forbidden. "He's a doctor friend." *Why did I sound so defensive?*

"Oh?" Papi pursed his lips with a hand on his hip.

Damn! He picked up on it, too. What is wrong with me? "I don't want to talk about Jensen. Just know you won't have to worry about the bill." I was anxious enough for all of us because paying Jensen back would take forever—especially if I took two weeks off for finals.

Dad's dark eyebrows shot above his thick-rimmed glasses. "What do you mean *we don't need to worry*? You only have catastrophic insurance. That won't cover an emergency room visit and surgery."

I fought a grimace and focused on adjusting my hospital gown by smoothing the creases, my stomach in knots.

Dad threw a hand in the air. "Oh, good grief. This *Jensen* character paid for the bill, didn't he?"

I gusted the air from my lungs. Getting out of this conversation wasn't an option—I needed to confess. "Um…yes?" A bead of sweat trickled down my temple. *How will I explain this right when even I don't understand the situation?*

Papi's hands flew to his cheeks. "Please tell me it's not for the benefits?"

My nose crinkled. What was he talking about? "Benefits?" I couldn't fathom what Jensen would get from his generosity, but then a sickening thought occurred. Was I part of Jensen's required hospital philanthropy work? If I was, would his paying the bill change how I felt about him? I wasn't sure. But either way, I didn't want to be a charity case out of pity or vocational obligation. Both reasons went against my vow for independence.

"You know"—Papi waved a hand in the air, his face scrunched—"friends with benefits?"

Fire scorched my cheeks. I hadn't even considered that option, but now my imagination went wild. "What? Papi, noooo!" All my previous worries about Jensen evaporated, replaced with forbidden thoughts about what Jensen would look like naked—which was the last thing I wanted to do in front of my parents. Picturing that was the last thing I *should* do—period.

Dad jabbed a finger. "What's that face?"

I recoiled, irrationally angry that Dad's twenty-seven years as a trial attorney made him an expert at reading body language. "What's what face?" I schooled my features.

Dad's lips spread in a slow smile. "You like him."

"What?" My insides turned to ice, and my heartbeat pulsed in my ears. "No. We're just friends, Dad." Why did those words feel wrong? Yeah, Jensen was hot, but he was a client. Nothing *could* happen. Even if I wanted more, I couldn't, right? Regardless of my ambiguous feelings, I needed to convince my dads nothing was going on. An idea formed. "He's a doctor, and I want to be a nurse. Jensen's just helping me with my studies. That's all." I focused on a loose thread in my bedding. I hated to lie, but the truth wasn't an option per my Plus One contract.

I'd broken so many personal and professional rules. Thanks to my appendicitis, Jensen knew where I lived and my true identity. Not to mention, because he'd seen me at the docks, the cat was out of the bag for my second job, too. But *Jensen's* confidentiality wasn't an option. Besides, he *had* offered to help me study before, so taking him up on his offer might wash away my guilt from omitting the truth to my dads.

"Your *study buddy* paid the bill?"

Dad's tone sounded like an accusation rather than a question. The hair on the back of my neck rose.

"I don't know any friends who shell out thousands of dollars for each other." Dad tucked his blue, grid-checked dress shirt into his gray suit slacks. "I hope you plan on paying him back."

Papi held up a finger. "With money."

I rolled my eyes. Did he even realize what he was saying? "Of course, I plan on paying Jensen back." I tugged on one of Papi's dreadlocks. "With money. I'm not a freeloader or a prostitute." If I owed Jensen money, I'd work my butt off at Plus One until we were even.

Papi shrugged. "I wasn't accusing, just being your father."

Dad shook his head, then shifted my IV tube out of the way, and sat on the edge of my hospital bed. "You're under a lot of stress right now, sweetheart. How about we reimburse Jensen, and you can repay us after you graduate and have a job?"

Tempting. But I needed to pay someone back, regardless of who it was. And my dads had already done so much. "No, Dad." I set my jaw. "I will pay Jensen back on my own."

Dad eyeballed me over his glasses. "Then maybe you'll reconsider letting us pay for your tuition?"

"Nope." I could never do that to my dads again.

Dad huffed. "You're so stubborn."

Papi scoffed. "Gee, I wonder who she got that from?"

Dad pursed his lips with an eye roll, then took my hand. "If you change your mind…"

"I won't." With a final nod, I made a mental note to call Ruth tomorrow.

****

After being discharged from the hospital, I relished the feel of my apartment. I was grateful the pain had reduced to an aching throb as long as I didn't bend over. Which was good, considering my roommate was still out of town. If I needed help, I'd be forced to call my dads because, after their suspicions, I'd never live it down if I called Jensen. I shuffled into the kitchen and grabbed myself a bowl of cereal. My books from studying with Lilly were still on the rickety wooden table sitting atop the mail I hadn't gone through. Rather than relocate the heavy stuff, I shoved the items aside and sat, wincing when I slouched. Sitting straight-backed, I dug in, crunching on the sugary bran flakes. I heard my phone ping. Glancing, I read Jensen's name on the screen, and a lightness filled my chest, followed quickly by an overwhelming sense of dread. Was he contacting me about the money?

—*How's the patient?*—

The dread in my stomach dissipated a fraction. *Small talk first, I guess?*

—*Doing great, thanks!*—

Lies! My goal was to ignore the pain and continue

as usual. Plus, the hospital sent me home with pain pills. If needed, I could pop some, grit my teeth, and bear the discomfort for midterms.

—Make sure you get plenty of rest—

Huh. He didn't mention the money. Should I?

—I wish I could. Midterms—

—You're going for your BSN. If any department would understand the need to reschedule, it's them—

Probably, but I would wait until my first exam on Tuesday before I decided.

—Maybe—

—Not maybe. You need to take care of yourself. If you're in pain, you won't perform well—

—Yes, doctor—

A thrill ran through me at my coy response. However, calling him by his title got me thinking—our contract was over; Jensen didn't need to contact me. Was he really texting out of concern as a doctor or a friend? Or was the chitchat a gateway to remind me of my financial obligation? If his reason was the latter, then I needed to nip it in the bud.

—BTW, I plan to repay you for the hospital bill—

—Are you always this lousy at accepting help?—

I scowled. Getting me to the hospital *was* help. Paying through the nose to cover my surgery was a whole different ballgame.

—You barely know me, Jensen—

—But I like what I've learned so far. As long as everything on our dates wasn't a lie…—

I never lied…to him.

—So, I always try to stay close to the truth during contracts, but you got the whole of it—

I hung my head. *Why did I tell him that? Can I*

break any more Plus One rules?
—*You just made me smile.* Smiley face emoji—
For some reason, I grinned, too. *Great!* Now I was breaking my own rules.

Chapter 18

Jensen

Sitting on my living room couch, I waited for the dots to appear on my phone screen, but Autumn never responded to my last text. While checking in after her surgery was a genuine inquiry, I also used the opportunity to stay in contact. I was on cloud nine knowing Autumn was genuine on our dates. The only façade was her pretending to be my girlfriend.

I couldn't deny the physical chemistry—both hers and mine—was real. The body's basic reflexes and core responses couldn't be faked. My desire for Autumn was more than an innate attraction. The feeling was a combo—desire along with how I felt in her presence. Time moved faster, I was drawn to her energy, and I forgot all about Kayla and the drama at work. Autumn was the whole package. In fact, I wanted to build on those feelings and ask her out on an actual date. My shared interests with Autumn, like hiking, watching Orcas games, and our love of medicine, made us extremely compatible. "But then there's that damn hospital bill." My dopamine levels dropped a few clouds, and I let my shoulders slump.

A knock sounded at the door.

My dinner. Too bad, I'd already lost my appetite. Retrieving the bag of Mexican food from my brick porch, I carried it into the kitchen. I set the contents on the counter, and the scent of chipotle peppers stung my nose. I'd eat later when my hunger returned. Standing in front of my kitchen sink, I gazed past my living room, watching the sailboats floating on the Sound, and reflected on my text conversation with Autumn. For some reason, reimbursement for her hospital invoice was her top priority, regardless of my insistence she didn't need to worry. I didn't expect her to pay me back or want her to. Why couldn't Autumn accept that, as both a doctor and a decent human being, helping her out was the right thing to do? I closed my eyes and shook my head, gusting out a breath. Who was I kidding? If Dan knew I'd taken care of Autumn's debt, he'd either have me committed or assume I was one step away from proposing.

Over my career as a pediatric hospitalist, I'd seen numerous families struggle with follow-up care for financial reasons. As much as I wanted to help, I treated too many impoverished people, and as their physician, offering financial assistance was unethical. However, Autumn was an exception—I wasn't her doctor. Paying her bill hadn't broken any rules.

Besides, if she had her way, Autumn wouldn't have even gone to the hospital to save the money. While she might be upset that I insisted she seek medical treatment because my oath and morals wouldn't let her die on her entryway floor—the guilt weighed on my conscience. In the end, looking back over my actions, I stood by my decision. The situation still came down to the basic fact that I liked Autumn and wanted to help. However, while I knew initially she would be upset, I hoped by now she would have recognized my feelings behind the gesture and accepted my generosity. Scrubbing my face with a hand, I groaned. *Apparently not*. I needed to think of a way to alleviate Autumn's indebtedness. But how?

****

The following day when my alarm sounded, I had to gather all my strength to drag myself out of bed. I'd spent the night tossing and turning, wracking my brain for ideas on how to placate Autumn, but by morning, I still came up empty. Of course, when I received her offer, I could always refuse the money. However, doing so wouldn't change how she would have earned the large sum of cash—contracts with other guys. I couldn't picture a scenario where we were both happy.

I made a breakfast burrito from last night's takeout and got ready for work. My worries over Autumn were like a chirping smoke detector completely out of reach—sending intermittent waves of anxiety through my veins. Assuaging Autumn was like a double-edge sword—I wanted her free of guilt and obligation, but her acceptance would also end our correspondence. I'd never expected to feel this way about a woman again, especially considering I'd become jaded after my experience with Kayla. But after two weeks with Autumn, I realized my heart was ready to try a new relationship.

By the time I finally arrived at the hospital, I had rationalized an excuse to text Autumn. I was a doctor, and she'd just had surgery. Of course, I'd want to check on her again. Unfortunately, as I got out my phone and entered the breakroom, I spotted Dan at the counter.

"Hey, buddy. Texting your girlfriend?"

His razzing made me feel like a twelve-year-old with the way my heart stuttered. Sadly, I was only texting the woman I *wished* was my girlfriend. "As a matter of fact, I was about to."

Dan poured himself a cup of coffee from the percolator. "Kristine was sad y'all didn't stay longer at the benefit."

I trapped the earthy scent from his cup in my lungs for a few beats before releasing. "Thank goodness, we didn't."

"Oh?" Dan waggled his eyebrows and elbowed my side.

I rolled my eyes. *Pfft. If only.* "Not like that. Her appendix ruptured."

The creases in Dan's forehead deepened, and he straightened to his full six feet. "Oh, man. Is she okay?"

I felt my chest tighten thinking about how it could have gone sideways. "Thankfully, yes." I recapped how Autumn called last night, asking for a second opinion on her diagnosis and the subsequent trip to the emergency room.

"Good thing you weren't already on the ferry." Dan perched on the edge of the leather couch and sipped his coffee.

I pushed a hand through my hair. "You're telling me. Just thinking of what could have happened had Autumn called thirty minutes later makes me nauseous."

Dan's cheek hitched in a half-smile. "You really like this woman, don't you?"

More than I should. "Yeah, I do." He had no idea how much.

"Excuse me, Dr. Falkner?"

The familiar Russian accent of a pediatric nurse interrupted our conversation.

"Cooper is back from his MRI."

"Thanks, Katia. I'll be right there." Dan watched the woman's retreating figure, then turned to meet my gaze. "Don't forget we have a double date in our future. Expect to hear from Kristine soon."

My stomach swooped. "You got it." Dan was clueless about the opportunity he'd just presented—a reason to contact Autumn when I ran out of questions about her surgery or Plus One. The potential of a genuine get-together was all the motivation I needed to make this thing between Autumn and me happen.

As I strode with a buoyant step to my office with renewed confidence, I refused to let my jealousy and Autumn's pride derail a possible relationship. Closing the door, I retrieved my phone and opened our thread. Launching into a possible double date with Dan and Kristine would seem abrupt, so I went with my earlier plan as an opener, saving Dan's invitation for another time—if I had the courage. One step at a time.

—How are the incisions? Are you still in a lot of pain?—

I waited for a response, even though the time was early. A few minutes before eight a.m. Chances were, she was still sleeping. When I didn't get a reply, I switched over to check my email, and a text alert flashed on my screen. I tapped on her response with a smile.

—A lot better. Thank you. The meds they sent me home with helped. I slept like a rock—

I was glad she was doing better, but now I needed to think of something else to text to keep the conversation going.

—When is your follow-up visit?—

—In four weeks—
Standard time frame.
—Just make sure to take it easy until then—
My subsequent thought was selfish, but I couldn't help myself.
—As a doctor, I'd recommend taking some time off work—both jobs. At least until you've had your checkup—
—Well, I need the money, so I'll still be working the toll booths, but no more Plus One until after midterms—

I relaxed my shoulders. While I had no right to keep her from companioning, hearing Autumn was taking a break for her exams made me happy as a clam. I knew my next question would cross the line, but since I'd decided to pursue a relationship with Autumn, I realized the only way to know if she was interested was to put myself out there. After wiping my sweaty palms on my lab coat, I typed.

—Hey, I know you're still recuperating. I get off at four p.m. Do you want me to come by with dinner?—

Chapter 19

Autumn

I stared at my phone screen, still lying in my soft, warm bed. Sitting would mean using my abdominal muscles and disturbing my incisions—they still smarted. I knew that made me a wuss, but I couldn't help it. On top of that, I had Jensen's offer to provide dinner, tightening my chest like a vice. I wanted to say *yes*. Because friends could make friends food, right? And that's all he was—a good friend. Or was his offer simply because he was a good doctor? Who was I kidding? Why he texted didn't matter; I was just glad he did.

Jensen was no longer a client, so I didn't need to remain professional. Since he wasn't my doctor, he didn't, either. He'd already saved my life, paid my medical bill, and knew where I lived. I had no reason to reject his dinner offer—other than the fact I was attracted to Jensen and promised myself I'd graduate before I started dating again. As I hovered my thumbs over my keyboard, I chewed on my lip, ready to type out my refusal. I shouldn't allow him to stop by with food. Period. But saying *no* would seem ungrateful, considering how generous he'd been. Besides, Jensen was most likely just following up, as his texts indicated.

Wrong. I was lying to myself again. Considering the sparks I felt in his presence, if I allowed Jensen to come over, it'd be like a date, which would be a mistake I couldn't let happen. I heaved a sigh and reached behind me to readjust my pillows, and as the healing cuts on my belly pulled, I winced. "Stick to your guns, Autumn."

—I appreciate the offer, but I'll be fine—

Sitting here alone in my bed, wishing you were here, feeling sorry for myself.

—If you're being polite, stop. It's not a big deal to run over some food—

The act was a big deal—full of confusing feelings and complications.

—No, really. My dads are coming over this evening, and I'm pretty sure Papi is cooking his famous curried mutton—

I was lying again, but I salivated at the mention, and I wondered if Papi would be willing to make some if I asked.

—Okay, as long as you're being taken care of. If anything changes, shoot me a text; remember, I get off at four p.m.—

Damn it, Jensen. Why are you such a nice guy?

—Thanks, I'll keep that in mind—

As a heaviness sank into my gut, I threw my phone on my bed. The possibility I'd never see or talk to Jensen again was high, and to my surprise, I didn't like it.

Braving the pain, I stepped into the kitchen, opened the freezer, and grabbed the pint of pink bubblegum ice cream and a spoon from the drawer. I pressed the icy container against my stomach and eased myself onto the couch. The memories of Jensen's examination, while kneeling on the floor, before taking me to the hospital ran through my head. The concern in his eyes and the gentleness of his touch warmed my heart. No wonder he'd made the Best Doctors in Seattle list.

Thinking back to his award ceremony, when I watched Jensen step on stage to receive his plaque, I felt genuine pride. He was so humble. I could see his flushed cheeks from where I sat in the audience. As I remembered myself swaying against him on the dance floor, I recalled the image of his face morphing from an embarrassed pink to the red of desire. Heat washed over me, remembering Jensen's hand on my butt and the way his lips tasted. I twisted the spoon against my tongue, feeling like my limbs weighed a thousand pounds—I shouldn't have rejected Jensen's offer. The jingle of keys in the lock knocked me out of my reverie, and I replaced the lid on my ice cream.

Alyssa bustled through the door, wearing her ever-present athletic wear, holding her coffee tumbler, and dragging her suitcase.

"Welcome back! How was your visit with your folks?"

Her smile was as tight as her ponytail.

"Fine, thanks, but I'm exhausted. I work at six, so I'm taking a nap." She strode toward her room but froze in the hallway, glancing over her shoulder. "How was your week?"

I knew she was asking to be polite. Telling her about my surgery would be a moot point. "Uneventful."

Alyssa opened her bedroom door. "That's good." Stepping inside, she closed it without even a second glance.

"Okay, then. Good talk." I rolled my eyes, used to Alyssa's aloof personality. Deciding wallowing over

Jensen wasn't good for my mental health, I returned the ice cream to the freezer and padded into the bathroom to shower. The thought of Papi's sweet and spicy curry haunted my taste buds, and I couldn't get it out of my head. I toweled off, donned my sweats, and broke out my study materials before texting him with my request.

A knock sounded on my door. I glanced at the clock: 4:50 p.m., only fifty minutes later than he said he'd be over. Not bad for Papi. If Dad weren't working, he'd have ensured Papi was on time. Unfortunately, Dad was still at the office and wouldn't be here for a few more hours.

Unlocking the deadbolt, I opened the door. "Hey, Papi!" As I reached to relieve him of one of his reusable shopping bags dangling from his arms, I kissed his cheek.

"Oh no, you don't!" He pivoted out of my reach, sending his dreadlocks swinging. "You've just had surgery, and I'm pretty sure carrying groceries is a no-no."

I huffed. Papi knew I was a wimp, so I stepped back and watched him deposit his things onto the counter. After I requested my favorite home-cooked meal, I accepted Papi's offer to make dinner at my place so we could spend the prep time visiting. Normally, I would be thrilled to spend that time with my dad, but I suspected Jensen would come up in conversation. Chewing on the inside of my cheek, I put it out of my head. I'd cross that bridge when we came to it. Standing opposite Papi behind the counter, I rubbed my palms together. "Okay, what can I help with?"

"You'll find a bottle of wine in the Van Gogh bag."

Papi pointed to his *Starry Night* tote. "Why don't you pour us a couple of glasses while I work on dinner?" He tied his dreadlocks back before unloading the other bags.

I grabbed two glasses from the cupboard and the corkscrew. After opening the bottle, I sniffed the heady, fruity aroma and poured the wine. Handing Papi a goblet, I sat at the kitchen table. "When's your next gig? I'd love to come. It's been too long."

As he glanced away from dicing an onion, Papi squinted, his dark denim shirt rolled up his forearms. "It's during your midterms, so you'll be busy." He dabbed his watering eyes on the cuff of his sleeve. "So, this Jensen guy? Tell me more about him."

Really? We're diving right in? He'd only been here five minutes. That question must have been burning on the edge of his tongue. If I thought he'd go for it, I'd plead the fifth and beg him to change the subject, but I knew better. "I told you before; he's just helping me study."

Papi pursed his lips, the gold chains around his neck glistening in the overhead lights. "And taking care of your bills."

Prickling heat crept up my spine, and I held up a hand. "I'm planning on paying Jensen back." Maybe I could exchange my Fridays at the tollbooth for Plus One contracts. That would speed up the process.

"Mmm hmm. No man just pays your bills." Scooping the onions, Papi threw them into the frying pan. The sizzling and popping intensified the scent of oil and vegetable caramelizing. He spun, pointing the knife in my direction. "He likes you."

He does? Stop. Papi was just projecting. I willed

my cheeks not to flush and failed. "Papi, it's not like that." Well, perhaps the situation could be, if I'd let it.

"Maybe for you." Papi pressed a garlic clove over the pan.

The scent, combined with the onions, filled the tiny space. "For him, too. I'm just Jensen's friend, and after graduation, I want to work at his hospital." I should just come clean. "Even if I wanted more, I couldn't. You know what Dad always says—don't cut the branch you're sitting on." I fiddled with the stack of brown takeout napkins in the middle of the table, unable to meet Papi's gaze. Hearing my phone buzz, I glanced at the screen, suppressing a smile at Jensen's name, and swiped the message clear.

"Autumn, you've got the worst poker face I've ever seen."

I gawked at my father.

Papi removed the pan from the burner before nabbing my phone, waking the screen, and angling it at my face. Unlocked, he tapped on my messages. "Hmm, just the person I'd expected after your dopey expression." He returned my device. "So, this *friend* knows I'm making you dinner?"

Dammit. I forgot I'd used Papi as my excuse to turn Jensen down. "Earlier, he asked if I needed food, and I told him you were bringing it."

"Sounds like a *very* good *friend* to me." Papi opened the bag of potatoes and rinsed them in the sink.

"Exactly. A good *friend*." The flush I felt in my cheeks negated my words.

He gave a cock-eyebrowed smirk. "How old is Jensen, and where did you meet prior to the hospital?"

As Papi waited for me to spill the tea, he couldn't

hide his smile. Unfortunately, because Jensen was a previous client, I couldn't tell him the truth, but I hated lying to my father. "He's thirty-seven, and we met through a mutual friend." I took a gulp of my chardonnay, both the alcohol and lie burning the back of my throat.

Dragging the stainless steel trashcan over to the table, Papi sat and peeled a potato. "You've never thought about taking the relationship further? Because you obviously like him."

I inhaled a deep breath. If only my situation with Jensen was that easy. "Doctors and nurses." I grimaced. "It's a bit cliché, don't you think?" My attempt to sell this excuse was weak. I didn't even buy it myself.

Papi shrugged and grabbed another spud. "I don't know. It seems to work for McDreamy."

I shoved his shoulder. "Student doctors also perform major surgery on that show. It's not reality."

He stood and carried the potatoes to the cutting board. "Fathers can dream"—he glanced over his shoulder, the *thunk* of his knife hitting the hard plastic—"Dad and I wouldn't mind seeing our daughter marry a doctor."

Papi would say that, but if he knew Jensen was a previous Plus One client, he probably wouldn't be so encouraging. Besides, I didn't expect to talk to Jensen again other than to repay him. A small part of my brain rationalized other ways to see him, but I told it to shut up. Jensen should never have paid my bill. I needed to sever all ties to move forward and forget him. Ignoring the knot in my stomach, I forced myself to voice my decision before I could overthink. "You know what, Papi? I *will* take your and Dad's offer to repay Jensen."

Chapter 20

Jensen

I sat on Dan and Kristine's couch in front of the seventy-two-inch flatscreen, staring at my phone. A week passed since I'd last texted Autumn, and I couldn't think of another reason to reach out other than her surgery. But at this point, she'd be all but healed. I tapped my chin. Or maybe…if Kristine followed through with her double date idea, I could call in another favor. Then again, I could also hire Autumn for another event. I shook my head. A contract would give the wrong impression. I could deliberately bump into her at the ferries. However, she usually worked at the Bainbridge Port, and if I showed up there, she'd know I'd gone out of my way, and I'd come across as a creepy stalker. I kneaded my forehead. None of these options were ideal. Besides, Autumn had given no indication she wanted more.

Dan handed me a brown bottle and sat on the adjoining cushion.

The condensation from the glass dripped onto my jeans, leaving navy spots on the denim.

"Sorry about the lite beer." He patted the Orcas' logo stretched over his stomach. "Kristine's got me on a diet."

I laughed. *Poor guy.* "No problem." Taking a swig, I tried not to wince at its hollow taste.

Dan slapped my shoulder. "You get used to it."

"I don't believe you." I glanced at the TV, only half-focusing on the panel of ex-players discussing the lineup. "Next week, I'm buying my own."

"Ah, man. You gotta share."

Kristine stomped into the room and swatted her husband on the shoulder. "No, don't even think about it." She set a plate of whole grain pita chips and hummus on the rustic chest coffee table in front of Dan before handing me a plate of nachos.

The scent of melted cheese and jalapenos had me salivating.

Dan scowled at the hummus.

With her back to the screen, Kristine pointed a finger in my face. "Don't you even think of sharing your beer." She straightened the stack of napkins piled on the chest. "Where's Autumn tonight? I thought for sure she'd come since she's such an Orcas fan."

My gut twisted. "Um, she has midterms." *At least, that's the truth.* "So she's...recording the game." *Possibly another lie—I'm going to hell.*

Kristine put her hands on her hips, bunching her jersey, and making the shirt appear like a dress on her small frame. "Are you saying you'll be watching the game again tonight at Autumn's? Because good luck keeping the score a secret until morning. The final outcome will be all over the Internet."

I shifted on the tan leather couch, not meeting her gaze. "Nah, I won't be seeing Autumn tonight." *Unless I took the Bainbridge ferry.... No, I already decided that was a bad idea.*

Kristine strode to the adjoining kitchen but glanced over her shoulder. "Well, she's got to take her nose out of her books at some point. What about next week's game? Can she make it then?"

Uninvited tension seized my shoulders, but I was grateful that, at least this time, my excuse was valid. "I work next week."

Walking back in front of the coffee table, she twisted a corkscrew into the top of a wine bottle. "What about the week after?"

Clutching my beer, I shoved a chip in my mouth with a shrug.

"Why don't you text her now?" Kristine poured herself a glass of wine and sat between me and her husband. "Let's make it a date."

And there it was—my excuse to contact Autumn. Sweat beaded in my pits. "She's studying, and I don't want to interrupt." Would Autumn even answer my texts?

Kristine kicked my foot. "Don't be silly. She's your girlfriend. She'd love to hear from you, and I'm sure she could use the break. Go on"—she jabbed with an elbow—"text her now. It'll be nice to have one of your girlfriends come who actually enjoys football."

Dan furrowed his brow. "Kristine."

"What?" She shot him a sideways glare. "It's true. Kayla hated football. She ruined game nights."

Dan bobbled his head. "Well, to be fair, she ruined everything."

My friends weren't wrong. Watching a game with someone who liked the Orcas and got along with Dan and Kristine would be a nice change of pace. But, when Kristine got something in her head, she was like a dog with a bone. Getting out of texting Autumn wasn't an option. With my pulse pounding in my ears, I unlocked my phone. "Okay." Letting my thumbs hover over the keyboard, I realized Kristine's request would take more than a short text to explain. "You know what? I'll just give her a call instead." I rose from the couch. "Be right back."

I slipped through the short hall filled with wedding and honeymoon photos to Dan's office and closed the door with a soft *click*. Running a hand through my hair, I wracked my brain for something to say. The jitters in my stomach were two-fold—I was excited I now had an excuse to call, but the circumstances were less than ideal. I decided to rehearse the conversation before I dialed. "Hey, Autumn, I know you're super busy studying for midterms, and I'm no longer your client, but Kristine and Dan want to see you." I shook my head. *So dumb.* "Hey, Autumn, can I hire you again to join me at Dan and Kristine's to watch an Orcas game in two weeks?" I pinched the bridge of my nose. I didn't want her to agree to that one; the objective was voluntary participation. Pacing the length of the small runner in front of Dan's desk, I dissected every scenario I could think of, but each came back to the same conclusion—I should just go with the truth. I took a deep breath and tapped the *call* icon.

"Hello?"

Her voice was music to my ears. "Hey, Autumn, it's Jensen."

She laughed. "I know who you are."

Warmth exploded beneath my skin. "Oh, I wasn't sure if you would still have my contact saved in your phone."

Autumn scoffed. "Like I'd delete the number of my personal physician."

I smiled, and my whole body hummed. "Personal physician, huh?" *I'm game, if she is.* Sitting at Dan's desk, I pulled on the last cool metal ball on his five-sphere pendulum and released. The steel clacks resounded around the room.

"Don't get me wrong, I'd never bother you for another house call... I don't expect more medical treatment for free." She sighed. "I mean, you've already done enough, and I still need to pay you back."

Autumn just provided the perfect opportunity, and I jumped on it. "Speaking of which, I need to ask a favor, and it's a big ask. But if you're willing to do this, then we can call it even."

"I'm intrigued. What do you need?"

Autumn's tone sounded sincere, and I hoped she wasn't feeling guilty. "I'm over at Dan and Kristine's to watch the Orcas game, and they don't understand why I haven't brought my girlfriend, AKA you."

"Oh, they're so sweet."

Thank goodness, they are. "Yeah, Kristine likes you, and she insisted I bring you to the game the week after next. So, how about it?" I cringed, awaiting her answer, then decided to sweeten the deal. "And we can stage an official breakup after the game—see this to the end so I don't get caught in the lie. Then I won't bother you again. I promise." *That was dumb.* I regretted the last words as soon as they left my mouth.

"Wow, you're just going to break my heart like that? As if I meant nothing? I even stripped for you— well, metaphorically speaking." She giggled. "At least, Kayla thinks so."

Hearing her reference the conversation in front of my ex and, recalling the subsequent kiss, sent a ripple through my torso. I laughed nervously. "I can't deny I fake loved your striptease." I slapped my hand over my forehead, and I squeezed my eyes closed. *What is wrong with me?* "Wait, what I meant was, I loved our fictional relationship?" I hung my head. "I'm not sounding any better, am I?"

"It's okay, Jensen. I appreciate you saying I wasn't just a fling."

I pushed off the corner of Dan's desk, spinning the chair, feeling buoyant that she overlooked my fumbling behavior. "So, you'll come with me in two weeks?" *Please say yes.*

"Of course, I will. I never miss an Orcas game."

I pulled the phone away from my mouth. "Yes!" I fist-pumped the air.

"About the breakup."

Catching the term *breakup*, I smashed my ear back to the screen. "Yes?"

"Do you want to end things in front of your friends? Because if I had to choose, I wouldn't want to ruin the game. Seeing as you'd be breaking my heart, I'd be expected to cry, and I don't cry unless the Orcas lose."

"Oh no." Sitting straight, I grabbed the desk and steadied the chair, swallowing the lump in my throat. "I would be devastated to watch you cry. The last thing I want to do is make you uncomfortable in front of my friends. In fact, we don't even need to break up, if you don't want to…." *Shut up!* I was rambling now.

"Jensen, it's okay. We can discuss the details in two weeks after the game. Speaking of which, if we don't hang up, we'll miss tonight's kickoff."

"Good call." I felt a weight lift from my shoulders,

realizing I now had a two-week's reprieve. "I'll be in touch tomorrow with the specifics." Rising from my seat, I felt lighter than air, knowing I had an excuse to contact her throughout the next fourteen days and more opportunities might arise to see her. "Enjoy the game."

"Go, Orcas!"

With a bounce in my step, I returned to the family room to rejoin Dan and Kristine.

"So?" Kristine nabbed a cheese-loaded chip from my abandoned plate. "Can I count on the two of you for the nineteenth?"

"Hey! I thought we were dieting together." Dan glared, gesturing at the nacho.

"*I* work out." She shoved the chip into her mouth and returned her attention to me, eyebrows raised.

Grabbing my now-warm beer, I settled into the couch. "Yep, she said she'd love to come."

Kristine gave a mini clap. "Yay!"

The whistle blared from the TV, ending our conversation, but my mind wouldn't stop. I replayed my phone call with Autumn in my head. When I extended the invitation, I couldn't recall any hesitation in her voice, only enthusiasm. Then again, her light tone could have been anticipation over watching the Orcas play—she was an avid fan. But Autumn could watch the game from home like she was doing tonight. Perhaps she was simply excited to see Kristine again. The ladies *had* hit it off the two times they'd seen each other. *Whatever*. I didn't care. Regardless of what caused Autumn's excitement, the point was *I'd* get to see her again.

Glancing at Kristine, I smiled. In most situations, I wasn't too fond of my friend's aggressive attitude, because it usually involved her setting me up with one of her friends. This time, I was grateful. As long as Autumn was still in the picture, Kristine could meddle as much as she wanted.

Chapter 21

Autumn

I placed my phone on my white-laminate kitchen counter and grabbed the bag of popcorn from the microwave. By attending the Orcas game at Kristine and Dan's, Jensen promised my debt would be repaid. Even though the monetary value wasn't equal, Jensen implied that upholding his reputation in front of his friends made up the difference. I struggled to accept his terms. While Jensen was being kind, and being debt-free would be nice, I'd already asked for a loan from my dads. How would I explain I didn't need their money anymore? I shuddered. *Nope*. The idea of explaining Jensen's compromise to my dads was out of the question. I rubbed my forehead. Perhaps I could take the money from Papi and Dad and hold on to it in case Jensen allowed me to repay him—the best-case scenario. However, if Jensen continued to refuse, I'd reimburse my fathers little by little with their own money, so they'd be none the wiser.

Satisfied with my devious plan, I curled up on the couch under my super-soft minky Blast the Orca blanket and waited for the game to start. I felt my phone buzz against my thigh. Checking the screen, I smiled at Jensen's name and opened his text.

—*Thanks again for agreeing to the nineteenth. Kristine can't wait to see you again. Neither can I—*

Excitement bubbled in my chest. *Why am I so elated he wants to see me again?* I shouldn't be. Liking Jensen was a bad idea.

—*My pleasure. I'm looking forward to seeing you, too*—

Wow, I guess my subconscious decided I'm going with honesty tonight. The whistle blew, and I returned my focus to the TV.

The first quarter of the game was intense, but neither team scored. However, two minutes into the second quarter, the Orcas made a touchdown, and I felt my phone buzz again. This time, Jensen sent a GIF of an Orcas running back, flexing. I smiled, texting back.

—*#Go, Orcs!*—

But after the kicker missed the goalpost by miles for the extra point, Jensen sent another Gif—the Orcas' coach with a gobsmacked expression, followed by a text.

—*Really? He only had one job*—

I erupted in laughter. Jensen was hilarious.

—*Yeah, my grandma could have made that shot*—
—*I could have made it—blindfolded!*—

Readjusting my blanket to cover my icy toes, I shook my head.

—*Too far, Jensen. Too far*—
—*How do you know I'm not a football prodigy?*—

I bit my lip, searching for the perfect comeback.

—*Ha! I'm sure you sacrificed a career in football to be a doctor*—

—*Doctor was the logical choice*—

My banter with Jensen continued throughout all four quarters, making the game a thousand times more enjoyable, and considering I never missed a game, that was saying something. When I watched the Orcas score the final touchdown in the last forty seconds, sealing the win, Jensen lit up my screen.

—Thank goodness, they won; I'd hate to think of you crying alone in your apartment—

—True. And in two weeks, if they lose, it's nice knowing you'll be there to comfort me—

Dammit! I sounded like a girlfriend. Without an audience, I should be making more of an effort to be just friends. Jabbing a finger on the screen, I was desperate to unsend the message, but the dots were blinking, and nausea rolled through my stomach. He'd already seen my text.

—I'll have tissues at the ready—

With an exhale, I let my shoulders relax. His casual response told me he'd read my comment as a joke. But I needed to be more careful in the future. With Jensen, letting my emotions get the better of me was too easy.

—How many midterms do you have left?—

I reviewed my schedule in my head.

—Two. The first on Tuesday and the other on Thursday. Then I'm done. Just three more semesters!—

—Which classes?—

—Anatomy of Circulation and Pathophysiology of the Endocrine System—

Thanks to Lilly's Hashimoto's disease, I was confident about the latter, but for some reason, the ins and outs of blood flow weren't sticking in my brain.

—I'm off work tomorrow morning. Do you want a study partner?—

Chewing on the inside of my cheek, I couldn't deny I needed help. But if I was alone in my apartment with Jensen, I'd struggle to fight off his magnetic pull, making it difficult to keep him in the friend zone. *Perhaps somewhere public?* An indecent exposure citation would be the perfect motivation to behave myself.

—*Sure, Jensen. That sounds great. Want to meet at the campus library? The Nancy Parker Memorial?*—

—*What time?*—

—*How about ten a.m.?*—

—*Perfect. And if our studying goes until lunch, I'll treat. But I need to leave for the hospital by four*—

Joy sparked my insides at his chivalrous gesture, and as much as I wanted to, I couldn't allow him to buy me food—too date-like. Plus, lunch would only add to my growing tab.

—*Thanks, but you're the one helping* me *study. The least I can do is pay for* your *food*—

I was a glutton for punishment.

—*Well, I'm not keeping track, but I'm also not stupid enough to turn down a beautiful woman offering to buy me lunch*—

Pinching my lips, I contained my squeal.

—*See you tomorrow*—

I set my phone to charge on my nightstand and grabbed my pajamas. That I was so amped about tomorrow was ridiculous; we were only studying, for Pete's sake. But he'd been so flirty all night with his texts and GIF during the game that I couldn't help myself.

After finishing my nighttime routine, I opened my closet and shifted through my shirts and dresses. I wanted something comfortable yet flattering for tomorrow. Because while I wasn't trying to impress Jensen, I didn't want to look frumpy, either. I settled on skinny jeans with a cropped cream sweater and my retro sneakers. Setting the outfit on my chair for the morning, I repeated my motto in the mirror, "No men until my BSN." A text from Jensen lit my screen.

—Sweet dreams—

If I didn't know better, I'd think he was determined to test my resolve.

Chapter 22

Jensen

I stood on the stone steps of the ornate Gothic entrance to the Nancy Parker Memorial Library, staring at my phone. From the corner of my eye, I scanned the campus, searching for Autumn, trying my best to appear cool and relaxed, like I belonged on a student campus and wasn't a mid-thirties perv; hence why I kept my gaze zeroed in on my screen. As I spotted Autumn scurrying across the central brick plaza, juggling several books and a bag on her shoulder, I burned with a flare of exhilaration. I jogged down the steps. "Here, let me take those." I held out my hands.

"Thank you." As she handed over the stack, she groaned. "They wouldn't all fit in my bag."

I smiled. "Yeah, *War and Peace* has nothing on medical textbooks." I gave myself a mental slap for the dad joke. "Sorry, I have a lame sense of humor."

"While the joke wasn't funny, you're not wrong." Autumn shifted her backpack.

A flash of silver around her midsection caught my eye. I glanced at her navel and spotted the belly button ring. Heat like a five-alarm fire engulfed my torso. I tried to look away, but my gaze snagged on the metal like a magnet.

"Once this week is over, I'll definitely need to see my chiropractor."

"How rude of me. You're still recuperating from surgery." I reached for her bag. "Let me take this, too."

She spun sideways and waved a hand. "Please, my incision's long since healed. I can't even feel it anymore. I'm fine."

The hairs on the back of my neck prickled. I wanted to protest.

But Autumn quickened her pace and entered the library. She led the way to the research commons on the ground floor to study area *B*.

The space consisted of two bright-blue booths on either side of a light-gray laminate table.

Autumn dropped her backpack on the adjacent seat.

I sat across, placing her textbooks in the middle of the table. "What do you want to start on first?"

Autumn pulled the *Anatomy of Circulation Volume Two* from the stack. "For some reason, cardiac disorders will be the death of me." A ghost of a smile touched the corners of her lips. "Pun intended."

"Lucky for you, I've treated tons of patients with heart problems." I closed my eyes and let my chest deflate. "That sounded better in my head."

She extended a hand across the table and squeezed my forearm.

Ironically, my heartbeat erupted in a frenzy.

"It's okay. I know what you meant." Autumn opened her book, flipping through a couple of pages before stopping. "Maybe we can start with you quizzing me on the various disorders, their symptoms, and treatment options?"

"Can do." I dragged the heavy textbook toward me, glad to focus on the medical jargon instead of her sexy brown eyes. "Arrhythmia, tell me about it."

An hour later, Autumn had nailed every disorder I'd listed, and we'd progressed to physiology and circulation. "What's the difference between pulmonary and systemic circulation?"

A crease formed on Autumn's brow. "Pulmonary circulation is a closed circuit between the lungs and heart, while systemic circulation is the transfer of blood from the heart to the whole body." She squeezed her eyes shut, then peeked out of the corner.

"Correct." I watched as her shoulders visibly relaxed. So far, my presence was redundant. Had Autumn agreed to this study date because she wanted to see me again? *Man, I hope so.* "And where are the strongest pulse points on a person's body?"

Autumn stared at the table and licked her lips, touching just below her palm. "Radial artery, on the inside of the wrist." Her fingers shifted to the side of her throat. "The carotid artery, in the neck."

Every brush of her hand against her skin had me wishing I could interchange her fingers with my lips. "And what about the lesser-known pulse points?" As she demonstrated six more spots on her body, I followed the movements with a hungry gaze. Each touch turned up the heat of my desire.

Autumn shimmied against the back of her booth, holding her chin high.

I hated to burst her bubble, but she missed one—the popliteal. Her mistake gave me a purpose for being there. Hyperaware of her knees just inches from mine below the laminate work surface, I raised my eyebrows, waiting for her to realize her mistake.

Her smile faded. "What?"

"You missed one." Extending my right hand under the table, I gently caressed the side of her left knee, pressing my fingertips into the soft flesh on the backside of the joint.

Autumn's lips parted, and her gaze locked on mine.

Her pulse quickened under my touch, matching my own hammering heart.

Clearing her throat, she readjusted on the blue vinyl, maneuvering her knee out from under my hand.

As she shifted away, cold invaded my fingers, but I smiled. I'd obviously affected her—the circulatory system didn't lie.

"Oh, ha-ha. Yeah, how could I have forgotten the popliteal?" Pink crept up her neck, and she tucked a lock of hair behind her ear.

Knowing I had some skin in the game, I continued quizzing Autumn, touching her every chance I got to demonstrate some principle or another. I'd even gone as far as using Autumn's hand to trace the path of my subclavian vein along my collarbone, even though I'd have rather outlined hers.

Autumn's fingers trembled against the cotton of my shirt, and she couldn't meet my gaze. I tugged on her wrist to get her attention.

Her gaze lifted to mine.

Autumn's stare radiated desire, and I decided to make my move. Leaning across the table, I pulled her closer.

She didn't break eye contact and didn't resist.

A good sign. Inches apart, I let my gaze fall to her mouth, and my gut clenched.

Autumn's stomach audibly growled. She blinked several times, shaking her head. Glancing to the side, she exhaled a laugh and sat back.

Feeling like I'd had the rug pulled out from under me, I begrudgingly released her wrist.

"It would appear I'm hungry."

"Sounds like it." I infused my voice with false cheeriness. *Is she as disappointed as I am?* I closed her book and added the tome to the pile. With a heavy heart, I wiped my hands down my thighs. "Where are you taking me for lunch?" I mustered all my willpower not to cringe at my own words. Even though she'd offered to pay on the phone last night, my question sounded rude and presumptuous.

Autumn's eyes sparkled. "I know a great little Vietnamese restaurant just off campus."

My paralyzed lungs relaxed.

She stuffed her things into her bag. "How does pho sound?"

I'd prefer to have you served on a plate. Since my fantasies needed to stay in my head, her company and a brothy bowl of noodles, beef, and vegetables would suffice as a consolation prize.

As I ambled next to Autumn down the library steps, I stopped at the bottom, squinting in the bright sunlight. I had no intention of offering to take separate cars. "Do you want to drive together or walk?" The more time we spent with each other, the better. I watched Autumn's teeth sink into her lip, and I repressed a growl.

"It's close enough to walk, but I don't want to carry my backpack and books. Would you mind following me to my car so I can drop off my stuff? Plus, I need to feed the meter. I paid for two hours; lunch will be at least one more." She shrugged. "Can't afford to get another ticket."

My interest was piqued. "Another ticket? Is this a habit of yours?"

Her cheeks flushed. "Let's just say they're part of my budget and never mention it again."

I snorted a laugh. This confession was the closest Autumn came to living up to her carefree hippie name.

She tilted her head with narrowed eyes. "What? Like you've never gotten a ticket?"

Saying I hadn't would sound self-righteous but denying I'd never been stopped by the police would have been a lie.

"Oh my gosh! What?" Autumn's mouth fell open. "You've never gotten a ticket?"

Her tone suggested it wasn't a question. "Let's just say I enjoy my insurance's good driver discount and never mention it again." I winked, hoping my mimicked response sounded flirty and not condescending.

She rolled her eyes, her lips lifting at the corners. "Whatever." Autumn gestured with her head at the brick plaza spanning out before the library. "I'm just on the other side of the far building. It's on the way to the restaurant."

"Perfect. I'll follow you." I strode beside Autumn across the quad, matching her brisk pace.

"I'm just over there." She pointed to a small parking lot behind one of the buildings. "The blue, four-door sedan."

The car was an older model but still in good shape. As we approached, she dug the keys out of her backpack and disarmed the alarm, unlocking the doors. Autumn opened the passenger side and put her bag on the seat before turning to retrieve the last of her textbooks from my hands. After stacking them on the car floor, she stood, reaching for the door.

"I've got it." I stepped forward, shutting the car. Leaving a hand on the roof, I put Autumn between me and her vehicle.

Autumn's breath hitched.

Fire flared through my veins. Could I take her reaction as an invitation? All I needed to do was tilt my head, and I could kiss her. But should I? I could think of only one way to find out.

Chapter 23

Autumn

In the university parking lot with my back against the car, I stood so close, my lips were almost touching Jensen's, and the way his gaze focused on my mouth told me he was about to close the gap. A large part of me wanted him to, but a vision of my ex, Matteo, flashed before my eyes, saving me. I repeated my promise to myself—no men until my BSN. I cleared my throat and glanced down, slapping my forehead. "Oh my gosh! I can't believe I forgot!"

Jensen reared backward, taking a step away and dropping his hand from the roof of the car. "What? What did you forget?"

"I'm supposed to pick up my roommate from work in twenty minutes." I was one hundred percent lying, and I was sure Jensen knew it. "She needs to take her car into the shop, and I'm her ride home. It broke down on Alaskan Way last week, clogging traffic." I screamed at myself in my head, knowing the more I was prattling on, the less convincing I sounded, but I couldn't stop. The adrenaline from the almost-kiss thrust all common sense from my brain. "Traffic was a huge mess. She caused delays for hours." I was talking with my hands now, making the lie so much worse.

"Is that so?" He tilted his head to the side and squinted, putting his left hand into his pocket. "How had I missed such a huge accident when I boarded the ferry heading home?"

Damn! He's on to me. I needed to sell this. "What time were you there?"

He tapped his chin. "Around three p.m." Jensen peered from the corner of his eye.

I wafted a hand in the air. "Oh, this happened much later."

"Wait"—Jensen held up a finger, gazing upward—"my last appointment was at three p.m., so I would have been on the four p.m. ferry."

"You know…" I could hear my heart pounding in my ears. Sidestepping from between him and my car, I gave myself some much-needed breathing room from his delicious musky scent. "I think I had the timing mixed-up. She'd said the car stalled earlier in the morning." I fiddled with my keys, twisting them in time with my churning gut. *Can the earth swallow me now? Please?*

"Really? Hmmm." He drew his lips into a tight line, crinkles in the corner of his eyes. "Sounds like serious car trouble. Do you all need any help? Would you like me to come with you?"

Jensen's teasing tone and half-smile were the cherry on top of my guilt sundae. He knew I was lying, so why was he being so nice? *Damn him!* "No, um"—I patted my pockets, checking for my phone, unable to meet his gaze—"we'll be fine. But thank you."

He tsked and rubbed the back of his neck. "Is that a rain check for lunch?"

I hurried to the driver's side and opened the door. "Yeah, sure. Of course." I put one foot in the car. "I'll be in touch." As if I'd just robbed a bank, I launched into my getaway vehicle and started the engine, desperate to put as much space between me and the guy whose mere presence thwarted both my motto and rattled my brain. Backing out of my spot, I put my foot on the brake to change gears when I heard a knock on my passenger side window, which made me jump. Jensen's glorious face stared through the glass, taking my breath away. I rolled down the window. *He's milking this for all its worth.*

He placed a hand on the roof of the car.

The tight gray short sleeve on his tee highlighted the definition in his bicep. My heart skipped a beat. If he kept this up, then I couldn't resist him much longer.

"Good luck with your final tomorrow, and let me know if you want to study for the one on Thursday." He winked.

I bit my lip, feeling a little lightheaded. Even if I needed Jensen's help, I couldn't take him up on it. His undeniable magnetism would make the nineteenth hard enough. This man was my kryptonite, and the last thing I could handle was more exposure.

"Thanks, gotta run!" I slammed the car into Drive and took off, not even bothering to close the window. Back home, I slumped against the entry door to my apartment.

"Long day?" Alyssa collected her black chef-style apron from the kitchen table and put the garment into her bag.

I rolled my eyes. "You could say that." Not really, but I didn't want to share my man problems.

"Well, you'll have to relocate your respite from the entry to the couch because I gotta run to work."

"Oh yes, sorry." I peeled myself off the door and

stepped out of her way.

As Alyssa bustled past into the hallway, she gave a tight-lipped smile. "Bye."

"Bye." The door closed, and I stared at the white-painted wood. "Thanks for the sympathy." I dumped my books on the kitchen table and got out my phone before flopping onto the couch. Jabbing the power off on the TV controller, I sneered at the door. Alyssa never turned anything off. I tapped on Lilly's contact, laid my head back into the soft cushion, and waited for my best friend to answer.

"Hey, girl, what's up?"

I rubbed my forehead. "Nothing much." I winced at the lie. "Just got back from studying at the library."

"Tomorrow's test will be a beast. Are you ready?"

I squeezed my eyes shut, knowing a reprimand was coming, but I needed to talk about what happened with Jensen. Lilly was like my sponsor—my love sponsor, giving me the advice I needed even when I didn't want it. "The Hot Doc thinks so." I held my breath.

A moment of silence passed. "Are you freaking kidding me? First, you tell him where you live, he knows your real name, and he paid your hospital bill. Now, what? Are you dating? What happened to 'no men until your BSN?'"

I ducked my head between my shoulders, instantly regretting I'd shared so much with Lilly. "We're not dating. He was helping me study." As I remembered his proximity at my car, I bit my lip, and liquid heat spread through my veins. "Until he almost kissed me."

"He almost *kissed* you? What? How? So much for studying!"

The stress Lilly put on the word *kissed* made me

feel like a scolded toddler. After clearing my lungs, I talked her through the morning, detailing Jensen's check-ins and his offer to help me study and all that went down at the library.

"So, that's it then, right? You're not seeing him again?"

My overwhelming guilt made me feel trapped, like I'd been harnessed in a straitjacket. "Well..."

"Oh geez, what now?"

Ignoring the exasperation I heard in Lilly's tone, I recounted Jensen's repayment bargain for the date at Kristine and Dan's.

"Hmm, girl. For someone who's sworn off men, you're playing with fire."

Resting my head in a hand, I couldn't deny she had a point. "I know. I know." *But I want to get burned.*

"Do you think you can handle the game at his friend's house?" She laughed. "The other couple thinks you and Jensen are a thing, and they've seen you all in action—they'll expect some physical contact. Perhaps even a kiss if the Orcas score a touchdown. Which you know they will since Washington's having a great season."

My fingers traced over my lips, and I suppressed a moan of longing. "It'll be fine. I avoided kissing him this time. I can do it again." *If I put my mind to it.* And I would—I had to.

"Um, I don't think using Alyssa as your excuse will work a second time. I doubt he believed your nonsense. Plus, it's not like you can leave his friend's house. He'll be driving you there, won't he?"

I frowned at the ceiling, swiping at a stray hair tickling my cheek. "Good point. But there's not much I can do since this is my way of paying him back." If I did Jensen this favor, perhaps he'd soften and allow me to pay him back monetarily.

"True, but you can also tell Ruth you're ready to work again. Maybe if you go on a Plus One, it will put some distance between you and Jensen and give you some rational perspective."

Lilly made sense. While a Plus One wouldn't be a rebound, the distraction might be just what I needed to get myself back on track. Although forgetting about Jensen would take a lot more than one date. "I'll give your suggestion some thought. But I don't know if I can handle a date this weekend right after midterms. I'll need to decompress before I can put on a show."

She sighed into her speaker, sending a crackling noise through the line. "What you need is a boomer, like my Sunday dates with Gerald."

My chest warmed, picturing Lilly getting schooled at chess by the old man in the park. "Ha! I wish more people like Gerald lived in Seattle."

"You could ask Ruth about it…."

Lilly's persistence was never-ending. She was lucky I loved her so much. "Whatever, I'll speak to you tomorrow."

"No men until the BSN!"

Shaking my head, I ended the call, knowing I had no intention of contacting Ruth. While I knew Lilly meant well, more dates would be too much pressure. I had enough on my plate studying for midterms, working the tollbooth, and figuring out the Jensen-debt situation. Plus, my brain would be completely fried by the weekend. I'd be poor company for anyone, let alone a paying client expecting me to be on my A-game. I rubbed my forehead. There was no way. I just couldn't do it. Calling Ruth was out of the question. At least, that's what I kept telling myself. Maybe, with enough repetition, I'd believe it.

Chapter 24

Jensen

I slid my favorite Orcas hoodie over my head, then stepped into the still-steamy bathroom to gel my hair. Over a week had passed since I'd seen Autumn at the library. I texted her last Wednesday about helping her study for her final midterm. She never responded. I rationalized she'd decided to ignore her phone until her exams were over—the decision I would have made. But the niggling feeling in the back of my head told me I was lying to myself.

By Friday, Autumn responded, but my relief was short-lived because her texts were brief or consisted of single-word answers with days in between. The longest text exchange was for the essential details for the game at Kristine and Dan's. While her lack of engagement had me questioning my every move, I took courage from the fact she hadn't canceled.

During our contracted dates, Autumn and I kissed twice. Both instances had my body burning and my skin tight. However, I'd convinced myself they were for show—she'd been doing her job and nothing more. But I couldn't forget the study session when her pulse quickened under my touch, not to mention the charged tension I felt in the parking lot. Those encounters gave me hope our previous kisses were more than a requirement to fulfill my contract. Plus, she agreed to do me a solid and attend the game at my friends' house. Yet, she flat-out lied to get out of lunch. Her actions weren't adding up and had me scratching my head, confused on how to interpret the situation. I felt my phone vibrate in my pocket, and I scrubbed the remaining hair gel from my hands on a towel, then unlocked the screen. Reading the name on the message, I hung my head, wishing the text was from Autumn and not my best friend.

—Kristine wants me to remind you not to forget the chips and salsa. But if you bring regular chips instead of multigrain, I won't be upset—

I sighed at the ceiling. Kristine was particular when entertaining. She always wanted everything perfect, as if my Dan-diet-friendly chips and salsa would define the rest of the night.

—Too late. They're packed and ready to go. Be there soon—

I parked at the curb in front of Autumn's well-labeled student housing complex and pulled at the collar of my hoodie. *You've got this. It will be fine.* I rolled my head to loosen my neck. *Being friends is better than nothing—for now.* After moving the bag of chips and salsa to the back seat, I grabbed a mint and crunched it between my teeth, not wasting time sucking, before exiting the car and ignoring the meter. A few minutes without paying wouldn't hurt. Catching the door as another resident left the building, I strode along the white-walled minimalistic hallway toward Autumn's apartment, and memories from the last time flitted through my head, kicking my heart into overdrive. As I knocked on her door, I felt a bead of sweat trickle down my back.

"Coming!"

I could just make out her muffled voice, and I slowly exhaled while smoothing a hand down the front of my sweatshirt, fingers snagging on the logo's stitching. When the door swung open, I felt my breath catch.

Autumn stood in the entryway, with a smile in navy blue leggings and a white Orcas top which laced over her chest.

I swallowed hard. "You look great." *Sexy as hell.*

She glanced at her outfit. "Thanks."

"Sorry I didn't push the buzzer. Someone was leaving when I arrived." I didn't know why I felt the need to explain myself. She probably guessed as much from the casual way she answered the door.

Autumn shrugged one shoulder. "Yeah, I figured." Grabbing her keys and a six-pack of beer from the kitchen counter, she stepped forward.

I squinted at the bottles and raised an eyebrow.

"For us to share." Autumn shrugged. "Since you complained about the lite beer last time." Pink crept up her neck.

Very thoughtful. I forgot I'd mentioned that in a text earlier. "Thank you. I appreciate it." The gesture showed she'd paid attention to our conversations and remembered. Was she acting? I had no idea, and I debated for a moment on whether to take her hand.

Autumn bustled past and strode down the hall.

Okay, then. This was a business transaction. My heart pinched. Her actions were clear as mud.

Stints of chitchat made the car ride to Dan and Kristine's awkward. When I asked Autumn about her weekend, she replied, "Fine," with no elaboration. I tried a few follow-up questions, but she gave minimal responses, just like her texts over the past week and a half. Overcompensating, I babbled about how the hospital had changed the brand of coffee in our break room and hadn't provided enough cream or sugar to balance out the cheap flavor. Finally, as I parked in front of my friends' house, I couldn't deny the nerves clawing their way through my stomach. *Did I really talk about coffee for twenty minutes?* If she harbored any feelings for me before, she had to be questioning them now.

Autumn gripped the beer, exited the car, and approached the front door.

I trailed behind. *Please be more personable in front of Kristine and Dan.*

"Autumn, Jensen!" Kristine's expression was as bright as her bleached-blonde hair. "Come in!" She opened the door wide, letting Autumn pass and giving me a squeeze on my forearm.

I lifted the bag of appetizers. "Where do you want me to put these?"

"On the island." Kristine waved a hand at the kitchen at the end of the hall.

Placing the food on the cool granite counter, I followed Autumn into the living room, which branched off the kitchen as part of the great room floor plan.

Dan was already on the couch, lite beer in hand. Glancing away from the pregame show, he raised his bottle. "Hey, you two. How's it going?"

I sat next to Dan, patting the cushion beside me for Autumn.

Turning her nose up with a sniff, she settled into the corner of the couch, as far from me as possible.

Ugh. Not a good sign. I was supposed to be her boyfriend, but the two feet between Autumn and myself screamed otherwise, giving me flashbacks of Kayla. *What did I do?*

Kristine carried in the chips and salsa, having transferred them into a large sombrero-shaped, red-and-orange bowl.

Dan hit mute on the TV. "The Mustangs have been doing surprisingly well this season with their new quarterback. Do you think we'll still beat them?"

Autumn scooted to the edge of her cushion, eyes alight. "It'll take more than one new player to beat the Orcas. Because our defense is second to none right now." She waved a hand at the screen. "Even if our kicker pulls his usual stunt and misses the goalposts, we've still got this in the bag."

I was impressed with Autumn's passion for our team. "You don't have a lot of faith in our kicker, do you?"

She crossed her legs, pursing her lips and averting her gaze. "No."

I waited for her to expand as she had with Dan, but a chill ran through me, as if the room dropped several degrees. Nothing but the sounds of the television filled the room. I watched her tense posture as she focused on the pregame. Was this the difference between a contract and a favor? Or was her behavior a precursor setup for ending the fake relationship? Either way, I had no choice but to roll with it. "Do you think this defense is as good as the one in 2014?"

She kept her focus on the TV. "Better." Autumn rose from the couch. "I'm going to help Kristine in the kitchen."

I let my gaze follow her and felt my gut twist.

Dan punched my shoulder. "Dude, what'd you do?"

I shrugged, massaging my arm. "Nothing. I didn't do anything." I was just as clueless as Dan.

"All I know is, when you get one-word answers from a woman, you did something wrong." Dan glanced at the kitchen and leaned in. "Just apologize. Whatever you did, it doesn't matter; just say you're sorry. I can't deal with another Kayla."

Neither could I. My ex had wrecked me. I regarded Autumn while she smiled and chatted with Kristine and replayed every interaction we'd had over the past two weeks. Nothing stood out, and I couldn't think of anything offensive I'd done. Unless her coldness had something to do with our almost-kiss back at the University? Maybe I'd crossed a line? But nothing *happened.* I didn't think simply *wanting* to kiss her was offensive. I pinched my eyes shut. As feminist as I was, I still didn't understand women. This had to be about the breakup.

Kristine carried in a bowl of trail mix and set it on the coffee table before sitting next to Dan.

Autumn placed a plate of veggies and dip next to the chips and salsa, then took a seat but left a foot of personal space between us.

Nabbing a cold carrot, I leaned across the chasm. "Have I done something wrong? If I have, I'm sorry." I kept my voice low.

She closed her eyes, pinching her lips for a beat before her shoulders relaxed. "No"—she exhaled—"it's not you."

I smirked, and a hollow feeling engulfed my chest.

"If you finish that sentence with 'it's me'…." I watched as a genuine smile spread across her lips, melting her frosty edges.

"I wouldn't dare."

The tension in my muscles evaporated. "Then what's wrong? Dan and Kristine think we're fighting."

Autumn glanced over my shoulder and stood. "Excuse us for a minute." She pulled me to my feet, took my hand, and led me into the kitchen.

Releasing my grip, I crossed my arms and leaned my butt against the island. "Um, don't you think taking me out of the room is a bit conspicuous?"

She stood opposite, her back against the gas range, matching my tone and stance. "Well, you said it yourself, they already think we're fighting."

Are we? "Good point." I glanced over my shoulder into the living room to see Kristine and Dan jerk their heads back to the screen. Deciding to play on Dan's suggested scenario, I took Autumn's hand again. "So, what's wrong if I haven't done anything?" I traced my gaze over her teeth as she sank them into her bottom lip, hesitating as if debating what to say next. After another minute, I tugged her hand, drawing her gaze back to mine, and raised my brows.

"Actually, Jensen, it is you."

Chapter 25

Autumn

Jensen's jaw went slack, and he released his grip, bracing himself against Kristine's kitchen counter. "What? What do you mean?"

His voice was even quieter than before. I reached forward and laced my fingers with his, my grip tight. What I was about to explain went against everything I wanted for this period in my life, but he deserved to know. "The problem is"—I focused on our intertwined hands—"I like you."

Jensen's head jerked up, and the corner of his mouth twitched. "How is that a problem?"

I took a deep breath. "I have this motto, 'no men before my BSN.'"

Jensen breathed out a laugh. "What?"

Shaking my head, I stepped closer so Kristine and Dan couldn't hear us over the football commentary. "I know. Somehow, when I say the motto to *you*, it sounds stupid, but when I say it to *my best friend*, the phrase makes sense." I cradled his soft, strong hand in both of mine. "Before, when you were just my client, I found separating work from my feelings was easy, but after my appendectomy, lines got blurred, and the contract wasn't there to keep me in check. Which I know was *my* fault, but at that moment, I didn't call you because I was attracted to you; I called you because I was in pain.

I didn't think through the consequences."

He dipped his head and glanced through his lashes. "And the consequences are…you like me?"

The hope in his voice had my head and heart battling for domination. I shrugged and nodded. "Yes, but it's complicated." I explained about Matteo, how I'd centered my future on him, how he'd left me high and dry, and how I'd vowed never to make the same mistake again.

Jensen placed a finger under my chin. "But I'm not asking you to center your future around me. I just want to date you—for real."

I bit my lip and met his gaze. Jensen was like a chocolate-covered, cream-filled donut, and my New Year's resolution was to avoid carbs. "I know because I feel the same, but I made a promise, and I'd never forgive myself if I broke it." I watched Jensen's posture deflate like a popped balloon.

"So, where do *we* stand? Just friends?"

As much as I wanted to, I couldn't offer anything more. "For now."

He hung his head. "Every guy's dream."

Heavy sarcasm laced Jensen's tone, and his disappointment was like a knife to my heart. I cupped his cheek, feeling his stubble on my right palm. "I know it's cliché, but it's all I'm capable of right now."

Jensen nodded and rubbed a thumb across the back of my hand. "What about situations like this?" He tilted his head toward Kristine and Dan. "Do we stage a breakup?"

"No!" I felt my heart squeeze at the idea of never seeing Jenson again, and my answer came out louder than I intended. I lowered my voice. "No, we can continue the charade in front of your friends, but outside of them, we'll just be ourselves."

"Are you saying we get to hang out as friends, too?"

I couldn't fathom the hopeful spark in his eyes, considering I had just friend-zoned him. Throwing him a bone couldn't hurt, right? I put a gag around my inner voice, even though I knew I would regret this. "I guess we could meet for coffee sometime."

Jensen bobbled his head. "Okay, if that's what you want, I'll take what I can get."

My limbs felt light, and I could finally breathe. "Thanks for being so understanding."

"Of course."

The Orcas' siren blared from the living room.

"We missed kickoff." Jensen thumbed over his shoulder. "We should go back in."

"Yes, but first." I jutted my chin toward Dan and Kristine, who I'd seen shoot furtive glances periodically over the back of the couch. "We need to *make up*." I made air quotes with my fingers.

"Right." He drew me into his chest with a smirk and cock of his brow. "I, for one, like to make up with a kiss."

I could feel my heart pounding against my ribs. "Do ya, now?" *Damn him, being so irresistible. And why do his abs have to be rock hard?*

"Always."

His gaze grew dark. While I rolled my eyes, the action didn't match the excitement in my veins, and as I watched him lean forward and touch his lips to mine, I didn't stop him. The kiss started slow and gentle at first, but when I felt Jensen's hands tighten on my waist, I wrapped my arms around his neck, letting the passion overtake me.

His lips parted, and his tongue tasted mine.

I tangled my fingers into his hair, and heat flooded my skin.

A whistle shrilled from the television.

Startled, I broke apart, Jensen's heavy breathing matching my own.

He stepped back, swallowing hard before running a hand over his mouth. "Sorry. Got carried away."

I felt my cheeks burn, and I straightened my shirt. "It's okay. Me, too." Even though he'd agreed to our friendship, his kiss told me this wouldn't be easy.

He took my hand. "Shall we?"

I followed him into the living room, and I took my position on the couch, this time snuggled right next to Jensen.

"Sorry about that." Jensen took a handful of trail mix. "What did we miss?"

"Not much." Dan chewed a salsa-laden chip. "It's the third down, and Mustangs have six yards to go."

"How's their new quarterback?" I nabbed the bottle opener, snatched one of my beers from the carton on the floor, and popped off the cap. Taking a swig, I swallowed, the bitter bubbles tingling my taste buds.

"So far, he's only been running the ball." Kristine handed her husband a napkin. "Nothing worth noting yet."

The game continued, the Orcas taking the lead by the end of the first quarter. With every good play, I high-fived Jensen and his friends, talked smack against the Mustangs, and toasted the Orca players with my beer. By half-time, Jensen and I let our last slap of hands linger, entwining our fingers and leaving them together. The contact was both electrifying and made me sweat at the same time.

When the game cut for the break, Kristine asked me to accompany her to the kitchen.

Eagerly, I joined her, giving me some much-needed space from Jensen.

"Looks like you and your man made up." She wagged her brows.

More like we'd reached an agreement. "Oh, you know how it is—just a little disagreement."

Kristine retrieved some hot wings out of the oven. "Jensen's a good guy."

As if I hadn't already figured *that* out. Inhaling the tangy aroma of the hot sauce, I felt my mouth water. "Yeah, I know. He's one of the best."

"He seems taken with you." She transferred the wings onto a white ceramic platter.

"The feeling's mutual." The timing was what sucked.

Kristine's smile glowed. "Good, because Dan and I think you're awesome and enjoy spending time with the two of you." She grabbed the blue cheese and fat-free ranch bottles from the fridge along with two bowls and shoved them into my hands. "Are you outdoorsy? Do you like to hike?"

"I *love* hiking. The Hoh Rainforest is one of my favorite places." I set the ramekins on the island and poured the salad dressings into each. "Have you been to Ruby Beach or Shi Shi?"

Kristine wiped a splash of hot sauce from the edge of the plate with a rag. "Yeah, a long time ago when Dan and I first dated."

I could never be away from the coast for that long. "Where do you hike now?"

She rolled her eyes. "Unlike back then, now I'm lucky if I can get Dan to go twenty feet from the couch. But maybe if you and Jensen agreed to a double date"—Kristine clasped her hands together and held them against her chest—"I could persuade him to do something more adventurous."

My body's reactions were undermining my brain's common sense. Hiking with Jensen and his friends sent fire through my veins, but how would I keep my heart in check if I kept agreeing to dates?

She rounded the island and squeezed my forearm. "What do you say? Please?" Kristine bounced on her toes, biting her lip.

Seeing her excitement, I couldn't say *no*. Plus, I kind of wanted to. "I'm sure we can make it work."

She pressed her palms together and clapped her fingertips. "Yay!" Lifting the tray of wings, Kristine carried them into the living room.

I trailed behind with the dips.

"Hey, Dan, Autumn and Jensen asked us to go hiking with them next weekend."

Jensen cocked an eyebrow.

I shrugged in response, heat creeping up my neck. The twinkle in Jensen's eye told me he would have a field day with this.

Dan glared at his friend. "Yay, hiking. Thanks, man." He slapped Jensen's left shoulder with a loud *thwack*.

The quirk of Jensen's mouth told me he didn't seem to mind. *Great. I might as well throw out my motto now.*

"No problem." Jensen pulled me onto the couch, wrapped an arm around my shoulders, and hugged me close. "I know the perfect trail."

What had I gotten myself into?

Chapter 26

Jensen

The Orcas won, and Autumn and I hung around at Kristine and Dan's for the replays and post-game wrap-up. The four of us relaxed and laughed like we'd all been friends for years. After Autumn and I helped clean up the food—Autumn washed the bowls while I dried—then Kristine and her husband escorted us to the front door.

"Thanks so much for inviting me tonight. I had a great time." Autumn hugged each of them in turn.

Kristine patted the phone in her back pocket. "I have your number, Autumn, so I'll be in touch about next weekend." She wrapped her hands around her husband's bicep, bouncing. "It'll be so much fun."

Dan's smile was tight, giving me two shaky thumbs-ups.

His wife jostled him with a glare.

I laughed at my best friend's obvious discomfort. "Don't worry. We'll ensure the trail is short and flat, with a bakery at the end."

Dan dropped his gaze and scuffed at the doorjamb with his foot, rattling the metal. "Don't see why we can't just park at the bakery to begin with."

Kristine elbowed Dan in the ribs. "Stop!" She patted the beginnings of his beer belly. "It's not like you couldn't use the exercise."

Dan sucked in his gut. "What are you talking about? I'm like Adonis."

I joined in the laughter and watched Dan's jaw drop open as if he was physically wounded. "Keep telling yourself that, man." I waved at my friends. "We'll see you all later." Taking Autumn's hand, I led her to my car. After helping her into the front seat, I jogged to the driver's side, got in, and pressed the ignition button. The radio blared, and I shot out a hand to turn the volume down so I could address the elephant in the room—or car, if I were being literal. "We're hiking with Dan and Kristine next weekend, huh? How'd *that* happen?"

Autumn hung her head, hands over her face. "Your friend's wife is super persuasive."

As I pulled onto the street and drove out of their neighborhood, I hummed in agreement, pinching my lips to repress my smile. "I'm just surprised you're such a pushover."

Autumn's hands dropped, her shoulders slumping. "You weren't there! Kristine's very convincing." She readjusted in her seat, her lips twitching up at the corners. "Lucky for her, I enjoy hiking."

I glanced over, elbowing her arm. "Lucky for you, I do, too."

Autumn toyed with the laces in her shirt, drawing my gaze to her cleavage. Desire flooded my midsection, and I forced my gaze back to the road.

"Good. And since we can't back out of this, we should set some ground rules."

She wasn't getting out of this one. "But it's a *date in front of friends*." I used bunny ears with a hand for emphasis, and as I pointed out the loophole in her plan,

I couldn't hide my grin. "According to the rules, aren't we supposed to act like a couple?" Out of the corner of my eye, I noticed the intermittent flashes from the streetlamps reflect off her twisting lips, as if the two halves of her mouth were wrestling against each other—her brain the upper lip, her heart the lower.

"This is true." She nodded and held up a hand. "However, let's not make the situation harder on ourselves than necessary."

"Okay." Autumn's torn feelings spurred a taunting sense of hope, and I was curious what exactly she meant. "Shall we establish what's hard for you?" I laced my fingers through hers, relishing how delicate her hand felt. "What about this? Is holding hands acceptable?"

"Yes." She let out a sigh. "It's fine."

Hearing her exasperated tone, I recoiled, and I coughed a laugh. "Hey, I'm just making sure." Releasing her hand, I brushed my fingers along the silky-smooth skin of her arm.

She shuddered.

A warmth simmered low in my belly. I loved how my touch affected her. "What about this? You okay with this?"

She scooted infinitesimally away. "Yes, but I'm not sure caressing my forearm would be applicable during hiking."

"Well, you never know." I brushed the back of my fingers down her cheek.

Autumn swallowed hard. "Pretty sure *that* move can be avoided on the trail."

As I rolled the car to a stop at the light, I shifted, pushing her hair behind her shoulder, then wound my fingers into the locks at the base of her neck.

Autumn's breath caught, and her eyes closed.

My gut clenched.

"Okay, maybe that particular move is more than I can handle." Autumn's voice shook.

Her words were like a bucket of icy water ready to extinguish the inferno I wanted to ignite within her. I released Autumn's hair, and as I withdrew my hand, I let my fingers graze her back. "Fair enough." I arrived at Autumn's apartment building and parked at the curb. Getting out, I rounded the car, opened her door, and extended a hand.

She held my palm.

Pulling, I gathered her into my arms.

As she gripped my biceps, her eyes went wide, and her pupils dilated.

Autumn was flush with my chest. Her gaze dropped to my mouth, and she tilted her head.

An invitation? I ducked, my lips brushing against hers. "How about this? Is this too hard for you?"

Throwing her arms around my neck, she crushed her mouth to mine.

Blood thundered through my veins, and I dug my fingers into her back.

Autumn gasped, deepening the kiss.

I took a step, pinning her against my car. Leaning in, I shifted my lips to her jaw.

Firm hands pushed against my chest.

Fighting my inner animal for control, I complied, putting space between me and her.

"It appears your lips brushing mine was too much for *me*."

The soft curves of her chest rose and fell behind

the laces of her shirt, taunting me. I took another step back before I pushed my luck, followed my instincts, and kissed her again.

Autumn pulled on the hem of her shirt, covering her navel ring which had become exposed during our make-out session.

I wanted to pout and would have if I'd thought it would make a difference.

She peeled herself from the car and took a step toward her apartment. "For this to work, I think we'll need to keep kissing strictly to those times necessary when we're in front of friends."

I surveyed the sidewalk, pointing at a guy in rags and a dirty trench coat, pushing a squeaky shopping cart across the street. "He's my friend." I took her hand. "Do I get another kiss?"

Autumn rolled her eyes, the corners of her mouth twitching. "Oh yeah? Where'd you two meet?"

"At the soup kitchen where I volunteer." I rocked on my heels.

She cocked a brow. "Which one?"

I wracked my brain, picturing the homeless shelter down the street from the free clinic where I *did* volunteer. "What's the name of the one on Forty-First and Eleventh?"

Autumn tilted her head. "Our Lady of Grace?"

I snapped and pointed. "That's the one."

She pinched her lips and nodded with a sparkle in her eyes. "Ernie is a devout patron of Feed the Hungry on the corner of Thirty-Fifth Avenue and Fifty-Fifth Street."

"Oh, so, he's *your* friend." *Did I find another loophole?* "Does it still count?"

Autumn huffed and shook her head with a smirk, withdrawing her hand and folding her arms across her chest. "What do you think?"

I was struggling to see why the two of us couldn't just pursue a relationship. She liked me, together we had undeniable chemistry, and I no longer had contract constraints. Because, unlike Matteo, as a doctor, I would encourage Autumn's goals and dreams. I'd help her every step of the way. But she'd made her point clear. I would be her friend outside of pretend dates with the people in my circles. For once, I was grateful the hospital had benefit dinners on a regular basis. Plus, Kristine liked Autumn, and if next weekend went well, I'd have plenty of opportunities for more dates. "Okay, Ernie doesn't count." I shrugged my shoulders and lifted my palms. "I promise to behave myself." I used my pockets as hand restraints to keep from touching her again. "Although, you make it hard being so cute." Her face was too dark to see in the streetlamps, but I'd swear she was blushing by how she ducked her head.

"*You* make it hard being so stinking charming."

I took hope from the playful lilt in her tone.

Autumn stepped forward and shoved my shoulder, turning me toward my car. "Now go!" She nudged my back, propelling me forward. "Before I do something stupid."

Chapter 27

Autumn

Back in my apartment, I found Alyssa sitting on the couch, eating cereal and watching some reality TV show where a guy handed out roses to a group of women on the screen. "Hi." I beelined for my room, closing the door and cutting off her grunted response. Flopping on the bed, I groaned, muffling the sound with my pillow.

What was it about Jensen? He had me acting like a hormonal teenager. And the attraction wasn't just because of his looks—being around him gave me a greater high than when the Orcas last won the season title. Whenever I glimpsed his name on my phone screen, I felt like my whole body glowed. Jensen was easy to talk to, and we shared a lot in common. Plus, when I had appendicitis, the way he cared for me made me feel the same as when I drank hot tea and wrapped myself in a warm blanket—safe and cared for—rare qualities in the guys I'd known and dated. The timing couldn't be worse, though—just my luck. I still had a year left in school while working the tollbooth five evenings a week and Plus One on the weekends. Now, as a personal favor, I'd agreed to keep up the charade of being Jensen's girlfriend. Considering all he'd done, it was the least I could do, even though, deep down, I liked doing it.

I ground my teeth. "Ugh!" What had I gotten myself into? Rolling onto my back, I dug my phone out of my pocket and called Lilly.

"How'd it go?"

She sang the question, clearly dying for details. I pinched the bridge of my nose. "It went well—too well."

"I'm afraid to ask what *too well* means."

"No"—I sat up, positioning myself against my headboard—"we didn't sleep together, if that's what you're asking."

"I wasn't specifically asking, but I *was* thinking it." She laughed. "So, what *did* happen?"

Recounting the evening's events, I ended with the part where I confessed my feelings.

"Wait a minute, you admitted you like him? What were you thinking?"

"That's the problem—I wasn't." I massaged my forehead, hoping to alleviate the throbbing threatening to turn into a headache. "Like I told you, when we first arrived, I'd been snippy with him, and his friends thought we were fighting. And when I tried explaining, the admission just slipped out." While I knew I shouldn't have, I couldn't make myself regret the decision.

Lilly blew out a breath. "How'd he take it?"

"Hot Doc was thrilled." I suppressed the bubble of excitement I shouldn't feel rising in my chest.

"He was? Wow, he's an anomaly. I've never met a guy who wanted to date me, knowing I worked for Plus One."

"Right?" Throwing my comforter over my head, I relished the spring breeze scent of my freshly washed bedding. "Obviously, he doesn't care." Jensen was a diamond in the rough.

"Okay, he's sweet, and you're into him. Are you sure you want to stick with your plan?"

I fiddled with a thread on my comforter. "Yes. I told him I wasn't in a position to date anyone right now." *Only because of my stupid pride. If he can just hang on until graduation....*

"Hot Doc was okay with that? He just dropped you at your place and left?"

Flipping over, I hugged my pillow. "Well...."

"Spill."

Screwing my eyes closed, I selectively chose what to share about the car ride, omitting the details I knew would disappoint Lilly.

"He kissed you, didn't he?"

I grimaced. Of course, she'd read between the lines. Lilly knew me too well. *I guess since the cat's out of the bag....* "No, *I* kissed *him*."

"Autumn!"

Her shriek hurt my ears, and I winced. Even though I couldn't see her, I could picture her shaking her head.

"Way to keep him in the friend zone."

"I know, but we set boundaries." Loose lines I wanted to blur.

"Umm hmm. Your boundaries are sounding pretty flexible."

Not as flexible as I want. I squeezed my pillow. "But how often do we find a good guy willing to date a companion?"

"I already agreed he's rare, but if Hot Doc likes you, he'll wait for you to achieve your goals."

My heart pinched. Lilly was right. "I know, I

know." Jensen wasn't the problem, I knew he would wait. The problem was me. Throwing back my covers, I rolled onto my back and stared at the ceiling, squinting from the onslaught of light. "But to keep my head straight, I need to put more space between me and the doctor."

"Like I said before. Call Ruth. Set up some dates. Make. Yourself. Unavailable."

As if I was a petulant teenager who wouldn't take her advice, I listened to her enunciate each word. I held my breath for four counts before exhaling. "Fine. I hear what you're saying. The more time I spend with this ex-client, the harder keeping my feelings in check will be. I'll call Ruth tomorrow."

"You know I love you, Autumn. But please, email her tonight."

I laughed half-heartedly. "Okay, I will."

"And BCC me on it."

"Good night, Lil." After ending the call, I grabbed my laptop, composed the letter, and shot off the email, ensuring Lilly got a copy. Biting my thumbnail, I was unable to pinpoint why contacting my boss filled me with unease. The discomfort didn't matter, though. If getting Jensen out of my head took filling my schedule with contracts, the deed was done.

****

With my midterms over, I had six weeks until classes began again. Ruth responded regarding my availability, and I'd changed my tollbooth hours to days, freeing my evenings and weekends for Plus Ones. On Thursday, I got an alert from Ruth about a contract for a family reunion brunch on Sunday. I was a little disappointed the date wasn't sooner. Jensen and I had been texting throughout the week, and I could have used the distraction of another man before the hike with Kristine and Dan tomorrow. After setting out my leggings, rain jacket, and boots, I crawled into bed. I felt my phone buzz beside me. Staring at the screen, I giggled.

Jensen sent a picture of his gear laid out and ready for tomorrow morning, too.

Biting my lip, I snapped a photo of my own pile of clothes and hit Send. I watched the dots appear on my screen.

—Love it! Look at you being prepared! Did you notice our outfits match?—

I studied his photo again and compared his clothes to my own ensemble. He'd also planned black pants and a gray shirt with a green jacket.

—Oh my gosh! They do! Look at us, totally selling ourselves as a couple—

—Our chemistry does that—

Desire blossomed low in my belly. He wasn't wrong, but I didn't want to encourage him.

—LOL! Good night, Jensen—

—Sweet dreams, Autumn—

He attached a picture of himself, shirtless in bed, one arm behind his head accentuating his bicep. A shiver traveled the length of my body, and I moaned. He was not making being friends easy. I thumbed through the Gifs on my screen as I searched for the perfect one to send in response, settling on an actor making a gagging motion.

Seconds later, Jensen returned my Gif with one of his own—a tween cocking a suggestive eyebrow.

He was so naughty. Laughing, I set my phone on

the charger, pulled my covers up to my chin and switched off the lights. After staring at the ceiling for a few minutes with the image of Jensen vivid in my mind, I gave up. One last look at his photo couldn't hurt.

Chapter 28

Autumn

On Saturday morning, when Jensen picked me up at nine, Dan and Kristine were already in the car. As I slid into the plush, black leather passenger seat, I turned to see Dan who sat behind Jensen, already mid-rant.

"I've seen Mount Rainier; they practice there for Everest. Those are professionals. Why are you taking an amateur?" Dan glared at each of us in turn. "I'm not going to make it."

Kristine patted his knee. "They have a trail for everyone."

He jerked his leg away from his wife. "Are you sure? How long is it? And what kind of elevation are we talking about?"

She blew a hair off her forehead. "It's a family-friendly trail for children of all ages—including thirty-seven-year-old toddlers."

Jensen winced with a grin, watching his friend in the rearview. "Ouch."

Kristine and Dan were a cute couple. Seeing how she handled his dry humor was fun, and their love was evident. I could tell by the softness in Jensen's gaze that he admired his friends' relationship, too.

Jensen pulled the car into the gravel lot next to the trailhead and parked.

I stepped out the passenger's door and joined the

others by the trunk.

"Look, Dan." Jensen motioned toward an elderly woman returning from the trail. "She has a cane. If a senior citizen can do it, so can you."

"Blah, blah, blah, very funny." Dan mimicked a caricature of Jensen's expression.

"Look! That kid can't be more than three, and he's managed to hike the trail." I kept my face stoic, forcing back the laughter, and ready to explode. Mocking Dan was too easy. Even though my group was still in the parking lot, I'd forgotten how much I loved being out in nature with friends. As I gazed out over the lush green forest, inhaling the earthy scent and seeing the happy faces of Kristine and Jensen, I let the reality of the situation sink into the pit of my stomach. My smile wavered, and I wrinkled my nose. Dan and Kristine weren't my friends. They were Jensen's, and I was only here because Jensen asked me for a favor. If his friends knew the truth, everything would change.

Dan rolled his eyes. "Not you, too!"

"Shush and help me with this." Kristine held an insulated bag toward her husband.

Jensen cocked his head to the side. "Why do you have such a big bag? Isn't the hike supposed to be two-point-nine-miles round trip?"

"Two-point-nine miles?" Dan froze, gripping his hair in his fist. "You didn't say the hike was two-point-nine miles." He huffed. "Leave me here."

Kristine sighed and gestured to her husband. "I brought the tote because of him."

Dan hefted the bag over his shoulder and zipped his jacket. "At least, she understood that if I'm being made to hike, I shouldn't do it hungry." With red-tipped ears, he pecked his wife on the cheek. "Thanks, babe."

I snorted. "But you just ate a granola bar in the car." Dan was hilarious. I leaned into Jensen's ear. "Is he always this dramatic?"

"Look, do you all want me to come? Because I'm happy to meet you here when you return." Dan cozied his back against the car.

Kristine squeezed her lips into a hard line and grabbed Dan's arm.

I stifled a laugh as I watched her tow him like a reluctant child to the trailhead.

Jensen held out a hand with a smile, his brows rose. "Ready?"

I laced my fingers through his, relishing the softness of his skin and curbing a need I didn't realize I had—like I was a junkie, and he was my fix. *I'm in trouble.* "Let's go."

The orange-and-red-dotted foliage was a stark contrast to the deep emerald of the evergreens along the trail. A slight breeze ruffled my hair.

"It's beautiful, isn't it?" Jensen swiveled, gaze darting from tree to tree.

"Gorgeous. This is why I love hiking." I usually relished the peace and tranquility of the outdoors, but today, my mind was cluttered with confusing thoughts of Jensen and our situationship.

"How often do you get to go? I imagine with school and work, it's been a while."

I was careful to step over a protruding tree root on the path. "Ooh, um, I think it's been since the beginning of summer when I hiked with Papi out to Marymere Falls."

"Oh yeah." Jensen stepped to the side for another

group of hikers. "I noticed a picture of the two of you on your fridge."

I widened my eyes as he pulled me with him. "Wow, I can't believe you remembered." He'd only been in my apartment one time, and it wasn't a casual visit. I was impressed.

"Sorry"—Jensen peered from under his lashes, his cheeks flushed pink—"I wasn't snooping. I promise."

"Oh, I know." I waved a hand. "They're in plain sight; I'm not surprised you noticed them." I paused to photograph a fern leaf.

Jensen grabbed my arm. "Quick, over there! A bald eagle."

I followed the direction he indicated, snapping a picture of the majestic creature circling an enormous pine tree, and landing on a thicket of sticks at the top. "Look! His home." I splayed my fingers against the rectangle of glass, expanding my screen. "Aww, there's another one already in the nest. He has a family." Lightness filled my chest.

Jensen put a hand on my waist, leaning close.

The heat from his body warmed my right side, and I savored his musky-citrus scent. I could smell him all day. After capturing the image, I slipped my phone back into my pocket.

Jensen didn't let go.

Tucked against his side, I lifted my chin.

He met my gaze for a second before focusing on my lips. "You know, since you're supposed to be my girlfriend today, I think I should kiss you."

I placed a hand on his chest, taking a moment to recognize its hardness before pointedly focusing on Kristine and Dan. "Hmm, nope. They're not looking."

"Ouch." Jensen frowned, his gaze narrowing and darting to his friends. "Maybe I should make some noise to get their attention."

Laughing, I forced myself to push him away and took his hand. "Come on, silly. Let's catch up." A few steps behind Kristine and Dan, I slowed my pace. "What about you, Jensen? How often do you get to hike?"

He bobbled his head. "I don't hike so much as run trails outside the city."

I bumped my shoulder against his. "Don't tell me you're one of those gazelles I see parkouring through the forest?" The image of Jensen—slick with sweat, his shirt plastered to his chest, ricocheting off trees—made my breathing hitch. I coughed to cover the sound.

Jensen's laugh echoed through the trees. "No, I'm more of a clumsy mountain goat."

I liked my image better. "Good thing you're a doctor, then. If you twist your ankle, you'll know how to care for yourself in the wild." We skirted a fallen tree. "Speaking of which, what made you decide to become a pediatric hospitalist?"

Jensen kicked a small rock on the path, sending it clicking and tumbling into the yellowing grass along the edge. "My dad was a surgeon, and I always loved hearing his stories from work. As a high school student, I got special permission to watch a few of his surgeries from the medical student observation area." He pointed at a bright-red-leaved tree and stopped.

I snapped another picture.

"They were so fascinating. That's when I decided I wanted to be a doctor."

I reached to put my phone away.

Jensen caught my wrist. "How about a selfie? Or an us-ie?"

I laughed at his sitcom reference, silently debating the pros and cons. Having a photo to commemorate this moment would be nice, but I was positive Lilly would frown on it. *Whatever. What the hell.* "Sure."

Jensen leaned, resting his cheek against mine.

I took the shot.

He grazed his nose along the edge of my ear. "Send me a copy?"

I couldn't stop the shudder running down my spine. "Of course."

His mouth cinched in a roguish grin.

"Anyway"—I stepped away along the trail, needing to get Jensen talking again before my desires got the better of me—"going back to our earlier conversation, why didn't you become a surgeon?"

"I thought about it, but when I was sixteen, my best friend, Kevin, was diagnosed with leukemia. Despite his valiant fight, he lost the battle a year later." Jensen rubbed the back of his neck. "Those doctors in the pediatric ward were so different from my father. They were always upbeat, ensuring those kids' spirits were high. They went the extra mile, ya know?"

Nodding, I recalled how my childhood pediatrician always smiled and wore cartoon-themed ties.

"After Kevin, I'd decided I wanted to work with kids, but I also knew my heart couldn't handle the mortality rate of cancer patients. So"—he shrugged—"I chose to be a pediatric hospitalist instead."

I rested a hand on my heart, yearning to envelop Jensen in a hug but knew I shouldn't.

"Hey, come have a snack. Crybaby over here is

whining he's hungry." Kristine smiled and thumbed over her shoulder at Dan, who was already splayed out in the grass.

Saved by Kristine.

Jensen squeezed my hand and led me over to his friends.

"Here." Kristine passed out some granola bars and fruit leather.

As I stared at the image of a strawberry on the packaging, I felt my mouth water. I didn't realize I was so hungry.

Dan shoved an entire granola bar into his mouth and reached for a second.

Kristine slapped the back of his hand. "Don't be a barbarian. Finish what's in your mouth first."

Her husband scowled and chewed faster.

"Isn't this beautiful?" Kristine sighed, her gaze lingering on the snow-capped peak of Mt. Rainier dominating the sky above the blanket of tall evergreens next to the trail.

"It is. I love the Pacific Northwest." I sat cross-legged on the scratchy grass, my knee burning where it touched Jensen's.

"We should do this again." Kristine's gaze focused on Jensen and me. "What are you all doing tomorrow?"

Jensen pursed his lips, cocking his head. "I'm free." He turned in my direction with a smug smile. "Autumn?"

His gaze was challenging, and I fidgeted with my ear, my insides churning like a boiling pot. "Sorry, but I work tomorrow."

Jensen's face fell. "But I thought you didn't work at…."

I could see the moment he realized I wasn't referring to the toll booth but rather to a Plus One contract, and my lungs froze.

"Oh, right. I forgot you were picking up extra hours over your break." A muscle in his jaw twitched.

Kristine's shoulders slumped. "Darn. That's unfortunate."

Looking at Jensen's crestfallen face, I agreed.

Chapter 29

Jensen

As we sat in the grass at the end of the hike, Kristine continued chatting with Autumn, who seemed oblivious to what just happened.

Realizing Autumn had a contract was like a punch in the gut. For me to assume she wouldn't be companioning because of our arrangement was irrational. If she worked at any other job, then I wouldn't expect her to quit because we were in a kinda-sorta-not relationship. Besides, Autumn was clear. Even though we liked each other, we couldn't be more than friends—at least, for now. But even she admitted lines had already gotten blurred. Images of some guy who resembled Dave Franco or Ian Somerhalder with his arms around Autumn's waist made my granola bar vie for a return appearance. I clenched my jaw to dispel the vivid thoughts, but my action had the opposite effect.

"Are you okay, Jensen? Do you need something to drink?" Kristine retrieved a water bottle from her bag and passed it over.

Cracking open the plastic top, I took a swig of the thankfully still-cold water and glanced at Autumn. She wouldn't make eye contact, but she placed a supportive hand on my back. The voice in my head screamed her action was contrived. Earlier, when I observed her hiking on the trail, her actions appeared natural. Now I could see the scene for what it was—an act—the exact thing I'd asked for. I plastered on a smile. "Thanks. Yeah, not sure what came over me." I stood to escape Autumn's touch, brushing the dirt off my pants. "Felt kinda like the wind was knocked out of me for a second there, but I'm fine now." Not really, but I had one and three-quarter miles left of the trail, not to mention the car ride home before I could own my jealousy.

"Here." Kristine handed me another snack. "Have another fruit leather. Maybe the sugar will help." She glared at her husband. "Ready to head back?"

"I just got comfortable." Dan spread his arms wide on the grass.

"You've been sitting on your backside for fifteen minutes." Kristine grabbed her husband's hand. "Any longer, and you'll take root."

Grunting, Dan stood and pouted. He grabbed Kristine's bag. "Fine, let's go."

A bitter part of me didn't want to help Autumn stand, but I was kidding myself. Even though she'd inadvertently hurt my feelings, I still wanted to touch her. I extended a hand.

Autumn responded, leveraging herself onto her feet. "Jensen, I—"

"It's fine." I dropped her hand and motioned for her to follow Kristine along the path. I wasn't ready to have the *I told you so* conversation I knew was coming.

She tramped along the trail.

I fell in step behind her, kneading at my chest. Somehow, learning of Autumn's contract for tomorrow seemed like a betrayal. I knew my reaction was ridiculous—she and I weren't a couple, and I had no claim on her heart—but the feelings I experienced mirrored the moment I'd learned about Kayla and Andrew. I took another swig from my water, letting the lukewarm liquid cool my hot head.

How could I have let myself get into this situation? I hadn't dated over the past year for only one reason—I didn't want to feel this way again. I should have known better. Even Molly warned me not to buy into the fake dating. Because even though Autumn said she liked me, nothing changed about our situation, and she'd still taken on a new client. Yanking a leaf from a nearby tree, I ripped the veined foliage, shedding the shrapnel along the trail. *Stupid let's be friends rule.* Why couldn't things be different? Autumn must know how good we were together. Even Dan and Kristine could see it. My ex burned me just as much as Autumn's ex burned her, but I was willing to put my fears aside and try again; couldn't she?

Autumn slowed her pace.

I caught up, matching her stride.

She elbowed me in the side. "I took the job because I need the money. You know that, right?"

My chest loosened infinitesimally, but not enough to be okay. "Hey, you can do what you want." Just because I understood her motives didn't make it hurt any less. "We're not together." My comment was flippant, but it was true.

She winced. "Wow. Harsh."

Scrubbing a hand down my face, I bit back my apology. "Hey, you're the one who set up the rules." Stupid rules I hated with everything I had.

"I have *those rules* because I like you and want to stay on track in my life." Her jaw was rigid.

Sighing, I stared at Kristine and Dan's backs, glad

they were yards ahead and couldn't hear. "Autumn, look. I don't want to throw you off track. But I'd be lying if I didn't say I'd like to join you on the journey."

Autumn reached for my hand.

I avoided her touch. She'd made her decision, and I was following her lead—distancing myself and rebuilding the walls around my heart.

Autumn's shoulders slumped, and she wrapped her arms across her torso. "Jensen, you know I can't right now."

I stopped and grasped her elbow, turning her to meet my gaze. "But why not?" Not wanting to draw my friends' attention, I kept my voice low.

A slight crease formed between Autumn's brows. "Because I'm working and attending school...."

"I'm not your ex. I can help you—support you through your whole program." And I would. Helping her achieve her goals would be one of my top priorities.

Autumn screwed her eyes shut and shook her head. "Jensen...."

I ground my teeth at her pleading tone and huffed. "Fine. Have it your way." I spun on my heel, jogging to catch Kristine and Dan.

Autumn's rapid footsteps crunched in the gravel, getting closer with each breath. "Jensen."

I ignored her whispered appeal for my attention.

"Jensen."

Ugh! You're better than this. Don't be a jerk. Pinching my lips, I extended a hand and wrapped my fingers around hers. "The parking lot is just ahead." With any luck, she took the hint. Now wasn't the time to discuss the situation further.

"Finally!" Dan held his hands over his head, fists

clenched. "I've got a beer calling my name."

Kristine swatted her husband's backside. "Stop. You had fun; admit it."

"Fine, the forever-long hike wasn't the worst way to spend a Saturday." Dan wrapped an arm around his wife and gave her a kiss.

I clenched my jaw. Dating etiquette would have dictated I should do the same with Autumn. However, I couldn't handle the intimate moment, knowing the gesture was futile. Instead, I unlocked the car and stomped to the driver's side. After I'd waited for my friends to buckle, I pulled onto the highway, turning the music just loud enough to make talking uncomfortable. To my dismay, Kristine asked me to turn the volume down.

"Wasn't that fun? Did you all have a good time?"

Gripping the steering wheel tighter, I fought to keep the scowl from my face. *I was until we stopped for a break.*

Autumn shifted in her seat. "I had a great time. Thank you so much for suggesting this, Kristine."

Her tone was full of an enthusiasm I didn't share.

"Hey!" Dan scowled at his wife. "I thought this was their idea."

Kristine waved a hand. "Who can remember who suggested what? I'm just glad we all got to go." She squeezed Dan's knee. "I know Autumn is busy tomorrow, but what about Monday night? Do you two want to join us again for the Orcas versus Scorpions game?"

Dan put a hand over his wife's. "Honey, I'm sure they're sick of us. Why don't we let them have some time alone?"

I raised a brow and peeked at Autumn, eager to hear her response but doubting she'd want to be alone with me.

"Jensen and I aren't sick of you, are we?" Autumn placed a hand on my bicep.

Her touch sent an ache to my core. "No, of course not." *Is she considering Kristine's offer for real?*

Autumn gave a curt nod. "Let me check my work calendar and get back to you."

"Perfect." Kristine gave a wide smile. "Speaking of alone time, you're welcome to drop us off first if you'd like, Jensen."

I shook my head. *Nope.* I wouldn't be a glutton for punishment. "It's fine. We're almost at Autumn's now. Doubling back doesn't make sense." In my rearview, I watched Kristine's gaze ping-pong between Autumn and me, her lips pressed into a hard line, but she didn't say anything. When I arrived at Autumn's apartment, I got out and rounded the car, maintaining the pretense of a couple. Opening her door, I helped Autumn onto the sidewalk.

"Can we talk later?" Autumn blinked rapidly with watery eyes.

My heart caved, but I resisted. Lifting a shoulder, I let my gaze drift to the side. "What's to talk about?"

"Jensen…."

Her brimming tears and wrinkled brow almost broke me. I leaned in, hesitating for a moment.

Autumn closed her eyes.

At the last second, I inhaled, my stomach curdling. I twisted my head, brushing my lips against her cheek. The salt from her tears burned my mouth. "Bye, Autumn."

Chapter 30

Autumn

As I watched Jensen's car drive away, I couldn't ignore the pain in my chest. Blinking back tears, I dragged myself to my apartment. Inside, I opened the fridge and yanked out a bottle of wine. I filled a goblet to the brim.

Alyssa marched out of her room. As she opened the front door, she eyed me. "You okay?"

Her squinty eyes were unusually suspicious. "Yeah, fine." Not like she really cared, and I wouldn't tell her, anyway. I downed half my glass, not even tasting the fruity bitterness on my tongue.

"Okay, see ya." The door slammed shut.

"Nice chat—as usual." I slumped into one of the kitchen chairs. Alyssa's indifference didn't really bother me, but I needed to talk to somebody. Grabbing my phone, I stared at the screen. I wanted to talk to Jensen. Knowing he was upset, I felt my shoulders tighten into knots. But as I located his contact details, I hesitated over his number. I couldn't call now; he'd still be with Kristine and Dan. But what would I say other than *sorry*, anyway? But was I sorry? I wouldn't change my mind.

Finishing off my red wine, I sighed, the alcohol warming my stomach. The burn felt good. I poured another glass. "Stupid Jensen. I'm doing the right thing.

Why did he make our relationship so complicated?" Opening my photos, I tapped on the picture of Jensen in his bed last night. My toes curled. The definition of his bare chest taunted me. Taking another gulp, I scowled at my screen. "You shouldn't be allowed to be so sexy. It's not fair." I flipped to the selfie we took on the trail a few hours ago, and my breath caught. The two of us were positioned cheek to cheek, with the trees in the background. Jensen's warm smile filled the whole screen, and I wished I could go back to the moment before I crushed him with news of my latest contract.

Finishing off my second glass, I could feel a buzz. I knew I shouldn't be drinking—I had a client brunch tomorrow. Staring at the black bottle on my counter, I pushed my lips into a pout. The hollowness I felt in my chest was too much. My eyes stung. *Screw it.* I poured a third. I drifted to the window overlooking my street and the high-rise complex across from my building. My apartment was a symbol of my independence I refused to give up. "I'm a modern woman, dammit." Working at Plus One was a requirement—I needed the money. Taking a sip from my goblet, I pressed a hand against the sun-warmed pane. If I didn't have my companion money, I couldn't afford to live in the city. It's not my fault Jensen doesn't understand. "Shortsighted man."

Going back into the kitchen, I topped off my glass. I stared at the red liquid, and my chin trembled. "Jensen does understand." He even offered to help me achieve my goals. Pressure built behind my eyes. "He's such a good guy." Ditching my goblet, I grabbed the bottle. I connected my phone to the wireless speaker in the kitchen and queued a song. Using the bottle as a microphone, I belted along with the love lyrics, crying with each word. My tears came in earnest, and I crumpled onto the couch. Sobbing, I cried until my eyes ran dry. "I'm a terrible person."

****

The following day, I arrived at the coffee shop down the street, wearing sunglasses despite the rainy weather. I was in dire need of some coffee to take the edge off my hangover. Opening the door, I inhaled and let the warm, thick, almost nutty aroma of the café wash over me, evoking a knowledge relief was on the way. I stepped to the register. "One espresso, please." As the grinder blared from behind the counter, I cringed, my head pounding.

"Name for the order?"

The rainbow-haired teen's tone screamed that they hated their job. "Autumn."

They scribbled on the side of the cup and passed the container along the row. "That'll be six dollars and fifty cents"

A tall man with hooded eyes and black hair, dressed in an impeccable, casual blue-suit with a collared floral button-up shirt, slid beside me. "Let me get your drink." He handed the teen his credit card.

"Thank you." I recognized my date, Chris Yang, from the photo attached to his contract. Judging from his outfit, my cream pants and textured, emerald-green, puff-sleeve blouse were a good choice for today's engagement.

"My pleasure." He added two lattes to the order and led me to a table where a redhead with a broad smile sat in a slim-fit cardigan.

I rested my elbow on the wooden surface and rubbed my throbbing temple with all the stealth of a rodeo clown. "And whom do we have here?" I didn't remember any photo or mention of this other man in the contract brief.

Chris sat on the edge of his chair, his back straight. "This is my husband."

I knitted my brows together. "Okay….What's my role then? I thought you hired me to be your girlfriend at a family reunion?"

Chris held up his palms. "Look, the truth is, my family doesn't know I'm gay, and my parents won't approve."

Every muscle in my body tensed. *How is this still a thing?* Memories of hearing my dads' struggles of acceptance weighed down my heart.

The redhead extended his right hand. "Hi, I'm Garrett."

I shook. "Nice to meet you." Tilting my head to the side, I gave him a warm smile. "You two make a cute couple. I'm sorry you feel the need to hide your relationship from your loved ones, but I think I get the gist of my role."

The barista called my name.

Garrett touched my shoulder and stood. "I got it."

Chris watched his husband wistfully, then met my gaze. "Sorry. This is hard on him because my parents think Garrett is my roommate and we're best friends. The situation sucks, but what can you do?" Chris sighed heavily. "As far as you and I"—he indicated between himself and me—"they think we've been dating a few weeks, but considering I'm thirty-five, they jump at the slightest chance to meet any lady friends I have."

Garrett set my espresso on the table. "Don't be surprised if his mother talks kids and marriage with you." He sat next to Chris and rubbed his husband's back.

I winced. "Ooh, that bad, huh?" Poor guy was under a lot of pressure. I pulled my espresso close, and the hot cardboard cup warmed my palm.

The two men exchanged a look. "Worse," they replied in unison.

"So, how do you want me to play it? Am I to be the perfect fit? Or should I turn her off?" I'd come across this kind of situation before, and each one was delicate and unpredictable.

Chris set his coffee on the table. "Just be the strong, independent woman you appear to be. That'll be enough."

I reared my head. "All right. I'm excited to meet her, I think?" I rolled my eyes and took a sip. The caffeine rush and bitter flavor of my espresso lightened my mood and took the edge off my headache. "Let's do some rapid-fire facts about ourselves." I shivered against the prickle on my skin at the memory of doing this exercise with Jensen. I rubbed my forearm.

Chris scratched his chin. "Okay…."

Seeing his blank expression, I expanded. "You know"—I waved a vague hand—"things we would know about each other if we were dating—get our stories straight."

Chris nodded slowly. "Oooh. Good thinking. What should we share?"

"I'll go first." I slid my sunglasses on top of my head, the caffeine clearing the rest of my headache. "My favorite color is red, I like all types of music except jazz"—my heart pinched—"my favorite food is Indian, I'm a sucker for the movie *Dirty Dancing*, and

I'm an only child of two dads." I beamed at the two men, hoping they would take courage from my parents.

Chris grabbed Garrett's hand, meeting his partner's gaze. "I can't wait for the day when we can start our own family."

Garrett sighed, pursing his lips. "Mmm hmm. If *someone* admitted to his parents I'm the love of his life, then we could tell them we're married and start sooner."

Chris ripped his hand from Garrett's and angled himself away. "You know I can't get into this today."

Garrett's features softened. "You're right. I'm sorry. You promised you'd do this on your own time when you're ready."

Chris nodded, mouthing *thank you*, then returned his gaze to mine. "Sorry, Autumn."

"No need to apologize, but if we want to make the brunch on time, we'd better get a move on." I waved a hand in a hurry-up motion. "What are your favorites?"

Chris rattled off his answers.

Garrett filled in the gaps.

Hearing the two men play off one another, I bit my lip, my heart melting. With the details memorized, I followed the gentlemen out of the café to Chris's car.

Arriving at the International District Chinese Restaurant, I looped an arm through Chris's, as he led me inside.

Garrett followed.

A model-esque woman with slicked-back black hair in a crisp white button-down and black pants led Chris, Garrett, and me to the outdoor patio. Wisteria vines covered the pergola, spanning half of the reception area and filling the air with their sweet, floral scent. Several round, white-clothed tables with pink orchids lined the concrete at various intervals. The wall bordering the interior of the restaurant held a variety of succulents and mosses, giving the space an intimate feel despite the size. I scanned the crowd of at least thirty people. Groups of twos, threes, and more laughed and talked with one another. I let my shoulders relax, taking in the friendly atmosphere.

Chris nodded at a tall, salt-and-pepper-haired man standing in an embroidered silk vest. "That's my uncle Chung. I'll introduce you to him first. He's the least nosey of the family."

Garrett rolled his eyes. "To your face, he's not nosey. I've heard him gossiping with your aunties plenty of times."

"Whatever." Chris squinted at his husband. "Come on."

As I shook hands with Chung, I felt like a third wheel. During the conversation, Chris and Garrett shared inside jokes and finished each other's sentences. The connection between the two men seemed apparent, and the fact Chris's family hadn't figured out he and Garrett were a couple surprised me. Even when Garrett wasn't in my circle of conversation, I noticed Chris was aware of his partner, shooting him furtive glances from across the room. Love radiated off the two of them.

Watching the exchanges made my heart ache. I wanted a relationship like theirs. Because I'd been so preoccupied with being strong and sticking to my plan, I'd lost balance in my life. Getting my degree didn't mean I needed to forfeit love. Not every relationship would be like mine with Matteo—especially with Jensen being the complete opposite. Besides, I'd already broken one of my rules and taken money from my dads. Even though I hadn't paid Jensen back, I didn't feel indebted because he went out of his way not to pressure me. If I was honest, the only obstacle was my stupid pride. My headache came back with a vengeance.

Chris pulled me to a stop in front of a gray-haired woman in a maroon kimono-type top with black, tapered slacks.

I blinked to clear my thoughts and forced a smile for the matriarch.

As if he was afraid to touch me, I could feel the heat from Chris's hand hovering over the middle of my back.

"Autumn, this is my *nai nai*." Chris bowed to his grandmother and spoke in her native tongue.

I dipped my head and shook his grandmother's withered hand. She spoke Mandarin—the only non-English-speaking relative I'd met so far at the reunion. The tension in my muscles dissipated, knowing the language barrier meant I wouldn't have to put on a show. As Chris led me around the quaint restaurant, introducing me to cousin after cousin—he had to have a hundred of them—I found myself almost giddy at the lack of affection from my date. Not having to reciprocate loving gestures, I floated around the patio. The one time Chris kissed my cheek to assuage one of his aunties, I tensed the muscles in my jaw so hard I was afraid I'd cracked a tooth, and guilt, strong and swift, swept through me. My emotions made no sense. Pretending to be Chris's girlfriend wasn't betraying Jensen—I was just doing my job.

But by the time Chris dropped me at the coffee

shop, I'd come to a cold, hard truth: the contract with Chris was a mistake. The unwelcome kiss on my cheek weighed as heavy as a scarlet letter emblazoned across my chest. Chris's contract was the first time I'd felt disconnected from my role as a companion since joining Plus One. More importantly, meeting Jensen. *What am I going to do?*

Chapter 31

Jensen

Monday evening, as the second half of the Orca's game began, I cracked open another soda, wishing it was a beer. Repositioning myself on Dan and Kristine's couch, I couldn't get comfortable. The pillows were stiff behind my back. They poked me at odd angles, as did the images of Autumn on a date with another guy, possibly with his hands on her backside. The thoughts kept rioting in my brain and had been since yesterday. I was stupid and had no right to be jealous. But the feelings still assaulted me, nonetheless.

"Jensen! Dude." Dan shoved my shoulder with a hand. "Jensen!"

Startled out of my thoughts, I scowled. "What?"

"Did you see Latu's tackle? It was terrible. How could the ref not call that? The players were literally helmet to helmet."

I feigned interest at the screen. "What?"

He flung out an arm toward the TV. "Dude, you didn't see it?"

Shaking my head, I dropped my chin. "Sorry. I must have missed it." Not that I cared. I didn't care about a lot of things right now other than Autumn.

Dan smacked my back, then gripped my shoulder. "What's up with you, man?"

Kristine placed a hand on her husband's thigh.

"Give Jensen a break. He's missing Autumn." She leaned forward and met my gaze; her mouth angled down. "I'm sorry she's working, by the way."

Work was the excuse Autumn gave Kristine for not coming, which was probably true. Although, with the way I ended things on Saturday, I was probably the last person Autumn wanted to see anyway. "It's okay." I took another swig of sugary soda. "Bills gotta be paid." The green monster gnawed at my stomach, hoping if she was actually working, she was at the tollbooth. *Not that her whereabouts matters. We aren't together.*

Kristine stood. "I'll grab the pizzas. Hopefully, food will help."

Wallowing about Autumn made me lose my appetite, but if eating pizza stopped Kristine from asking too many questions, I'd force down a slice or two. "Thanks. Sounds great."

She left the room.

Dan watched his wife leave, then raised a brow in my direction. "Jense, you've got it bad."

I jerked my head back. "Pfft, whatever." He was right. "You don't know what you're talking about." I didn't understand why he razzed me—guys didn't discuss feelings.

He barked a laugh. "Do you even know who's winning the game?"

I turned toward the screen.

Dan shielded my eyes, blocking my view. "Nah, nah. Without looking."

Sighing, I dropped my head. "No." *He's as bad as Kristine tonight.*

"Uh-huh, I thought so." Dan leaned back and rested his feet on the coffee table. "Why don't you admit you're catching feelings for Autumn?"

Because the timing sucks, and she is likely on a date with some other guy. "You're right; I do have feelings for her. But I don't know if I see us going anywhere." *She won't let it.*

Dan sat straight, head rearing back. "What do you mean you don't see the relationship going anywhere? You two work really well together. Were you *there* Saturday?"

Sadly, my time with Autumn hadn't gone as smoothly as he thought. "I was there, and we do, but I don't think she sees me the same way I see her." I pinched my brows together, resting the back of my head on the cool leather sofa. "Pretty sure I've been friend zoned."

"Friend zoned?" He grimaced. "You never come back from that. You might as well cut all ties and end all communication now. Save yourself the heartbreak."

Tension seized my shoulders, and I winced. "Ouch." I didn't expect Dan to agree. "I don't know if I'm ready to cut her out of my life altogether." Stupidly, I was still racking my brain for a way to reach out.

"Fine, don't. Whatever. All I know is you're super distracted, and it's bumming me out." Dan took a swig of his diet soda, then grimaced, staring at the TV with a frown.

I felt my phone buzz. *Probably the hospital.* I dug my cell out of my pocket. A banner blaring Autumn's name glowed on the screen. My heart jumped.

—*Hey, can we talk?*—

A pit formed in my stomach. Those words were never a good sign.

—*Of course. Want to call when you're off work?*—

Preferably not after you've kissed another man.

—I'd rather not wait until then. But I was stupid and picked up a second shift at the Bainbridge booth. I don't get off until eleven p.m., so I guess I don't have a choice. Plus, when we talk, I'd like to see you—

A smile crept across my face. She was at the tollbooth, and she wanted to see me face to face—both were a good sign. At least, I hoped. My muscles relaxed.

—Sure. I'll be there at the end of your shift—

I let out a cleansing breath, unable to hide my smile.

"Let me guess"—Kristine shoved her husband's feet out of the way and set two pizza boxes on the coffee table—"you're texting Autumn?"

I righted myself, high on the endorphin rush. "Yeah, guilty." My appetite returned, and I reached for the top box. Opening the lid, I inhaled, garlic assaulting my senses, and I felt my eyes burn. "What is this?" I cringed at the flatbread pizza with olive oil, artichoke hearts, spinach, and fresh mozzarella.

"Oh"—Kristine switched the boxes—"that's Dan's."

"What the hell? Pizza is off-limits, too?" He ran a hand over his mouth. "A real pizza has all the food groups—it's good for you."

"Tell that to your cholesterol." Kristine opened the second box and handed me a piece of sausage and pepperoni on a paper plate. "Here you go, lover boy."

"Thanks." As I bit into the meaty-cheesy goodness, I couldn't even feel sorry for my friend. My head was full of ferry routes. Opening my app, I checked the departure times. If I wanted to be at the Bainbridge Port by the end of her shift, I should leave now to catch the ten p.m. boat. I set my half-eaten slice on the table. "Hey, do you all mind if I take off early?" I pointed at my phone. "Autumn texted she wants to see me."

"Wup-ah." Dan made a whipping motion.

"Shut up. He's cute."

The smug smile on Kristine's face made my cheeks hot.

"Of course, we don't mind. Go, shoo." She waved. "Tell her we say *hi*."

"Thanks." I sprinted out the door.

Driving toward the ferry leading to the Bainbridge Port, I couldn't ignore the niggling feeling in the back of my head telling me not to get my hopes up. Because even though I'd already convinced myself Autumn's request to see me was good news, I couldn't deny the possibility things could become worse. My insides froze, and I drummed my fingers on the steering wheel. These past two days, picturing her with another man killed me. *I* wanted to be the one to hold her hand, tell her she was beautiful, gaze into her eyes, claim her lips—those privileges should belong to *me*. But with Autumn working as a companion, I wouldn't have exclusive rights. Maybe I could handle those complications better if I knew I held her heart. In an ideal world, Autumn would quit Plus One, but that decision wasn't up to me, and I wouldn't hold my breath.

I waved my Puget Card at the reader and drove into the ferry queue, which, I was grateful, was already boarding the first two lanes. I followed the line of cars onto the deck and parked where the harbor worker directed. As soon as I cut the engine, I got out, too anxious to sit still for the twenty-minute ride to Bainbridge Island. Breathing in the briny air, I paced the length of the boat several times, which would have been great if I wanted to get in steps. I didn't, though, and the back and forth did nothing to calm my nerves.

When the ferry arrived at the opposite shore, I disembarked, but my insides still felt strangled. Scanning the lot, I swung into the nearest parking space and turned off my lights. Two booths sat at the entrance to the port. I studied them both, but in the dark, and with each worker wearing identical vests and hats, I couldn't tell which held Autumn. I got out my phone, glancing at the clock: 10:23 p.m.

—*I'm here. Parked and waiting*—

The figure in the tollbooth closest to my car retrieved a phone.

Smiling, I allowed my gaze to bounce between her silhouette and the dots flashing on my screen.

—*I still have just over half an hour. Are you sure you're okay waiting?*—

If I got to see her at the end, I'd have waited for her entire shift.

—*Of course*—

—*Okay, I'll find you as soon as I clock out*—

I searched the car, unsure what to do with myself for thirty minutes. A truck with an Orcas' sticker pulled into Autumn's line. Opening my sports app, I checked to see if the game was still going and if I could watch the last few plays. I was in luck. The next twenty minutes were frustrating and contained a lot of cussing as I watched Seattle lose twenty-eight to thirty-five. I glanced at the time in the corner. Knowing Autumn would be off in eight minutes reanimated my paralyzed lungs. I tried listening to the post-game wrap-up, but I couldn't concentrate. My focus stayed glued on Autumn's tollbooth, waiting for the moment she'd open the door. Those last few minutes took forever, but when I watched her finally switch off the light in her workspace, I got out of my car. "Autumn!" I waved a hand to get her attention.

Her head snapped to meet my gaze, and she gave me a nod, holding up a finger. She approached the second booth, and after a short exchange with the other harbor worker, Autumn strode in my direction. "Hey, thanks for waiting." She removed her hat, undid her ponytail, and shook out her hair.

Feeling as though I was watching one of those movies where the girl swings her head in slow motion, and my insides exploded like a firework. "No problem." I heard my heartbeat pounding in my ears. "Want to go somewhere and talk?"

"I'd love to, but we need to get in line." She thumbed over her shoulder. "This is the last ferry back to Seattle tonight."

"Oh, sure." I gestured to my car. "Get in, we can ride together, and I can drive you home on the other side." Her warm fingers touched my forearm.

She smirked. "My car is parked at the Seattle dock."

"Then I'll give you a lift to your car." I fought to hide the disappointment in my voice, knowing how short-lived our meeting would be.

"Perfect." She opened the passenger door and got into my vehicle.

I drove into the tollbooth queue, pulling to the window.

Autumn flashed her badge. "The ride's on me." Leaning across the console, she showed her ID to the harbor worker.

I was hyper-aware of her proximity, and I took a breath, inhaling her vanilla scent.

The red-haired woman in the booth flipped the lever and waved me through.

I drove forward. "Thanks." My voice cracked, and I coughed to clear my throat.

"It's the least I could do since you agreed to meet me."

With a hand, I waved off her comment. "What did you—"

"I wanted to—"

Speaking over each other's words, I laughed in embarrassment.

Autumn laughed, too.

"No, you go." I waved a hand. "You said you need to talk."

Staring at her clasped fingers, she took a deep breath. "I don't think we can be friends."

Chapter 32

Autumn

Out of the corner of my eye, I watched Jensen deflate into the driver's seat of his car. I shifted, placing both my hands on his sexy, sinewy forearm, the sleeves of his Orcas hoodie pushed to his elbows. "No, no, no. I didn't mean to sound ominous." What appeared to be hope replaced his anguished expression, and I watched his lips part. "I had a contract yesterday, which made me realize some things."

Jensen's throat bobbed once. "This isn't sounding any better."

None of my thoughts came out right. "It will; it'll make sense. I promise." *Get yourself together!* "Just hear me out."

He sighed, his face turning red from the brake lights of the sedan in front, revving to life and inching forward. Jensen pressed the ignition and shifted his car into gear, following the queue onto the ferry. "Okay, I'm listening."

I felt like my heart was lodged in my windpipe. "As you know, I like you, but I said we have to be friends because of my plan." I wasn't abandoning my goals, rather, I was just taking a different route.

Jensen's car crept toward the bumper of a green hatchback, and he shut off the engine before turning and clasping his hands in his lap. "Go on."

I swallowed hard, trying to relieve the dryness in my throat. "My client yesterday asked me to pretend to be his girlfriend, just like you. However, he was already in a committed relationship with a man he loves very much." As the boat sailed away from the dock, I leaned forward to slide out of my stiff, neon-yellow harbor-issued vest.

Jensen grabbed the polyester collar of my ferry uniform, and a crease formed between his brows.

I freed my arms. "Thank you."

He passed over the vest. "Then why did he hire you if he already had a boyfriend?"

"Because his parents won't accept his relationship." I folded the fluorescent fabric, placed it in my lap, and met his gaze.

Jensen nodded, a scowl on his lips. "Seriously, people, he's still your son."

I felt my chest warm. "I know. Don't get me started." I swiped my hair out of my face. My opinions of Chris's parents weren't what were important right then. I cleared my throat. "Watching those men deny their feelings during the brunch, I was heartbroken." As I remembered the moments I was about to describe, I couldn't hold back a smile, replacing my anger at his parents. "But when they thought no one was watching, the two men would catch each other's gaze, the love between them written all over their faces. Frankly, I'm surprised nobody else noticed." I traced the stitching on the edge of the leather seat with my nail, and my insides squirmed. "Watching them made me realize our situation wasn't unlike theirs." I chanced a glimpse at Jensen. *Does he see where this conversation is going?*

The corners of his lips twitched, and lights from

the islands shimmered in the darkness through the window behind him. "Huh, how so?"

I laced and unlaced my fingers, and hope simmered on the edge of my nerves. "Those men are denying themselves potential happiness because they're scared of what would happen if they were honest with their families." I filled my lungs, then released the breath in a sharp whoosh, letting my anxiety go. "Just like me. I'm doing the same thing. I'm forcing a friendship with you because I'm worried I'll repeat my past mistakes. But I'm not the same person I was." I blinked slowly, cupping Jensen's cheek, his stubble prickling under my palm. "I don't want to fight what I'm feeling anymore. It's not fair to either of us."

Jensen's gaze danced between my eyes, and he covered my hand with one of his. "So, we're doing this?"

I beamed. The hope I'd been fighting filled my chest. "I guess we are."

He leaned, slow and deliberate, over the center console, almost prowling. Jensen paused, his lips hovering over mine.

His smoldering gaze scorched my insides, and his distinctive scent, mixed with the brine of the ocean, washed over me. I let my gaze fall to his mouth.

With an upswell of the boat, he closed the gap between us.

The kiss was slow and sweet at first.

Jensen's hand slid to the nape of my neck, tangling in my hair. His tongue teased my lips.

I opened my mouth, needing more. Wrapping my arms around Jensen's neck, I was desperate to get closer, but the confines of the car frustrated my efforts.

Two clicks resounded in the silence, and Jensen removed the seatbelt strap from my shoulder. His hand slipped down my right arm, onto my side, and grasped my hip.

His grip stoked the growing inferno inside me, and I gasped.

Jensen devoured my mouth.

The sweeping strokes of his tongue fueled my desire.

He tugged on my lip with his teeth before moving his mouth along my jaw and making his way down my neck and to my collarbone, exploring with little nips along the ridge.

I closed my eyes, tilting my head to the side. The scruff of his stubble beard grazed my skin, and I shivered. A shadow fell across my lids, and I flung my eyes open.

A middle-aged man averted his gaze, while squeezing past Jensen's car, maneuvering between vehicles, and stopping at a white truck two cars forward.

I stiffened.

Jensen pulled back, studying my face. "What's wrong? Do you want me to stop?"

His pupils were at max capacity, but they didn't hide the concern in his expression. I tidied my flannel and pointed at the man in his truck a few cars down, watching me from his side mirror.

Jensen straightened in his seat, pinching the fabric over his thighs to readjust his jeans. "Right. Sorry. Guess I lost control for a moment."

He was sweet, being willing to take all the blame, but he wasn't the only one. "*We* lost control."

Jensen blew out a breath and shoved a hand through his hair. "Where do we go from here?"

I righted myself. "Maybe we should plan a real date—something fun, just the two of us." Butterflies filled my stomach. Thanks to the adrenaline in my body, I felt energized and wide awake. I was bummed it was after eleven. Otherwise, I would have suggested doing something together right then.

Jensen pulled my hand into his lap, tracing the lines on my palm with a finger.

Tingles skirted along my skin.

"We could get some Indian food." He winked.

I couldn't deny how my chest swelled, knowing he remembered my favorite cuisine.

"Or we can find a club and go dancing…" He brushed the back of his fingers along my jaw.

Goose bumps erupted on my arms.

"Or maybe the Pacific Science Center. Do any of those options sound good?"

The sexy rasp of his voice made all the suggestions sound good, but after that make out session, the last choice felt safest—I wanted to take my relationship with Jensen slowly. "Let's go to the science center. I've always wanted to see their planetarium but never made the time." Which was true.

Jensen's smile widened. "I'm glad you chose there. We'll have fun. I've always been fascinated with space. What's your schedule for tomorrow and Wednesday? My shifts start Thursday, and then I'm not available until the following Thursday."

I retrieved my phone and tapped on my calendar, praying for an open timeslot in the next seventy-two hours. Now that I was okay being a couple, waiting until next weekend to have our first official date would stink. I chewed on my thumbnail and swiped through my phone. "Um, I think I have some time Wednesday after three p.m." I eyed Jensen, electricity running through my veins.

"Perfect." He tapped on his screen, entering the details into his calendar. "The planetarium might be busy, so I'll call tomorrow morning and reserve a showtime." Jensen squeezed my thigh.

My insides blossomed like cherry trees in spring.

He leaned over the console again, his gaze on my mouth.

Heat rose up my neck.

The crackly loudspeaker blared the ferry's arrival in Seattle.

Jensen jumped.

I smiled and ducked my head, disappointment aching in the back of my throat.

Jensen's eyes sparkled. "Hold that thought."

Outside the car, the other commuters started their engines.

As the ferry pulled into the dock, I buckled my seatbelt.

Jensen followed suit, then gripped the wheel and drove forward.

Clearing the exit, I pointed at the staff parking lot on the left. "I'm in there." After giving Jensen directions to locate my car, I paused before getting out, running my sweaty palms down my thighs. "Do you want to follow me back to my place and come up for a drink?" I knew my question was forward, but I didn't want the night to end. Jensen's salacious half-smile sent a warmth low in my belly.

"More than anything."

I glanced toward Alaskan Way. The streets were abnormally quiet for a game night. "I'm guessing the Orcas lost?"

Jensen's shoulders slumped. "Yeah, but the game was close, so you don't need to cry."

I released a shaky laugh. Jensen had been my fake boyfriend for weeks now, so I shouldn't be so nervous. But up until then, we'd hidden our feelings behind the pretense of Plus One. Now, the relationship was all out in the open, and I felt vulnerable but excited at the same time.

"When I get there, do you want me to park at the meter?" Jensen's gaze flickered to my mouth.

I made languished strokes along his arm with my fingers. "Anything along the curb is fine. It's after eleven, so they won't check the meters until seven a.m." Jensen brandished a lazy grin.

"You're being a bit presumptuous, aren't you?"

My stomach barrel rolled. "That's not what I meant. I wasn't suggesting you stay the night...." As illicit thoughts ran through my mind, I trailed off, realizing I wasn't opposed to the idea.

He placed a finger under my chin. "I'm just teasing. But I can always set an alarm, just in case."

Jensen's husky voice, along with his thumb tugging on my bottom lip, sent a thrill up my spine. I was unwilling, or better, unable to leave his car and burst the perfect bubble he'd created, scared that when I opened my door, the cold wind outside would whip away the heat from our connection. Jensen's wanton expression pinned me to my seat.

He leaned across the console again, a hand

gripping the back of my neck.

My heart thudded against my ribs, his possessive gesture a complete turn on.

The buzzing vibration from his phone disrupted the charged silence.

Withdrawing, Jensen retrieved his cell. "Sorry. Let me just send this to voicemail." He glanced at his screen, and his lips drew into a hard line. "Of course, it's the hospital. I'm on call. Let me see what they need." Jensen turned toward the driver's side window. "This is Dr. Edwards."

A muffled, garbled response sounded from the other end.

"I see. Administer an IV and give her seven and a half milliliters of Tylenol." Jensen ran a hand through his hair with his eyes pinched shut, and his brow furrowed. "Yeah. I'm just a couple of miles away. I'll be there in a few."

So much for that drink.

Chapter 33

Jensen

When the hospital got a hold of me Monday night at the docks to cover Dr. Michaelson's shift, I was crushed the call forced my evening with Autumn to end early. She'd finally admitted her feelings, and now, she and I had a shot at a real relationship. Then my job ruined the moment. This was why the planetarium adventure—my first official date with Autumn—had to be perfect.

After attending to the one inconvenient incident which ripped me away from Autumn and finishing the on call shift, I returned home for the remainder of the night. Unfortunately, the thrill of my new relationship had me too amped for sleep. I tossed and turned until seven a.m., when I finally gave up and made myself breakfast. Grabbing a packet of blueberry oatmeal from the pantry, I added water and stuck the bowl in the microwave. Placing a pod in my coffee machine, I retrieved my NASA mug, the nutty dark roast aroma filling the kitchen. Jitters shook my insides.

I opened my phone, searched the web for the Pacific Science Center, and clicked on their show reservations page. Remembering Autumn would be available after three on Wednesday, I scheduled us for the Hubble Telescope show at four-thirty p.m. The time was late enough that she could freshen up after her shift at the tollbooth before I arrived at her apartment. With a hardy three hours of sleep under my belt, I counted down the minutes until our date.

****

Just before four the following day, I straightened my navy-blue sweater with clammy hands, unsticking the knitted fabric from my cotton undershirt, and pushed the button next to Autumn's apartment number.

"Yes?"

Hearing her voice, I felt my mouth go dry. I coughed to clear my throat. "It's Jensen."

"Come on up."

A buzzer sounded, and the wrought iron security door clicked open.

I headed up the steps and stopped at her apartment. Cracking my neck, I shook out my shoulders and knocked on the partially open entrance.

The door swung inward. "Hi." Autumn stood with a hand on the frame.

She looked hot in black skinny jeans, boots, and a rusty-orange sweater.

Grabbing her purse, she glanced over her shoulder. "Bye, Alyssa." Autumn paused with her ear cocked. Silence pierced the apartment. With a shrug, Autumn closed the door. "My roommate's not very talkative."

I laughed, then bent to kiss Autumn's cheek, inhaling the familiar perfume lingering on her skin. The fragrance sent my nerves into a frenzy. "You look beautiful."

Autumn put a hand on her hip, cocking it to the side. "I think we're past cheek kisses." Standing on her tiptoes, she leaned close.

Her lips were soft and inviting, and desire lurched

through my torso. I grasped her sides with eager fingers. All too soon, my moves were thwarted as I felt Autumn's hand on my chest.

She gently pushed.

I stepped away.

"We should get moving. I don't want to let your reservations go to waste."

I knew she was right; the show started in thirty minutes, but I would've been just fine to have stood on her doorstep kissing for the rest of the night. "As you wish."

Alone in the car with Autumn was new territory. While the ride to the Pacific Science Center wasn't my first solo excursion with her, this time, neither of us had a script or an agenda. I peeked out of the corner of my eye, unsure what to say.

Autumn smoothed her shirt with a hand.

I let my mind drift to thoughts of touching her taut torso after her appendectomy and the awkward encounter with her parents. "So, um, your dads. They seemed nice." Actually, I was kind of scared of them—at least of Karl.

Autumn's shoulders curled, and she smiled broadly. "They're the best. I don't know what I'd do without them. Papi called this"—she motioned between herself and me—"by the way. He's a hopeless romantic. I think he was rooting for you." She poked my shoulder with a finger.

I was surprised Rob was on my team. "I'm glad he'll approve." The fact Autumn hadn't mentioned Karl's endorsement wasn't a shock. *What has she told them about me since I met them at the hospital?*

Autumn rested her head against the seat and tilted

her gaze my way. "Dad will come around. He's just cynical about everything."

I gripped the steering wheel, rubbing my thumb over the rough stitching on the underside, and pulled to a stop at the red light. "He's the lawyer, right?"

"Yep. He's a partner at Parker, Wickens, and Goldstein."

One of the most prestigious law firms in Seattle. I raised my brows. "And he married a musician. How did *that* happen?" Apparently, oil and water did mix.

"They first encountered each other at Dad's law school graduation party. He and his classmates rented out a dive bar close to the university where Papi's band always played." Autumn paused, a glint in her eyes. "Here's where the story diverges, depending on which of my dads you're talking to."

I sputtered a laugh and accelerated through the intersection, the momentum pressing me into my seat. "They don't agree with how they met?"

"No, they both agree their first encounter was the same night at the bar, but who came onto whom is a different story."

I reared my head back. "Now, *this* I have to hear." Knowing Karl hadn't won this debate in the decades they'd been together said a lot about Rob.

She scooched farther into her seat. "Papi claims, Dad rooted himself at the edge of the stage, white-dancing the Carlton and drooling at Papi's feet." Autumn mimed the hand motions and finger snaps.

Laughter burst from my lips. "Karl? Dancing and drooling? The same man in the button-down and slacks at the hospital?" I shook my head. "Sorry, but I'm not buying it."

Autumn tilted her head, gaze shifting to the side. "Agreed. But Papi's adamant."

"What's Karl's version?" Knowing he was a lawyer, I was positive his story would sound more convincing than Rob's.

"Papi spotted Dad across the room, lounging at the bar, and sent him a drink. Then, after watching Papi's set, Dad strode—not danced—to the front of the crowd to thank Papi when he got off stage." She giggled. "Dad insists Papi was the one drooling."

"Now *that* I can picture." From my brief encounter at the hospital, noting Rob's dramatic reactions and Karl's stoic expression, Karl's version sounded more plausible.

Autumn scoffed. "Probably because it's the truth. I'd love to believe Papi"—she placed a hand over her heart—"but he romanticizes *everything*."

Her emphatic inflection told me she took after Rob. "How long have they been together?"

"Just over thirty-two years. They had a whirlwind romance—dating for only eight months, then held an unofficial ceremony to celebrate their love at the end of the same year and made the marriage official in 2004. Meanwhile, Dad was defending a date rape victim, who'd ended up pregnant."

A cold chill ripped through my spine, and I gripped the steering wheel with white knuckles. "Whoa." Was Autumn saying what I thought she was? If so, her biological parentage was a heavy truth. I was speechless.

Autumn shook a finger. "I know what you're thinking, and everyone feels sorry for me when they hear my story. But I love my dads, and they've given me a great life. I wouldn't change a thing."

My hold on the wheel loosened, warmth returning to my core. "You know who your biological mother is, then?"

"No, she opted for a closed adoption, which I've respected. I've never asked my dads about her."

Her smile was unapologetic. I widened my eyes. "No way! In all this time, you've never been curious?" I stole another sideways glance before pulling to a stop at the next light.

"No." Autumn shrugged. A cloud passed over the sun, darkening her features. "Don't get me wrong, I'm grateful for her sacrifice, but I have everything I need. Because of her, I've got two wonderful dads."

I loved how she was so at peace with herself. Autumn's confidence was a rare quality nowadays.

"What about the Edwards family? How much longer until your brother graduates dental school?" She reached over the console and rested her left hand on my leg.

My skin tingled, but I ignored the rush of desire and concentrated on the conversation. I couldn't believe Autumn remembered that detail about my brother. "Billy's got another semester; then he begins his residency."

"Is he staying in California?"

Damn, she has a good memory. I'd only mentioned Billy attended UCLA during the rapid-fire questions during my first contract. "No, he can't afford rent since residencies don't pay enough, and he'll no longer have financial aid." I pulled into the parking lot of the science center. "He's planning on returning home to stay with my mom until he's matched with a practice."

Getting out of the car, I rounded the bumper and took Autumn's hand. "Did you take notes for the contract or something?"

She sputtered a laugh. "What kind of fake girlfriend would I have been if I couldn't remember information about your family?"

I bumped her shoulder with mine, sending a spark of electricity through my right side. "Can I expect that same type of vigilance now we're official?" I stopped, waiting in the queue to scan our tickets.

Autumn turned and traced a finger down my chest. When her hand reached the top of my belt, she peered from under her lashes. "Oh, honey, you have no idea how attentive I can be."

My insides ignited, and I swallowed hard, allowing my mind to run wild with the possibilities. "I like where your focus is going."

"Tickets."

I turned to see a gray-haired teen girl in a green blazer holding a scan gun with a vacant gaze. *Someone hates her job.* Flustered by Autumn's comment, I fumbled, almost dropping my phone. After locating the QR codes, I waved each under the laser.

The beep signaled. The attendant waved a hand at the next woman. "Tickets."

I flashed Autumn a wide-eyed *alrighty then* look and escorted her inside. A dark-blue sign hanging from the ceiling indicated the planetarium was down the hallway to my left. Nodding in the same direction, I pulled Autumn along.

She pointed at the mural of the solar system adorning the wall. "What's your favorite planet?"

I pinched my brow. "Do people have favorite

planets?"

She lightly slapped my shoulder with a hand. "Yes, of course they do."

Her inflection and playful chastisement made the assumption sound obvious. I laughed. "Okay, then, what's yours?"

Autumn beamed, running a hand across the painted azure sphere on her right. "Neptune, because it's blue."

"I thought your favorite color was red."

Her eyes widened, and her jaw dropped. "Now look at who's remembering details." Autumn paused.

I waggled my brows and held the door to the auditorium, gesturing to enter.

She flicked her hair over her shoulder with a smirk. "Thank you."

I followed Autumn along the outside of the coliseum-style seats, retaking her hand.

"Red is my favorite color, but when you compare pictures of Mars and Neptune side by side, Neptune just stands out."

"Good thing no one's comparing you to those planets, or neither of them would stand out." I repressed a cringe.

Autumn rolled her eyes with a smile. "Really?"

I mocked offense. "What? Too cheesy?" I knew I'd covered my comment in layers of mozzarella and cheddar with a dash of parmesan, but the compliment was true nonetheless.

She pinched a thumb and forefinger together. "Lil' bit." Autumn turned down one of the aisles, choosing a row halfway to the stage and scooting in before taking a seat.

Settling beside her in the stiff, deep-red velour

chair, I released a dramatic sigh. "Man, that was one of my best chat-up lines." I smacked my palm against my forehead in theatrical frustration. "No wonder I've been single for so long."

She winced. "Have you used that line on other women?" Autumn stroked her chin. "That explains a lot."

The contemplative gesture couldn't conceal the amusement in her squinting eyes.

Feeling warmth fill my chest, I squeezed her hand and watched several other couples and families fill in the seats.

When the presenter entered, strode to the stage, and checked the equipment, the room was half-full. The dark purple-blazered, bespectacled man made a few more clicks on the control panel and a sound check before dimming the lights.

As we laid in the semi-reclined seats holding hands, I felt almost like Autumn and I were lying in bed together, and I relished the thought. I shifted my head to face her.

She mirrored my action.

Studying her features, I felt my pulse race. Even though we were in public, the moment was oddly intimate, probably because of the visions in my head. Releasing her hand, I brushed the back of my fingers down her cheek. The touch seared my skin.

Autumn smiled, turning to kiss my palm.

"Welcome to Seattle's Pacific Science Center Planetarium." The presenter's voice resounded over the speakers.

Autumn shifted to stare at the ceiling.

I remained where I was, gazing over her dimly lit

form. Drinking in her features, I laced my fingers with hers again.

She squeezed my hand and shot me a quick smile.

Having Autumn beside me, knowing she chose to be here, was a huge distraction. I couldn't focus on the planets projected on the domed ceiling. Recalling my conversation with Molly from a few weeks ago and her insistence Autumn's feelings were fake, I marveled at my luck. Could Molly and I both have been fortunate enough to find unicorns? The chances seemed unlikely, but Molly was happy in a committed relationship, and I was on my first official date with Autumn. My situation was too good to be true.

The presenter described the planets one by one, displaying images from the Hubble telescope and facts about each. Mars filled the screen, and I made a mental note and compared the likeness with Neptune when they projected the planet a few minutes later. Autumn was right; the blue planet put the others to shame.

Autumn nudged my shoulder, shifting in her chair. "See? Isn't she beautiful?"

Her warm breath tickled my neck. I nodded and slid closer. "Yes, she is." I knew Autumn referred to the projected planet, but my words were meant for her.

She snuggled in, leaning her head on my shoulder and wrapping her free hand over my bicep.

I mustered all my energy not to flex because the gesture would have been too obvious. But I was desperate to impress Autumn. I settled for kissing her on the head. Her hair smelled of citrus—orange or grapefruit—which complemented her skin's vanilla. The scent permeated my nose and messed with my head. Everything about this woman riled my senses.

For the last twenty minutes of the show, Autumn's featherlight touch grazed idly on the back of my hand.

Electricity shot straight to my core. I forced myself to remain in my chair and not whisk her away somewhere private where I could be alone with her—one-on-one time would come later.

Chapter 34

Autumn

The Hubble show was fascinating, but it paled in comparison to the butterfly sanctuary located in the south wing of the Pacific Science Center. As Jensen and I meandered hand in hand through the lush greenhouse building, I couldn't keep my jaw from falling. Sweat trickled down my back. Around me sat various tropical plants and hundreds of beautiful butterflies and moths fluttering through the humid air.

"Who knew so many different species existed?" Jensen gaped, his gaze following the delicate insects dancing through the air. "How do you even tell the difference between them, whether the insect is a moth or a butterfly?"

His question was valid. "I don't know. Let me grab a pamphlet." Nabbing a tri-folded paper from the display table by the doors, I perused the information.

"Autumn."

Jensen's whispered tone caught my attention. I whirled to see him frozen like a statue, eyeing a butterfly perched on his chest with beautiful iridescent blue on the inside of its wings that matched Jensen's sweater and a dull brown pattern on the outside.

"Quick, take a picture." He stood stiffly.

I retrieved my phone and snapped a photo.

Jensen inhaled and held his breath.

I bit my cheek to hold in my laughter. "Look at you, acting like a proud papa." He was so cute, like a toddler with a balloon—awestruck and excited. His mouth hitched in a cheeky grin.

"How could I not be proud to host this little guy?" Jensen pursed his lips. "I shall name him Phillip."

I screwed up my face. "What? That's a weird name for a butterfly."

Jensen scoffed. "Oh, come on. You don't think he looks like a Phillip?"

Rolling my eyes, I shook my head as warm fuzzies filled my insides, and I scanned the index of butterflies on the wilted paper. "It's called a common blue morpho."

A young boy in a puffy, green jacket pointed at Jensen. "Dad, look! This guy has a butterfly on his sweater."

Taking his son by the hand, the dad nodded. "I bet if we sit on the bench, one might land on you, too."

The boy with floppy, red hair squealed and sprinted toward the wooden seat, yanking his father along.

I smiled at the little family.

Jensen pointed to my pamphlet. "What did you say Phillip is again?"

Looking back at the list of winged insect names, I found the corresponding picture. "A common blue morpho."

He scoffed. "How dare you call my kid common." Jensen turned up his nose, the corners of his mouth twitching. "He's exceptional."

I crushed on Jensen and his reference to the butterfly as his son and repressed a grin, my insides turning to goo. Unable to help myself, I stood on my tiptoes and gave him a peck. "You're adorable."

Phillip flew away.

Jensen pursed his lips and raised a brow, wrapping his arms around my waist. "It's a good thing you are, too, since you've scared away the most *uncommon* blue morpho in this place." His mouth claimed mine possessively.

My legs trembled.

His fingers caressed the small of my back.

Normally, I would have felt self-conscious about the damp sweat covering my body from the humidity, but I didn't care. I was lost in Jensen, and I wondered how I'd managed to resist him for so long. When I came up for air a moment later, I recognized the burn of desire in Jensen's gaze which rivaled my own.

He leaned in, gripping my hips and grazing his nose along my ear. "Do you want to get out of here?"

Every nerve in my body ignited. So much for slow. *Desperately*. "Yes." My answer was breathy. "I do." He flashed me a sexy smirk.

Releasing his hold on my waist, Jensen grabbed my hand, marched toward the exit, and opened the door.

A cool breeze washed over me, and I all but flew across the wet parking lot to his car.

Jensen was hot on my heels with the Space Needle's regal presence standing guardian over the science center.

Inside the vehicle, Jensen leaned across the center console. His hand found the back of my neck, tangling in my hair, and he drew me in.

As his mouth collided with mine and I parted my lips to deepen the kiss, I gripped his shoulders.

Jensen broke away, nibbling along my jaw.

I angled my head, desperate for more.

He nipped at the tender skin under my ear.

I gasped, and a shiver reverberated along my spine.

Jensen captured my mouth again with a sexy growl.

My insides ached with longing.

He tugged on my bottom lip with his teeth. "Sorry, I just can't seem to keep my hands off you." His thumb grazed my cheekbone.

Breathing heavily, I shook my head. "Don't be." I glanced around the parking lot. "But I think we should go someplace more private."

"Your place or mine?"

Hearing his husky tone had anticipation thick in my throat. "Mine's closer." *I need him now.*

"What about your roommate?"

I glanced at the clock on the center display. "Her shift starts in ten minutes."

"Deal." Jensen started the car and drove onto the street. "It's about dinner time. Should we grab some food along the way?"

I cocked an eyebrow. "Food? *That's* what you're thinking about?" The hunger in my belly was for one reason and one reason only.

He focused on the road, but his hand squeezed my thigh. "I plan on working up an appetite."

My breath hitched, and I bit my lip.

"Any cravings?"

The wicked glint in his eyes made my toes curl. "Any place with a drive-through."

****

With fumbling fingers, Jensen hastily paid the meter in front of my building.

After flashing my entry gate fob, I raced to my apartment, dragging Jensen along. The to-go bags banged against my legs. I retrieved my keys from my purse, but I couldn't get the lock while Jensen nibbled the back of my neck. My whole body quivered. After turning the bolt, I flung open the door, spinning and wrapping my arms around Jensen's neck. Locking my lips with his, I stumbled into my living room.

Jensen followed, dropping the takeout bags on the floor before he kicked the door shut.

Grabbing the hem of his sweater, I shoved the fabric over his chest. I scowled at his undershirt.

His collar got caught on his chin, and Jensen raised a hand to help.

The deep sound of a throat clearing from over my shoulder was like an ice bath. I froze.

"Friends, huh?"

Jensen scrambled to yank his sweater down.

Closing my eyes, I cringed into Jensen's chest, wishing with everything in me that I didn't recognize the deep, stern voice.

"Autumn?"

Taking a fortifying breath, I glanced at Jensen, and my stomach tensed at his round, saucer-like eyes. I mouthed the word *sorry* before turning to face my father. "Dad." I felt my chest loosen at seeing Papi, in his favorite navy-and-pink flamingo shirt, sitting on the couch, too. "What a nice surprise."

Dad crossed his arms over his coral button-down. "Is it, though?"

Papi nudged my father. "Stop. It's not any of our business."

Dad frowned. "It is when it's in front of my face."

Papi rolled his eyes, scooting forward on the couch to peer around Dad. "Ignore him. He's had a long day at work."

My sentimental father regarded Dad with a soft gaze, and my heart pinched.

"Besides"—Papi squeezed Dad's knee—"he seems to have forgotten how hands-y he was when we were first dating."

I covered my ears. "La, la, la, la, la. I don't want to hear it."

Dad smoothed a hand down his stomach. "Well, I don't want to see it."

"So sorry." Jensen put his left hand on my back, leaning around and extending his right toward my parents. "Rob, Karl. It's nice to see you again."

Papi rose and gave Jensen the typical guy hug-pat-on-the-back greeting.

Dad merely stood from the couch and nodded his acknowledgment.

I huffed at this unfortunate change of plans, retrieved the takeout bags from the floor, and set them on the table. "What are you all doing here, by the way? Did Alyssa let you in?"

Jensen shifted from foot to foot at my side.

I unpacked the food, the salty scent of fries filling the small space.

Dad rounded the couch and entered the kitchen. "Your roommate is a strange one." He slid his hands into the pocket of his gray slacks. "I don't think she said two words to us before she sped out the door." Dad jutted a chin at the table. "The plan was to take you out to dinner because you've been so down lately."

Jensen's attention cut to me with furrowed brows.

I gave him a weak smile, shaking my head. Denying my feelings for Jensen was the cause for my previous sulky behavior. Now, I would have to explain that to Jensen and have a conversation I'd hoped to avoid. *Thank you, Dad.*

"But apparently, you're doing better." Papi eyed Jensen with a smirk. "And you've brought us dinner. How convenient."

I smiled through gritted teeth, knowing my dads weren't going anywhere. "Perfect." Repressing a sigh, I squeezed Jensen's hand. We should have gone to his place.

Chapter 35

Jensen

"I am so sorry, Jensen."

Autumn's tone was full of remorse on the other end of the line.

"Last night was embarrassing, to say the least. Please don't take Dad to heart. He loves me and gets overprotective."

Following the line of cars onto the ferry also heading into Seattle to start their workday, I shook my head, even though she couldn't see me because we weren't video chatting. "Stop apologizing; I get it. It's fine." I had to be. After dinner, her dads were obvious, setting up camp on the couch to show they weren't leaving Autumn's place until after I left, despite their daughter's less-than-subtle hints for them to do so.

"Thank you for being so understanding."

"Of course, they're your dads. But I am still confused about one thing: Karl said he and Rob were there because you were sad." I followed the harbor worker's directions onto the ramp, the salty air leaking through my vents. "Why were you feeling so down?"

"Oh, um…" She paused. "I, uh…well…." Autumn huffed. "My sulky behavior was because I kept denying my feelings for you."

Adrenaline coursed through my veins, and I sat straighter. "Is that so?" I made my tone flirty. Knowing

I hadn't imagined my feelings were reciprocated was like dreaming with my eyes open.

"Being around you as your friend while pretending to act like your girlfriend was hard."

I could hear the humor in her voice, and I relished the fact these past few weeks were difficult for her, too.

"You don't seem to understand how attractive you are."

"Really?" I smiled at the console display bearing her name. "What do you find attractive about me?" Placing my car in Park, I cracked a window to let in the breeze. I gave her my full attention, allowing my mind to form a list of Autumn's best qualities.

"I'm going to stop this right here." Autumn laughed. "Because someone's getting a big head."

"Oh, come on. You're telling me you don't want to stroke my ego?" I pinched my lips together to keep from laughing at my innuendo.

"Pfft. I won't even humor you with a response, and for the record, I'm rolling my eyes right now."

I could picture her big brown eyes twisting upward, with a smile on her lips, and my insides flared with desire.

"But now I'm sad because of your hospital shifts. I won't see you until next weekend."

Warmth filled my chest when I heard the pouty lilt in her voice. "I'll plan something romantic for Friday. Sound good?" I cataloged a series of possibilities in my head.

"Ugh, I work Friday at the Bainbridge Port."

I glanced in my rearview and watched the cars line up on the deck behind mine. "Hmm." I tapped idly on my steering wheel. "Isn't there an Orcas home game next Sunday?"

"Yeah, against the Pilgrims. Why? Are Kristine and Dan having people over to watch?"

I had something better in mind. "They are, but if I can get my hands on some tickets, what would you think about seeing the game at the stadium, just the two of us? Are you up for it?"

Autumn squealed.

My ears rang, and I turned down the volume on the display.

"Oh my gosh! You have no idea how long it's been since I've seen a game in the flesh."

"Is that a *yes* then?" I held my breath, praying I could make this plan come to fruition.

"Yes, of course! I'd love to go!"

My heart sped like a cheetah, and I fist-pumped the air with a smile. "Good. I'll see what I can do." I mentally ran through my calendar for Leon's next follow-up appointment so I could ask his father about the tickets.

"I can't wait." She hesitated. "But dammit, I've got to go. I've got a shift in an hour, and I haven't even showered yet."

Spikes of heat prickled my skin at the image she'd conjured with her words.

"Text me later?"

At this point, I wouldn't let a day go by without contacting her. "My break's at two. Am I allowed to call you while you're working?"

"Hmm, better stick to texting. But I get off at five, so you can call after my shift ends."

I said goodbye and hit the End button. The screen lit again—this time with my mother's name. I sighed heavily. "Hi, Mom."

"Is there something you want to tell me?"

Her clipped tone made my shoulders tense, and for the life of me, I couldn't figure out what she was talking about. "Um…no?"

"Are you sure? You're just going to keep lying to my face?"

I rolled my eyes. We were on a phone call, so we weren't technically face-to-face, but I was still clueless. "What lie are you accusing me of, Mom?"

"Autumn."

Cold sweat broke out across my brow. *My mother found out Autumn works for Plus One?* This conversation was heading nowhere good—fast. "Mom, I can explain…."

"You'd better. I don't like being made a fool."

"Mom, you're not a fool. I told you Autumn was my date for the dinner." *Please let that be the only thing she knows about her.*

"So, Darla's the misinformed one? Dan's mother said he told her you and Autumn were dating for several weeks before the recognition dinner, was he wrong? What about Molly? Either you're lying about dating Autumn for weeks, or you should never have asked Gillian's daughter to be your date to the banquet."

I let my head fall against the smooth, leather headrest, and I blew out a long breath. Her call had nothing to do with Autumn being a companion. *Thank goodness.* My mother referred to the story I'd concocted and told Dan as my meet-cute with Autumn that he'd clearly passed onto his mother. My brain kicked into overdrive, thinking of alibis before settling on a partial truth. "You railroaded me into asking Molly, Mom. And so, yes, I *did* lie to Dan and Kristine about Autumn. But that was on me." I leaned toward the console, glad she couldn't see my face. "Because the other option was for your loser son to admit the woman he did ask to attend the Best Doctor's event backed out and then proceeded to set him up with someone else at the last minute."

Mom tsked into the phone. "You're not a loser, Jensen. You're a handsome, successful doctor, and if you weren't so picky, any number of girls would have gone."

I knew she meant well, but my mother didn't understand. Yes, I'll admit, I was a good-looking guy. Plenty of nurses at the hospital weren't shy with their compliments. But after what happened with Kayla, I swore I'd never date anyone at work ever again. "Finding the right date isn't as easy as you'd think, Mom."

"Darla says you're still seeing Autumn. Is that a lie, too?"

I scrubbed a hand through my hair, deciding how much I wanted to tell my mother. "We've gone out a couple of times since then. But it's still very early days; don't go and start making plans for my future."

"You've got to give me something because, at this rate, when you get engaged, Darla will be the one who'll tell me."

I rubbed my temple. "Mom, stop. Like I'd ever keep a big life event from you." The ferry reached the Seattle Port, jostling my car. "If I ever get engaged, you'll be the first to know."

"Wait! Is the relationship heading toward marriage,

then?"

Her condescending hopefulness grated my nerves. "Mom!" I let my exasperation lace my tone. She was the last person I'd tell about my feelings for Autumn. "The ferry just docked. I've got to go."

"Fine. But keep me updated."

"Of course, but please, don't say anything to Darla." I knew the request was in vain.

"You know me; my lips are sealed."

Like hell they are.

"Talk to you soon, honey."

"Bye, Mom." I ended the call, but the conversation left a bad taste in my mouth. Putting the car into Drive, I followed the line of vehicles into port. My mother was worse than a tabloid magazine. At some point, I needed to confess to Dan—not about Autumn being a companion, but the part about Molly's rejection and subsequent setup. I gripped the steering wheel, exhaling through my nose. Dan's shifts started earlier this week, so when I arrived, I knew he'd already be at the hospital. I had to find time to talk to my friend and tell him the half-truth I mentioned to my mom before she spilled all her assumptions to Darla. Dan was a good friend; I didn't want him to hear my story secondhand.

Since Seattle was heading into the colder months, the first part of my shift was busy with fevers, sinus issues, and broken bones from early winter activities gone wrong, making the hours fly. By break time, I was in dire need of a coffee pick-me-up. When I entered the break room, I was startled to find Dan shoving a vending machine sandwich into his mouth at the circular table in the corner. "You have a break right now, too?" I grabbed the pot of coffee and poured myself a mug, the nutty aroma already soothing my frayed nerves.

"Just fifteen"—Dan shoved in another bite—"I have ten left."

Ten minutes was long enough. Plus, with a time limit, I wouldn't have to endure the awkwardness after my admission. A perfect window. "Hey," I scooted the chair out opposite him at the little, white table and sat. "I need to confess something."

Dan's eyebrows shot up. "Will this make me mad?" He wiped his mouth on a napkin. "Because I want to have my drink ready to throw in your face if need be." The corner of his lips twitched before he took a swig of his soda.

I kicked his foot under the table. "Shut up. It's not a big deal."

Dan laughed before eating the last of his sandwich and licking his fingers.

"It's about Autumn." I focused on my coffee, deciding to throw the truth out there. "I lied at the Best Doctors event. She and I weren't dating before then."

Dan narrowed his eyes. "Why'd you lie about you and Autumn?"

I took a deep breath. "Because we were set up last-minute by the woman I *had* asked who'd rejected my offer. I was embarrassed." Heat rose in my cheeks, still uncomfortable about how the situation went down.

Dan chuckled, balling the napkin and stuffing it into the sandwich container. "But you admitted you were set up; I don't understand why you lied about the timing."

"For Kayla's benefit. I didn't want her to find out I couldn't get a date to my *own* recognition dinner." I pictured Autumn at the dinner in her silky red dress, and my excitement about my budding relationship overshadowed my humiliating confession.

Dan nodded, teeth scraping at the peeling skin on his chapped bottom lip. "Okay, that makes sense." He collected his trash and stood. "But next time, give me some credit, okay? We've been friends for years; you can be honest with me." He scooted his chair in, making the legs screech against the linoleum, then turned toward the door. "Besides, a setup isn't a big deal. It's not like you paid for a date."

"Ha!" My laugh was forced, and I avoided his gaze. My stomach soured. "Yeah, that would be worse."

Chapter 36

Autumn

I flipped the last pancake in the pan—golden perfection. Smiling, I admired the fluffy stack on my kitchen counter beside the stove and stirred the scrambled eggs. I didn't often fix myself a big breakfast. Making one I intended to share with my roommate was even more rare, but I'd received the results of my midterms yesterday, and I was on cloud nine.

Alyssa opened her bedroom door.

Noticing she was already dressed for the day in jeans, a beige sweater, curled hair, and full makeup, I jerked my head back. *Is she going somewhere? The roommate calendar says she doesn't work until one p.m.* "Hey, perfect timing. I made us breakfast." I waved a hand at the table laden with food, the smell of warm maple syrup saturating the small area.

She turned up her nose. "I don't like eggs."

"Okay...." My neck prickled, but I quickly swallowed my pride. "I made pancakes, too."

As she grabbed her keys from the counter, Alyssa huffed, one hand on her hip. "I was just trying to be nice." She sneered at the food. "I don't eat breakfast."

That was her way of being nice? "Oh, I didn't know. I'll make a mental note for next time."

"Whatever, I'm leaving to meet my boyfriend."

She left with a slam of the door.

She *has a boyfriend? Poor guy.* I sat and served myself some eggs, glancing at the clock—6:52 a.m. Jensen would text in eight minutes. With his twelve-hour shifts this week, he'd developed a routine—if he got off at a reasonable hour and wasn't too tired, he'd text me in the evenings. But since his start times remained the same each day, he'd contact me as soon as he woke, which always happened to be at seven a.m. on the dot. Clicking on the University of Washington student portal and rechecking my grades, I drummed my fingers on the smooth tabletop. Just this once, I wished Jensen wasn't such a stickler about his routine. I was dying to share my good news. Two pancakes later, I heard my phone ping.

—*Good morning, beautiful*—

Beaming at my screen, I was too excited to deal with the niceties of conversation.

—*I PASSED MY MIDTERMS!!!!*—

—*Congrats!* Confetti and horn emoji. *I knew you would!*—

—*Thanks! I appreciate your confidence, but as my boyfriend, you're biased*—

I bit my lip to contain my squeal, and not just because I'd aced my tests. *He's my boyfriend!*

—*Can I take you out this weekend for a proper celebration?* Tongue out winky face emoji—

The heat in my midsection headed south.

—*Yes, I'll hold you to that. The* naan *at Tandoori Central is my favorite*—

I couldn't help teasing him.

—*Well, I wasn't thinking of eating* naan*, but that can be on the menu, too*—

I pinched my lips to keep from spitting out my orange juice. Here I was, doing my best to keep the conversation on the high road, but he dragged it right back into the gutter. Although, I'd be lying if I said I minded. I smiled, tapping out my response.

—*It's nice to know you don't shy away from spicy*—

—*Now I'm really regretting I have work today*—

—*Don't. Today wouldn't have worked for me anyway. My tollbooth shift starts at nine a.m.*—

—*Then Sunday can't get here fast enough. Can I take you out after the game?*—

I stood to place my plate in the sink and box the leftovers, typing one-handed.

—*Sadly, I'm at Bainbridge from five to eleven p.m.*—

—*Bummer. Okay then, let me know your schedule for the following week so I can make reservations to celebrate*—

—*Will do! Gotta run. I need to shower before my shift.* Kissy face emoji—

—Fire emoji—

Giggling, I put the plastic container of pancakes in the fridge, then wiped the table. Striding into the bathroom, I turned the knob for the shower. I debated leaving the temperature on cold, thanks to my conversation with Jensen, but I decided not to. I'd had a good morning and deserved to bask in the glory of the endorphin rush.

I'd savored the steamy, sauna-like shower for too long and rushed to prepare for work. I held the mascara wand near my lashes.

The loud ring of my phone rent the air.

I jumped and almost poked my eye out. I tapped the speaker icon. "Hey, Lil. What's up?"

"Long time no hear. Where have you been?"

I cringed, hating myself for neglecting my best friend. "Just busy lying to myself. You know, nothing big."

"Whoa, whoa. Lying to yourself? About what?"

Lilly's bubbly voice was like an extra energy boost. "Love, relationships, what my goals are." I switched eyes and coated my left lashes. "Let's just say I've been reevaluating my life's decisions."

"Like what?" She sputtered a laugh.

Fighting the strangled feeling in my chest, I puckered my lips to slide on some gloss, then smacked them together. "Hot Doc. I'm giving him a chance."

Silence lingered on the end of the line. "The same man you swore you wouldn't date because it would derail your goals?"

I clenched my jaw and threw my lip gloss into my purse, grabbed my neon-yellow vest and keys, and stalked to the door, phone in hand. "Yep, that's him—his name is Jensen." Struggling to keep the irritation from my tone at being called out, I took her off speaker and pinched my phone between my cheek and shoulder to lock my apartment. "We went on our first official date last week."

"What happened to your mantra?"

I opened the door to the stairwell, not wanting to lose my signal in the elevator. The chill of the corridor raised goose bumps on my skin. "I know I said 'no men until my BSN,' but Jensen is different."

"Please." Lilly dragged out the word. "I thought you learned from your experience with Matteo."

I could almost hear her eyes rolling. "Yeah, but I was young and stupid back then. I'm older and wiser now." I rubbed my forehead. *That sounds mature.* I knew Lilly was only doing what a best friend should do, but I needed her to understand my point of view. "Jensen's supportive. He encourages me to pursue my goals, he doesn't expect me to chase him, he's respectful, and he's invested in my success."

Lilly sighed into her phone. "Okay, I trust your judgment. But be careful; I don't want to see you get hurt again."

My throat tightened at the sincerity in her tone. I opened my car and slid behind the wheel. "He won't hurt me." While my mind was set, my heart still willed the words to be true.

"If you say so. What about being a companion? Is he okay with you working for Ruth?"

I turned over the ignition, and the car rumbled to life. "He is, but about Plus One, I've been thinking…."

Chapter 37

Jensen

After my text conversation with Autumn, I decided I couldn't wait three days to congratulate her for passing her exams, but I wasn't sure what to get as a present. So, I called Kristine, and taking her suggestion, I stopped at a bakery, bought a cupcake, and made the circuitous route to work in order to see Autumn at her tollbooth. She'd signed up for double shifts Thursday through Saturday to have the Sunday evening shift off to attend the Orcas' game. I tapped my thumbs against the steering wheel, waiting in the ferry queue. The extra thirty minutes I'd allotted on my drive to work would still be tight, but seeing Autumn was worth the risk of being late.

Thankfully, the rare sunny skies made spotting her through the clear glass windows of her booth easy. Glancing at the passenger seat, I retrieved my purchase and held the domed plastic. Hints of the decadent, pumpkin-latte cupcake with rich, piped-vanilla frosting and a cinnamon stick wafted through the container. I'd debated ordering a double chocolate mocha bomb, but considering the season, I bought the fall option instead. The last car in front of me pulled ahead, and I inched forward to Autumn's window.

She did a double take before a wide smile spread across her lips. "Jensen, what are you doing here?"

Her whole face brightened. Despite her slight frame, Autumn's beauty filled the tollbooth. I retrieved the plastic container and held the treat through the window, the sun warming my skin. "Congrats on passing your midterms."

Autumn placed a hand over her heart. "Mmm." She took the cupcake. "You're so sweet. Thank you." She lifted the lid, sniffing the dessert, and flinched. "Oh, pumpkin."

Fake enthusiasm infused her tone. I flashed an amused smile. "I take it you're not a pumpkin spice person?"

"Oh, no, no, no. I like it."

I lifted a suspicious eyebrow.

Her cheeks flushed. "Well, it's not my number one choice, but I *do* like it."

I clucked my tongue. "I knew I should have listened to Kristine and gone with the chocolate."

Autumn put a fist over her mouth, stifling a giggle. "You asked Kristine's advice?"

Heat invaded my face. "I didn't want to mess this up, but…here we are."

"You didn't—"

The car behind mine honked, and I scowled at my rearview. "I did. But I'll make it up to you." I scanned my Puget Card. "I promise." With a wink, I drove forward, stopping behind a shiny silver sedan. Huffing, I noted the time on the display. If only I could return to the bakery and buy the mocha bomb. *Oh, well.* Whatever I did to make up for my blunder needed to be good. I grabbed my phone and found Kristine's contact details.

—You were right. I should have gone with the

chocolate—

—Let that be a lesson—

Kristine's answer tracked.

—Noted—

When I arrived at the hospital, I checked my schedule. Seeing Leon's name as my first patient gave me an idea. While the compensation gift couldn't happen until Sunday, the wait would be worth it if I could make my new plan happen. Grabbing the kid's chart, I pushed the cold metal handle and entered the room of my first appointment. "Leon!"

The six-year-old sat on the edge of the exam table in an Orcas' hoodie, spinning a football in his hands.

"How's the season going?"

Rashaan, Leon's dad and the punter for the Orcas, stood in the corner, wearing his team's skull cap.

Leon's newly acquired adult teeth dwarfed the rest of his grin. "Made a touchdown last game!"

I held out my fist. "Niiice."

As he bumped his curled fingers against mine, Leon tilted his head up, jutting his chin in my direction.

I noted Leon's lab results. "And your sugars, they're great, too. Good job keeping these logs." I tapped my pen against his personal journal of foods and glucose levels.

Rashaan clapped his son on the back. "Right on, buddy. We make a good team."

As I watched the father and son, I rocked on my toes, recognizing how far they'd come, and beamed. Last year, I diagnosed Leon with type 1 diabetes, and he'd had a rough start, but these past few months were like night and day. The father-and-son duo listened and followed my every instruction to the letter, and the results spoke for themselves. "You sure do." I flipped through the rest of Leon's chart. "I1C is right where it should be." Walking to his side, I examined the boy's fingertips. "How's the glucose testing going?"

Leon averted his gaze and shrugged.

Rashaan frowned. "Use your words, son."

The boy deflated. "I hate it; it's stupid. My fingertips hurt."

Poor kid. His sulky tone and comments were a common response from my younger patients. "Not so good, huh?"

Rashaan glared at Leon before meeting my gaze. "Excuse my son, Doc. What he meant to ask was, is there another location where we can check his levels to give his fingers a break?"

I nodded, indicating for Leon to hop off the exam table so I could check his insulin injection sites.

Leon scooted to the edge of the cushioned surface, rustling and bunching the medical table paper before jumping to the linoleum floor.

I shifted his clothes to inspect his skin. "There are a few other options since you've been doing so well with management; your insurance should cover all of them." I lifted Leon back onto the table. "I'll have the nurse grab some information for you to review, then I'll return, and we can discuss them together." I watched the tense features of Rashaan's face soften.

"Thanks, Doc. And before I forget." He retrieved his wallet from the pocket of his baggy, black jeans. "Here are those tickets you asked for. Sunday should be a good game."

I took the passes from Rashaan and infused my smile with sincerity. "Thanks, I appreciate this."

Having contacts was a nice perk of my job.

"I'm just glad you finally accepted my offer." He patted my shoulder. "Let me know if I can do anything else."

Taking a deep breath, I rubbed the back of my neck. *Here goes nothing.* "Come to mention it, if I brought in a jersey, would you autograph it? I want to impress my new girlfriend." *And make up for the lame cupcake.*

Rashaan's hand hovered over his mouth. "Ahhh, boy! Pullin' out the big guns!" He pursed his lips and nodded. "I'll do you one better. Tell me her size, and I'll get the whole team to sign it. I'll have the jersey waiting at will call on Sunday."

Scooping my jaw off the linoleum, I shook his hand with a firm grip. "Thanks, man. Let me know how much I owe you." Seeing Autumn's reaction would be worth any price I had to pay.

Rashaan shook his head. "Naw, I still owe you for what you've done for Leon—I got you, boy."

I held up a hand. "Rashaan, no. I'm just doing my job."

"Pfft." He pursed his lips with a scowl. "Please. I don't know any other doctors who've attended their patient's games."

Leon was a great kid, and I loved football. Why wouldn't I go? I grasped the boy's shoulder, smiling and meeting his father's gaze. "I don't deserve your credit. It's for selfish reasons—I want to say I knew Leon before he became a famous running back." With a wave of goodbye, I left the room, walking to the nurses' station. I made my notes on Leon's chart and sent in a pink scrub-wearing nurse with the information Rashaan requested.

"There's the man I was looking for." My chief of staff stopped at the counter, nodding a *hello* to the nurses before turning. "Meg's gotten on the whole November gratitude social media train." He rolled his eyes. "Now, she's insisting on hosting thank-you brunches for the senior staff who have raised money for the hospital and their significant others. Are you up for it?"

I noticed my thoughts flew straight to Autumn, and a burst of energy ran through my veins. *Another opportunity to show her off? Count me in!* "Absolutely. When is it?"

Gary blew out his breath. "This Monday at eleven thirty a.m."

I knew I was available, but I wasn't sure about Autumn. "Let me double-check with my girlfriend, but I'll be there."

"Sounds good." Gary slapped my back. "Keep me posted on"—he ducked his head, snapping his fingers—"what's her name again? Autumn?"

She must have left a good impression, if Gary remembered her name. "Yes, that's her."

"Lovely girl. Shoot me an email with your RSVP."

I gave a curt nod. "Will do, sir."

Dr. Anderson sauntered away.

Eagerly, I got out my phone.

—*Hey, beautiful. Do you have any plans for this Monday, late morning?*—

I put my cell into my pocket, not expecting an immediate response. When I felt the device vibrate against my thigh, I retrieved my phone again.

—*No, I'm free. What do you have in mind?*—

I had no doubt my heart swelled, knowing this would be our first official outing with my peers as a couple—no more lies.

—Dr. Anderson and his wife, Meg, invited us to a gratitude brunch—

—How sweet of them. Where and what time?—

I jumped and slapped the sign for the *B* wing with a whoop.

—Their house. I'll pick you up at eleven—

—Can't wait!—

I pocketed my phone, unable to contain the smile on my face. Two days in a row seeing Autumn—the weekend looked better and better.

Chapter 38

Autumn

Jensen was adorable, wrapped in his Orcas' beanie and scarf. Even better, as I stood beside him in line at will call outside the Orcas' stadium, he'd pointed out we wore matching snow caps. "I thought you already had the tickets."

He scratched the back of his neck. "I do; this is something else."

The conversation piqued my interest. I didn't realize will call had any other purpose than holding tickets.

Jensen reached the front of the line and smiled at the balding, gray-haired man with his matching mustache. "There should be a package on hold for Dr. Jensen Edwards."

For the life of me, I couldn't figure out what he'd be collecting. Seeing the man drift away from the counter, I leaned into the warm air filtering from his window.

The gentleman returned with a large, brown grocery bag. "May I see some identification?"

I watched with interest as Jensen brandished his license.

The man squinted at the card and nodded at the side door of the building.

"Wait right here." Jensen jogged around the brick

structure.

After a moment, he returned, looking like he was ready to burst.

Jensen held out the bag. "Congratulations again on your midterms."

I took the gift, my thoughts in a frenzy, wondering what he could have gotten. With a broad smile, I unrolled the top of the brown paper sack. "An Orcas' jersey!" I held the garment with reverent awe.

"Not just any jersey. Here." He took the shirt and turned it around. "All the players signed it."

As I inspected the synthetic fabric closer, examining all the scribbles dotted across the back along with the odd Bible reference, I gasped, my heart thrashing. I clutched the gift to my chest. "Jensen, this is crazy! Thank you! I love it!" I threw my arms around his neck. "How will I ever top this?"

After a tight squeeze, he pulled back to meet my gaze. "It's not a competition." Jensen shrugged one shoulder. "I wanted to show you how proud I was of you, that's all."

All my doubts about throwing aside my motto washed away. Jensen was the perfect guy, supporting me in my goals, and he was happy I was succeeding—the complete opposite of Matteo. I was an idiot for depriving myself of this kind of happiness for so long. Standing on my tiptoes, I gave Jensen a quick peck on the lips before thrusting the brown bag into his hands. "Hold this." Wrestling off my coat, I pinched it between my knees and slid the new jersey over my head. After adjusting the hem of the slick fabric, I held my hands out to my sides. "How's it look?" A smile flirted on Jensen's lips.

"Like I should kiss you right now." He stepped forward, took my jacket from between my legs, and wrapped it around my shoulders, using the collar to draw me closer. "Who knew a jersey could be so sexy?"

His kiss was tender, full of suppressed passion. For a moment, because I worked tonight, I almost wanted to skip the game—almost.

After helping me into my coat, Jensen took my hand. "Ready?"

I nodded, unable to remove my stupid smile.

Jensen and I drifted hand in hand, following the signs to Section 235. I felt energized, watching the beaming, merch-adorned fans rushing through the halls. As I passed the concession stands reading the names, I relished their unique scents—the spiciness of Burrito Bar, the nutty aroma of Seattle's Coffee Cafe, the zing of ginger from Dumpling Express, and the comforting scent of bread from Substation, among many others.

He pulled to a stop. "Would you like to get some refreshments before we take a seat?"

"Um." Tapping my lips, I assessed the state of my stomach. "Let's find our seats first. I'm not hungry just yet."

"Sounds good." Jensen rechecked the tickets. "We're just over here." He led me through the entryway to Section 235 and down the stadium stairs toward the field.

I gaped at my surroundings—the blue and green seats, the cloudy open sky overhead, and the bleachers leading to the big screen backdropped by the Seattle skyline. My body felt electric, the view vastly different from my usual nosebleed section. The seats were so close to the sideline that as the athletes stretched, jumped, and threw the ball back and forth, I could make out each player's and staff's faces. I was lucky Jensen paid attention to where we were going, or I would have stumbled over the cement barrier between sections.

Tugging me along row *A*, Jensen stopped at seats ten and eleven. "This is us." He gestured at the chairs.

"I don't want to know how much you spent on these tickets." I unfolded the cold, hard plastic and sat.

Jensen followed, dipping his head. "I can't take the credit. They were a gift from one of my patients."

My heart glowed. "I hope I get patients like them one day." *Only three more semesters to go!*

Jensen squeezed my knee. "You will."

As the stadium filled, the energy amplified, and I couldn't sit still. By kickoff, I was on my feet, cheering with the crowd. I watched the Orcas' offense assemble along the Grizzlies' forty-one yard line. Despite the chill in the air, I wasn't cold watching the game. Between the numerous first downs, a fumble, and an interception by one of our players, I'd been too mesmerized to pay attention to the weather. At the beginning of the second quarter, Jensen nudged my side.

"Do you want a drink or something?" he yelled over the surrounding fans.

I stared into his warm, emerald eyes, noting his cheeks and nose were pink, probably from the cold. Jensen was too cute, and with the charge in my veins, I couldn't stop myself from giving him a kiss. When I broke away, seeing his cocky grin made me giddy.

"What was that for?"

I shrugged. "Just because." *You're everything I've*

dreamed of and more.

Jensen put his hands on my hips, drawing me closer. "Mmm, an excuse I'll take any time." He leaned forward and brushed his lips against mine again.

My body flushed with heat. Although, to his credit, despite his fingers digging into my skin, Jensen kept the kiss brief. While I understood the short lip-lock was because people surrounded us, I had to admit the disappointment still pinched.

"Sorry, I got sidetracked there." He thumbed over his shoulder toward the back of the stadium. "Did you want a drink or a snack?"

You'd make a great snack. "Sure, I could go for some food."

Jensen took my hand.

Following his delicious backside, I hiked the thirty steps to the concession area.

He stopped at the top. "What do you feel like?"

I scanned the area. The scent of grilled jalapenos made my stomach growl. Spotting the Burrito Bar, I pointed. "Mexican."

Jensen nodded. "Ooh, *barbacoa* does sound good."

After ordering my food, I stood to the side and waited for Jensen.

He paid the cashier and joined me among the small crowd also holding receipts.

I looped my arm through Jensen's and snuggled into his side. "I can't believe you got the hot salsa on your burrito."

His head reared back. "Why? Don't I seem like a 'hot salsa' kind of guy?"

Hell yeah, you do. I slapped him on his chest. "Oh, stop." *Please don't.*

Jensen turned and wrapped me in his arms. "I thought you'd have known I like hot things." He squeezed my backside. "I like you, don't I?"

The sound of blood pumping in my veins reverberated in my ears. Static pulsed under my skin. I toyed with the collar of Jensen's jacket. Feeling reckless and playful, I kicked the parental rating on our conversation up a notch. "I know you like hot things"—I gave him a forceful yank until our lips were only inches apart—"but what about spicy?" Warmth pooled low in my belly.

Jensen's grip tightened, and a low groan came from his throat. He stared at my lips but didn't claim them.

The tension of the moment grew thick, and the smell of his earthy cologne filled my senses. Despite the layers of padding and fabric I wore, I could feel every inch of his hard body against mine. Right then, the game didn't feel important anymore, and I longed to be somewhere—anywhere—alone with him.

"Number twenty-nine, *barbacoa* burrito and chicken bowl."

Jensen stepped back, his Adam's apple bobbing.

The shrill voice of the Burrito Bar worker repeated themselves.

I watched him grab the food, and his boyish grin and pink cheeks were almost too much to handle.

"Do you want to eat this at our seats or watch the game over there?" Jensen pointed to a high, thin, bar-like table where we could stand and eat our food with monitors displaying the game overhead.

If I were being honest, I would have told him we should take our food to go, and I could test his spicy limits, but I didn't. "We can eat over there."

Striding to the tall table, Jensen set the aluminum bowls on the bar.

I watched the game on the overhead TV and unwrapped my fork. The end of the second quarter flew by with the Orcas ahead, twenty-seven to thirteen.

The crowd rushed to the concession stands for halftime.

Jensen gathered our empty containers and carried them to the trash.

"Dr. Edwards!"

A young blond boy attacked Jensen's leg with a hug.

Squatting, Jensen squeezed the kid to his chest.

The little guy wrapped his arms around Jensen's neck, the puffy collar of the boy's jacket pressing against his round cheeks.

"Beckham! So great to see you!" Jensen held the kid at arm's length and gave his frame a once-over. "How's the asthma?"

"Great! I made it through my whole soccer game Thursday night without a single attack." The boy smiled a toothy grin, thumping his chest. "I even scored a goal."

Beckham's parents, both with matching white-blond hair, joined the little reunion.

Jensen stood but continued to focus on their son. "I'm so proud of you. The new treatment plan's working then?" He glanced at the boy's parents with raised brows.

The couple nodded and launched into praising Jensen with as much enthusiasm as their son.

Watching the foursome interact made my eyes sting. Jensen was so good with people—kids and adults.

Everyone appeared to love him, no matter what social event he attended—except for Kayla, who had her own issues.

"Hey, Autumn." Jensen's smile widened, and he beckoned me to join the group. "Come meet my favorite patient."

As I strode over, I felt my cheek flush. I extended a hand to the blue-eyed boy. "Hello, I'm Autumn."

"Hi, I'm Beckham."

His little hand gripped mine with a force I didn't think capable from such a small kid. I snickered. "I heard you tell Dr. Edwards you scored a goal. Great job!"

Beckham proceeded to give a play-by-play of the event with animated features.

I listened adoringly. *He is too cute.*

"Then the ball flew over the goalie's hands and into the net."

I held out my fist for Beckham to bump. "Wow, sounds like quite the game."

"It was." He tapped his knuckles against mine, then spread his fingers wide as he withdrew. "Hey, do you want to buy a team shirt?" Beckham motioned to Jensen. "Dr. Edwards already has one. You two could match."

Jensen ruffled the boy's hair. "I'm a huge Kent Koalas fan."

Such an innocent suggestion. I exchanged a proud look with Jensen before turning to Beckham. "I'd be honored to wear one of your team's shirts."

After arranging for Jensen to be my Kent Koala Tee's go-between, I followed Jensen as we returned to our seats.

Sitting, he took my gloved hand. "Thank you for making Beckham feel special. I know he ate it up, but don't feel obliged to buy the shirt."

I wanted to, though. The Orcas jersey would be in a frame by the weekend, so the soccer tee would be a great reminder of today. "It's fine. I can wear it to work."

"You mean at the tollbooth?" He didn't meet my gaze.

Jensen fished without being too obvious. I decided to put him at ease, but not without teasing him first. "I would never wear a Kent Koalas Tee on a Plus One date."

"Of course not." Jensen shook his head, his attention on the Orcas' Fin Girls dancing on the field. "That would be ridiculous."

My muscles tightened with the news I was about to share. "Yeah, it would be. Especially since I've quit."

Chapter 39

Jensen

"Wait, what?" My heart stuttered, and I faced Autumn head-on, ignoring the Orcas' game. "You quit companioning?"

She sunk her teeth into her bottom lip and nodded. "Yep. The day we decided to make our relationship official."

All the tension in my body evaporated, and the walls around my heart crumbled to dust. "You know I never expected you to quit your job." I held a halting hand. "Don't get me wrong, I'm grateful, but still. I know this is a huge financial sacrifice." Grasping I was the reason she'd left Plus One was a heady thing.

Autumn's gloved hand cupped my cheek. "True, but I'll figure it out. Besides, pretending to date other men when my heart belongs to you didn't feel right."

"I…I don't know what to say." Swallowing hard, I let out a breath, my heartbeat blaring like a siren in my ears, and the crowd around me melted away. Her admission was more than I dared hope for. If she had continued, while I wouldn't have stopped her, I honestly don't know if I could have coped, knowing she was out with other men, regardless of the contracted circumstances. Not to mention, if my family or friends had spotted her with a client, my reputation would have been ruined—again. But Autumn was worth the risk.

Thankfully, those possibilities were no longer a concern. The stadium slowly came back into focus, like adjusting the lens on a camera, and I met her gaze. "I'm so relieved. Is *thank you* an appropriate response?"

Autumn beamed. "No thanks necessary. I didn't do it for *you*. I did it for *us*."

Leaning in, I crushed my lips against hers, and for the millionth time, I wished we weren't in public. I didn't want to hold back from showing her my gratitude. But since we were surrounded by a crowd of people, I broke the kiss. Taking her hand from my cheek, I held it instead, and stared as I entwined my fingers with hers. "I'm not gonna lie—it killed me—the thought of you out with other guys." Even now, the thought made my stomach turn.

She ducked her head, peeking from under her lashes. "You know my contracts wouldn't have meant anything."

I grimaced and focused on tracing the seam of her glove with my thumbnail. "My contract wasn't supposed to mean anything, either."

Autumn shrugged. "You're right, Jensen. But..."

Knowing the implications behind that single word hanging in the air put my whole body on edge. Autumn must have noticed because she squeezed my hand and gave me an encouraging smile.

"You were different. Being with you felt natural. Your contract was the first time I could be myself instead of putting on a persona. Plus, from the moment I met you, I couldn't deny the instant chemistry, and I know you felt it, too. By the time you'd dropped me at The Stalker's Tango, I was captivated." Autumn leaned close and rested her forehead against mine. "But after my appendectomy, how concerned you were, and your adorable follow-up texts—that's when I started falling for you."

Warmth heated my insides and blocked out the icy air in the stadium. I breathed out a sigh of relief, the knot in my stomach loosening. "I knew I was a goner the first moment I laid eyes on you at the bar." I leaned in and tugged on her scarf, pulling her ear to my lips, and pictured that first night. "The way your hair fell over your sexy shoulders." I grazed my nose along her jaw. "The way the red dress clung to your curves."

The crowd erupted.

But I ignored the noise. "The no-nonsense way you handled our arrangement and the ambition regarding the nursing goals you'd set for yourself—all of it." I pushed her hair behind her shoulder and nibbled on her ear. "You were the whole package; yet, I wasn't allowed to make you mine."

Autumn's breath hitched.

A jolt of energy charged through my veins. "Now, you're saying you've quit Plus One, and you're falling for me? It feels too good to be true." I captured her mouth again, the heat within my core building, and I was desperate to be closer.

The crowd leaped to their feet, and the jersey-wearing man beside Autumn jostled into her side, breaking the kiss.

"You okay?" As popcorn rained from the fans in the row behind, I steadied Autumn with a hand.

"Yeah, I'm fine." She stood, brushing the kernels off her jacket and hair. "I guess we missed the touchdown." Laughing, she pointed at the Orcas' running back doing a celebratory dance in the end zone.

"Hmm, I hadn't noticed." As the extra point cleared, I brushed the popcorn from the back of her coat. Then, I shook out my scarf, shooting Autumn a sarcastic smile. "Maybe we should pay attention to the game?"

"I could"—she gave me a hip check—"if you'd stop being so distracting."

Autumn and I watched the rest of the game like the loyal fans we were, and when the final whistle blew, I buzzed with excitement. The Orcas won forty to twenty. On the way to my car, I shared my favorite plays and my projections for the rest of the season.

"Agreed. I don't think we'll have trouble getting into the playoffs, either, but we're relying too much on our defense right now." Autumn opened the passenger door and slid inside.

I settled behind the wheel, buckling my seatbelt. "Yeah, our offensive line needs to start pulling their weight." Extending my right hand over the console, I squeezed Autumn's thigh. "It's great how you love football, too."

A line formed between her brows. "I can't be your first girlfriend to like football."

I barked out a laugh. "Ha! Sadly, yes. You are." I'd dated a few girls who hadn't minded watching a game but weren't *into* football like Autumn. "Seeing your enthusiasm, knowing you're a genuine fan—not just because I am—feels good. Right." I wasn't sure I should have voiced that last part, but what I'd said was true. I liked being with Autumn. What I'd told her during halftime was the truth—Autumn was the whole package. Admiring her delicate profile, I couldn't believe how lucky I'd gotten. "What time does your shift start?" Stopping at the curb of her building, I glanced at the clock: 3:48 p.m. I hated that she worked tonight. Letting her go would be hard.

Autumn jutted her bottom lip in a pout. "Five p.m."

Damn. We were out of time. "Want me to walk you to the elevator?"

"Yes, please."

I exited the warmth of the car and met Autumn on the curb. Taking her hand, I stepped toward the apartment building.

Autumn yanked me to a stop. "You're not going to feed the meter?"

I shook my head. "Nah, I'll only be ten minutes." I turned toward the entrance.

Autumn stood firm. "But what if you get a ticket?" She put a hand over her heart. "I'd feel horrible."

I didn't want to waste time downloading an app and securing a ticket when I could be kissing her at her door. "It's my choice." I guided her fingers to my lips, kissing each one. "Besides, I won't." And I wouldn't care if I did get a parking violation, although it'd be a memorable first.

"You can't predict what might or might not happen." She withdrew her hand and wrapped her arms around my waist. "Let's say our goodbyes here."

I wanted to object and get her out of the cold, but this seemed to be a hill she was prepared to die on. Instead, I turned and leaned against the cold metal of my car, drawing her into my arms. "There, are you more comfortable if we stay here?"

"Well"—she rolled her eyes with a smile—"as comfortable as we can get right now."

I loved where her mind went. "Please tell me you

don't work tomorrow night, too?"

Autumn bit the tip of her gloves, removing each, then unwrapped the scarf around my neck. She ran a finger along my collarbone.

A dizzying current of electricity ran up my spine.

"Why?" A smile played at the corners of her mouth. "What do you want to do tomorrow night?"

As I captured her mouth with mine, I couldn't stop the primal growl emanating from deep within my chest. Autumn melted into me.

Undoing my jacket, she glided her hands over the front of my hoodie.

I worked my way down her jaw and neck to the hollow of her throat, following the edge of her clavicle with my tongue.

She gasped and arched against my chest.

I let my mouth trace her neck, just above the collar of her shirt.

A loud ringing blared from the direction of her pocket.

Stepping away, Autumn groped her coat with frenzied motions and wide eyes. "Stupid thing!" Finding her cell, she silenced the alarm. She gave a heavy sigh. "I gotta go."

I wanted to beg her not to, but that request would be irrational and unreasonable. Instead, I wrapped her in a final hug. "Okay." I sulked, but I couldn't help myself. "Text me later?"

"As soon as my shift ends at eleven thirty p.m."

I raised my brows, buoyancy filling my chest. "Is that too late for visitors?"

Autumn pecked my cheek and sauntered backward toward her building. "Maybe."

Chapter 40

Autumn

Monday morning, Jensen was abnormally quiet on the ride to his boss's house in Bellevue for the gratitude brunch, which wasn't like him. He'd blown up my phone last night during my tollbooth shift, and his texts this morning were flirty enough. Covertly, I reviewed the conversation thread on my phone. *Hmm.* Nothing in the texts indicated a reason for his silence. *Is he upset I didn't invite him over last night?* I reached over the middle console and let my left hand settle on Jensen's warm thigh.

He flashed a tight smile and turned the car onto West Lake Sammamish Parkway.

I squeezed. "You don't seem yourself. You okay?"

He cleared his throat. "I'm fine." Jensen shot a sideward glance. "Just not used to attending brunches at the chief of staff's house."

"Huh, I'm surprised. Dr. Anderson and Meg were pleasant at the awards dinner, and they seemed very impressed by you." The gleam in his boss's eye and his huge smile at the Best Doctor's dinner screamed nothing but pride in Jensen. "Haven't you attended numerous events with them before?"

Jensen slowed the car as he made a right onto Mallard Lane. "He appreciates my work ethic and my bedside manner." He cruised south along the street lined with orange-and-yellow-leaved trees. "It's not the same as a brunch at his home, though."

I shook my head. *How does he not see how great he is?* "You don't have anything to worry about. They clearly adore you."

Jensen lowered the volume on the stereo and squinted at the house numbers.

I held back a snort of laughter, knowing this was something everybody did, but the action made no sense.

His gaze darted between the map on his navigation screen and the residences. "If you say so, but I'm still intimidated."

I lifted my hand from his thigh and massaged the nape of Jensen's neck just above the collar of his white button-down shirt and navy blazer. His muscles were tight. "You'll be fine. You've got this."

He pulled into a driveway in front of a cream-colored, nondescript set of garages. Jensen exited and strode around the front bumper, opened the passenger door, and held out a hand.

After exiting the car, I stared at the four-car parking structure, then met Jensen's gaze with knitted brows.

He shrugged. "It must be more impressive on the inside." Jensen chuckled.

I covered my laugh with a hand.

Jensen led me past the side of the garage along a path to a set of frosted glass front doors. He rang the bell.

After a moment, Meg greeted Jensen and me with her wide approximation of a smile—the best her enhanced cheeks allowed.

"Jensen. Autumn. How nice to see you both again."

She stepped to the side, holding open the door with the exposed arm protruding from her asymmetrical gray blouse. "Come in. Everyone is downstairs."

With a hand on the small of my back, Jensen escorted me into the house.

I shrugged off my jacket, passing it into Meg's outstretched arms. The salty scent of ham and onions hung in the air, and I realized I was hungry.

Meg hung the coat on a peg by the door and gestured for me to enter.

I padded down a small flight of wooden steps of the split-level floor plan into a great room area. Stopping at the bottom of the stairs, I gaped at the back side of the house overlooking Lake Washington. Two sections of twelve-foot picture windows spanned the wall, one a step below where I stood in the living room and another by the dining area, which included a sliding door leading out to a small balcony. The view put the front of the house to shame.

Meg scooted past, batting her fake long lashes. "Gorgeous, right?" She leaned in. "It's the reason I made Gary buy this house."

I wasn't sure why Meg kept her voice low. Anyone could see the view made this property prime real estate.

"It's impressive." Jensen nodded.

She waved a hand in the air. "I'm sure yours is just as nice, living on Bremerton and all."

Jensen stretched his neck, loosening his collar. "Not quite, but I'm not complaining."

Meg opened her mouth, but the doorbell rang again. "Excuse me." She scuttled away.

Jensen nodded toward the kitchen.

I tracked the motion with my gaze and spotted

Kristine and Dan standing off to my left, pouring themselves drinks at the bar.

"Shall we go say *hi*?"

Agreeing, I followed Jensen over to his friends. "Hey, you two." I grabbed a couple of glasses sitting on a tray by the booze and poured two mimosas. "I'm so glad you're here." I glanced around, took a sip, letting the bubbles tickle my tongue, then leaned into Kristine. "It's nice to have friends at these small social events."

"Amen." Kristine squeezed my arm.

She looked absolutely stunning in a cashmere, cream sweater and pale-pink tulle, maxi skirt.

"Love your green jumpsuit, by the way."

"Thanks. I got it off Twice Buy." I smoothed a hand down the front of the polyester fabric, pleased with my bargain purchase. Without that website, I would never have afforded the outfits necessary for most of my Plus One occasions. And although I was no longer a companion, I was even more grateful for Twice Buy, knowing it would be essential now I was a part of Jensen's social circles.

"I love that site. They have the best selection."

"Agreed." I gestured around the room. "Can you believe this house?"

"I know." Kristine put a hand on her chest. "It's incredible. I would never have guessed this hid behind those dull garages out front."

"When we arrived, Jensen and I thought the same thing." I thumbed between Jensen and myself. "It shows how wrong first impressions can be." The house's twelve-foot ceilings, combined with the neutral colors and natural wood trim, were simple yet elegant. But the light fixture hanging over the couches took my breath away. The intricate silver structure resembled an illuminated dandelion puff.

Jensen cupped my elbow and jutted his chin at the couple in the entry. "That's Lisa Hall, head of the pediatrics department, and her husband, Gareth."

I reared my head. "Gareth?"

He smiled. "They're from England."

"Ahh." I nodded. "Got it." Gareth was so unusual. Hopefully, the name would stick.

"They've been in the States for about six years; this is her second hospital. The first was in Tacoma. She's a great boss. A no-nonsense kind of person who doesn't tolerate gossip." He slid an arm around my waist, leaning close. "She was one of the few people who wasn't impressed with Kayla's behavior."

Jensen's voice was full of reverence, and his breath tickled my ear. After learning what happened with his ex, I understood why he respected Lisa. I zeroed in on the petite brunette in the rosy-pink gingham dress under a white cardigan. Even though I hadn't even spoken to Lisa, I liked her already. "And her husband?"

"He's a stay-at-home dad of their two daughters." The corners of Jensen's eyes crinkled. "Lisa has a picture of him and the girls in matching crowns on her desk."

"Aww." I couldn't stop my heart from melting. Loving, attentive, present fathers who stayed home with their children were rare. "What a sweet family."

"Yeah, they're great."

The English couple spotted Jensen and excused themselves from Meg.

"Hey up, Jensen. Good to see you." A dimple sank into Lisa's cheek.

Gareth jutted out a vitiligo-spotted hand. "Dr. Edwards."

"I've told you before, call me Jensen." He shook the man's hand.

Gareth dipped his chin in a curt nod.

Lisa gave me once-over with a half-smile. "So, are you going to introduce us to your beautiful date?"

Her directness was endearing.

Jensen bowed his head, squeezing my hip. "Lisa, Gareth, this is my girlfriend, Autumn." He waved a hand at the couple. "Autumn, meet my boss and her husband."

"Pfft." Lisa swatted Jensen's arm. "Don't call me the b-word. We're not at work right now."

Jensen chuckled low in his chest, his ears turning pink. "Fair enough."

He looked so sweet that I thought I'd get a cavity.

Lisa readjusted her sweater to cover her ample cleavage. "So, you're the reason Jensen's been so nice at work recently?"

Jensen's back stiffened.

Lisa leaned close to my ear. "Whatever you're doing, keep it up."

She spoke loud enough that Jensen heard the compliment. I patted his chest, wafting his earthy cologne in my face, awakening all my senses. "Don't worry, I don't plan on going anywhere." I felt Jensen's muscles relax under my touch, and his expression softened. The heat from his chest radiated into my palm, and my body filled with a bottomless sense of peace and satisfaction. I was glad I broke my *no men before my BSN* rule. Missing out on Jensen would have been such a waste.

The sound of cutlery against a glass resounded through the room.

Meg and Gary stood at the bottom of the stairs by the entrance. Gary held a champagne flute and knife while Meg stood at his side, clutching her husband's bicep.

"Thank you all for coming." Gary's smile was wide. "Brunch is ready."

"Please take a seat." Meg directed everyone to the long white stone table with natural wood legs, grabbing two glass pitchers and placing them in the middle of the smooth marble surface. "Cucumber gin and tonic and strawberry limoncello Rosé sangria. Help yourselves while I grab the food."

I downed the rest of my mimosa, set the glass in the kitchen, and followed Jensen to the table. Dan, Lisa, and Jensen sat on one side, while Kristine, Gareth, and I sat opposite, with Gary at the head.

Meg hurried around the kitchen, grabbing serving utensils from random drawers.

Two women, who appeared to be in their early- to mid-twenties, in chef's coats and tight buns, materialized out of nowhere and helped Meg take the already prepared dishes out of the oven.

The three of them placed a broccoli-and-cheese quiche, a basket of blueberry muffins, a plate of apple crisp ginger scones, and some ham-and-potato hash on the table.

I salivated at the spread. Everything smelled delicious. *How much can I put on my plate without looking like a pig? Probably not enough.*

Jensen leaned forward, hand hovering over the pitcher with the floating, sliced, green vegetables. "I'm guessing since I know a dirty martini is your favorite, cucumber gin and tonic is your preference?"

Again, I felt touched Jensen remembered such a small detail from our first encounter. I shouldn't have been surprised. He'd been nothing but thoughtful since the day I'd met him. "Yes, please." I extended my goblet.

Jensen filled my glass halfway, then proceeded to pour himself some sangria.

Meg sat at the opposite end of the table from her husband. She nodded at Dr. Anderson.

Gary raised his glass. "I know I tease how my wife forced me to have this brunch, but in truth, I am grateful for all of you, and those who couldn't be here, for the hard work this team puts into making the pediatric unit the best in Seattle." He swooped his goblet toward the table.

I mimicked his gesture, then raised the glass to my lips.

"And I want to recognize Kristine, Autumn, and Gareth."

Biting my lip, I quickly lowered my glass and swiped my fingers across my mouth. Straightening, I gave my full attention back to Gary.

"Thank you for supporting my staff."

"Here, here." Dan toasted his wife with a huge smile.

Jensen shot me a wink.

Heat dotted my cheeks. Gary's praise felt undeserved. I hadn't dated Jensen for more than five minutes, and for most of that time, I'd resisted my feelings.

Gary set his glass on the table and clapped his

hands once. "Now dig in."

I limited myself to a single serving of hash and one blueberry muffin. Taking my first bite of the savory portion of my brunch, I suppressed a moan. The crunch of the bell peppers was just the right addition to the salty ham and sausage. I needed to convince my stomach I was full so I wouldn't take seconds.

The discussion over brunch flowed easily. Each doctor shared stories about their favorite inspirational patients, and my conviction for my chosen profession increased with every tale.

When brunch was finished, the two kitchen staff cleared the table.

Meg encouraged everyone to relocate to the living room.

I perched on the edge of the velvety, soft, tan leather couch.

Jensen sat on my right.

Kristine and Dan were on his right at the end of the sofa.

Dr. Anderson, Meg, Lisa, and Gareth each took a club chair on the other side of the stone coffee table.

Dan continued the conversation by transitioning to when he extracted a pair of fashion doll shoes from a kid's nose.

I cringed, my heart going out to that kid, while at the same time wondering how the tiny heels fit into their nostril in the first place.

Lisa held up a finger. "No, no, no. That's nothing. Back in Tacoma, I had a patient who ate her own hair. Her condition got so bad, I had to surgically remove the hairball from the little girl's stomach because she couldn't eat or digest her food."

I gagged, covering my mouth. These examples were why I didn't want to go into internal medicine.

Meg dipped her head and held up a hand. "Okay, we just ate. No more gross medical emergencies."

Gary and Dan chuckled.

I joined in with their laughter, grateful I wouldn't have to hear another nauseating story on a full stomach.

Jensen pivoted the conversation by recounting his time helping treat kids in The Gambia. Halfway through his story, the front door burst open.

I felt like my heart stopped, and a cold sweat engulfed my body.

Josh Anderson swayed in the foyer, stumbling toward the stairs and slamming the front door.

Dammit! How could I not have put this together sooner? He and Dr. Anderson shared the same sharp jaw and heavy brows. But when I'd first met Gary, Anderson was such a common surname, I hadn't given it a second thought. Now, noticing the similarities between the two, I wondered how I could have been so stupid—Josh was Gary's son. I let my hair fall forward, shielding my face from my former client. Nerves clawed their way through my stomach. Watching Josh sway and stagger, I knew he was completely intoxicated. If I were lucky, then Gary and Meg would usher him out of the room before I was recognized.

Dr. Anderson marched up the steps to the landing, steadying Josh with a hand on his arm. "Son, we've got company. Maybe you should head to your room. I'll send Savannah up with some coffee."

As Josh scanned his surroundings, his head bobbled. "Hey, it's Dan and his super-hot wife." He leaned into his father. "She's out of his league."

His attempt at a whisper failed. I was sure the neighbors could have heard him.

Red flushed Kristine's face.

A muscle in Dan's jaw flexed.

"Enough, Josh." Gary maneuvered his son toward the upper staircase.

Josh tripped to the side. "What? It's true! Everyone knows it—except Kristine."

"Move." Gary shoved Josh.

"Wait!" Josh grabbed the banister and swiveled back. "Who's Jensen's date? That's not Kayla, is it?"

Cursing under my breath, I dry swallowed and turned to face the window. *This can't be happening!* I felt a bead of sweat trickle down my back.

"No, Josh. Her name is Autumn, Jensen's new girlfriend." *Why the hell did Gary tell him my name? I'm doomed!*

"Autumn? I thought I recognized her!"

Josh pointed in my direction like a sailor who'd just spotted land. *No! No! No! No! No!*

"She's an escort. She works at…"—he pinched his eyes shut and snapped his fingers—"Plus One!"

Dammit! The cat's out of the bag. How the hell would I get out of this one?

Chapter 41

Jensen

As I watched my boss manhandle his son, pushing him upstairs to his room after his outburst, I couldn't stop my stomach from bottoming out. *How the hell does he know she worked at Plus One?*

"Shut your mouth, Josh. You don't know what you're saying. Get into your room." Gary grasped both of his son's arms, shoving him forward.

Yes, please! Get him out of here before he makes more of a scene. The situation is still salvageable. I was suddenly aware of the damp perspiration seeping into my shirt.

Josh held firm. "Stop, Dad! I'm telling you, it's her!" He held out a hand in Autumn's direction, his brows lowered. "She's the same chick Brett dared me to hire for my birthday."

Wait! Josh was one of Autumn's clients? I froze as an icy sensation speared down my spine.

"Don't be ridiculous, son." Gary shielded Josh from our view. "You're the only one in this room pathetic enough to hire a date."

Gary's words stung, and I almost missed the side-eye he shot Autumn. *Great! Gary believed his son, or, at the very least, he had doubts.* I was such an idiot. Digging my fingers into my palms, I felt my nails pinch my skin and winced. Because of my feelings for

Autumn, I jumped into a relationship without thinking through the consequences. I should have known an encounter with a former client was a possibility. But even then, I would never have expected the confrontation to happen at my boss's house—and with his son, no less.

Josh shook his head and barked a laugh. "Wow, I didn't realize Jensen was so desperate."

Everyone's gaze was on me, and a cold sweat trickled down my back. I swallowed, my throat thick with embarrassment. *What a nightmare!* I wanted to say something to cut the tension building in the room, but I couldn't decide if sticking up for Autumn would help or make the situation worse. The last thing I wanted was another Kayla debacle.

"Just so you know, Jensen, she won't put out. I tried. It's against"—Josh made rabbit ears with his fingers—"company policy."

Meg bolted to her feet. "Josh!"

"You're done." Gary forced his son up the stairs, almost dragging his drunken form, and shoved him down the hall, muttering profanities at Josh the whole way.

I noticed Meg's chest heaved just as hard and fast as mine.

She cleared her throat. "I'm sorry, everyone." Meg smiled at each of our stunned faces in turn. "He's been under a lot of stress with his Life Guru workshops."

Kristine gave me a pointed look, jerking her head toward Autumn.

The stillness radiating from the cushion beside me was hard to ignore, but Kristine was right. I needed to say something, given I'd frozen during the entire interaction. Licking my lips did nothing to relieve the dryness permeating my mouth, but I forced a smile. Afraid to see Autumn's expression, I took her hand and focused on my coworkers. "Josh doesn't know what he's talking about. Autumn would never…she's not…" I felt her rip her hand away.

"Would never what, Jensen?" Autumn spoke the words through tight lips with narrowed eyes.

The disgust in her tone made my insides squirm. I opened and closed my mouth like a fish, but no words came out.

She sat straight. "You don't have anything to say?"

Feeling unmoored with my erratic heartbeat in my ears, I felt my head spin. The overhead light became a spotlight fixed on me. I couldn't think of anything to say that wouldn't sound damning.

"I knew it!" Autumn's nostrils flared. "I knew you weren't okay with what I did for a living."

The hair on the back of my neck prickled, and I felt my body go rigid. "I thought you quit."

Autumn threw her hands in the air, rolling her head and scoffing. "I did, Einstein. Now, you're just splitting hairs."

"Look, I don't even know what I've done wrong here." I kneaded my forehead.

"You're embarrassed I was a companion."

I felt the vein in my temple throb and barked a one-syllable laugh. "This has nothing to do with Plus One. It's about Josh and everything going down in front of my boss and co-workers." I waved a hand around the room, and my movements were jerky, my anger and humiliation bubbling over like a pot releasing steam. "Are you telling me you're okay that one of your previous clients just waltzed in and embarrassed us in front of everyone?"

Autumn stood and planted one hand on her hip, glaring as she hovered above me, the other hand pointed in my face. "Embarrassed *us*, or embarrassed *you*?"

All of the above. I ground my teeth, trying to regulate my breathing and sort my thoughts.

"Jensen"—Dan nudged my thigh—"quit while you're ahead, man."

Frowning at my best friend, I stood. I had to find a way to salvage my predicament. "Embarrassed *us*. I care about your integrity, too." I reached for Autumn's arm.

She maneuvered out of the way. "My integrity was never compromised."

I released a breath slowly through my nose, counting to ten. "Look, I don't care what you *used* to do, but you've got to see this from my side." I couldn't think of one man who would want to admit his girlfriend used to be a companion. Even though I trusted my coworkers in the room, Josh was a loose cannon, and I had no doubt this would get back to the staff at the hospital. "I knew you had ex-clients, but I didn't think we'd bump into them around every corner."

A crack rang in my ears. I couldn't feel my face at first, but then a rush of throbbing heat flooded my cheek, and a shock wave jolted through my system. *Autumn slapped me.* Bile rose in my throat. *What must my friends and boss think?*

Autumn dropped her hand and stalked toward the front door with tears in her eyes.

Nausea roiled in my stomach. "Autumn, wait." She couldn't leave. We'd barely become official. This couldn't be how the date ended.

Autumn didn't stop. Glancing over her shoulder, she grabbed her coat. "Screw you, Jensen."

The front door slammed, echoing throughout the large space. I stared at the reverberating oak-and-glass surface. My brain hesitated, but I sensed my heart would force my feet to move. I was torn. *If I don't go after her, could I ever make things right?* The back of my neck seared with the gazes I knew were boring into me. I pinched the bridge of my nose, my heart plummeting. First things first—deal with the here and now. I needed to smooth things over with my boss because living in a fishbowl at work again was out of the question. Turning from the bottom of the stairs, I dropped my gaze to the floor. My lungs felt paralyzed. I didn't want to see the looks on my friends' and colleagues' faces. *What the hell do I say?*

"Jensen!"

I cringed at the accusatory edge in Kristine's tone.

"Could you *be* a bigger jerk?"

I snapped my focus toward Dan's wife. The scowl on her face pinned me to the spot, but I couldn't think—like all the roads in my head were barricaded.

Meg shook her head. "Very disappointing, Jensen."

Lisa shrugged, nodding along with Meg's words.

I glanced between the three women, feeling as transparent as plastic wrap. Desperate to justify my behavior, I grasped the first excuse that came to mind. "Come on. You have to admit nobody likes confronting their partner's ex." My words even sounded lame to my own ears.

"Please." Kristine dragged out the word. "That's not even close to this situation. Josh wasn't her ex-boyfriend." Her eyes narrowed. "He was an *ex-client*."

My friend's obvious judgment was like poison thumping through my veins, infecting my insides with guilt. Kristine was right, but my pride forced me to defend myself. "I know, but—"

"But nothing, Jense." Kristine huffed. "We all have a past. I just thought you were better than this." She gestured at the front door and then the room in general.

The fight fizzled out of me like a flat soda, and I let my shoulders drop. Shame churned in my stomach. *I have no excuse for my behavior.* "You're right. I was an idiot." I ran a hand through my hair. "But after the whole fiasco with Kayla, I stupidly worried what you all would think if you knew Autumn previously worked as a companion. Whereas I should have been focused on Autumn and her feelings." I dropped onto the entry's hard, wooden step and rested my head in my hands. I acted so selfishly. The least I could do after everything they'd just witnessed was to come clean. Taking a deep breath, I pushed my pride aside. "I met Autumn when I hired her for the Best Doctor's dinner. But I lied about my relationship because I worried the truth would be another strike against me—more ammunition for gossip around the hospital." Rumors were still possible, but I'd brought them on myself this time.

Dan's brow wrinkled. "Wait, Autumn's not your girlfriend?"

"She is." I ran a hand down my face as the reality of the situation sunk in. "Or at least she was. We'd hit it off after the ceremony and, not long ago, made our relationship official." I couldn't fathom she'd take me back after how I'd acted. Autumn deserved someone better. My stupid ego ruined everything. I massaged my temples, trying to alleviate the pounding in my head.

Meg strode to my side and put a hand on my shoulder. "Oh, hon. Gary and I know all about Plus One. Josh wouldn't shut up when his contract was canceled because of the no-sex policy." She rolled her eyes and motioned toward the upstairs, where her husband and son were sequestered in one of the bedrooms. "There's nothing disreputable about what Autumn does." She laughed. "It's no worse than when I worked at High Beams putting Gary through medical school."

Dan's eyes widened. "*You* worked at High Beams?"

Kristine slapped her husband's arm. "Shush."

"What?" Dan gave a wide-eyed shrug.

"Let her finish." Kristine settled into the couch and gestured at Meg.

"Yes, Dan. I worked at High Beams." Meg puffed out her chest. "And while maintenance has cost me a fortune, I've still got it."

"Yeah, you do, honey." Gary descended the steps, stopping at the bottom behind where I sat. "Where's Autumn?"

Meg pointed at the front door. "She left, and I can't say I blame her." She pursed her lips and shot me a squinty glare.

Gary's brow furrowed, giving me the same look. "How's she getting home? Didn't she come with you?"

Rubbing at the ache in my chest, I let my shoulders fall. I was even more of a jerk than I thought. As I willed back angry tears, I squinted at the blue sky through the windows in the ceiling, warm sunlight caressing my cheeks. "Great. Autumn's so mad she'd rather walk home than get inside a car with me." *I'm no better than Josh.*

"You like her, don't you?"

Kristine's soft tone was like a punch in the gut. "More than you know."

"Enough to swallow your pride?"

My heart caved in. "Of course." *But will that be enough?*

"Well then, what are you waiting for?" Kristine flung an arm at the door. "Go!"

"Yes, go!" Meg echoed.

"Get out of here!" Lisa made a shooing motion with her hands.

Hope filled my chest. If these three women thought I still stood a chance with Autumn, maybe they were right. Standing, I thanked Meg and waved at the others before sprinting up the steps past Gary and out the front entrance.

The crisp fall air filled my lungs and allowed the icy chill to clear my head as I raced along the sidewalk leading toward the street. "Autumn!" I rounded the side of the garage, scanning the front of the house. "Autumn!" The driveway was empty, except for the cars. I jogged along the street toward the highway, the dead leaves crunching under my feet. Gary's road was relatively secluded, but I was sure Autumn wouldn't have waited for a ride where I could have found her. When she left, she made it clear she wanted to be anywhere but around me. Rounding the bend leading to West Sammamish Parkway, I stopped. The road was empty. A void swallowed my chest. She was gone.

Chapter 42

Autumn

I slammed the door to the rideshare that drove me home from Dr. Anderson's and stood on the sidewalk in front of my building. Blinking, I pushed away the stinging behind my eyes. Just a few more minutes, and I could let the dam break. Losing my control over a guy in the back of some stranger's car that reeked of weed wasn't my style. I wanted to be in the solace of my bedroom before I fell apart.

As I opened my front door, I couldn't stop my bottom lip from trembling. Alyssa's room was dark and empty, as was the apartment. I was grateful I wouldn't have to face her. Flipping on the lights, I allowed the floodgates to open. Dark clouds gathered over the city, blocking out the sunlight coming from the window—the dismal weather was a good analogy for my mood.

When Jensen became my boyfriend, I believed he wasn't bothered by my work for Plus One. But after the way he behaved at Gary and Meg's, his attitude implied I was wrong, and my previous occupation embarrassed him. I understood why Jensen didn't want his coworkers to know, but his fear didn't excuse his lack of a backbone. He could have defended me or, at the very least, kept his mouth shut. "How could I have been so stupid?" Venting my frustrations out loud always helped me process. "If I'd just stuck to my original plan, 'no men until my BSN'"—I made sarcastic air quotes—"none of this would have happened. But noooo, I followed my stupid heart again." I yanked off my coat and threw it over one of the kitchen chairs. Gripping the wood, I glared at the table. "He even met my dads." I threw my hands in the air. "What would I tell *them*? Jensen was embarrassed of me?" Imagining the looks of shock and disapproval on my dads' faces filled my stomach with unease. "I wouldn't put it past Dad to hire some mobster and put a hit out on Jensen." While the idea was over the top, the thought did lift my spirits a fraction.

Stalking to my room, I flung my heels at my closet. As they hit with a *thunk* and dented the back wall, I didn't even flinch. I groped for the zipper at the side of my jumpsuit, yanking the metal tab, and shoving the green polyester off my shoulders and past my hips. When I could step out of the pile of fabric, I flung the outfit toward my hamper with my foot. Next, my bra, but like my jumpsuit, the lightweight fabric didn't quite make the entire distance to the basket in the corner, but I didn't care.

I opened my dresser and grabbed some sweats, yanking them on before flopping face-first onto my bed. After a few moments, I couldn't breathe through the overstuffed scatter cushions anymore, and I rotated my head. The angry tears subsided, but the pain in my chest wouldn't let up. Rolling onto my back, I rubbed my palms into my eyes, curbing the ache in my sockets. I was naïve to think a confrontation with one of my previous clients wouldn't be inevitable at some point. Working at a companion agency for almost a year increased the odds with each contract. When I did consider the possibility, I assumed I would bump into one client in front of another, and neither of them would want to out the other. Never in my wildest dreams had I imagined a client would break the Plus One confidentiality clause. Sadly, I'd underestimated Josh. I filled my lungs, ignoring the tightness in my chest, and exhaled.

The moment I saw him at Gary's, I knew I was in trouble. Josh's behavior wasn't surprising, though, considering how he'd acted during our contract—just like the pompous rich kid he was. What I didn't expect was Jensen's reaction. He had no problem pursuing a relationship while I was still a companion. So, why did my past matter now? And did he have to be such a jerk? Then again, I was at his boss's house with his best friend and colleagues. If roles were reversed, would I have behaved any better?

When I heard Josh point out his connection to me, I witnessed sheer panic on Jensen's face, and I should have been warned his brain had shut off. But did that excuse Jensen's behavior? I silently replayed the morning's events, feeling fresh tears leak out of the corners of my eyes and puddle in my ears. I rubbed the salt water away.

I heard my phone ping a text alert from the other room. Sighing, I glanced at the clock: twelve thirty p.m. The message was most likely from Lilly dropping me today's location pin for her contract. I pulled one of my satin throw pillows over my face. Two minutes passed, and my phone dinged again, sending my brain into overthinking mode. What if the text wasn't Lilly? What if the message was Papi? With a groan, I hauled myself off the bed, knowing he'd send out a search party if I didn't answer. Entering the kitchen, I dug my cell out of my jacket pocket.

—Living it up again today! Another client chose Buffet Garden—

Poor Lilly. While she didn't need my help, she was a germaphobe, and the all-you-can-eat buffet restaurant would test her limits. She was a diligent companion, though, and pushed past her fears for the job. I felt my phone vibrate in my grip, and another message appeared on my screen.

—I might or might not have primed myself with a mimosa before calling my rideshare—

Hitching up a cheek, I couldn't quite finish the smile. If anyone would understand my situation, Lilly would. I tapped her contact picture.

"Hey, gurl!"

She'd answered on the first ring.

"If you're calling to tease me about snotty hands or spittle in my food, I'm hanging up now."

"No." I shook my head, even though she couldn't see me. While normally I would have given her a hard time, I couldn't muster the effort. I just wanted to talk. "It's not about that."

"What's wrong?"

Lilly must have picked up on my melancholy tone because her question contained a protective edge that soothed my wounded ego. The tears began again in earnest. "You were right. Jensen couldn't get past Plus One." Feeling numb, I flopped into one of the hard kitchen chairs during the beat of silence that followed my admission.

"He's a moron!"

I could hear Lilly's heavy breathing on the other

end of the line. She was mad, and my heart lodged in my throat. She was such a good friend.

"What happened? I need the whole story—pictures, diagrams, everything."

Sniffling, I swatted away my tears with the back of a hand. "I don't know where to start."

"I've got twenty minutes; start at the beginning."

As I recounted what happened with Josh and Jensen's response, which ended with me storming out of the Anderson's house and running toward the highway to call a ride, I sensed a heaviness in my limbs.

"Jealous much? It's not like we're escorts. He was one of your clients; he knows how it works. And he's the reason you quit Plus One."

Lilly continued her defensive rant, and while I wasn't taking all of her words in, I couldn't deny the warm sensation in my heart. She had my back. Lilly wasn't wrong, though. I thought I'd learned from Matteo that I deserved better. Apparently, the lesson hadn't sunk in. *Never again.* "Thanks, Lil. I love you; you always know what to say." I stood to retrieve a paper towel and mopped my face.

A loud knock sounded at the door, and I jumped. "Lil, shh. Someone's at my door."

"How did they get past the gate? Who is it? A neighbor?"

"I don't know." No one rang for me to buzz them into the building. Although, someone could have simply held the door for my visitor. This was one of those times when I wished I'd let Dad install a hallway camera.

"Autumn!" Jensen's voice resounded alongside his

pounding.

"It's him." I kept my voice low as a combination of heat and cold trickled down my spine. "What do I do?"

"Don't you dare open that door!"

Lilly's voice was stern. I chewed on my thumbnail and padded toward the peephole. "But what if he's here to apologize?" I felt my chest glow at the prospect but was quickly extinguished by my hurt and humiliation.

"Sure. That's easy to do now that he doesn't have an audience. The real issue is, he shouldn't have anything to apologize for in the first place."

Lilly had a point. I peered through the peephole, my heart in my throat.

Jensen stood, slumped against the door, braced by his left forearm, and pounding with the other, his head bowed. "Autumn, please? I'm truly sorry."

The remorse in Jensen's tone was evident.

"I know what you're thinking right now, and don't you dare."

Lilly's whisper in my ear was like a shoulder angel. As I watched Jensen's warped image rub a fist over his eyes, I felt as though my heart splintered. "But, Lil…"

"No, Autumn. Don't you remember when you said Matteo did this, too? Nothing but heartache will come if you open that door."

I couldn't really compare Jensen to Matteo. The only thing the two men had in common was Jensen's behavior this morning. While Matteo was controlling, selfish, and egotistical, Jensen merely spoke without thinking.

Lilly huffed. "Autumn Summer Haze, I know you're buckling. Stand strong."

My nerves were taut like one of Papi's guitar strings. One wrong pluck and I would snap. I had too many conflicting emotions to make a rational decision. Lilly, however, came from an outsider's perspective. *You better be right, Lil.* With all the strength I could muster, I squared my shoulders, staring at the entrance to my apartment. "Go away, Jensen." *Dammit!* My tone sounded weak.

"Autumn, please? I'm begging you. Allow me to apologize." His voice cracked.

I felt my heart stall.

"Autumn."

Lilly's voice crackled in my ear. Thank goodness, I had her on the line, or I'd have caved. "No, Jensen. Just go." I choked on the last word, a sob building in my throat.

"Is that what you *really* want?"

Hearing the devastation in his pitch about did me in. I sank to my knees and watched my tears dot the wood laminate. My arms dropped to my sides, and I let my phone thud onto the floor, steeling my resolve. "Yes."

Chapter 43

Jensen

Behind me, the door to my patient's room closed, and I let my smile and shoulders fall simultaneously. The effort of putting on a show in the hospital for the last two days was exhausting. I was lucky I hadn't worked the day following the gratitude brunch. After my catastrophic blunder at Dr. Anderson's on Monday and Autumn's refusal of my apology, I was in no shape to see anyone, let alone help ailing kids. I spent the day surviving on toaster pastries and caffeine while watching football in my sweats. "Here's Eisley's chart." I dropped it, letting the clipboard clatter onto the nurses' station counter.

Nicole scowled from over her glasses. "Someone's still in a foul mood."

I scrubbed a hand through my hair. "Sorry. You don't deserve to be on the receiving end." I wasn't mad at Nicole. I was mad at myself. If only I had stuck up for Autumn or said something different, anything would have been better than what happened.

"Maybe if you told me what's bothering you, then I wouldn't want to strangle you with the stethoscope around your neck." She made a circling motion with a finger, pursing her full, dark lips.

Nicole was one of my favorite nurses. Most days, her bright, sunny disposition matched her smile full of straight white teeth, which contrasted beautifully against her rich brown skin. Knowing I upset her hurt my heart, but admitting my blunder was just too humiliating. Again, I was a coward, but I didn't want Nicole to think less of me. I couldn't imagine she wouldn't if I told her. "Sorry, Nicole. I'll be better next time." And I vowed I would.

With a half-hearted smile, I trudged to the break room, hoping another caffeine hit would lift my mood. I opened the door, and when I spotted Dan sprawled on the light brown couch, an arm over his eyes, I came to a halt. I debated leaving, but the pull from the hypnotic aroma of the coffee was too strong, so I crept past. After the brunch fiasco, I'd avoided contact with everyone, including Dan. While I knew my best friend wasn't one for holding grudges, I wasn't in the mood to hear the secondhand lecture from Kristine. Not yet, anyway. Stepping to the counter, I poured my coffee, added some cream and sugar, then tiptoed toward the door.

"Not even a *hello*?"

I squeezed my eyes shut for a moment before turning. *No avoiding him now*. "Hey, Dan."

"You look horrible."

Between my disheveled hair, the bags under my eyes, and two-day beard growth, his observation was spot on. "I know. Feel horrible, too." Rounding the front of the couch, I shoved his feet off the sofa and slumped beside my friend.

He righted himself. "Maybe because you messed up—big time."

I winced. "Wow. Don't sugarcoat it."

"If Kristine knew I was talking to you, she'd be

mad."

I should have figured she'd tell him to avoid me—womanly solidarity and all—but I couldn't blame her. I deserved her wrath. "Then I shouldn't come to the game night this Sunday?" I sipped my coffee, relishing the bitter taste on my tongue.

Dan barked a laugh. "Not unless you figure out a way to bring Autumn."

I set my cup on the coffee table and rested my head in my hands. "If I knew how to get her there, I would." Replaying the scene at Autumn's door made my lungs feel tight—like I was out of oxygen. I'd begged for forgiveness, but she still turned me away. My heart twisted, and I rubbed at my chest.

"You've tried to apologize?" Dan stretched his arms over his head.

"Yes, the same day as the brunch. But she wouldn't even open the door—didn't even want to listen." I felt helpless like I was adrift in a boat without an oar.

He cracked his knuckles. "What about calling her or texting?"

Leaning back, I shook my head. "I'm pretty sure she's blocked my number."

A frown appeared on Dan's forehead. "Dude, how do you know?"

"Well, when I tried calling, I got her voicemail. When I texted"—each of the twenty-something times—"the screen didn't even show the little writing saying *read* or *delivered*."

Dan nodded, drawing his lips into a hard line. "Hmm, then what are you gonna do?"

I scoffed. "What can I do?" Standing, I rounded the couch and paced the length of the room. "If she's done with me, do I even have a choice?" I stopped and gripped my hair, leaning against the coffee counter, feeling defeated. My relationship with Autumn had only just started. It couldn't be over so soon. "I don't know what got into me at Gary's." What I said wasn't entirely true. Thanks to Kayla, I'd become paranoid about the hospital knowing my personal business. So, when Autumn's previous profession came to light, as did my involvement with Plus One, I jumped to the worst-case scenario—more rumors.

"Josh Anderson; that's what got into you." Dan retrieved his stethoscope from the coffee table and looped the instrument around his neck. "He'll get under anyone's skin."

"You're damn right." *That douche ruined everything.* Rubbing my eyelids with my fingers, I was still shocked at how fast I'd fallen for Autumn. Because even though I'd only known her a short time, she'd been the only woman I'd connected with in a long while. "Still. I overreacted. I blew it. I have no choice but to move on." Dread washed over my body, coating me like a second skin.

"Ha! Good luck."

Dan's tone was heavy with sarcasm, but he was right—I needed all the luck I could get. I'd thought of nothing but Autumn since the day I'd met her; getting over this relationship would take forever.

"When Kristine's forgiven you"—he rose from the couch and straightened his lab coat—"I'll let you know."

"Tell her I tried, will ya?" I grabbed my now-cold coffee, drained the cup in the sink, and tossed the container into the trash can. "And if she's got any advice, let me know." I couldn't think of any way to win Autumn back or even get her to listen. If anyone could devise a plan, it would be Kristine.

"Will do." Dan gave a two-finger salute and stepped into the corridor.

I opened the door and patted down my hair. Three steps down the hallway, I spotted Lisa talking to Nicole. I hesitated. Taylor's chart was at the nurses' station, but so was Lisa. I was embarrassed to face her after she'd witnessed my display at Gary's. *Swallow your pride. You brought this on yourself. Face the music.* I squared my shoulders, took a deep breath, and forged ahead. Taylor couldn't wait forever.

"If and when he's ready to tell you why he's in a bad mood, he will." Lisa's toe tapped against the linoleum.

As I approached the two women, I didn't need to have heard Nicole's question to know what she'd asked my department head. My ears warmed. *Here we go again.*

Lisa must have spotted me first because she shuffled some papers, and I heard, "Let it go," hiss out of the corner of her mouth.

"Ladies." I could hardly get the word past the tightness in my throat. Grabbing the needed chart, I marched toward Taylor's room around the corner from the nurses' station. When I could no longer see the women, I paused and sagged against the wall. How could I have gotten myself in this predicament again? Sweat trickled down my back, and my hands trembled. Gossip was the one thing I'd wanted to avoid after Kayla. Yet here I was, cowering in the hallway as Nicole fished for information about my personal life for the second time in less than two years. Then again, if I controlled my emotions, none of this would be an issue. But I couldn't because I was heartbroken.

I wished I could go back to Monday and have a do-over—I would have defended Autumn and behaved better. I pinched the bridge of my nose. The situation was more complicated, though. Since Monday, I'd given the brunch a lot of thought. Even when I imagined a scenario where I'd come to Autumn's defense, none of my projected outcomes worked any better than where I'd ended up. If I'd admitted my relationship with Autumn began with a Plus One contract, then I'd have outed her as a companion, which wasn't my secret to tell. I'd signed a non-disclosure, for Pete's sake.

But when I'd stayed quiet, I was guilty of not defending Autumn, and Josh's accusations stood like an elephant in the room. However, if I'd acted surprised, that, too, would have been hurtful and outed Autumn. Regardless of how I'd handled the situation, I had no excuse for my jealous behavior and clumsy words. Both reactions fueled the fire that consumed my relationship with Autumn and reduced it to ashes. Shaking my head, I couldn't win or see a way to come back from my mistake. I felt my phone vibrate in my pocket, and I hurried to check the message on the off chance the text was from Autumn. I tensed; no such luck. My mother's timing was impeccable.

—Don't forget the pie for Thanksgiving dinner next Thursday. Supercenter is open twenty-four hours. Smiley face emoji—

I leaned my head against the wall. First the nurses, now my mother. This day just got better and better.

Chapter 44

Autumn

My apartment intercom buzzed. I stared at my bedroom door; I didn't have enough energy to get out of bed or even care who insistently rang. I didn't know if Alyssa was home, but I low-key hoped she wasn't and whoever was outside my apartment would go away. The buzzing continued. This person wasn't giving up, so if I had to guess, I'd say they were either Jensen, Papi, or Lilly at my door—none of whom I wanted to see at the moment.

After a few seconds of glorious silence, I felt my chest loosen, and I sank back into the safety of my down comforter. The bedroom door flung open. *What the hell?* I felt like my heart nearly jumped out of my ribcage.

Lilly entered, gaze darting every which way, then released a breath with a frown. "Oh my gosh. You're worse than I thought." She marched to the side of the bed and flung back my covers, sending wadded-up tissues scattering to the floor. "Eww. Are you lying in piles of your own snot?"

I watched my eyes glaze over with fresh tears. "Yes, I'm disgusting." I fumbled for the toilet paper—the tissue box ran out days ago—and blew my nose. While I was grateful Lilly loved me enough to utilize my spare key and check on me since I'd called out of work all week and ignored everyone's texts and calls, I didn't want her here—wallowing was a one-person job.

"Well, let's put an end to that." She tugged on my arm, hoisting me out of bed. "I've let you sulk for a week, which is more than enough. Go get in the shower."

I don't want to. Crossing my arms, I glared and stood my ground.

Lilly pursed her lips and shoved my shoulder, pushing me toward the door.

I tripped over the clothes and empty candy bar wrappers on the floor. "Why do I need to shower?" My voice was rough, not having spoken much in the past seven days. "School doesn't start again for another week—after Thanksgiving." My plan was to sit in the dark, eat ice cream, and watch chick flicks to make myself cry until I left for turkey dinner with my dads.

Lilly grabbed my trash can and a magazine, herding the paper snot balls into the bin. "Because I'm taking you out. I should have done this days ago—right after you called and told me what happened." She paused, pointing a finger. "It's time to get over Jensen."

I let my face crumple. "But I'm not ready yet." I knew I sounded immature, but I didn't care. Getting dressed up and going out to a bar sounded like a terrible idea. Surely, I deserved to bask in misery for a few more days.

"Wallowing isn't an option. This behavior"—she swatted another wadded up tissue into the trashcan and shuddered—"isn't healthy."

"You can't make me." I planted my feet and tugged on my baggy sweatshirt. A peaceful protest was an appropriate response, right?

Lilly narrowed her eyes.

I braced myself for judgment.

"You know how this works. You can make it easy on yourself and get in the shower of your own fruition, or you choose the hard way, and we can argue for another ten minutes until I force you under the water. What's it gonna be?"

She wouldn't let this go. Lilly was so pushy. "Ugh! Fine!" I balled my hands into fists. "I hate you."

Lilly turned up her nose, straightening the covers on my bed. "I hate you more."

I stormed through the door.

An hour later, I climbed into a rideshare behind Lilly to head downtown. Zipping my jacket over my white blouse and skinny jeans, I blew into my hands, rubbing them together for warmth. The crisp November air was colder than usual, making me even more reluctant to be out. "I can't believe you convinced me to do this."

Lilly smirked, staring out the window. "I can't believe you put up such a fight." She shifted her gaze to meet mine. "You'd have done the same for me."

She was right. Ever since I'd started at Plus One, we'd had each other's back. Thanks to school and work, maintaining other friendships was hard. Lilly was the one person who never gave up on me and the sole reason I had any social life at all this past year. I should be grateful, but all I wanted was to go home.

The driver pulled to the curb.

Shock sucked the air from my lungs.

Lilly hopped out, leaving the door open, and beckoned with a hand.

"No." I shook my head, eyes stinging. "Not here." I

couldn't prevent my mind from spinning like a record and felt dread wash over me.

Lilly glanced back at the dark brick building with gold Edison bulbs. The lights from The Stalker's Tango illuminated the sidewalk. "Why? What's wrong with this place? It's hot right now."

I scooted farther into the car, and I couldn't stop my mind from filling with memories of my time with Jensen at that establishment. A sob built in my chest. "NO!"

Lilly winced.

My tone sounded harsher than I'd intended, but I needed her to understand—I was not going inside.

"Okay, okay." Lilly pushed her hands out, palms up. "We'll go somewhere else." She got into the car. "Can you drop us off at O'Sullivan's?" Lilly threw a twenty over the driver's shoulder, even though the bar was less than two blocks away.

"You got it." The balding man with a Middle Eastern accent took the bill and weaved into traffic.

Lilly turned, resting a hand over mine. "Want to explain what you have against The Stalker's Tango?"

As I struggled to wrangle my feelings and keep from bursting into tears, I strove to control my heaving chest. "The bar was my neutral location where I first met Jensen for his contract." The same place he picked me up for the second contract. And at the end of the evening, the place where he insisted on taking me home due to appendicitis. Jensen was such a nice guy. Was his blunder at Dr. Anderson's so unforgivable? Perhaps I was too hasty in my judgment. I was so confused.

Lilly's head dropped. "I can't believe I forgot. You even sent me a pin drop and everything." She wrapped me in her arms. "I'm so sorry. Now, I owe you some chips and guac to go with the drinks."

Feeling the moisture, I wiped my nose on the sleeve of my jacket. "Fish and chips."

Lilly released her grip and met my gaze, rubbing a hand up and down my arm. "What?"

When the car had arrived at the Irish Pub, I pointed out the window, and forced a smile. "They don't have chips and guac here." Which was fine. Fried food sounded good. Slamming the car door, I followed Lilly into the bar to a booth in the back, the scent of ale and grease heavy in the air assaulting my senses.

The server, dressed in a green Irish rugby shirt, stopped at the table and asked for our drink orders.

Lilly requested a fruity cocktail along with my dirty martini and added an order of fish and chips to the tab. She leaned back, toying with a cardboard coaster, her gaze raking over my face. "He's really gotten to you, hasn't he?"

I took a deep, shuddering breath. "He's done more than that." Jensen took care of me in the hospital and paid my bill—things I would always be grateful for. But then he ripped my heart out and humiliated me in front of his friends. *Can his actions be more contradictory?*

Lilly cocked an eyebrow.

Clearly, she wasn't satisfied with my partial answer and wanted me to spill my truth. I let my shoulders drop. "I think I was falling in love with him." In reality, I knew I loved Jensen, but saying the words out loud now seemed pointless.

She scoffed. "After just over a month?" Lilly leaned forward, laying her hands flat on the smooth black table. "Two weeks of which, may I add, were contract weeks."

"I know, I know." Shameful heat washed over me, and I slouched out of my jacket, then buttoned my shirt to cover my cleavage. "I never thought I'd fall so hard and fast either." Whenever I watched a rom-com, I would be the first to laugh at the instantaneous love between the two main characters. Yet, here I was, unable to deny my feelings and eating my words.

Lilly reached across the table and undid the button I'd just fastened.

"Hey!" I slapped the back of her hand.

Lilly batted me away. "We're trying to attract men, not ward them off."

I rolled my eyes. "Maybe *you* are." The last thing I wanted was some drunk guy hitting on me while focused on my chest. Regardless, my heart felt too tender to deal with whatever Lilly pictured.

The dirty-blond server arrived with the drinks, set them on the table, and left.

Lilly took a sip of her cocktail. "You thought Jensen was the real deal, huh?"

Another crack fissured my heart. "Yes"—I swirled my martini—"I did."

"Why? What made him different from Matteo?" She took another swallow. "Because what he did at his boss's house sounds very Matteo-esque."

"That's just it—why I'm still so upset—the reaction was out of character for Jensen." I couldn't stop my lip from quivering, but I held back the tears.

The same server returned with my fish and chips and a bottle of malt vinegar. "Anything else, ladies?"

Lilly flashed a smile at the tall, burly man. "No,

we're fine. Thanks."

With a nod, he left.

She stole one of my fries before I could douse my plate in vinegar. "Maybe, that *is* his character; he'd just been hiding it before."

My stomach lurched. What if Lilly was right? What if Jensen's kindness was because of the contract or because he had an audience? On the other hand, Jensen began as a client, which put him in charge of the agreement, so those encounters didn't count. Come to think of it, I hadn't spent much time alone with him. Even on our first actual date, while he'd been a gentleman at the Pacific Science Center, we both knew where the evening was headed. Maybe, his kindness had all been a ploy to get me into bed. If my dads hadn't interrupted the evening and lingered, would Jensen have even called the next day? But then, he gave me the Orcas jersey. He'd called in favors to get that generous present. He wouldn't have made such a grand gesture if he didn't like me, right?

And what about my appendectomy? Jensen didn't need to pay my bill or continue to check-in. Plus, I'd witnessed him with the little boy, Beckham, at the football game. No one could fake Jensen's sincerity for his patient. However, I knew plenty of people who could separate work from home life. Dad, for example. He was a shark in the courtroom with a no-nonsense reputation and nothing but professional in the office. But at home, with Papi, he was a complete cinnamon roll.

"Hey." Lilly tapped my leg with her foot under the table.

Yanked from my reverie, I jumped.

"I lost ya there for a second."

"Sorry. I was just thinking about what you said." More like *overthinking*.

"And?" She wrapped her hands around her drink, lacing her fingers on the opposite side.

"I don't know. After all, we barely know each other. I'm unsure if I can forgive what he did at the brunch. However, I struggle to believe that behavior was a reflection of Jensen's true self. But, if you're right, I'm better off without him." If only I could make my heart believe the latter.

"Amen! If he were the good guy he claims to be, last Monday wouldn't have gone the way it did. You're better off." Lilly raised her glass in a toast. "No men until our BSN."

Reluctantly, I lifted my glass, then hesitated, scowling at my half-buttoned blouse exposing my chest. "If we're swearing off men, why did you make me bust out the ladies?"

A slow smile crossed Lilly's face. "*No men* doesn't mean you can't have fun. It just means nothing permanent—if you catch my drift." She winked.

Unease filled my stomach. "If you expect me to have a fling, you'd better buy me a shot." I had no intention of having *fun* with anybody tonight, but I'd humor Lilly by having a few more drinks and bashing on the men in the bar.

"Done!" She snapped her fingers toward the waiter. "Hey, can we get some shots over here?"

I plastered on a smile, ready to drown my sorrows, one shot at a time.

Chapter 45

Jensen

As I stopped on the driveway of my mom's brick-and-cream rambler home in Poulsbo with my pumpkin pie in the passenger seat, I heard the deafening sound of the gravel crunching under my tires. I was positive my mother would be upset that I hadn't brought any vanilla ice cream to go with my dessert. However, considering I still lamented my breakup with Autumn almost two weeks ago, she was lucky I was attending Thanksgiving dinner at all. I'd even chosen the land route to my mother's rather than the ferry to ensure I wouldn't have a possible encounter with Autumn.

Parking beside a dark silver, non-descript, mid-size rental, I knew my brother was already inside. I heaved a sigh, unsure I was prepared for how complicated dinner would be. Maintaining my I'm-unfazed-by-my-breakup façade in front of my mother was one thing—she saw what she wanted to see.

But Billy was another story. He wasn't more intuitive; no, we were just closer. Even more so since my dad's passing. My brother and I were a team—united against my meddling mother—which meant Billy knew all the telltale signs of my lies. Dinner would be rough. I grabbed the pie and trudged to the front door, taking one last deep breath of the fresh-cut grass, pine needles, and freedom before facing the

Spanish Inquisition. "Hello?" Shutting the door, I followed the tiled entryway toward the voices and the delicious smell of stuffing wafting from the kitchen. I entered the bright room with yellow walls lined with light pine cabinets and smiled at my mother and Billy.

"Hey, Sweetie!" Mom grabbed the pie and kissed my cheek. "Take your coat off and stay a while. The turkey's almost done."

Hanging my jacket over the back of a kitchen chair, I hugged Billy with a backslap. "Hey, man. How's it going?"

Billy returned the embrace. "Great! My residency application was accepted. I'm with Dr. Richardson." He stepped back, crossing his arms over his puffed-up chest. "I'm all set for spring."

"Well done. Although, I bet Dr. Richardson is scared to let you back into his office." I punched his arm, letting my pride seep into my tone. "He's got to remember when you bit him during a cleaning as a kid." The rumor was, he needed a tetanus shot afterward.

Billy laughed. "I hope not, so don't you go and remind him!"

Mom dished stuffing into a serving bowl on the counter. "I'm sure your teeth marks have long since healed."

I tilted my head, watching. "Mom, why was the stuffing in a disposable container?"

Her cheeks flushed.

"It's not just the stuffing; it's everything." Billy opened the trash can lid to reveal several other aluminum pans. "The potatoes, the gravy, the green beans, even the turkey."

I gave my mother a quizzical look. "Wait, I thought you said the turkey was almost done?"

She busied herself by putting the gravy and cranberry sauce on the kitchen table. "It is. It's almost done *reheating*."

I shook my head. "When did you start buying Thanksgiving dinner?"

Mom wafted a hand in the air. "Oh, honey. I've been doing this for years. But in the past, I've been better at hiding the containers."

So much for our traditional family dinner. I knew the premade, store-bought food shouldn't have mattered, but somehow, it did. Almost like finding out Santa wasn't real. My limbs felt heavy, and I narrowed my eyes at my mother. What else had she been lying about? Putting my concerns on the back burner, I set the last of the food on the table.

Billy grabbed the wine. "Looks great, Mom." He sat and toasted her with his goblet.

I took the seat opposite and raised mine half-heartedly in turn. "Hopefully, it tastes as good as your cooking. I'm sure you spent a pretty penny on this meal." I'd be upset if the food were as bitter as my attitude. While I knew my anger was irrational, learning her falsehood wasn't helping my current mindset. Gulping my wine, I relished the gentle burn in my throat.

Mom lowered her glass and threw her napkin on the table. "What, Jensen? Are you *that* offended I bought dinner, or did something go wrong with Autumn since she's not here?"

Of course, she would jump to that conclusion—her way of asking for information without actually asking.

Too bad, she'd hit the nail on the head. Two weeks ago, right before the brunch at Gary's, Mom asked me to invite Autumn to Thanksgiving dinner, but I messed up everything and never got the chance.

"Autumn?" Billy shoved a forkful of turkey into his mouth.

"You haven't bothered to tell your brother about your girlfriend?"

My neck prickled at the judgment in Mom's question. I pushed my potatoes around with my fork. Clearing my throat, I kept my focus on my plate. "We just went on a few dates; nothing came of it. We're not even together anymore." My tone was supposed to be nonchalant—but wasn't.

Billy's eyes narrowed.

I pleaded with my eyes, knowing I would have to have a private conversation later.

"Yeah, Mom. If the relationship was serious, Jensen would have mentioned her."

I appreciated how Billy played along in front of our mother, and I felt too angry to feel guilty about lying. These past two weeks were a nightmare. First, Autumn refused to let me apologize and ended things. Then, I heard Nicole asking about my sulky behavior at the hospital, followed by finding out Thanksgiving dinner was a hoax. Now we were discussing the one topic I desperately wanted to avoid. What was next, I'd get fired?

Mom reached for her napkin and wiped the fabric over her mouth, her brow wrinkled. "What did you do?"

Indignation filled my chest. I was never good enough.

Billy waved his glass in my direction. "Why do you assume Jensen was at fault?"

Gratitude filled my heart, hearing my brother come to my defense. If only he were right.

Mom pursed her lips.

She leveled Billy with a look I knew all too well.

"Because Dan told Darla"—she shook her head—"actually, Kristine raved to Darla, insisting Autumn was a gem—perfect for my boy. So, whatever went wrong had to be Jensen's fault."

"Wow." I shot out of my chair, knocking the table with my thighs and rattling the dishes, my appetite gone. "I'm glad you have so much faith in me, Mom." Without another word, I stormed toward the bedrooms. I felt too vulnerable to sit at the table and defend myself when I knew I was clearly in the wrong.

Entering the first guest room, I closed the door and slumped onto the edge of the bed, leaning my elbows on my thighs. I hated that Mom was right this time. What happened with Autumn *was* all my fault, and I couldn't fix anything. Even Dan's mom had been spot on—Autumn *was* a gem. She was perfect. We'd been good together, but I messed up, and going back wasn't an option. Resting my head in my hands, I heard a slight knock at the door.

"Jensen?"

Billy's whisper was almost inaudible through the wood. *Thank goodness, it's not Mom.* "Come in."

He entered the room, hovering by the door. "This Thanksgiving is full of surprises."

The humor and sarcasm lacing his words raked my nerves. "Ugh, seriously, Billy?" I shook my head, feeling my chest tighten. "Just don't."

"I'm just messing with ya." Billy took a small step forward. "Wanna talk about it?"

An odd twinge twisted my belly. "Not really."

"Okay. I'll leave you alone." He grabbed the door handle.

Before I lost sight of him, I suddenly wanted to get the truth off my chest. "On second thought, Billy. Just stay."

He lowered himself beside me, slightly rocking the bed, mimicking my hunched-over posture, and clasping his hands. "What's going on, Jense?"

I sat up, staring at the ceiling, and huffed an exasperated breath. "Mom called it." My lips burned—the admission was painful.

"You're upset because she bought dinner?"

I elbowed him in the ribs. "No, because I messed up with Autumn—royally." I'd never been so ashamed of my behavior.

"Explain."

His tone held no judgment, so I briefed Billy on everything—from the canceled date with Molly to the contract to how Autumn and I decided we both wanted more, up until when I'd put my foot in my mouth at Dr. Anderson's.

"Dude, could you have been a bigger tool?"

"I know. I know." I ran a hand through my hair. "But I was on the spot and wasn't thinking."

"You might as well have accused her of sleeping with her clients."

The door to the room swung open. "Autumn's sleeping with clients?" Mom stood just inside the room, her face as white as the wall behind her.

Defensive, I vaulted off the bed. "No. Of course,

she's not." I shook from the anger burning under my skin. Not only had Mom listened at the door, but she also interrupted a private conversation with Billy and jumped to the wrong conclusion. *I might as well have sat at the table and had this discussion.*

"Then why did you accuse her?" She put her hands on her hips. "There must be some truth to it."

Billy stood, putting himself between me and Mom. "She's a companion. Just like Molly's fiancé, Jared."

Mom's brow pinched. "Like rebranding makes what she does any better—dating for money. It's disgusting."

My blood boiled in my veins at the revulsion radiating off her body. "Mom!" I hadn't expected her to understand, but I thought she could have at least kept her judgments to herself.

She released a maniacal laugh. "Sugarcoat the truth all you want, Jensen. She's still selling herself as an income."

"What about Jared?" I made my tone challenging. "You don't seem to have a problem with him." At least, not to his face or Gillian's.

Mom's expression hardened. "Because Molly's not my daughter. And I won't have you embarrassing our family by dating a companion."

I don't need your permission, although that ship has sailed. "Then it's good I screwed things up." My words came out through clenched teeth.

"Thank goodness, you did." Her gaze was cold. "You dodged a bullet, if you ask me."

"Mom…" Billy cupped her elbow.

She yanked away.

"It's okay, Billy." I met Mom's hard stare. "Is that

what you think? I dodged a bullet?"

"Yes, I do." She stood in the doorway with her arms crossed and her feet planted.

I exhaled a sharp breath. "You're wrong. Autumn is the kindest, smartest woman I've ever dated. I was lucky to have her in my life, and I won't let you talk about her like that. I've already made the mistake of keeping my mouth shut once. I won't do it again."

She threw her hands into the air. "Why do you care if you're no longer together?"

"Because I love her!" The words erupted from my lips before I could think them through, but they felt right.

Mom gasped.

Billy's mouth fell open.

Mom put a hand on her chest with a scowl. "What did you say?"

"I. Love. Her." As I enunciated each word, I couldn't deny how my heart swelled, and my resolve fell into place. I couldn't give up. Not now that I'd realized how much Autumn meant. She was worth fighting for. Asking her forgiveness only one time in person and the subsequent declined calls and texts weren't enough. I needed to do more. "Excuse me." Sidestepping past the two, I marched from the room toward the front door.

"Jensen!"

I heard Billy's footsteps jogging down the hall, and I turned to see him stop a few feet away. With a hand on the open front door, I paused.

"Where are you going?"

"I can't give up on her, Billy." I clenched a fist. Hope and adrenaline coursed through my veins.

He put a hand in his pocket and shrugged. "But you said she won't talk to you."

"I know. That doesn't mean I shouldn't try."

Chapter 46

Jensen

After leaving my mother's house, I sped to the port and queued at the light leading to the ferry, tapping my fingers on the steering wheel. Bainbridge was Autumn's usual ferry terminal, but I wasn't sure what I would do if she were working. Would showing up at her window be better, or should I avoid her booth until I had a plan? Then again, if I queued in another line and she spotted me, she might be offended, making my situation worse.

However, I'd be in the same predicament if I showed up at Autumn's booth and she wasn't ready to talk. I let my head fall against the seat. The light turned green, and the cars inched forward, allowing me to glimpse the tollbooths. I relaxed in my chair; Autumn wasn't working—hurdle one cleared. Waving my Puget Card at the terminal, I decided I couldn't wait any longer. As I boarded the ferry to Seattle, I called Dan.

"We're not talking to you right now."

Kristine's brisk tone held no room for argument. I double-checked the contact on my phone. "I called Dan."

"I did say *we* weren't speaking to you."

Great! I'd hoped to talk to Dan, get him on my side, and together, we could face Kristine. Guess I'd fly solo on this mission. "Fine, will *you* hear me out?"

"Why?"

I rubbed the back of my neck, wishing I'd prepared a speech. "Look, Kristine. You know I'm not a fool."

"You were at Dr. Anderson's."

Let me talk! "True, I'll give you that, but I'm asking you to give me the benefit of the doubt because we've been friends for years." As the harbor drifted away, my car rocked. "I have a plan to win Autumn back." Well, not really. But I still had the drive to Dan's house to come up with one.

"Okay, I'm listening."

The touch of life reentering Kristine's voice was like a shot of adrenaline.

"What's this brilliant plan?"

Her sarcasm was back, and I felt like some of the air was knocked from my lungs, but I soldiered on. "Please, I need your help." I did my best to emphasize the pathetic tone in my voice. Begging was still an option.

Kristine scoffed. "I figured as much since you called my husband."

"Right." She wasn't giving me anything. I shoved a hand through my hair. "So, can I come over to hash out the details?"

"Ugh."

I could picture her pinched expression, but I knew she was considering my plea. "Please, Kristine? As a favor to your old friend?" Adding a little guilt couldn't hurt.

"Fine."

"Thank you!" A weight lifted from my chest. "I'll see you in twenty."

Parking in front of Dan's house, I was grateful

Kristine relented because I couldn't think much beyond *get Autumn back*, which didn't remotely resemble a plan. Hopefully, Kristine would have pity, and together, the three of us would have an epiphany.

Kristine opened the door, her eyebrows pinched low on her forehead. "Come in." She gestured toward the kitchen.

I met Dan sitting at the table. Catching my eye, I watched him mouth the words *good luck*. As I took a chair beside him, I felt my gut twist.

Kristine sat across the table, folding her arms on the wooden surface. "Okay, let's hear what you're thinking—and it better be a huge, grand gesture."

I inhaled a deep breath, saying the first idea that came to mind. "I could go through Autumn's tollbooth with flowers and chocolate." The idea was lame, but it was all I had.

Kristine shook her head before I'd even finished. "Nope. Too cliché."

I wiped my sweaty palms down my thighs. "Okay, what if I showed up at Autumn's school? Would that be better?" I envisioned myself hunting down her car and waiting there until she arrived.

"No." Kristine cocked her head to the side. "Showing up at the university would be as bad as her showing up when you're with a patient."

I frowned. She had a point. "Then I've got nothing." Meeting Kristine's gaze, I gave her my best puppy dog eyes. "Please help me? I've tried calling and texting to no avail. I even went to her apartment on the day of the brunch to apologize, but she ignored me. I can't do this on my own."

Dan rubbed his wife's shoulder. "He's trying,

babe."

I shot my friend a grateful smile.

"Fine." Kristine rolled her eyes. "Is she still working at Plus One?"

I shook my head. "I don't think so. When Autumn agreed we'd make our relationship official, she'd quit. But for all I know, she could've gone back." *Damn!* I should have checked the website. Mentally, I kicked myself for not thinking of that. I retrieved my phone from my pocket.

Kristine was faster and made a few taps on her screen. "She's not on the website."

I unclenched my jaw. "Great, but what difference does that make?" I gestured at her cell.

"Well, I planned to tell you to book her available appointments for the next few weeks—show her you won't take *no* for an answer."

I barked a laugh. "Ha! Who has that kind of money?" While the suggestion was unreasonable, a small part of my brain calculated loan possibilities and credit card limits since I'd emptied most of my savings for Autumn's hospital bill.

Kristine pursed her lips, leveling me with a stare. "Do you want her back or not?"

"I do, I do." Autumn was the whole reason I was there, subjecting myself to Kristine's ridicule. "But maybe something that won't put me in the poorhouse?" The three of us were smart, and I was positive that, together, we would think of a better plan.

"You're not willing to spend money on Autumn?"

I could hear Kristine's shoe tapping against the tile floor. "Of course, I am. But what good would I be if I'm homeless?" Again, another way had to be found.

Dan nodded. "He's right."

"Shut up." Kristine shoved her husband, almost knocking him out of his chair. She blew out a breath. "What could you do?" Her eyes lit up. "How's your singing voice?"

Dan exploded in laughter.

Fixing him with a cold stare, I shook my head. "Sadly, he's right to laugh. I'm tone deaf."

Her eyebrows shot to her hairline, and she straightened in her chair.

I held up a halting hand. "And before you even ask, I'm not holding a boom box over my head below Autumn's apartment window." Or any of the other rom-com grand gestures. Whatever I did required originality.

Kristine slumped, screwing her lips to the side.

With music on my brain, I thought of Autumn's photo taped to her fridge. "Although I could talk to Rob, he's musical." Snippets of a plan swirled through my thoughts.

Kristine leaned forward, a hand splayed on the table. "Who's Rob?"

I forgot how little they knew of Autumn's personal life. "One of her dads. He sings and plays the guitar in a band—or at least he used to." I silently replayed conversations with Autumn, trying to remember if she mentioned whether or not Rob was retired. Nothing came to mind.

Dan scoffed. "You needed to beg to get Kristine to help you. What makes you think that after insulting their daughter, one of her dads would be on board?"

I swallowed, scrubbing at my scalp. "I don't know, but I have to try *something*." I pictured Karl's militant face and cringed.

Kristine stood and grabbed a diet cola from the fridge. "Do you even know how to get ahold of either of them?"

I still wasn't sold I wanted to. "That's the tricky part." I chewed on my lip. "I don't know their last names, but I'm pretty sure it's not Haze, like Autumn's. But Karl is a big-time defense attorney." Gritting my teeth, I tapped on my forehead. "I wish I could remember the name of the firm." When I first met Autumn, she mentioned the name of the company. "The law office has three last names, one of which is Goldstein."

"No problem!" Kristine cracked open her soda. "Let's look him up."

"Yeah…" I hesitated. "He's the dad who won't be too keen on helping." I honestly didn't think Karl would answer if I called.

"But you think Rob would?" She took a sip from the can.

"Autumn mentioned Rob was the sentimental one. When I met them in the hospital, and at her apartment, I realized Rob was definitely the softie." His friendly demeanor and romantic side were my only hope. Retrieving my phone, I opened my search engine and tried variations of *Rob and band, Rob performer,* and *Rob vocalist*, but I came up empty. *No surprise there.*

Kristine glanced at my screen. "Any luck locating him?"

I shook my head. "No, I'm finding nothing without a last name."

"Then I don't think you have a choice. We're locating Karl, and you're calling."

Kristine shrugged like the decision was a done deal.

Nausea roiled in my stomach.

Dan skidded his phone across the table. "Is this him?"

I felt like my eyes were frozen wide. The picture on his screen was indeed Karl, under a *Seattle Post* headline reading, *Washington Attorney Wins Triple Homicide Case*. I forced myself to blink. Even Karl's hard stare in the photo made me as uncomfortable as a fish out of water. I could feel my heart pounding and the sweat trickling down my back. "Yeah, that's him."

Dan scratched his scruff. "Looks like you've got your work cut out for you." He gestured at his phone. "He's a partner at Parker, Wickens, and Goldstein."

I almost laughed. Even Dan could tell Karl was no pushover. Scrolling through the phone screen, I found the firm's contact number. "They'll be closed. Should I leave a voicemail?"

Kristine nodded. "But first, let's figure out what you're going to say."

We spent the next fifteen minutes brainstorming until Kristine was satisfied the message would be persuasive enough for Karl to respond and I wouldn't sound like a chump.

Taking a deep breath, I looked over my script and steeled my shoulders. "Wish me luck." I tapped the call icon, the sweat on my back turning to ice. "Here goes nothing."

Chapter 47

Autumn

"Students!" Professor Sharma slid his arms into his threadbare, tweed coat with leather elbow patches. "One more thing."

I closed my laptop and numbly shoved it into my bag, only vaguely listening. Since my night out with Lilly last week, I'd shut off my feelings, robotically going through the motions of life, classes, and the toll booth. I hoped if I ignored my emotions, the throbbing ache and pain gnawing my insides from Jensen's absence would eventually go away. So far, though, I'd had no such luck.

"Next Thursday evening, the nursing department will do their annual holiday present drop-off to the patients in Seattle Children's and St. Jude's pediatric wards. This is both an excellent service and networking opportunity. Plus, it's extra credit."

He shot the class a pointed look over his round-rimmed glasses, the gleam from the overhead florescent lights bouncing off his shiny golden head.

"I'd block off my calendars if I were you."

Feeling my heart seize, I raised a hand.

"Yes, Miss Haze?"

"Do we get to choose which hospital?" Seattle Children's was Jensen's workplace. A cold sweat enveloped my body, and I thought I might throw up.

Bumping into Jensen would set me back in my healing process.

Professor Sharma slung his leather messenger bag over his shoulder. "No. We made the assignments randomly, and there will be no changes." He grabbed his phone from his table at the front and gave it a shake. "The list of assignments is posted in the classroom portal." He left without another word.

My classmates and I retrieved our devices, searching for the allocations. It took a few minutes to locate the list of names, but I finally opened the spreadsheet. I could feel my heart pounding in my ears, and I skimmed my gaze over the list.

Autumn Haze—Seattle Children's Hospital.

The surrounding sounds dulled, and I narrowed my vision to a point while my mind spun. *I knew I'd get Jensen's hospital. Why do these things always happen to me? So unfair!* On wobbly legs, I shoved my way past my peers and dashed into the hallway, darting my gaze in every direction for Professor Sharma. I know he said *no changes*, but surely, he would make an exception if I found the right excuse. Three-quarters of the way through the hall, I spotted his balding head. "Professor!" I waved my arm in the air.

He spun in a half circle. When his gaze met mine, his features brightened, and he waited.

"What can I do for you, Miss Haze?"

I swallowed hard. "Um…About the hospital assignments—"

He held up a hand. "I'll stop you right there. No changes."

Staring into his stern features, I blanked for any excuse other than the truth. But I was out of time. "I know this will sound terrible, but I used to date one of the doctors at Seattle Children's—"

"You think you're the first nurse to date a doctor?" Professor Sharma shook his head. "When you apply for jobs, will you avoid Seattle Children's? Is that how this is going to work?"

His condescending tone inspired a wave of guilt. "Well, no…" Fiddling with the zipper of my hoodie, I couldn't meet my professor's gaze.

He heaved a sigh. "I suggest you sort out your private life and keep any drama away from your professional one." Readjusting his bag on his shoulder, Professor Sharma cleared his throat. "Now, if you don't mind, I have more pressing issues." He spun on his heel and stomped away.

I watched his retreating figure, mortified and alone in the hallway. Slumping against the wall, I leaned my head back and closed my eyes. "Great." Avoiding Jensen if he was at work would be difficult, and since we were no longer together, I didn't know his schedule. My only guarantee of not seeing him was if I didn't go. However, missing out on this networking opportunity might prove fatal to my career. "Ugh!" I peeled myself off the brick wall, feeling the fabric of my hoodie tug against the rough surface, and retrieved my phone from my pocket. Finding Lilly's profile, I tapped the green phone icon.

"Hey, Autumn. What's up?"

"Are you done with classes? Can you meet me at the coffee shop on the corner of Fourth and Madison? I need to talk." With my hands full, I used my butt to open the double doors to the outside, trotting down the steps and across the quad toward my car.

"Sure, but don't forget I've got a contract at four."

I glanced at my watch: 2:43 p.m. *Dammit*. I forgot about her client, which didn't give me much time, but I didn't have a choice. I had to get my predicament off my chest. "Okay. See you soon."

Taking my chai with vanilla from the counter, I found a table by the window and waited for Lilly, blowing the steam off the creamy sweet tea.

A few minutes later, she slipped through the door in a dark-gray duster coat over her sheer, button-down white blouse and black sweater vest, her hair in her usual bubble braid. "Hey, gurl. Where's mine?" Lilly smiled with a wink.

Even though she was joking, I felt my gut twist. I was so entrenched in my own drama that I forgot to buy her a drink. Motioning toward the counter, I raised my brows. "Do you want something?"

She slunk out of her coat, draping the duster over the back of her chair. "Naw, I'm fine." She rested her chin in her palm and rolled her eyes. "I've got an office Christmas party tonight. It's a buffet and, if I understood the client right, an open bar." Lilly wiggled her eyebrows. "I plan on getting my money's worth."

I was always surprised at Lilly's ability to hold her liquor, given how she was so petite. Shaking my head, I ran a finger along the lid of my cup. "I need you to convince me to do the extra credit." Tell me I'm being overly dramatic, and nothing will go wrong.

Lilly's head reared back. "You mean the present drop-off? Yeah, you should do it. There, job done." She made a mic-dropping gesture.

I forced a laugh. "It's not that simple." I reminded her how Jensen worked at Seattle Children's and shot her a pointed look.

Lilly sucked in a breath through her teeth. "Oh, yeah. That's right. Talk about awkward." She grabbed my cup and took a sip. "I got assigned to the same hospital. Otherwise, I'd switch. Do you know anyone who's been assigned St. Jude's?"

"I didn't even bother asking." I heaved a sigh. "Professor Sharma was clear—he won't change anything. He even said I needed to *sort out my private life*." I mocked his words while making air quotes, feeling like I was at the end of my rope.

Lilly winced. "Ooh, savage."

"I know." Until today, he was one of my favorite instructors, but now….

"So, what are you gonna do?"

I scoffed. "That's why I called you!" I held up my hands. My intentions should have been obvious. "I have two choices—the one I want to do and the one I should." If Lilly agreed with my gut that I should stay home, then I would—in a heartbeat.

"Not go or risk seeing Jensen while making invaluable connections and earning extra credit." She tilted her head to the side. "There's not really a choice."

Thanks for stating the obvious. "But I've got an A in his class. I don't need the grade boost." *Great! Now, I was making irrational bargains with myself.*

"But what about the networking?" She cocked a brow. "Connections are priceless."

I frowned, staring at my now-cold tea on the table, hating her logic. "I'm one of the top students; superior grades will get me noticed, right?" Hospitals hired staff because of their qualifications all the time, not solely on their connections.

Lilly barked a laugh. "Yeah, sure. Supernerd is a weak argument—even for you. We both know getting a job is more about politics and who you know, not the grades." She leaned across the little round table and touched my arm. "The real question is, why are you letting a man—who was a complete jerk, by the way—dictate your life again?"

Scowling, I felt my chest deflate. I knew I had no defense. By not attending, I would let Jensen control my decision, which wasn't okay. "Fine. You suck."

Her dark almond-shaped eyes sparkled. "You love me." She trapped her tongue with her teeth and gave a broad smile. "Now, let's rehearse what you'll say if you see him."

Chapter 48

Autumn

Spotting my classmates at Seattle Children's Hospital was easy. They were the large group of scrubs-wearers with Santa hats and the occasional holiday sweater. The festive crowd assembled in the lobby, buzzing with excitement. Even Professor Sharma stood in the middle of my peers, wearing the ugliest sweater known to man with dancing lights no one could ignore.

He handed out large sacks to the students. "Here's your bag, Miss Haze." He wore a hint of a smile on his lips. "Glad you decided to join us."

Like I had a choice. I smoothed the fur of the giant reindeer on my sweater, which still paled compared to his gaudy attire. "You were right. I need to be here."

He patted my shoulder, then turned to face the crowd. "Okay, there are only two floors we're allowed to visit. Who can tell me why?"

Jonah, a scorching brunette with ice-blue eyes who—unfortunately for the ladies in my class—didn't swing our way, raised a hand.

Professor Sharma nodded.

Jonah beamed. "Because some children will have compromised immune systems or contagious diseases."

"Very good, Mr. Brooks. They'll get their presents from their doctors." Professor Sharma strode toward the elevators just past a giant chessboard. "There are plenty of us and plenty of kids on floors two and three. We'll stop on two first"—he pressed the call button—"where we'll fan out, visit each room, then meet back at the elevators to do the same on floor three." The doors pinged open. "Just be sure to knock before you enter any of the rooms, and when you leave, don't forget to place a holiday sticker on the door. We don't have enough gifts to double up."

Half of the group got onto the elevator while I waited with the rest for the doors to close before jabbing the button again.

Lilly wormed her way through the crowd to my side.

Her presence was like a sunny spot on a chilly day. I tapped a hand against my thigh to the beat of the Christmas jingle playing over the speakers, scanning the area for Jensen.

"Stop fidgeting. It'll be great." Lilly wrapped me in a one-armed hug. "Chances are, you won't see him."

I forced a smile and scanned the faces of my peers. From their expressions, I appeared to be the only person in the group who dreaded being here. "Fingers crossed." I exaggerated the gesture. An elevator behind me opened, and Lilly and I held back, allowing the others to board first. I couldn't deal with being in the midst of their enthusiasm in my current state of mind.

Stepping onto the second floor, I scoured the halls, scrutinizing every male in a lab coat. Noting that none of them were Jensen, the knot in my stomach loosened. However, just because he wasn't in eyeshot didn't mean he wasn't in the hospital. He could be in a patient's room or on another level. Either way, I remained vigilant, fortifying the walls around my heart.

Lilly squeezed my hand.

Her touch was a silent reminder of the rules she and I prepared for a chance run-in with Jensen—stay professional, smile, and have an exit strategy ready. The bravado seemed easy before I'd arrived, but now that I was at the hospital, I panicked. Feeling the heat in my armpits, I set the bag of presents on the floor to shake out my hands and wipe my clammy palms on my thighs. I retrieved the red velour sack, squared my shoulders, strode to the nearest door without a sticker, and knocked.

"Come in."

The high, breathy voice gave me courage. Edging the door open, I stepped into the room, peeking around the corner bathroom to the bed against the wall on my right. The pale girl, whose hair almost matched her light skin, had the mattress set to a sitting position, oxygen tubes in her nose. She wore a blue nightshirt with a fuzzy polar bear on the front.

Sitting straight, the girl leaned forward, her green eyes darting toward my bag.

"Hi, I'm Autumn; I'm a student nurse." The title felt weird on my tongue, considering I was still a year away from my degree. Professor Sharma was adamant we used the moniker to introduce ourselves. "I've come to deliver a gift from the North Pole." Knowing Christmas was only a week away, I felt a slight twinge in my chest, realizing this little girl would spend the holidays in a hospital bed and not at home around a festive tree.

Deep dimples sank into the child's cheeks, and she gasped, her shoulders lifting.

Seeing the excitement in her expression reminded

me how magical the holidays were. I could see my childhood memories of Papi dressed as Santa lighting the menorah flashing through my mind, and my smile widened. "What's your name?"

She rasped a breath. "I'm Winnie."

"Hello, Winnie." I gave her a little wave. "It's nice to meet you." Placing the sack of presents on the floor, I rummaged through the stash of gifts. "How old are you, Winnie?"

She scooched forward in her bed, peeking into the bag of goodies. "I'm nine."

"Nine? Wow, almost double digits." I found a red-and-green-striped package labeled *girl ages eight-ten,* peeled off the tag, and rubbed away the sticky residue with a finger. Handing her the gift, I beamed. "Happy Holidays!" The generic well-wish was another line scripted for the students. The university required me to stay neutral with my words to avoid offending different beliefs, which I didn't mind, considering my dads were from different faith backgrounds. Not that I or my parents were particularly religious, but I appreciated the sentiment.

Winnie took the box with grabby hands, examining and rotating the present. She gaped with wide eyes. "Can I open it now?"

I smiled. "Yeah. Have at it."

Biting her bottom lip, she tore into the paper. Inside was a colorful, bead bracelet-making set. Winnie squealed. "Thank you."

Overwhelmed by the girl's gratitude, I willed away the tears threatening to surface. I needed to develop tougher skin before graduating—a necessity if I worked in oncology pediatrics. "You're welcome. Enjoy the gift." I waved goodbye.

She dragged over her rolling bedside table and tore the plastic off the beads.

I was already forgotten. After putting a sticker on the door, I walked into the hallway and spotted Professor Sharma.

He waved toward Room 205. "This patient hasn't had a visit." He made a note on his tablet.

Knocking, I ventured into the room but kept my emotions at bay. I knew each gift I delivered would be hard. However, I couldn't help but wonder if my threatening tears were because of the sick kiddos in combination with the season or the stress of knowing I could bump into Jensen at any moment. When I got through the entirety of the second floor without a sighting, I felt the knot in my stomach ease. But I still had one more floor to go.

On the next level, everything was pretty much the same—rooms of adorable kids delighted to see my sack of toys and me reining in my emotions. Thankfully, luck was on my side because Jensen was nowhere to be seen. My energy was high as I gathered with my peers at the nurses' station and swapped stories. I watched everyone laugh and give each other hugs with flushed, smiling faces. Even a few happy tears, other than my own, flowed among my classmates. As I spotted Lilly and stepped beside her, I felt my chest fill with warmth.

"See?" She bumped her shoulder against mine, grinning from ear to ear. "It worked out. You worried for nothing."

"You were right; I was less right." Despite the anxiety of being in Jensen's hospital, I was grateful I'd come. The experience was a fantastic learning opportunity and made me excited for next year.

"Ho, ho, ho!"

The tenor voice boomed through the halls, halting my buzz of excitement. I turned to see Santa waving to the children who'd gotten out of bed. I gaped as he stopped a few feet from my group and focused his gaze on me. My chest constricted, and I could barely breathe. Beyond the white hair and beard, those green eyes were unmistakable—Jensen.

Chapter 49

Jensen

Now that I stood in front of Autumn, past the "ho, ho, ho," I wasn't sure what to say. She hadn't run away, so I took the sign as a win. I'd first seen her twenty minutes ago, entering one of my patients' rooms. Even though I'd read the memo about the university nursing students visiting today, I hadn't had time to check the sign-in sheet to search for Autumn's name. Seeing her both thrilled and filled me with trepidation.

Last week, Dan, Kristine, and I devised a plan to win Autumn back. I'd even braved calling Karl to persuade him to let me get Rob on board. After an hour of conversation and a whole bottle of antacid, I'd convinced them. But my original idea wasn't supposed to come to fruition until I was off work over the weekend. Autumn's appearance in my hospital wasn't part of the plan. However, I could feel in my heart that if I'd let this opportunity pass without trying, I would have regretted it.

But getting Rob to the hospital in time before Autumn left wasn't feasible. Having witnessed the charity event for several years, I knew the group was about to leave. But I wasn't brave enough to approach Autumn in front of her professor and classmates with no plan. So, I jogged through the corridor and caught Dan at the west nurses' station. "Hey, I need your help." Hopefully, he'd have a brilliant idea.

Dan dropped off a chart and turned, his brows drawn together. "What's going on?"

I struggled to catch my breath. "Autumn." Between the excitement of knowing she was in the hospital and searching for my best friend, I panted. "She's here."

Dan glanced around the hallways. "Where?"

"With the nursing students"—I clutched at a stitch in my side—"delivering presents."

"That's *her* group?" He cracked a smile. "Did you know she'd be here?"

I shook my head. "No, but now that she is, I can't wait until the weekend." The situation wasn't ideal, but groveling in front of her peers felt less humiliating than begging in front of her dads despite Rob's brilliant song.

Dan motioned to follow him. "Okay, are you going to call Rob and get him to come to the hospital?"

"I don't have time." I thumbed over my shoulder. "They were already congregating at the nurse's station in the *B* wing."

Dan halted. "Then what's the plan?"

I blew out a breath through my lips. "No clue. I hoped you'd have an idea?"

Dan's eyes narrowed. "You mentioned they're here delivering presents…hmmm."

I could see the wheels turning in his head, and I chewed on my cheek.

He snapped his fingers. "Got it." With a curt nod, Dan spun on his heel. "Follow me."

Ten minutes later, I found myself drowning in a scratchy Santa suit, tightening the belt over the padded jacket. "I feel like an idiot." *Why did I ever agree to this?*

Dan chuckled, throwing the wig over my hair. "You look like one, too, but if you want to get close to Autumn, the disguise will be necessary."

I couldn't argue. After the way I'd acted, seeing me without the costume, she'd probably run for the hills. "But dressing up as Santa?"

Dan huffed, his shoulders sagging. "Do you want this girl back or not?"

"I do." *More than anything.*

"Then suck it up, Santa, and get on out there."

With tense shoulders, I played along with Dan's asinine plan, which was how I ended up in front of Autumn with nothing to say.

"How come he gets to dress up as Santa, and we're required to say *Happy Holidays*?" A short woman with a black bun and a thick Columbian accent put her hands on her hips with a huff.

A balding Indian man in round glasses, whom I assumed to be her professor, stepped forward.

"He's not affiliated with the school." The man glanced over his shoulder. "You're with the hospital?"

I cleared my throat. "Yeah…I, uh…came to ask what this young lady"—I gestured at Autumn—"wants for Christmas." *What am I saying?* I wasn't coming across as professional or mature. My Santa suit felt like a straitjacket.

Autumn's dark eyes were huge, her gaze bouncing between me and her professor.

The teacher opened his mouth.

Dan grasped the man's elbow and whispered something in his ear.

A light dawned in the professor's eyes, and he

nodded. "Of course, Santa. Ask away."

I scratched at my fake beard and focused on Autumn. "What's your—" I stopped and cleared the high pitch from my voice. "What's your Christmas wish, Autumn?"

She folded her arms across her chest. "For you to leave me alone."

A collective gasp resounded from the crowd, including the doctors and nurses who were gathered to see what the fuss was about.

Her cold tone cut through my confidence, and I chortled. An uncomfortable prickle ran along my scalp, and I mustered all my energy to keep the Santa persona and not fall apart. "Oh, come now. Don't be sour. Aren't the holidays all about charity, forgiveness, and coming together as loved ones?" I pictured the green furry Christmas character when his heart grew three sizes larger and hoped Autumn would have the same experience.

She pursed her lips and kicked at the linoleum floor. "It depends on what those loved ones have done. Not everyone deserves to get off the naughty list. Some people are just giant"—she pinched her lips and paused—"jerks."

I watched the surrounding students' gazes bounce between me and Autumn, as if they were watching a tennis match.

My limbs felt heavy, and sweat beaded on my forehead. This couldn't be the end. She needed to listen. "Even giant jerks deserve second chances, especially if the apology is from the bottom of his heart." Maybe she couldn't see the sincerity in my expression past the stupid costume.

Autumn squinted and grasped my elbow, dragging me into a side hallway. "And what about the next time, Jensen? Will you stick up for me? Defend my honor? Be jealous and possessive? Or will you worry about everyone else's opinion?" She pointedly glanced at her peers and the surrounding hospital staff just out of earshot.

I swallowed hard. Her concerns were valid, but I needed to convince Autumn I wanted to be a better man, get over my ego and insecurities, and focus on what really mattered in my life—her. "I'm sorry I hurt you, and I recognize my mistake. From here on out, I promise to put your feelings and well-being above my own."

Autumn's gaze searched my face, her eyes brimming with unshed tears. She fiddled with the drawstring on the empty sack in her hands. "I want to believe you, but I don't know if I can."

A chill like liquid nitrogen ran up my spine. "What do I need to do to convince you?"

She gestured at the onlookers. "Prove it. Show me their opinions about our relationship don't matter." Autumn nodded toward the entrance of the hall.

I glanced at the crowd. If declaring those things in public was what I needed to win Autumn back, then that's what I would do. Taking off the wig and beard, I gripped them tightly in one hand, painfully aware of how ridiculous I must look with my sweat-matted hair, and pulled Autumn along as I walked to meet my fate. "Two weeks ago, at Dr. Anderson's house, I was embarrassed to admit how I came to know this amazing woman." I locked my gaze on Autumn, feeling my heart thunder like a storm in my chest. "I lied to my friends, my family, and my colleagues." I took a step closer. "Because I'd been hurt before, I was worried about my career and social standing, and I'd lost sight of what was important." I swallowed hard. "I should have defended you, Autumn. You're the woman I love. I was an idiot—"

"Wait!" Autumn's arms fell limp, and the gift bag dropped to the floor, her lips agape. "The woman you *love*?"

Her words were almost a whisper. I felt hope simmering like molten lava just under my skin, ready to erupt. "Yes, Autumn." I raised my voice so everyone could hear. "I love you, and I promise, with these people as my witnesses, if you accept my apology, I will never again let my ego come between us." I took her hand, wishing to feel her warmth through my glove. "What do you say? Since I literally can't leave you alone, will you grant *my* Christmas wish and forgive me?"

Autumn pinched her eyes shut, a tear dropping onto her cheek.

I ground my teeth, letting the guilt and shame wash over me, as I leaned closer to her ear. "I know I hurt you, and I'm sorry. Believe me, I am. I have no doubt I will mess up a thousand more times, but my mistakes don't reflect how I feel about you. I'm just a human—and a stupid one at that."

The corner of her mouth twitched. "True. You were pretty stupid."

I swallowed, and I felt the tension in my shoulders ease a fraction. "I was—I am." *Please give me another chance.*

Autumn locked her gaze with mine. "I can't be

with someone who's ashamed of me or the life I've lived."

Her voice was pitched low. "The only person I'm ashamed of is myself." Taking off my glove, I hesitantly cupped her face, brushing the moisture from her cheekbone with my thumb. "I love you, Autumn—with all my heart. Please give me another chance."

Her lips quivered, and the tears flowed freely.

"Will you forgive him and kiss him already?"

I froze at the familiar voice and turned to spot Dan holding his phone over the crowd, Kristine's face on the screen.

Autumn sputtered a laugh.

Pointing at the mobile device, I gave Autumn a tentative smile. "I like Kristine's idea."

"I do, too." She threw her arms around my neck and crushed her mouth to mine.

The salt on her lips ripped at my insides but solidified my resolve. I never wanted to hurt Autumn again, and I promised myself I'd spend the rest of my life being the man she deserved.

Chapter 50

Autumn

Returning home after the hospital charity event, I opened the door to my apartment and noticed the space seemed brighter. In fact, everything seemed brighter: my mood, my outlook, even my roommate. "Wow, Alyssa. That sweater looks great."

She stood by the fridge and smoothed the pale-blue knitted front with a hand and a ghost of a smile on her lips. "Um, thank you?"

"You should wear that color more often." As I hung my coat and dropped my purse by the door, I gave her a thumbs-up. "The blue brings out your eyes."

Alyssa collected her things from the kitchen table and shuffled to her room, humming an upbeat melody.

I considered the lack of snark a win. Grabbing the chilled container of leftover pasta salad from the fridge, I retrieved a fork from the drawer. I sat at the table, feeling like a kettle simmering on the stove about to whistle. The happiness inside me was ready to burst. When I first spotted Jensen dressed as Santa, I wanted to smack him on the head with my stupid gift sack. But then, when he declared his love, the fact I didn't faint on the spot was a Christmas miracle. If I were being honest, I'd thought Jensen and I were done. Never in a million years would I have imagined he'd make the rom-com big gesture—especially in front of the hospital staff. The whole situation was a lot more uncomfortable in real life than romance movies portrayed. Bravo to those actors who kept a straight face during filming. While I appreciated the humiliation Jensen must have experienced in his costume, I could have done without the audience. But I had to admit the gesture said a lot about Jensen's feelings—he really did love me. I felt my phone buzz, and I dropped my fork. Buoyancy bubbled in my chest, but I deflated just a bit when I spotted Papi's name on the screen. I had hoped the call would be from Jensen. "Hey, Papi."

"Hey, sweetie. You're on speaker. Dad's here, too."

"Hi, pumpkin. How was the present drop-off?"

Leaning forward, I cradled my phone, smiling and unable to sit still. "You'll never guess what happened!"

"Oh, do tell."

Dad's tone was curious. He loved his gossip. "Well, first things first." I shoved the plastic container of pasta away. "My assignment was at Jensen's hospital." I bit my lip and paused for the dramatic response I knew was coming.

"Wait! What?"

Papi didn't disappoint as disbelief saturated his exaggerated tone. "I know! And I asked to get my hospital placement changed at first, but Professor Sharma wouldn't let me, so I didn't have a choice." I emphasized the drama, knowing my dads would eat it up.

"Were you able to avoid him?"

Dad's voice got louder, and I could picture him taking control of the phone from Papi. "Not quite." I repeated the events from earlier, ending with Jensen's declaration of love. Silence pierced the other end of the line like the calm before a storm. *This went over like a lead balloon.* "Are you all still there?"

Dad cleared his throat. "Um, yes. We're still here."

I chewed on my thumbnail. "What are you thinking?" Wincing into the phone, I wasn't sure I wanted to hear what they had to say. Their reactions when I'd told them about the fallout at Dr. Anderson's had them spitting vitriol on my behalf. Yet here I was telling them we were back together. *This is not going well.*

"Dammit. I can't believe he didn't wait."

Papi sounded wounded, and I straightened. His words didn't make sense. "What do you mean *he didn't wait*? Wait for what?" For the life of me, I couldn't figure out what Papi was talking about.

"I composed a whole song and everything."

A song? What the hell?

"It's okay, Rob. It's not the end of the world."

Pinching my eyes shut, I rubbed my forehead. I was so confused. "What are you two talking about?"

"Last week"—Dad sighed—"Jensen reached out."

I let my mouth fall open, and I felt like my brain glitched. "He did what?" The shock of his words pinned me to my seat.

"Jensen called me at the office."

Hearing Dad's words sent a trill of ice up my spine. I shot up, the legs of my chair scraping across the floor, and I paced the room. I could feel my heart beating a million miles a minute. "Why did he call *you*?"

"Autumn, if you'd let me speak, I can tell you."

Huffing, I leaned against the back of the couch. "Fine. Go ahead."

Dad explained that in Jensen's message, he'd apologized, being more than honest in explaining what happened at Dr. Anderson's, how he messed up, and how sorry he'd been. Jensen even professed his love for me to both my dads, endearing them to his cause. Dad even admitted Papi broke him down and convinced him to return Jensen's call. During that phone conversation, Jensen proposed the idea of Papi helping in Jensen's apology. The idea of a grand gesture enamored Papi, and he composed an apology song, conveying Jensen's words into music. The plan was for Papi to come over Saturday, play his new song, and have Jensen arrive at my door with flowers. But my unexpected appearance at the hospital derailed Jensen's original course of action. I placed a hand over my heart. "Jensen wanted to do that for me?"

"He did. And I must say, considering I'm not very approachable—for him to call me, at my workplace, was a courageous and bold move."

Dad wasn't kidding. Most of my friends growing up were terrified of him. Hell, even Lilly still couldn't hold his gaze, and she was twenty-eight.

"I've got to hand it to him. He's got my vote."

"Thanks, Dad. Jensen is pretty great." My eyes stung with tears. "Is Papi still around?"

"Yes, honey. I'm here."

I swiped the moisture from my cheek. "Will you play the song for me sometime?" The idea of hearing Papi sing a song inspired by Jensen made me giddy.

Papi scoffed. "With all the time and effort I put in—someone's gonna hear it."

"I've heard it."

"You don't count, Karl."

I laughed at my parents' banter. "Thanks, Papi. Thanks, Dad. I love you both."

"We love you, too." Dad paused. "What's the plan now? When do you see him next?"

I glanced at the clock on the microwave. "He's coming over after his shift to talk." *Three more hours.*

"Excellent. I'm glad things worked out, sweetie."

Genuine joy infused Papi's tone.

"I am, too, Autumn. But know, if Jensen breaks your heart again, a phone call asking for a favor won't cut it."

My chest warmed. "Yes, Dad." While his tone sounded gruff, I knew the inflection was because he loved me and meant well. After saying my goodbyes, scarfing down my pasta, and putting the dishes into the dishwasher, I marched straight for the bathroom. I wanted to look nice when Jensen arrived because, despite Lilly's efforts to fix my makeup at the hospital, I was still an obvious mess.

Bathed and with my hair dry, I went to my room and stood in front of my closet, debating what to wear. A pair of sweats indicated I was too comfortable and not taking the situation seriously. Whereas Jensen might consider my silk pajama set an invitation to skip the conversation and go straight to making up in my bedroom. A dress was out of the question—his stopping by after work wasn't a date. I settled on jeans and a sweater.

The last forty-five minutes before Jensen arrived were excruciating. I spent my time wiping nonexistent crumbs from the counter, mopping a spotless floor, and reapplying the lipstick I'd nervously chewed off. After I'd fluffed each cushion on the couch for at least the hundredth time, I heard a knock at the door. Breathing into my right hand to check my breath, I scurried to answer.

Jensen stood in the doorway, holding a *Get Well* teddy bear. "Hi."

What the...? I cocked an eyebrow at the plushy toy. "My appendix has long since healed."

He shrugged. "Sorry. I know, but I couldn't find anything better at the hospital gift shop, and no florists are open this late."

I took the bear, stroking the velvety, soft brown fur. "It's perfect." The gesture was unnecessary but sweet nonetheless.

"May I come in?" He peered from under his lashes.

Damn, he looks sexy. Yanking him by the collar of his jacket, I dragged him inside. "I thought you'd never ask."

Epilogue

Autumn

I shoved another bobby pin into my hair, and as the metal scraped my scalp to hold my mortarboard cap in place, I winced. A lot happened over the past year, and my final two semesters of nursing school were the hardest of all. Which was why when Jensen asked me to move in with him six months ago, I'd declined. Focusing on my studies was hard enough without him being around as a constant distraction. Plus, I'd already broken my motto, 'no men until my BSN.' I wanted to keep at least some independence until I'd achieved my goal. I had a hard enough time using the money my parents loaned me to pay Jensen back to cover my bills instead, but they were generous, knowing working at the tollbooth alone wouldn't cover all my expenses.

Jensen insisted he'd be okay if I returned to Plus One to pay my dads back.

But I couldn't. The thought of even pretending to be with another man was out of the question—something I'd learned from my contract with Chris. Thankfully, Dad and Papi agreed.

At last, graduation arrived and was held at the Eco-Friendly Arena. As I awaited the graduation ceremony to begin, I sat in front of the stage among my peers, cast in a green glow from the marquee lights overhead. Somewhere in the audience behind me were my dads and Jensen. I felt my phone buzz in my pocket. Gathering the side of my black polyester gown, I retrieved my cell from my dress, glad designers finally realized the need for storage capacity in women's clothing. Joy engulfed me at seeing Jensen's name on the screen.

—You look beautiful—

I scoffed with a sharp exhale through my nose.

—We're all dressed exactly the same. I'm sure you don't even know which cap is mine—

—You're fourth from the aisle, three rows back—

I counted the seats. He was right; Jensen found me. Happy tears sprang to my eyes. The stupid ceremony had me all emotional. I tried to convince myself the waterworks weren't connected to my study sessions with Jensen, his vigilance in keeping me on track, or how his support was instrumental to how I'd gotten to this point. But I knew better. I loved him so much.

—Lucky guess—

—I'd know my nurse anywhere—

Pinching my lips together, I stared at the ceiling. *No tears until after pictures.*

****

Jensen

The Dean of Students stepped to the podium. "Welcome, graduates and Family."

I tapped out a quick *I love you* and closed out of the conversation with Autumn to open my camera, snapping a picture of the monumental moment. Something white flashed in my peripheral, and I flinched.

Rob patted my arm. "Sorry. I didn't mean to startle you. Want a tissue?" He leaned across Karl, proffering the thin white paper as he blotted the corners of his wet brown eyes.

With a gentle prod, I nudged his hand away. "Thank you, Rob, but you'll probably need the tissue more than me." At least, he would after I got the courage to ask for their daughter's hand.

"Of course, he will." Karl elbowed Rob, forcing him back into his chair.

He had no idea. I silently ran over the script I'd prepared while counting my breaths to slow my racing heart. Soon, the faculty speeches would end, and the dean would start calling the names of the graduates. Considering Dr. Mattinson was kind enough to cover me for the first half of the day to attend Autumn's graduation, I'd have less than thirty minutes to return to the hospital after the ceremony concluded. The opportunity was now or never. Leaning forward, I squeezed my leg to keep it from bouncing. "Karl, Rob." My voice was a shaky whisper. "Before the formalities get too chaotic, I wanted to ask you both a question."

Rob's breath hitched, and his hand flew to his mouth with a yip.

Karl braced his palm against Rob's leg. "Let him talk." Karl tilted his head.

Ignoring his stern glare from down his nose, I was grateful I'd gotten to know Autumn's parents pretty well over the past year, or Karl's look alone would have cowed my courage. I swallowed, but the action did little to help the dryness in my throat. I soldiered on anyway. "You know I love your daughter with all my heart. And even though I threw off her motto and convinced her to date me, I'm not apologizing. We're good together. I have and will always promise to continue to support her aspirations and goals." As I retrieved the black velvet box from my suit jacket pocket, I watched my hands shake. I opened the lid, displaying the diamond solitaire in a platinum band.

Rob gripped Karl's arm.

Karl put a hand over his husband's, his forehead creased and eyes blinking.

"With your permission, I'd like to support her as her husband." I looked into each of their eyes—Karl's round over his glasses and Rob's running like waterfalls. I felt my chest loosen and the top of my ears burn. "Do I have your blessing to ask Autumn to be my wife?"

****

After the ceremony, I followed Rob and Karl through the crowd to the plaza in front of the arena to wait for Autumn. As graduates found their families, groups gathered into small clusters, everyone smiling and taking pictures.

"Do you see her?" Rob braced a hand on Karl's arm as he craned his neck, scanning the crowd.

"Not yet." Karl swiveled his head, searching, too.

"Let me call her." I was anxious to find Autumn. Before long I would have to return to the hospital, but I was not leaving without proposing. I hit her contact in my phone. The call rang several times, and I felt the adrenaline spike my heartbeat.

"Hello? Where are you all?"

Her voice was hard to hear over the boisterous crowd. "We exited through the doors labeled *South 2B*. Where are you?" I examined every brunette in a cap and gown.

"No idea."

I shook my head. To say Autumn was horrible with directions was an understatement. "What do you see?"

"Um, a lot of people?" She laughed. "I see the big cement support coming out of the roof."

I motioned for both dads to follow and weaved through the crowd toward where she described, spotting her just under the concrete buttress.

Autumn faced the opposite direction, standing on her tiptoes, her cell pressed to her ear.

Stopping just behind her, I knelt on one knee, motioning for her dads to queue over my shoulders. "Turn around." I held the velvet box open.

She spun, gaze dropping to where I knelt.

"Autumn Summer Haze."

Her hand flew over her mouth, eyes shining.

"Will you marry me?" Autumn let out a squeal only dogs could hear.

She blinked rapidly, and a single tear fell to her cheek. "Yes! Oh my gosh, yes! Yes!" Reaching forward, Autumn cupped my face and smashed her lips against mine.

I rose, never breaking the kiss. Eighteen months ago, I would never have guessed that Molly hiring Autumn would be just what *this* doctor needed.

Praise for Amanda Nelson and Lisa-Marie Potter

Men In Books Aren't Better

"Funny with great banter between the two main characters, light-hearted, and has sexual tension in spades!"

~Sally Craft

~*~

"Everything you want in a romance—sparkling with chemistry, sharp wit, and sizzling tension!"

~Liz Kessick, MG author

~*~

"The authors nailed the tension and passion, making the romance feel both hot and heartfelt."

~Holly M.

~*~

Just What the Doctor Hired

"If Amanda Nelson and Lisa-Marie Potter write it, I'm going to read it. And now they're serving us the fake dating trope set in a hospital! Pick this one up STAT!"

~Jackie Khalilieh, YA author

~*~

"Amanda and Lisa Marie deliver another fabulously smart and sweet romcom! I can't wait for more from these two authors!"

~Lindsay Maple, Romcom author

~*~

"A delectable mash-up of Grey's Anatomy and Pretty Woman!"

~Bonnie Jo Pierson, Romcom author

A word about the author…

We're a co-writing team of best friends who share imaginary worlds, including a short story, Shivers, published in Moments Between. Lisa Marie Potter (BIPOC) is a mom of four who grew up in Nottingham, England, and now resides in Alaska with her husband and golden retriever. Amanda Nelson grew up in Maryland and moved to Arizona, where she attended college and currently lives with her husband and four kids. Both women are members of the Author's Guild, belong to a Manuscript Academy Podcast featured writing and critique group, and have a X/Twitter following of over 12,000. Each of their other social media platforms, Instagram and TikTok, have a combined following of over 1,700. They attend writing conferences, Manuscript Academy classes, and are beta reading ninjas. They also review books on their blog, hike the Olympic National Park, and fight over the same fictional crushes. NelsonPotter.com

Another Title by the Authors
Men in Books Aren't Better, Plus One book 1

Thank you for purchasing
this publication of The Wild Rose Press, Inc.

For questions or more information
contact us at
info@thewildrosepress.com.

The Wild Rose Press, Inc.
www.thewildrosepress.com